Thin Blue Smoke

DOUG WORGUL

Thin Blue Smoke

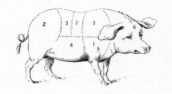

Macmillan New Writing

First published 2009 by Macmillan New Writing
an imprint of Pan Macmillan Ltd
Pan Macmillan, 20 New Wharf Road, London N1 9RR
Basingstoke and Oxford
Associated companies throughout the world
www.panmacmillan.com

ISBN 978-0-230-73708-2

1 3 5 7 9 8 6 4 2

A CIP catalogue record for this book is available
from the British Library.

Typeset by Intype Libra Ltd
Printed and bound in the UK by CPI Mackays, Chatham ME5 8TD

To Rebecca

Acknowledgements

This book comes as a complete surprise to me. Even after three years of research, writing, and editing, I'm still astonished that it exists. It most certainly would not if it weren't for the love, support, and inspiration of others.

My sister Jan and my daughter Lindsey were my two most avid supporters and readers during the writing of *Thin Blue Smoke*. Their unwavering enthusiasm for and loving critique of the story as it evolved, propelled me forward, and held me up when I faltered. I am deeply and gratefully in their debt.

My father and mother, Bob and Shirley, have given me unconditional love and support during the crafting of the story, and throughout my life, and my brother Andrew's love of books is a constant source of inspiration.

My daughters Corinn, Emma and Halla have been my joyful and relentless champions, as have my in-laws, especially Andrea and Duncan.

Special thanks go to my editor Will Atkins and the good people at Macmillan New Writing. It is no understatement to say that they have changed my life for ever.

Finally, I must acknowledge the blessings I have received from the writings of Frederick Buechner, and the preaching, teaching and pastoral ministries of Reverend Robert Meneilly and Father Rob Lord. Their wisdom and insight inform not only my work, but my life.

Then there's Rebecca, whose heart is the room where I go to write.

Author's Note

Passages of Frederick Buechner's book *Wishful Thinking* are paraphrased or quoted by the character Ferguson Glen in Chapter 26. Buechner is the 'friend' referred to by the character Ferguson Glen in his homily. In Chapter 13, details of the story of Satchel Paige's last game come from a story written by reporter Richard J. Olive in the *Kansas City Star*, September 26, 1965.

Prologue

SMOKE MEAT

The name of the place is LaVerne Williams' Genuine BBQ and City Grocery, but everyone calls it Smoke Meat, because – even though 'LaVerne Williams' Genuine BBQ and City Grocery' is handpainted in red letters on the restaurant's front window – outside, over the front door, painted right on the bricks, are the words 'SMOKE MEAT' in big white capital letters about two feet tall.

Smoke Meat is a block away from the *Kansas City Star*, on the southwest corner of 17th and Walnut. It's a favorite of reporters and editors at the paper, especially the copy desk, which has a tradition of taking its new staffers there for lunch on their first day on the job. The punchline of this initiation rite comes when it's time to pay, and all the veteran copy editors pretend as if they assumed all along the new hire was picking up the tab.

Cochran Rooney's first-day Smoke Meat lunch got off to a shaky start.

Rooney was a short stocky redhead with close-cropped hair, a goatee, and a silver earring in his right ear. He came to the *Star* after having been 'downsized' from his previous position as a copy editor at the *Topeka Capital Journal*. He stepped up to the counter first as if he was a long-time regular at Smoke Meat.

Behind the counter a tall skinny black man with a graying Afro stepped up to the cash register. He wore a white apron over a black T-shirt.

'What'll it be?' he asked Rooney.

'How about a regular sausage sandwich with fries and a diet Coke,' said Rooney. 'And how about a D for your sign?'

Rooney snorted and turned and smirked at his new co-workers as if he were letting them in on a joke. None of them let on that they had any idea what he was talking about. But the guy at the cash register knew exactly what Rooney meant. His eyes narrowed.

'What did you say?' he asked Rooney.

'You need a D for your sign outside,' said Rooney. 'It says "smoke meat". Shouldn't it say "smoked meat"? Smoke*d*, with a D?' He wasn't smirking anymore and appeared to have developed a severe blinking disorder.

'You work over there at the *Star*, don't you?' asked the guy behind the counter.

Rooney gave a quick little nod.

'I knew it. Every once in a while one of you smartass writers from the newspaper comes over here and tells me I need to fix my sign. Just because you know about words doesn't mean you know everything. You don't know *shit*. My *son* painted that sign the way it is. And it's staying the way it is.'

Rooney choked out an apology, but the guy behind the counter wasn't having any of it.

'And we don't serve fries here,' he said. He turned to take the next order.

Rooney was quiet while he ate.

On the way back up 17th Street to the *Star*, Rooney walked a bit behind the group smoking a cigarette.

Later that day one of the senior copy editors stopped by Rooney's cube. He leaned in and pointed at Rooney's computer screen. 'I think you need a D there at the end of that word,' he said.

Hanging on the wall by the restaurant's front door are some framed yellowed newspaper clippings. One is a story about LaVerne Williams, a promising young outfielder for the Kansas City Athletics. The article is dated April 9, 1967 and includes a photo of a tall skinny black kid in a baggy cotton baseball uniform, holding his bat over his right shoulder. He looks intently into the camera.

Another framed clipping is an obituary for a Raymond Williams. It reads:

On February 28, 1986, Raymond L. Williams passed into the loving arms of his beloved savior Jesus Christ. He was 19 years old. He leaves to mourn his passing his grieving parents, LaVerne E. and Angela R. Williams, his maternal grandmother, Alberta H. Newton, and many aunts, uncles, cousins, and friends.

Raymond died due to a cardiac irregularity while playing varsity basketball for Prairie View A&M University.

Raymond was loved by all who knew him. He graduated with honors from Central High School and was selected to the All-Missouri basketball team. He received a scholarship to Prairie View Agriculture and Mining University in Prairie View, Texas, and planned to attend seminary and enter the ministry upon matriculation from his undergraduate studies. Funeral services will be held at New Jerusalem Baptist Church at noon on March 4, the Rev. Orville P. Harris officiating.

Two of the framed articles are favorable reviews of the restaurant's food – both from 1982. One praises the ribs and pulled pork. The other includes the restaurant in a list of

'Recommended Joints' in Kansas City, awarding it three 'rib bones' on the basis of its 'tangy sauce and smoky brisket'.

The last frame contains a plain white sheet of paper on which twelve lines of verse have been typed:

'Peace' by Ronald Ross

Now slowly sinks the day-long labouring Sun
Behind the tranquil trees and old church-tower;
And we who watch him know our day is done;
For us too comes the evening – and the hour.

Golden the river brims beneath the west,
And holy peace to all the world is given;
The songless stockdove preens her ruddied breast;
The blue smoke windeth like a prayer to heaven.

Underneath the typed lines is a handwritten note:

To LW from FG
(The stockdove is songless because she's afraid you'll put her on the menu!)

I

A New Life

The day Raymond Williams painted the words 'SMOKE MEAT' above the front door of his father's barbecue restaurant, A.B. Clayton's second stepfather was arrested for bigamy, after it was discovered he had another wife and three young children up in St Joe.

When the detectives arrived at A.B.'s house and announced their intentions, A.B.'s mother became agitated and began throwing wild punches at her husband and also at the police who had come to take him away. A.B. was fifteen years old.

When the fracas spilled out onto the front porch A.B. slipped out the back door, walked down to the corner of 23rd and Chelsea and stood there wondering what to do. A preacher he saw on TV once said to pray when your heart is troubled. But A.B. Clayton didn't know how to pray so he lit up a cigarette instead.

As he stood there, a squad car drove past. His stepfather was in the back seat bleeding from the nose. A.B. flicked his cigarette out into the street and started walking. He wondered what the next guy would be like.

17th and Walnut is a good four miles from 23rd and Chelsea, but A.B. didn't notice how far or how long he'd walked or even where he was going. At one point he just happened to look up and there was Raymond Williams on a ladder, putting the final touches on the K. He smoked a cigarette and watched Ray start in on the E.

Ray looked down at A.B. 'Hey.'

A.B. returned the 'Hey'. He figured that the kid on the ladder was about his same age, but a lot taller.

LaVerne Williams came out to inspect his son's work. 'Lookin' good there, boy. You almost finished?'

'About halfway,' said Ray.

'Well, there's plenty to do inside when you're done. Don't be up there all day.'

LaVerne looked over at A.B. 'May I help you, son?' he said, sizing up the smallish white kid with dirty blond hair, wondering what it was that had made him so sad.

'Probably not,' mumbled A.B. looking away. He dropped his cigarette butt to the sidewalk and stepped on it. 'I need a new life.'

'I don't have one to give,' said LaVerne. 'But how about a job?'

A.B. agreed without a second thought, surprising himself. 'When do I start?'

'How about now?' said LaVerne. 'We got a lot of clean-up to do before we open. Then we're going to need some help in the kitchen.'

A.B. followed LaVerne into the restaurant, went to work, and has worked there ever since. During that time, A.B has been absorbed into the Williams family. Before Raymond died, he and A.B. were especially close, even as the gap widened separating A.B.'s smoky greasy world in the back of the restaurant from Ray's shining academic and athletic achievements.

A.B. is now supervisor of the kitchen crew and the primary operator of the restaurant's smoke pit. People like the barbecue at Smoke Meat and he's the one who makes most of it. LaVerne Williams depends on him and trusts him. He was one of the six pallbearers at Raymond's funeral. The other five were members of the Prairie View A&M basketball team. They towered over A.B. – a scrawny white birch in a grove of black oaks.

When Angela Williams asked A.B. to help carry her son Raymond's casket, he said that of course he'd be honored, but thought maybe he'd have to pass.

'But why, A.B.?' asked Angela. 'You and Ray were like brothers.'

'Yes, ma'am,' he said. 'We were. But I don't have a suit or a tie. I wouldn't look right. I don't want to embarrass you.'

So Angela Williams brought A.B. over to Michael's Fine Clothes for Men and bought him his first-ever suit, a white shirt, a tie, and a nice pair of shoes.

After the funeral and the following meal at New Jerusalem Baptist Church, A.B. didn't know what to do or where to go so he drove to his mother's house. She was sitting on the front porch in an old recliner drinking a quart bottle of beer from a paper bag.

'I hardly recognized you all dressed up like that,' she said, taking a big hit from the quart. 'What's the occasion?'

'I was at Ray's funeral, Ma. I told you.'

'Oh, that's right. That colored kid at the restaurant. How'd he die, again? I forget.'

A.B. turned away, walked down to the corner of 23rd and Chelsea and lit up a cigarette.

2

As Seen on TV

After the lunch rush, LaVerne Williams sometimes takes a nap on the tattered teal-blue couch in the small windowless office in the back of the restaurant. Though LaVerne is a clean and tidy man, his office is a cluttered mess, in part because the space also serves as overflow storage for non-perishables. Bulk cartons of elbow macaroni, cases of vinegar, and #10 cans of tomato sauce, applesauce, and peaches are stacked around the perimeter of the room, except along the wall where the couch is. Having exhausted himself imposing order on all other aspects of his life, LaVerne Williams has neither the energy nor the impulse to clean his office. It is the one place where things are left just as they are.

The couch was the first piece of furniture he and Angela bought for their apartment after they got married, almost forty years ago. When they moved to their first house, the couch ended up in the rec room in the basement, then, eventually, Raymond and LaVerne hauled it over to the restaurant. In spite of the fact that it is too short by at least a foot for LaVerne to comfortably stretch out on, he has never indicated any desire for a newer or longer couch.

On the wall over the couch is a framed team photo of the 1967 Kansas City Athletics. Next to it is a framed picture of the old Municipal Stadium at 22nd and Brooklyn, where the

Athletics played, before Charlie O. Finley moved the team to Oakland in 1968.

On the gray metal desk in the middle of the room is a beige computer with a grimy keyboard and a fingerprint-smudged monitor screen. None of the restaurant's employees can say for sure that the computer actually works.

Functioning as a paperweight, perched atop a pile of pink and yellow invoices, is a bottle of deep red barbecue sauce. The label says, 'LaVerne Williams' Genuine BBQ Sauce KANSAS CITY STYLE as featured on the *Morty Pavlich Show*.'

On the way back from filming a show in Branson in 1991, TV personality Morty Pavlich and his production crew stopped in Kansas City for some barbecue before flying on to Chicago. The show's soundman was a baseball trivia buff and, during deliberations over which barbecue restaurant the crew would visit, he was flipping through the yellow pages and saw the listing for LaVerne Williams' Genuine BBQ and City Grocery. The soundman figured it must be the same LaVerne Williams who played for the Athletics in Kansas City back in the late sixties and he convinced the group to pass up the better-known joints, Bryant's and Gates, for a visit to LaVerne's place.

A.B. Clayton was working the counter that day and was the one who took Morty Pavlich's order – ribs with two sides, greens and red potatoes. A.B. recognized him immediately. Sometimes when he got home late, A.B. drank beer in his underwear in front of the TV and watched the *Morty Pavlich Show* if there was nothing else on.

When Morty Pavlich and his crew sat down, A.B. scurried back to the office to tell LaVerne.

'It's Morty Pavlich!' he whispered loudly to his boss, who was counting boxes of paper napkins, and making notes on a clipboard.

'It's *what*?' said LaVerne vaguely, without looking up.

'It's Morty Pavlich! He's here! He's out front eating.'

'Morty Pavlich, the guy on TV, is *here*?' LaVerne asked, half smiling.

A.B. restated the facts and the two men went out to have a look. There was Morty Pavlich, gnawing contently on a rib bone.

LaVerne went over and introduced himself. Morty Pavlich was gracious and seemed delighted to meet LaVerne, but inasmuch as his fingers were covered in sauce, he didn't shake hands. The soundman wanted to know if LaVerne had in fact played for the Athletics. When LaVerne confirmed this, the soundman asked for an autograph.

LaVerne wouldn't let Morty Pavlich and his crew pay for lunch. As the group was leaving, A.B. rounded up the other employees and they applauded from behind the counter as if they were an audience at an actual *Morty Pavlich Show*.

A.B. watched the *Morty Pavlich Show* every night after that. On a Wednesday two weeks after his visit to the restaurant, Morty Pavlich mentioned the visit during the broadcast, specifically saying how good the sauce was. A.B was so excited when he told LaVerne about it he got choked up.

LaVerne had previously contemplated bottling and retailing his barbecue sauce, and this latest development seemed to present a perfect marketing opportunity. A few weeks later he signed a contract with a bottler in St Louis to distribute LaVerne Williams' Genuine BBQ Sauce KANSAS CITY STYLE as featured on the *Morty Pavlich Show*. When the first shipment arrived at the restaurant, LaVerne right away sent a bottle to Morty Pavlich with a thank-you note.

Three months later, LaVerne received in the mail an autographed photo of Morty Pavlich. No note. Just the picture.

About a week after that, LaVerne received a certified letter from a law firm representing the *Morty Pavlich Show*, informing LaVerne that he must cease and desist the distribution and/or sale of any and all products using the name Morty Pavlich in packaging or promotion, and that all existing such products must be immediately destroyed.

A.B. swore and cursed continuously as he and LaVerne heaved crates of the barbecue sauce into the dumpster behind the restaurant. In his rage, A.B. miscalculated the distance to the top of the dumpster and one of the crates bounced off the edge and landed on his foot. He couldn't work the next day and hobbled around for a week after that. Whenever anybody asked him about his foot he snorted and mumbled, '*Damn* that Morty Pavlich.'

LaVerne didn't say much about the whole affair, so it was hard to tell if he was angry or embarrassed.

In spite of this disappointment, on the wall of the restaurant, opposite the wall where Raymond's obituary is displayed, and among photographs of Kansas City Chiefs, and Royals, local politicians, and radio personalities, is the autographed photo of Morty Pavlich.

3

Lone Star

LaVerne Williams was born and raised in Plum Grove, Texas, north of Houston. Like all Texans he is inordinately proud to be a Texan, as if it is somehow a crowning achievement, not a simple accident of birth. So when LaVerne first got the idea to bottle and sell his barbecue sauce, which was well before the Morty Pavlich incident, he wanted to call it 'LaVerne Williams' Genuine TexiKan BBQ Sauce'.

'It combines "Texas" and "Kansas City",' he said, explaining his idea to A.B. 'And it sounds like the word "Mexican". TexiKan. Mexican.'

A.B. looked at his boss, expecting further explanation. When none was offered, A.B. nodded vigorously and told LaVerne it was a great name for a barbecue sauce. LaVerne took his idea, along with A.B.'s endorsement, to Angela.

'TexiKan is *not* a word,' she said. She was quite sure LaVerne already knew this but thought a reminder might help.

'I *know* it's not a word,' he said. 'We'll *make* it a word. It combines "Texas" and "Kansas City". It's the best of both worlds. The best of Texas barbecue and Kansas City barbecue in one bottle. And it sounds like Mexican.'

'Will the sauce be Mexican?' asked Angela.

LaVerne was exasperated with his wife's failure to perceive the cleverness and marketing savvy of the TexiKan concept and concluded that he needed to explain it a few more times.

'No, the sauce won't be *Mex*ican. It'll be *Texi*Kan,' LaVerne said with exaggerated patience. 'It'll be Texas *and* Kansas City.'

'But LaVerne,' said Angela, 'you've never promoted your sauce or your barbecue as having anything to do with Texas. We don't have any signs in the restaurant saying, "We serve genuine Texas barbecue." None of your customers even *know* you're from Texas. If you start selling sauce that's TexiKan, people won't know what that means. It'll just confuse people.'

'But *everybody* knows Texas barbecue is the best,' LaVerne said, as if the point was so obvious it hardly need be made.

'Well, *that's* just silly,' Angela laughed derisively. Angela was born and raised in Kansas City. 'There's not a single person in this town, not a *one*, who would agree with you on that. Kansas City is the barbecue *capital*. And in case you've forgotten, our restaurant is in Kansas City, not Texas. TexiKan is a *horrible* name for a barbecue sauce. Especially if you want people in Kansas City to buy it.'

LaVerne always got mad when Angela was right and he was wrong, a circumstance that was all too common as far as he was concerned. He grabbed a beer from the refrigerator and stomped out of the house slamming the door behind him.

If Angela Newton had known the specifics of what 'for better, for worse, for richer, for poorer, in sickness and in health' actually meant in the case of her marriage to LaVerne Williams she might have reconsidered marrying him. Loving

LaVerne had been easy. Living with him had only recently become, if not exactly easy, at least less difficult.

The marriage got off to a bad start. Angela's father, the Rev. Dr Clarence E. Newton, senior pastor of New Jerusalem Baptist Church, strongly disapproved of LaVerne, who he felt had an unsavory past and a questionable future. Both of Angela's older brothers had gone into the ministry and, without it ever expressly being said, it was expected that Angela would marry a minister, which LaVerne definitely was not.

Angela's mother, Alberta H. Newton, was only a little more accepting of LaVerne, but this was more strategic than heartfelt on her part. Mrs Newton feared she would incite her strong-willed daughter to all-out rebellion if she joined her husband in opposing LaVerne.

LaVerne naturally resented his in-laws' negativity towards him and rightly felt that it undermined his relationship with Angela.

Things improved slightly in late 1966 when the Athletics offered LaVerne a contract. The Rev. Dr Newton was a dedicated fan and learned scholar of baseball and it was hard to deny that his son-in-law was a talented ballplayer. However, when LaVerne blew out his shoulder in spring training in 1968, and was subsequently waived by the Athletics, Rev. Newton's support began to wane. It further eroded when LaVerne stopped attending church services and his moods darkened.

Angela, however, did not love LaVerne because he was a baseball player or even because he went to church. She didn't really care that much about baseball. Angela loved LaVerne for what he was, a sweet and soulful man. She loves him still for the same reasons. And when LaVerne had finished his beer and came sulking back into the house she reminded him of that.

'I love you, LaVerne. There's nothing you can say or do that will *ever* change that. But TexiKan is a *lame-ass* idea. And there's nothing you can say or do that will ever change *that*.'

4

Vinegar Pie

Smoke Meat is a small place, but it's not what you would call cozy. The building is about a hundred years old. And though it is located in what is now Kansas City's hip and increasingly upscale arts district, its decor is decidedly pre-hip. The interior walls are not exposed brick. They are cinderblock, painted with a heavy white enamel. The ceiling is not exposed heating and ventilation ductwork painted flat black. It's a 1970s-era dropped ceiling of once-white acoustic tiles now stained yellow. The floor is black industrial-grade linoleum tile worn down in spots to the wood underneath.

When encouraged by friends and well-meaning cus-tomers to redecorate or restore the building, so as to bring it in line with other recently rehabilitated buildings in the neighborhood, LaVerne takes the opportunity to expound on his barbecue philosophy.

'Barbecue is not fancy food. It's plain and it's simple. And that's how it should be served – plain and simple. If you're selling barbecue you serve it up in a barbecue joint. If you're selling fancy food then it's fine to serve it in a fancy place. The only thing fancy about this place is the damn rent.'

There are nine tables with mismatched chairs that seat a total of forty-four customers in LaVerne's plain and simple place. In the winter it is usually too warm inside. In the summer it's too cold.

And it's clean. Cleanliness being LaVerne Williams' big bugaboo.

'White folks assume that black people are not as clean and neat as they are,' he says. 'In spite of the fact that we've been cleaning their houses for the last three hundred years. So we always have to go the extra mile just to make sure our places are spotless.'

LaVerne keeps one employee on every shift busy clearing and wiping tables, sweeping and mopping floors, and scouring the washrooms.

Cleanliness is also a part of LaVerne's overall effort to set his restaurant apart from other barbecue establishments in town. 'Other joints are greasy and proud of it. I never understood that.'

The primary element of LaVerne's differentiation strategy, however, is his menu.

Smoke Meat is at least as well known in the neighborhood for the food it does *not* serve as for the food it serves. This is a source of mild irritation for LaVerne in that he would rather his restaurant be known for its fine smoked meats. But his strongly held and quite specific opinions regarding the kinds of food – especially side dishes – that ought and ought not to be served in a barbecue joint have positioned his menu somewhat outside the mainstream of Kansas City barbecue tradition. LaVerne understands this and steadfastly refuses to do anything about it.

This intransigence has been a source of irritation for LaVerne's right-hand man, A.B. Clayton.

When groups of workers in nearby office buildings discuss where to go for lunch, and someone suggests Smoke Meat, someone else will inevitably ask, 'Is that the place that doesn't serve fries?'

Smoke Meat does *not* serve fries. Neither does it serve onion rings, coleslaw, potato salad, or any kind of chicken – reliable standbys at almost all other Kansas City barbecue joints.

There are more than 120 barbecue joints in the greater Kansas City metropolitan region, and once in a while you'll come across one that doesn't have one or another of these items on its menu. But only Smoke Meat doesn't offer any of them.

Smoke Meat *does* serve beans, but not barbecue beans the way most people think of them, which is navy beans, baked in brown sugar and barbecue sauce, with bits of brisket tossed in. For that reason, LaVerne doesn't call his beans 'barbecue beans'. He calls them 'beans'. The recipe is straightforward: pinto beans cooked with chopped onions and jalapeño peppers, enormous amounts of garlic, way too much salt, and a pinch of cumin. Just the way LaVerne's grandmother made them down in Plum Grove, Texas. But not the way most customers expect when they order beans. When A.B. or one of the other employees puts a bowl of beans on a patron's tray it's not unusual for the customer to say, 'Excuse me, I ordered the beans.' At which point the employee is obliged to explain, 'These *are* the beans. They're *Texas* beans.' This is what annoys A.B.

'Why don't we just give people what they want, boss?' A.B. has pleaded on numerous occasions.

'Because they only want it because they're used to it,' LaVerne says. 'Kansas City beans are too sweet and too rich. They compete with the meat and the meat ought to be the star of the show. Once people get used to *our* beans, they'll start asking the *other* joints to make 'em *our* way.'

A.B. remains skeptical of this possibility. 'Well, boss, we've been open since 1982 and we're still the only place in town serving your grandma's beans.'

LaVerne will then explain that in order for a barbecue joint to compete successfully in a crowded marketplace it needs a unique personality, an identity all its own, which is why Smoke Meat has, in LaVerne's words, 'steered its own course' with regard to its menu.

'Our side dishes all taste good with barbecue meat,' he says. 'If people want the "same old, same old" they can go somewhere else.'

At which point A.B. sighs, shakes his head and returns to his work mumbling something on the order of, 'Yeah, but *you're* not the one who has to explain a hundred times a day why we don't have fries.'

Once A.B. put up a sign next to the menu letterboard that said, *'If you don't see it here, don't order it and don't ask for it because we don't serve it.'*

LaVerne made him take it down.

The items on Smoke Meat's menu are as follows, listed as they appear on the letterboard:

SMOKED MEATS
Brisket, sliced thick
Pulled chuck
Burnt Ends
Sausage
Pulled pork
Turkey breast
Reg. sandwich $3.95 Lg. $5.25
By the pound 11.00
Ribs
Full slab $17.95
Long end 10.50
Short end 11.50

SIDE DISHES
Greens $2.50

Red potatoes 2.50
Onions and cabbage 2.50
Beans 2.50
Applesauce 1.25

DESSERT
Sweet potato pie $2.25
Peach cobbler 2.25
Vinegar pie 225

BEVERAGE
Reg. 1.79 Lg. 2.25
Ice Tea
Coke product
Lone Star longneck 2.50
Boulevard Wheat 3.25

The vinegar pie doesn't actually cost two hundred and twenty-five dollars per slice. The little letterboard dot used for a decimal point fell off during a spring cleaning and was never found. This is the kind of thing Cochran Rooney would make a big deal out of, but he's only been to Smoke Meat that one time.

Smoke Meat's sandwiches are served disassembled, which is to say that the raw materials of a sandwich are supplied – a mound of meat on a piece of red butcher paper with four slices of white bread on top. It's the customer's responsibility to construct the actual sandwich. This is the same way sandwiches are served at Arthur Bryant's – Kansas City's most famous barbecue joint – located a few miles east. But LaVerne makes a point of saying that this is not 'Bryant's style', but is, in fact, *Texas*-style. 'The Bryants came from Texas, just like me,' he says. 'And that's the way barbecue is served down there. They didn't invent it. They just brought it with them.'

A thick slice of white onion and a dill pickle are also provided. And the meat is served without sauce, though sauce is available at the table. LaVerne explains that these, too, are Texas traditions and cites them as further evidence that he is not imitating Bryant's in any way.

Though he won't admit it to his boss, A.B. has slowly, quietly, and grudgingly accepted that the eccentricities of Smoke Meat's menu do give the place a distinct character. When it comes to vinegar pie, however, he remains defiant. Knowing that it is another one of LaVerne's grandmother's recipes has not altered his opinion. 'It's just weird,' he says. 'People don't even know what vinegar pie is. We should at least change the name.'

LaVerne dismisses all such criticism, especially from A.B. 'Boy, you'd have a lot more credibility on the subject of vinegar pie if you'd just once try some.'

5

A Good Saver

Another thing you won't find on Smoke Meat's menu is any dish made with rice. 'I had enough rice in the first seventeen years of my life to last me the entire rest of my life,' LaVerne says. 'I don't care if I never have rice pudding, beans and rice, Mexican rice, fried rice or any other kind of rice ever again.'

This aversion stems from the fact that LaVerne was raised by his grandmother, Rose Williams, in Liberty County, Texas, which, before it was oil and cattle country, was rice country.

Rose Williams worked for Raylon Rice and Milling Enterprises for thirty years and was paid for her labors in part with a weekly bag of rice, which she put to good use feeding her grandson who came to live with her when his mother, Rose's daughter Loretta, gave him up. LaVerne was six months old.

Rose tried her best to prepare the rice in interesting new ways, but after long hours at the mill, it was hard to gather up the gumption to get fancy with her cooking. LaVerne was a good boy and didn't complain much, but the day he boarded the bus for Birmingham to join the Athletics' farm club was the last day he ever ate rice.

Rose paid for LaVerne's bus ticket and the suitcase full of new clothes he took with him to Birmingham. She had always been a good saver. Every two weeks after standing in line at the payroll window for her paycheck she'd walk into town and stand in line at the bank to put some of her money away. She had tried to be a good Christian and a good mother. So, when Loretta fell in with a bad bunch, started skipping school and stopped going to church, Rose felt that she had failed both God and her daughter. But she would not fail her grandson. When LaVerne's baseball coach told her that some scouts from Kansas City had been watching LaVerne play Rose understood that baseball could be her grandson's chance to better his lot. When the Athletics offered him a minor-league contract later that year she was determined he would go.

'I don't know much about baseball, child. But I know you're good at it,' she told LaVerne as they sat together on a bench at the bus station. 'Everyone in this town knows it. You'll do just fine. Stay out of trouble with the white folks, LaVerne. Be a gentleman at all times. Find a good church and you'll do fine.'

Rose was lonely that summer. She cherished her years with LaVerne and didn't know what to do with herself after he left. She kept track of the team in the newspaper and sometimes she would go next door to her brother Delbert's house and if they could find one of the games on the radio they'd listen out on the front porch and drink iced tea.

Once a week, usually on Monday nights, LaVerne called her and made her laugh with stories about his teammates. Twice a month, Rose wrote LaVerne a letter, folded a five-dollar bill inside it and sent it to him in a box of puffed rice candy she had made herself.

And twice a month LaVerne Williams was the most popular guy in the Birmingham A's clubhouse. His teammates crowded around him as he dispensed homemade puffed rice candy until it was gone. Which was fine with him. LaVerne hated puffed rice candy.

6

Silent Partner

It was an unlikely friendship. Delbert Douglass Merisier III was a black man whose father had moved his family from Louisiana to Texas to find work milling rice when Delbert was four years old; and Frederick Wilhelm Hartholz, a white man whose father moved his family to Texas from Germany to join his older brother's butchering and sausage-making business. Both were widowed at a young age. Hartholz's wife died giving birth to a boy who would have been their first child, had he not died a few hours after his mother. Delbert's wife left one morning for her job at Raylon Rice and never came home. She was found three days later floating face up in the Trinity River with a broken neck. The police said it was an accident.

When Hartholz's family came over from Germany they settled in New Braunfels. But after his wife died, Hartholz had a falling-out with his father that ended with him taking the butcher-shop truck and driving east. In Plum Grove he ran out of gas and slept the night in the truck. The next morning he answered a notice in the paper and was hired on as the second janitor at the school. Delbert was the other janitor. It was the job he went to after his shift at Raylon. Even though he'd been the main janitor for four years, when

Hartholz started work the school board made him Delbert's boss.

Hartholz was moody most of the time. Not a mean-spirited moody, just not happy. For that reason, and because most small-town native Texans had little patience for his heavily accented English, Hartholz made no friends in Plum Grove.

Delbert Merisier was as merry as Hartholz was morose. When Hartholz grumbled about having to mop up the pee in the boy's room Delbert smiled. 'Well, sir, their little peckers ain't big enough for them to get a hold of 'em and aim 'em right. And little boys is always in a hurry. They don't care much if some goes on the floor. Half the time they wouldn't even go if someone didn't remind 'em to. They ain't like you and me, having to piss every five minutes.'

When Hartholz complained about rain Delbert laughed. 'Mr Hartholz, maybe in Germany you had plenty of rain but this is Texas and we don't ever have enough of it. Maybe if you was a farmer you'd feel different about it. It's all in how you see things.'

Hartholz marveled at Delbert's positive outlook. He had observed that black people were mostly invisible to the whites in Plum Grove and elsewhere in Texas. Except when they were ordered about, cursed at, or mocked. He saw that though they worked as hard, or harder, than white people, the black residents of Plum Grove all lived in a cluster of small, poorly built houses at the edge of town, without benefit of paved streets. Delbert's good humor was an antidote to Hartholz's gloom and over time Hartholz developed an unspoken respect and affection for Delbert.

Delbert had learned to be wary of friendly white folks. More than once previously gregarious white men had bluntly reminded Delbert of his proper place upon taking offense at a remark or smile deemed uppity. But gradually he let down his guard with Hartholz and a genial familiarity formed between them.

Since there was no public place in Plum Grove, or anywhere else in Texas, where a black man and white man were allowed to drink together after work they would sometimes drive out to the dump and drink whiskey in the back of Hartholz's truck where they talked about their wives, their fathers, Germany and Louisiana. Delbert made Hartholz laugh with gossip about other black people in Plum Grove, though he thought it remarkable that Hartholz could laugh without actually smiling. Hartholz never smiled.

Sometimes when the whiskey had done its work, Delbert would take a harmonica from his back pocket and play the blues. The first time Hartholz heard Delbert play, a liberating loneliness welled up inside him and escaped in a big sob that stopped Delbert cold. 'You okay?' Delbert asked.

Hartholz jumped down from the truck bed and walked off into the night where he stayed until Delbert became concerned. 'I'm leaving without you,' he called. 'And I'm taking your truck and your whiskey too.'

This produced the desired result. But Delbert was reluctant to use his harmonica again. However, the next time they shared a bottle in the back of the truck, Hartholz asked him to play.

On Sunday afternoons they fished for bluegill on the pond behind the Raylon property or sometimes for catfish up on the San Jacinto. Delbert wouldn't fish in the Trinity River.

Delbert called Hartholz 'Fritz' once. But Hartholz put an end to that. 'Hartholz is good,' said Hartholz. 'Fred is good. But never Fritz.' Delbert wondered if maybe Hartholz's father was called Fritz.

One Sunday morning on the drive up to the San Jacinto, Hartholz confided in Delbert that he was saving money to open his own butcher shop.

'How much you think you need?' asked Delbert.

'Maybe a thousand dollars for a building and a thousand for equipment,' said Hartholz. 'And then the meat.'

'How much you got saved?'

'One thousand, two hundred and thirty-seven dollars.'

'Well, I got nine hundred and forty-six saved up, myself. Maybe you could use an investor.'

The residents of Plum Grove naturally assumed that Delbert was Hartholz's employee when the butcher shop opened up in the old filling station next to the post office, and neither man ever said different. But they were in fact business partners. And after a time they both quit their janitor jobs and Delbert gave notice at Raylon.

Hartholz butchered sides of beef, whole hogs and chickens, which were delivered each week from Houston. Delbert arranged the cuts neatly in a meat case they bought used from a grocery store over in Beaumont. In a shack Delbert built out behind the store, Hartholz cold-smoked hams and sausages he made himself. Beside the shack Delbert erected a brick pit four feet high and four feet square. About halfway up, between two courses of bricks, he crisscrossed two rows of steel rods, forming a grate. On Friday afternoons Delbert covered this grate with briskets Hartholz had set aside for this purpose. In a bisected oil drum next to the pit Delbert burned oak logs down to coals which he shoveled into the bottom of the pit. He then covered the structure with a piece of corrugated steel and let the briskets cook slowly over the coals for the next seventeen or nineteen hours.

Saturdays soon became the busiest day of the week at the butcher shop. Delbert sliced the smoked briskets in the back of the store while in front Hartholz wrapped and sold the meat by the pound.

*

After Delbert's sister Rose took her grandson LaVerne into her care she sometimes left the boy at the shop while she worked an extra shift at Raylon, or if she had a meeting at church.

LaVerne liked the butcher shop more than any other place in Plum Grove, and the men enjoyed his company. He was eager to help and did what he was told. When his great-uncle sliced the briskets he stood at the end of the table and snatched crispy pieces of the black smoky crust and shoved them quickly into his mouth.

Hartholz looked forward to LaVerne's visits. On the days when the boy didn't come by, Hartholz asked about him. 'The boy, LaVerne, he is okay?'

One evening Delbert and Hartholz sat on chairs behind the store sipping whiskey and watching smoke rise from the pit while LaVerne played with a yellowed baseball coming apart at the seams. Over and over he threw it high into the air and caught it barehanded.

'The boy is a good boy, Delbert,' said Hartholz. 'You and your sister should be proud. He is happy. You are doing good for him.'

Delbert looked over at his friend. Hartholz was smiling.

7

Double-wide

It was the big kid at the trailer park who gave A.B. his first cigarette. A.B. was twelve years old. So was the big kid.

When A.B. was little, his grade-school teachers had the kids make construction-paper posters saying that smoking was bad. When he got to middle school, his gym teacher showed a film with pictures of diseased lungs and people who had to talk through holes in their throats because they got cancer from smoking. But A.B. didn't know any grown-ups who didn't smoke, including his gym teacher, who he'd seen smoking out in the school parking lot. Sooner or later someone would have given him his first cigarette. It just happened to be the big kid.

A.B.'s mother took him with her to a trailer park up on Sterling Road in Sugar Creek a few times, to visit a boyfriend. She was between husbands at the time – a condition she disliked and was always in a hurry to remedy – and the man in the yellow double-wide showed promise. He had a good job at the landfill, was separated from his wife, was a good pool player, and generous, too. At the bars, he was always buying pitchers of beer for his friends.

The boyfriend's kids lived with their mother so there wasn't anyone for A.B. to do anything with when he was there and the boyfriend didn't want him watching TV.

'When I get home from work the only sound I want to hear is my finger popping open a can of beer,' he said. 'We didn't have a TV when we was kids and we did okay so why don't you just find yourself something else to do and let me and your mom be.'

A.B. understood this wasn't a request.

A deep concrete drainage ditch ran along the back of the trailer park. Sometimes A.B. threw sticks in the water and watched them float away. Other times he wandered over to the park playground and knocked the tether ball around the pole.

One time when A.B. went down to the ditch a big kid was there adding trash paper and scrap wood to a fire he'd built. A.B. stood at a distance and watched.

After a few minutes the kid turned to A.B. and grinned. 'Wanna see something?' A.B. shrugged and walked forward a few steps.

'That's as close as you wanna get,' said the kid. He threw something into the fire and scampered over to where A.B. stood. An instant later a puncturing blast from inside the fire sent sparks and cinders flying in all directions, causing A.B. and the kid to cower and shield themselves with their arms.

'What was *that?*' A.B. squealed, as something metallic fell from the sky landing with a clank on a rusted tire rim approximately a yard from A.B.'s feet.

'*That's* what that was,' laughed the kid, pointing to an exploded aerosol can of Faultless starch. 'That was excellent!'

A.B. tried to laugh in a cool nonchalant kind of way, but what emerged from his throat was a big hiccup. Followed by a fit of smaller hiccups. The kid took a pack of Camels from the back pocket of his jeans and pulled one out. 'You want one?'

What A.B. wanted was to not look like such a scaredy

31

cat. So he said yes. He put the cigarette between his lips and let the big kid light it.

He'd seen his mother and her friends take long hard drags on their cigarettes so that's what he did, resulting in an instantaneous spasm of coughing which propelled his Camel out of his mouth in a high arc, into the ditch where it was carried downstream alongside an empty Pabst can.

The kid looked at A.B. with disgust. 'What a wuss.'

The next time A.B.'s mom took him with her to the trailer park, A.B. went down to the drainage ditch again but the big kid wasn't there. A.B. threw rocks into the ditch for a while. But it hadn't rained for several days so there was hardly any water. He walked over to the playground.

When he got there he saw that someone had cut open the tether ball. It hung there on the rope like a gutted fish on a stringer. He went over to the basketball court and lay down on one of the benches where players sit. He thought about his social studies teacher Mrs Norris and how pretty and young she was and how he had seen her at the grocery store holding hands with her husband and how she smiled up at him when he surprised her by kissing her neck. He fell asleep wondering if they had any children.

He woke up when the big kid kicked his feet off the bench.

'Hey, wuss,' he said. 'Taking your nappy? Where's your blankey?'

A.B. had learned that when big kids ask questions like this the answers never seem to satisfy them. He sat up.

'Hey,' he said, anticipating further provocation, perhaps with a painful conclusion. To A.B.'s surprise the big kid sat down next to him.

'So, do you live here or what? How come I only see you around once in a while?'

'My mom likes a guy who lives over there.' A.B. pointed in the direction of the yellow double-wide.

The big kid nodded. 'Do you have a basketball?'

A.B. shook his head.

They sat there on the bench without saying anything. A.B. wondered what would happen next. The big kid sighed and took a pack of Camels out of his T-shirt pocket. A.B. noticed that the kid was missing his index finger on his left hand. He didn't ask about it.

'Are you going to hack out your lungs again,' the kid asked, 'or do you want one of these?'

A.B. reached for one. This time he took in the smoke slowly and breathed it back out evenly. It made him dizzy at first but then it went away.

'It's just the opposite with me,' said the kid. 'My old lady's here and it's the guys who come to see her.'

He stood up. 'Next time you come here, bring a basket-ball,' he said.

He flicked his cigarette butt into the grass and walked away.

When the big kid got back to his trailer, his mother's car was gone and the trailer door was locked. He knocked on the door, but no one answered. He yelled and pounded on the door, but still nobody came. He went down to the ditch and sat on a broken cinderblock and smoked another cigarette. Tall weeds grew in the soggy dirt along both sides of the ditch, and sometimes a stray dog or a rat would run out of the weeds and startle him. So when he saw the weeds moving he picked up a rock and stood, ready for whatever it might be. It was a turtle. About the size and shape of an overturned cereal bowl. The kid watched the turtle make its way down toward the ditch. He wondered where his mother had gone. He felt the weight and rough edges of the rock in his hand

and without thinking much about it heaved it at the turtle. He heard a thick smack and he could see that the rock had hit and cracked the turtle's shell. He could see bright red where the shell had split. He picked up the broken cinderblock and went and stood over the turtle. It had pulled its head and legs and tail inside its broken shell. The kid wondered if it was dead. He held the cinderblock up over his head and let it drop. A piece of shell with something white attached to it stuck out from under the block. Maybe his mom just went up to the store to get cigarettes and beer.

8

Feed My Sheep

Like robins returning in the spring, near the end of March the screamers return to the sidewalks and alleys around Smoke Meat. They don't come around much in the winter. They live on the streets and when it's cold they stay at the City Mission or other such places.

The black screamer is a young man. He strides the streets purposefully, driven by righteous wrath metastasized into madness. He wears an oversized army surplus jacket. His hair is matted and littered with crud. Customers on their way to Smoke Meat sometimes hear him coming from a distance, at which point they tend to pick up the pace, hoping to make it inside before he sees them.

A.B.'s first encounter with the black screamer came one morning when he was in front of the restaurant sweeping up. The black screamer saw A.B. from across the street, pointed an accusing finger at him and started yelling.

'You! You are going to die and burn in the fires of hell for eternity! You are a wretched and vile sinner and you and the rest of your cursed race must get right with God! Damn you! Damn you for the excesses of your life and your smugness and your promiscuity! Damn you for looking away! Damn you! Only Jesus can save you now!'

A.B. was so shaken by this he was immediately seized by

a violent case of the hiccups that lasted through the lunch hour. When customers began asking A.B. if he was all right, LaVerne got disgusted, and relieved A.B. of his counter duties.

Later A.B. sought reassurance from LaVerne. In 1987, a year after Raymond died, A.B. was baptized at the New Jerusalem Baptist Church and he wanted to know for sure that it took.

'You don't think that guy is like some kind of prophet or something, do you, boss? Like they talk about at church. I mean, he looked right at me, right in my eyes, and damned me and said I needed to get right with God. But I am right with God, aren't I? I'm saved aren't I? That's what me being baptized was all about, wasn't it? Being saved? He said I would burn in the fires of hell for eternity. But he's wrong, isn't he? I accepted Jesus Christ as my personal Lord and Savior so I know he's wrong. Right, boss? Besides, I don't even know what promiscuity is.'

LaVerne shook his head. 'That guy is no prophet, son. What he is, is full of crap.'

While the black screamer's grievances are mostly soteriological, the white screamer is just plain pissed off. In fact, compared to the white screamer, the black screamer is really only a shouter. The white screamer screams with such ferocity that his vocal cords and the bulging veins on his neck and forehead appear always near the rupture point. He is a roundish older man with short-cropped gray hair and a grayish complexion. His torn and worn-thin coat is gray and his stained and greasy trousers are gray. Sometimes he pushes a trashcan and a broom around in front of him. When he screams his face turns a bright purplish red. Then it goes beyond red to white hot. He calls down curses of death and dismemberment on all within the sound of his screeching voice.

Once or twice a week during what he calls 'screamer season', LaVerne will be disposing of trash at the dumpster behind the restaurant, when he'll first hear, and then see, the white screamer. It was after one of these sightings that LaVerne noticed that the white screamer never actually makes eye contact with the people in his vicinity.

One morning LaVerne was outside leaning against the back door drinking coffee when the white screamer approached from down the block pushing his trashcan. He started right in as soon as he saw LaVerne.

'Eat shit, you asshole! I hope a bomb falls on you and blows you up cuz you're a asshole and you know it! You don't deserve to live! I want you to die! You need to die! I hope you die! I'm going to send a bomb to drop on top of you and kill you! Kill you! You're a shit asshole and I'm going to throw a hand grenade at you and blow you up, you shit asshole!'

LaVerne went inside. A few minutes later he came back out and called to the screamer who was then fishing around in the trash behind the strip club across the alley.

'Hey! You! Screaming guy! Come on over here.'

The screamer looked over in LaVerne's general direction and resumed his cursing. 'A bomb! I'm going to drop a bomb on you and—'

LaVerne waved a hand dismissively. 'Yeah, yeah. You're going to kill me with a bomb,' he said wearily. 'Come over here a minute. You like barbecue?'

The screamer hesitated then pushed his trashcan, over to LaVerne, his eyes down.

'Here's some breakfast,' said LaVerne, handing the screamer a slab of ribs wrapped in red butcher paper.

The screamer looked at the package for a moment, raised it to his nose and inhaled deeply, then turned and continued

on his way pushing his trashcan, the ribs tucked up under his
arm.

'That ought to shut him up for a while,' LaVerne said as
he went inside.

9

Charles and Charlie

Ordinarily, after the lunch rush, LaVerne will go back to the office and take a nap and A.B. will work the counter, but on one particular Tuesday, A.B. had to take his mother to her podiatrist appointment, so LaVerne was out front. A handful of customers loitered at their tables, mostly regulars.

'Mother' Mary Weaver, a local blues legend, occupied her usual spot in the corner nursing a beer, having finished off an enormous mound of burnt ends, a double helping of greens, some cabbage and onions, and a piece of sweet potato pie. LaVerne always puts a small cruet of apple-cider vinegar on Mother Mary's table because she likes it on her greens.

Mary shops for her clothes in the plus-sizes department. Her wigs she buys at the House of Hair, downtown. Her particular model is blondeish and bonnet-like, manufactured from a supernaturally shiny synthetic. Mother is past her prime as a singer, but remains hugely popular among Kansas City's loyal blues fans.

Seated across from her, drinking coffee, was Pug Hale, her frequent lunch companion. Pug is a highly decorated detective in the Kansas City Police Department and the regular lead guitarist for the band that backs Mother on her local gigs. It's no mystery how Pug got his nickname. His trunk is squat, thick, and cylindrical, but his legs are short and slender, and his feet dainty. His hands are delicate and fine-boned, and his brown freckled face is kind of pushed in around his bulgy dark brown eyes. It's hard to imagine Pug's tiny fingers navigating the neck of an electric guitar, but anyone who's ever heard him play says he's one of the best in town. Nobody's ever asked Pug what his real name is.

Pug isn't young, but he's younger than Mother. And because she never married and has no family left, Pug looks out for her interests. Mother is trusting by nature and uninterested in the financial aspects of her career and has therefore been swindled more than once by exploitative promoters and conmen. Arthritis, aggravated by her weight, has begun to limit her mobility and Pug now drives her to church and to shop for groceries. Once or twice a week they have lunch together at Smoke Meat. Pug always gets a full slab of ribs. No sauce.

McKenzie Nelson was there with Suzanne Edwards at a table by the window. McKenzie sells ads for *KC.21*, the alternative news and entertainment weekly favored by the city's tattooed population. She's pretty in a black-lipstick, black-nail polish, multiple-piercings kind of way. A.B. used to have quite a crush on her.

Suzanne Edwards sells trendy furniture at a store across the street from Smoke Meat. Stores like Suzanne's are increasingly common up and down Walnut Street, and on Main, one block over. This is a source of aggravation and anxiety for LaVerne.

'It makes me nervous, all these hippie, yuppie stores comin' in here,' he says. 'Pretty soon someone's gonna want to throw us out and put some organic yoga thing in here.'

He tends to look with suspicion at anyone coming into the restaurant wearing a suit and tie, assuming he's a banker or developer with designs on the building.

Over by the door sat Ferguson Glen.

Ferguson comes in at least once or twice a week. Sometimes he'll spend the entire afternoon writing in a notebook, reading, or sometimes nodding off at the only other window table. Ferguson is an ordained Episcopal priest, though he has never pastored a parish. He is a literature and writing professor at St Columba Seminary of the Midwest on Truman Road.

A novel Ferguson Glen wrote in 1968, when he was twenty-four years old, was nominated for a Pulitzer. His publisher and the literary establishment at large expected great things to follow, which never came to pass. Subsequent novels were not forthcoming.

Since then he has written three respected, but largely ignored, volumes of essays exploring such themes as 'The Cold Hard Silence of God' and 'Jesus: My Savior Not My Friend'.

Ferguson is tall and slender. His thinning gray hair is long and combed back from his forehead. His weak blue eyes frequently look as if they've been crying. Ferguson admits he has a serious drinking problem, but shows no inclination to do anything about it. He lives alone in a loft across the street from Smoke Meat.

Del James also lives across the street. Del is a sculptor and has converted half of his loft into studio space. He's a burly guy with a beer gut, close-cropped white hair and is usually dressed in denim bib-overalls, white T-shirt, work boots, and a four-day beard. Del is nearly deaf and requires hearing aids in both ears. Even with this assistance, people still need to talk loudly and clearly to him in order to be understood.

Del has developed a strong regional following and on the Tuesday in question, his lunch guest was Charles, a gallery owner visiting from Los Angeles. Charles was in town to look at Del's work and discuss a possible show in LA.

Charles wore freshly pressed blue jeans torn just so at the knees, an oversized tooled-leather belt with an elaborate silver buckle inlaid with turquoise, and electric-blue snakeskin cowboy boots. This was topped off by a melon-colored Western-style shirt with mother-of-pearl snap buttons. Charles seemed to have expected the streets of Kansas City to be heaving with cattle and cowboys and wanted to be dressed appropriately if called upon to do-si-do or rope a stray.

Del wasn't the only customer entertaining an out-of-town guest. Bob Dunleavy, CEO of the engineering firm building the new downtown arena, was there with Whitey Skomacre, a sports marketing consultant from Oregon.

R.L. Dunleavy Engineering and Construction was founded by Bob Dunleavy's grandfather in 1934. It has since become one of the Midwest's leading design-build firms. The company has played a major part in nearly all the important building projects in Kansas City for the last sixty years.

Bob starting eating lunch at Smoke Meat on a regular basis when his firm was building a new parking garage for the convention center, located a few blocks north of 17th and Walnut. Sometimes he comes in alone and reads the *Wall Street Journal* over a pulled pork sandwich and a diet Coke. Other times he comes in with some of his crew. They linger over pie and coffee long after their lunches are finished, laughing loudly at crude inside jokes. Sometimes A.B. or LaVerne have to remind them that other people are waiting for tables. Bob is good-natured about this and always complies with a smile. He's one of LaVerne's favorite customers.

Bob's guest, Whitey Skomacre, was a short man with a heroic comb-over and a nose that looked like a red Bartlett pear. On the way in he saw the framed newspaper clipping about LaVerne's stint with the Athletics, which provided him with the opportunity to express his opinions about Charlie O. Finley, the owner of the Kansas City Athletics. Whitey felt strongly that Finley was the most brilliant and underappreciated innovator in the history of the National Pastime. Bob and Whitey stood in line behind Del and Charles.

As they approached the counter, Del asked Charles about his name. 'I'm a tad hard of hearing so I may have missed it. Is Charles your first name, or last?'

'Oh, I just go by Charles,' said Charles.

'Beg pardon?'

Charles spoke louder. 'Just *Charles*!'

Del got it this time. 'Justin Charles.'

'No! *Charles! Only* Charles. One name. Like *Cher*.'

Del heard, but was unsure he understood. He discontinued his line of questioning.

'So, what'll you have?' Del motioned in the direction of the menu board behind the counter.

'Well, *whatever* I choose will be *wonderful*, I'm certain,' Charles said loudly. 'I'm *so* looking forward to this. An *authentic* Kansas City experience. You are *so* famous for your barbecue here. And this little place is, well, just *so* quaint.'

By the time Del and Charles stepped up to order, LaVerne already didn't like Charles. He didn't like his joint being called quaint, and he didn't like people with only one name, even though he'd never before met anyone with only one name.

Del ordered his usual. Pulled pork, applesauce, cabbage and onions, and a beer.

'What'll it be?' LaVerne asked Charles without looking up from his order pad.

'Hmmm,' said Charles, touching his chin lightly with his fingers. He wore a large turquoise ring. 'How about a grilled vegetable platter? But no onions, please.'

He smiled at LaVerne.

LaVerne did not smile back. 'First of all, we don't have platters. And next of all, we don't grill anything here.'

43

Charles was confused. 'I thought this was a *barbecue* restaurant.'

LaVerne clarified. 'It is a barbecue restaurant. It's not a *grilling* restaurant.'

Del picked up on bits and pieces of this exchange. 'The pulled pork is real good,' he told Charles. 'I recommend it.'

Charles was flustered. 'But I'm a *vegan*.'

'I'm a Texan,' snapped LaVerne. 'So? What'll it be?'

Charles scowled at the menu board and sighed. 'Oh, dear. I guess I'll have the greens. And maybe the red potatoes.'

While they waited to order Bob and Whitey continued their discussion about Charlie O. Finley. Whitey was doing most of the discussing.

'Finley was miles ahead of his time. That whole thing with the mule and the robot rabbit that supplied the umps with balls? Genius. Plus he had a real eye for talent. Rocky Colavito. Catfish Hunter. Reggie Jackson. Rickey Henderson. Some of the all-time greats.'

Whitey was on a roll. Bob nodded and glanced anxiously over to see if LaVerne was hearing any of it. He couldn't tell.

'Then the orange baseballs. It was a huge mistake that the league never adopted the orange baseball. The green uniforms, white shoes, and handlebar mustaches. Pure genius. He brought entertainment back to the game. That's why baseball is in the doldrums now; there's no one like Charlie Finley around anymore. He was one of a kind.'

Whitey hadn't expressed any curiosity about the young outfielder he'd read about in the newspaper clipping, and Bob had not had an opening into which he could squeeze the information that a former employee of Charlie Finley's was about to take their lunch order. When Del and Charles turned from the counter with their trays, Bob and Whitey stepped forward. LaVerne glared at Whitey. He'd heard every word. Bob rolled his eyes at LaVerne. LaVerne hated

Charlie Finley. The fact of which Bob Dunleavy was well aware.

LaVerne looked at Bob. 'What'll you have, Bob?'

Bob offered up a pained smile. 'We'll both have the brisket, with beans, and a couple pieces of sweet potato pie. And Diet Cokes.'

Whitey wasn't paying attention to the order. He was waiting to resume his oral arguments. LaVerne pushed their trays across the counter and walked off into the kitchen. Bob and Whitey took seats at a table next to Del and Charles. Charles was wolfing down his greens.

'Oh, *my*,' he said. 'These are *delicious*.'

'Beg pardon,' said Del.

'These greens are delicious,' said Charles loudly.

'Told you so,' Del said smugly.

Charles examined his greens. Then, in horror, he exclaimed, 'There is *meat* in here!'

Del nodded. 'That's what makes 'em so good.'

'But I'm a *vegan*,' wailed Charles.

'You said that before,' noted Del. 'What exactly *is* a vegan?'

'A vegan does not eat *meat*!' Charles appeared about to cry.

Mother Mary Weaver had been listening to all this from her corner table. 'Pug, if that idiot in the pink shirt don't shut up, I'm going to have to do something to shut him up.'

Pug sipped his coffee. 'I think they call that color melon, or maybe coral. Not pink.'

'Well, his ass is going to be pink after I'm through kickin' it.'

Pug laughed. 'Calm down, Mother.'

Charles stood up. 'Mr James, we have to go,' he said. 'This place is disgusting!'

Mother had had enough. 'You! You sit down and mind your manners.'

She picked up a rib bone from Pug's tray and flung it at Charles with a flick of her wrist.

The bone hit Charles on the right cheek, splattering his face and his coral shirt with sauce. This so startled Charles that he stumbled backward flailing his arms. He landed in Whitey Skomacre's lap sending both of them sprawling on the floor.

Whitey jumped back up ready for a fight. Except that in the tumble his big flap of hair had flopped over in the wrong direction. When he realized this, it became his primary concern. Charles was screaming, 'Oh! Oh! Oh!' still flailing his arms. Whitey interpreted this as combative behavior and as soon as he had reflapped his hair he assumed a fighting stance.

McKenzie and Suzanne were enjoying the show. Ferguson had fallen asleep – or had passed out – his forehead flat on the table.

Pug shot out of his seat and grabbed Charles by the back of his belt and trotted him out of the restaurant. 'Maybe it's time for you to find somewhere else to eat, sir. Someplace with carrots or broccoli.' Del followed, scratching his head, uncertain as to what had transpired.

Inside, Whitey puffed out his chest as if he'd just won fifteen rounds, and was about to sit back down to finish his meal. But LaVerne, who had emerged from the kitchen when Charles started screaming, had other plans. He took hold of Whitey by the arm and hustled him out the door. Bob slunk along behind.

'What are you doing?' Whitey protested. 'I didn't do anything wrong!'

'Go tell that to Charlie Finley,' LaVerne said. He turned

to Bob. 'Sorry, Bob. Hope this doesn't mess things up for you.'

'It's all right, LaVerne,' Bob said. 'I'm the one who ought to be apologizing.'

LaVerne went inside and began cleaning up the mess. Pug returned and retrieved Mother. As they left Mother said to LaVerne, 'They was both idiots, LaVerne. You don't need that kind of business.'

LaVerne nodded. 'See you next week, Mother. Later, Pug.'

Only McKenzie, Suzanne, and Ferguson were left in the place. The women got up to leave.

'Too much excitement, LaVerne,' said McKenzie. 'We're outta here.'

'Don't you put all this in that paper of yours,' he replied.

Suzanne paused at the door to check on Ferguson.

'He'll be all right,' said LaVerne. 'I'll see he gets home.'

The three of them looked at Ferguson.

That's when Ferguson farted. A long, sustained brap that rattled loud against the hard plastic chair.

'Jeez!' said McKenzie. She and Suzanne hurried out, fanning the air in front of their noses with their hands. LaVerne returned rather quickly to the kitchen.

About ten minutes later A.B. returned from his mother's podiatrist appointment.

'Did I miss anything, boss?' he asked.

LaVerne thought about it for a moment. 'Yeah. Ferguson farted.'

10

April 1968

The Athletics released LaVerne Williams from his contract on March 26, 1968. The GM called that morning with the news.

'You got a lot of talent, LaVerne, and we like you a lot. We hate to do this. We had big things in mind for you. But the docs say it looks bad. They say your shoulder's real iffy. Maybe it'll get better, but probably not. Either way, you're done for the season. And maybe for good. I don't like sayin' that. And you shouldn't take my word for it. You should get a second opinion. Maybe a third. And I encourage you to shop yourself around after you're healed up. You're real fast, LaVerne. There might be a club out there wanting a good base runner like yourself. Anyways, we wish you the best. This isn't personal. It's just baseball. We got to move on. And so do you. We wish you were comin' with us, but that's not how it worked out. So, we wish you the best. And Angela and little Raymond, too.'

And that was that.

LaVerne called every other team in the majors trying to 'shop himself around'. He emphasized his speed and his high on-base average. A couple of teams told him they'd be happy to maybe take a look at him next year when his shoulder had healed. None expressed any more interest than that.

When the team doctor, down in Winter Haven, explained how seriously LaVerne's shoulder was hurt and the long-term implications of the injury, LaVerne got on a Greyhound to Kansas City. He wanted the doctors at City General or maybe even St Luke's to take a look.

They all said the same thing.

LaVerne hung around the apartment for a few days, but he couldn't do much. His arm was in a sling and it hurt. He couldn't help Angela and he couldn't hold the baby. The slightest wrong move made him yelp and grit his teeth. He got headaches from clenching his jaw against the pain. He used his good arm primarily to drink beer, which frequently ended with him falling asleep in the recliner while watching TV, but more often resulted in him yelling at Angela for some minor or imagined infraction. When Angela had had enough of this she called down to Plum Grove and arranged for Rose and Delbert to ask LaVerne to come for a visit.

The Sunday after her call, LaVerne stayed in bed while Angela took Raymond to church. That afternoon, Angela drove LaVerne to the bus station and put him on a Greyhound for Texas.

'Maybe the time down there will help clear your head, and put your heart at peace,' she told him. 'I love you, La-Verne. And I need you. I don't need you to be a ball player. I need you to be my husband. And I need you to be Raymond's father. You've got a lot more to offer this world than baseball. So go home. Relax. When you come back, we'll figure this out.'

Angela held Raymond in her right arm and leaned in to give LaVerne a hug with her left, careful not to hurt his shoulder. LaVerne sobbed into Angela's neck and she cried, too. When Raymond joined in LaVerne kissed them both and boarded the bus.

He slept all the way to Joplin where he had to change buses. It was about 7:30 in the evening and the bus to Fort Smith wasn't leaving for another hour. LaVerne thought about walking down the block to buy some beer at a liquor store he'd seen on the way in, but he couldn't work up the energy. He went in and had coffee at the lunch counter in the bus station.

There were a few other passengers in the diner. A pregnant girl with her toddler son. She looked to be about eighteen. A soldier and a sailor in their uniforms. They sat together on the steps outside, talking and smoking cigarettes. A young man who might have been a college student reading a book. And a middle-aged Mexican couple. The woman rested her head on the man's shoulder and occasionally dabbed her eyes and nose with a handkerchief.

Through the night, down Highway 71 to Fort Smith, then on to DeQueen and Texarkana, LaVerne stared out into the dark, trying to empty his head. By the time the bus pulled in at Shreveport, he realized his efforts had had the opposite effect. All he could think about was how he hated his life and how cruel and wrong everything was.

He got off the bus, went to the men's room, then got his transfer at the ticket window. He wished he'd bought beer back in Joplin. He stepped outside and looked down the street in both directions, but there weren't any liquor stores he could see.

He slept the rest of the way to Beaumont.

Delbert and Rose were waiting for him at the bus station.

On the drive to Plum Grove, it became clear that Rose had decided ahead of time that her strategy to distract La-Verne from his sadness would be to provide him with detailed updates on the lives of each of the thirty-eight members of the Plum Grove Second Baptist Church. After about an hour of this, Delbert said, 'That's maybe all the church news LaVerne needs for now, Rose.' At which point Rose transitioned to news about the second shift at Raylon Rice and Milling.

When they arrived in Plum Grove, Delbert asked LaVerne what he wanted to do.

'Well, I've had enough sleep and being by myself,' he said. 'How about if we go up to the store and put some briskets and sausage in the smoker?'

'I thought you might say that,' said Delbert. 'Hartholz is up there already. He put some meat in this morning. Let's go see if he did it right.'

Hartholz had done it right. The little butcher shop was enveloped in a fragrant veil of thin blue smoke curling out of the big brick pit behind the store. Hartholz was sitting in a rocking chair on the back porch with two split cherry logs on his lap.

'Good morning, LaVerne,' he said. 'I apologize for your shoulder. Maybe it will improve.'

LaVerne nodded and took a seat on one side of the old German. Delbert sat down on the other side.

'Good to see you, Fred,' said LaVerne. 'I've missed you.'

'We miss you, too,' said Hartholz.

That was all anyone said for the rest of the morning.

At about 12:05 in the afternoon Delbert went inside and retrieved a bottle of bourbon and three glasses. He poured drinks for them all, sat down, and took his harmonica out of his overalls' breast pocket and started in on some blues.

After a while, the whiskey and the music loosened LaVerne's hard-packed grief.

'Why, Uncle Delbert? Why did God do this to me?' LaVerne glared off into the distance beyond the smoker.

'He didn't *do* this to you, boy,' Delbert said quietly. 'He didn't have nothing to do with it.'

'Then why did he *let* this happen to me?'

'Because, son, God is a lot like me,' said Delbert. 'He doesn't give a shit if you play baseball. God is a lot more interested in who you are, and not much in what you do. Same with me, LaVerne. I don't really care if you play baseball or not, except for I know *you* care. It hurts me to see you so sad about this. That's 'cause I love you. And I know how much playing in the big leagues means to you. But you're still LaVerne if you play or if you don't play. You're still who you are. And it's times like these that can make you better. Or they can ruin you. That's up to you. That's your choice. Are you going to be a man? Are you going to stand up to this and not let it take you down? Are you going to find a way to make a life for that pretty wife and that new baby of yours? Those are the questions here.'

LaVerne sighed, drained his glass and poured himself another. Delbert waited in case LaVerne might want to say something, but his nephew just scowled and shook his head.

'Son, listen to me,' Delbert continued. 'God will work his way in our lives one way or another. If he wants something out of us, if he wants us to do something for him, it doesn't really matter what we happen to be doing at the time. He can use us if we're playing baseball, he can use us if we're farming. He can use us if we're butchering steers or working in the mill. It's all the same to him.'

Those were the things Delbert had planned to say on the subject and he had said them. He poured more whiskey.

'But, *why*? Why *can't* I play baseball?' LaVerne protested. 'Why can't *that* be God's way of working in my life?'

'Why can't I be the king of France?' asked Delbert, his voice rising a bit. 'Because I *can't*, that's why. Because I was born a Negro in Louisiana, America. And 'cause there ain't even a king of France no more. But I *can* be Delbert Douglass Merisier III. And that's all God wants me to be.'

Hartholz had been listening while he watched the fire. Finally he spoke up.

'You should not always be asking this "why" to yourself, LaVerne. There are mysteries. Some things that only God knows. Why did my Greta and my boy have to die? Why was Delbert's Madeleine killed? You should maybe ask of yourself, "What do you do now?"'

Hartholz got up and went over to the pit. He took one of the cherry splits he'd had on his lap and pushed it into the fire to make more coals. He lifted the corrugated-steel cover to check on the status of the briskets.

'Close that thing,' Delbert barked. 'You're lettin' all the smoke out.'

Hartholz returned to his chair. He grimaced a smile at LaVerne and cocked his head in Delbert's direction. 'He always says that to me.'

Hartholz went on. 'You can lose many years of life in bitter and sad, LaVerne. I did. And I was very alone. It is lonely when we make our own hearts like stones.'

He replenished his glass. LaVerne didn't say anything. Delbert looked over at his nephew in time to see a tear spill onto his cheek. Delbert cleared his throat and went over to the pit to check on the briskets.

Hartholz objected immediately. 'I just looked at those,' he snapped. 'You're going to let all the smoke out.'

Delbert returned to his chair. He winked at LaVerne. 'He always says that to me.'

LaVerne smiled slightly and nodded.

II

April 1968

In 1968, Ferguson Glen was the rock star of the Episcopal Church. The buzz of adulation within American Anglicanism surrounding his literary achievements and high-profile civil-rights activism had caught the attention of literary and liberal salons, and FBI director J. Edgar Hoover, who had taken a personal interest in learning as much as possible about 'that tall white boy with the girl hair' whose image had been recorded a few years earlier in surveillance photos taken of Freedom Riders and, later, with marchers en route from Selma to Montgomery.

In one of these photographs, Ferguson was seated in the back of a bus with other white college students laughing and smoking cigarettes. In another, he was kneeling in prayer with the Rev. Ralph David Abernathy and other ministers, black and white, on a road outside Montgomery. In a third, he was walking several rows behind Martin Luther King, arms linked with other marchers.

Ferguson Glen was ordained to the priesthood at Washington National Cathedral in September 1966. In November of that year, a series of short stories he wrote in seminary were published in the *New Yorker*. The stories featured four characters, Jesus, Satan, a white man, and a black man, traveling together on a train across the United States. The stories captured the imagination of Walker Briggs, an enterprising editor at a venerable New York publishing house. Briggs approached Ferguson with the idea of expanding the stories into a novel, a proposal which Ferguson eagerly accepted. In January 1968, the novel, *Traverse*, was published. That month, Ferguson's picture appeared on the covers of the *New York Times Book Review* and *Christianity Today*.

Ferguson's youth, good looks, wit, and intellect – all wrapped up in a clerical collar – proved irresistible to newspaper and television reporters who clamored for interviews. They wanted to know what drove this privileged son of an auto-industry heiress and a respected Episcopal bishop to challenge, in Ferguson's words, 'the complacency and complicity of American Christianity' by marching against segregation in the South.

Virtually every journalist writing about the young priest and his sudden success felt compelled to make note of his physical resemblance to popular depictions of Christ – shoulder-length brown hair, beard, high cheekbones. Ferguson's usual response to this was to say that he was disappointed by the comparison because he had actually been aiming for more of a John Lennon look.

The hierarchy of the Episcopal Church was quick to embrace and exploit Ferguson's popularity. In February the Seminary of the Holy Trinity, in Memphis, invited him to speak at its prestigious Hammarskjöld Lectures, held annually the first week in April. The Rev. William Slone Coffin was to deliver the keynote. And there were rumors that Dr King himself might attend and perhaps speak. Ferguson's address was titled 'Caesars, Pharisees, and Samaritans'.

On the first night of the lectures, the seminary hosted a reception for its guest speakers, faculty, and students. Ferguson nibbled hors d'oeuvres, simultaneously deflecting the flirtations of the lone female faculty member while calmly explaining to an agitated professor emeritus why it was no longer a viable strategy for 'Negroes' to 'work within the system' for change. When eventually his tormentors abandoned their efforts to win him over he excused himself to the chairman of the lectures committee and exited. He needed a drink.

He stood outside the lecture hall considering his next move. He knew there was a bar at his hotel and thought he remembered that the hotel was about four or five blocks to the east. He started walking in that direction. The night was cool and damp.

Ten or twelve blocks later Ferguson realized that he had proved yet again his father's frequent assertion that his sense of direction was seriously deficient. Though he sometimes suspected that his father was not always referring to the points on a compass.

He reversed course with a sigh, then noticed down a side street a neon sign in the window of a small cinderblock building advertising 'BBQ & Whiskey'.

Like most Michigan natives, Ferguson had a vague knowledge of a thing called barbecue, but had never actually eaten any. He was, however, intimately familiar with whiskey. He decided that this was as good a time as any to sample some of this barbecue and way past time for a glass of whiskey.

As he approached the building he saw over the front door a Coca-Cola sign that had been customized with the name of the restaurant – 'General Bar-B-Q Ribs Wet N Dry'.

Inside, the place was yellow and warm and filled with a smoky aroma more wonderful than anything he could remember. There were a few tables and a few booths, maybe twenty seats in all. Ferguson was the only customer.

Behind the bar was a young black woman. When she heard Ferguson come in, she turned toward the door. Ferguson saw that she was about his age and that her skin was the deep brown-red color of the sweet cherries he loved back home, and that her eyes were bright and curious and that her smile was open and knowing. He saw that her breasts were small and that under her white T-shirt she must be feeling a bit chilly, even though he was feeling suddenly quite warm.

A door behind the bar opened and in from the kitchen came a child, a girl, maybe eight years old. She carried a stack of white terrycloth hand towels. 'Here, Mom,' she said, reaching up to give the towels to her mother.

'Thank you, miss,' said the woman.

The girl looked at Ferguson. 'Who are you?' she demanded.

'I'm Ferguson.'

'Is that your first name or your last name?'

'Mind your manners, you,' said the girl's mother.

'My first,' said Ferguson. 'Glen is my last name. My name is Ferguson Glen.'

'Sounds to me like you got your names mixed up,' said the girl, frowning, hands on her hips.

'Sounds that way to me, too,' said Ferguson. 'So, what's *your* name?'

'My name's Wren. Like the bird,' she said. 'Wren Brown.'

'Well, I've heard of a brown wren. But I've never heard of a Wren Brown,' said Ferguson, frowning, hands on his hips.

The woman with the cherry-brown skin and white T-shirt spoke up. 'That's enough, Wren.' She put her hand on her daughter's head.

She smiled at Ferguson. 'I'm Peri,' she said. 'Pleased to meet you. And please forgive my daughter, here. Sometimes she expresses herself too freely.'

Ferguson took a seat at the bar. 'Perry. Is that your first name or your last?' he asked with a smile.

'First. It's short for Periwinkle,' she said. 'Like the color. Periwinkle Brown. Actually, it's two colors.'

Ferguson repeated the name. 'Periwinkle Brown. That's quite lovely,' he said.

'Thank you,' said Peri. Ferguson thought he detected that she was blushing.

Peri asked Ferguson if he wanted something to eat or drink. He ordered bourbon. Wren went back into the kitchen and Peri poured the whiskey.

'So, are you up there at the seminary?' asked Peri, noticing Ferguson's collar.

'I am,' he said. 'I'm giving a lecture.' He finished his drink and Peri poured him another.

'So,' he asked, 'what are wet and dry ribs?'

Peri laughed. 'You're not from around here, are you?'

Now Ferguson blushed. 'No, I'm not. Why? Did I say something stupid?'

Peri shook her head. 'It's not wet *and* dry ribs. It's wet *or* dry ribs. In Memphis, folks like them either one way or the other. *We* serve them both ways to make everybody happy.'

'What's the difference?' Ferguson asked. 'Other than, I guess, one's wet and the other's dry.'

'Well,' Peri said, with the exaggerated patience one uses to explain something elementary to a child. 'Wet ribs are smoked slow, for about four or five hours, over hickory coals, then, about an hour before they're done, you start mopping them with your barbecue sauce. And just when you put them on the plate to serve them, you brush some more sauce on, so they're wet.

'Dry ribs you smoke the same way. Slow, over hickory. But you don't use sauce. Instead, before you put them in the pit, you rub them down good with your secret recipe of herbs and spices. Then, before you serve them, you give them another hit of those herbs and spices. Here in Memphis, it's a never-ending battle between wet and dry. So? Which would you like?'

Ferguson shrugged. 'Wet, I guess.'

Periwinkle Brown went into the kitchen and came back out a few minutes later with a platter, on which lay a glistening, sticky slab of ribs. Ferguson paused, unsure as to the initial step of the rib-eating process. Peri reached over and separated one rib from the rest and held it out for him. He took it and bit into the meat clinging to the bone. Peri watched, smiling. From that point, until all that remained of the ribs was a pile of shiny bones, Ferguson said nothing. When he had finished a look of utter confusion came over his face.

'How could I have not known about ribs before now?' he said. 'This might be the best thing I've ever eaten.'

'I don't know,' laughed Peri. 'Where are you from?'

'Michigan. I grew up in Michigan.'

'Don't they have ribs in Michigan?'

'I guess not in the part of Michigan where I lived.' He took a deep breath. 'So? How about some of those dry ribs?'

Peri feigned shock. 'You want some *dry* ribs now?'

'Why not?' Ferguson smiled. Peri went into the kitchen and Wren came out.

She eyed Ferguson. 'You look like that Beatle,' she said. 'John Lennon.'

'Thank you, Wren.' Ferguson laughed. 'You like the Beatles?'

'Not really,' she said. 'I like Sam & Dave.' She went and sat in one of the booths and played with the tableside jukebox. Soon the Sam & Dave tune 'Everybody Got to Believe in Somebody' was playing. Wren sang along. Peri came out with the dry ribs and Ferguson started in on them. Halfway through the slab he notified Peri that he preferred dry over wet, and promptly returned to his work.

'I'm glad there are only two kinds of ribs,' he groaned, when he had cleaned the last bone. He wiped his mouth with his napkin. Peri poured him a third glass of whiskey.

'You and your husband own this place?' Ferguson asked.

'There is no husband,' Peri said. 'Just me and my daughter. I got the restaurant from my father.'

'Does "General Bar-B-Q" mean it's kind of an all-purpose barbecue restaurant?' Ferguson asked.

The small-talk nature of this question made Ferguson realize that he didn't want to leave. He was buying time.

'No,' said Peri. 'It means that my father's name was General Brown. And, no, he wasn't a general in the army. My grandmother named him General because she liked the name General. She said it sounded important and that people would give him respect with a name like that. She named my two uncles Royal and Ambassador, and she named my aunt Honor.'

Ferguson smiled. His small-talk strategy was working.

'I guess your father could have used his middle name for the restaurant,' he said.

'Except that his middle name was James,' said Peri. 'And if he'd called the place "James Brown's Bar-B-Q" there would have been a whole different kind of confusion. Unusual names are just a part of our family's tradition. Like barbecue.'

'My father's name is Angus,' said Ferguson. 'Like the cow. Better than Holstein, I guess.'

It went quiet between them. Ferguson sipped his drink.

'What's your speech about?' asked Peri. 'Over at the school.'

'It's about the Gospels,' said Ferguson. 'And what they have to say about white people and black people in America in 1968.'

'Well,' said Peri, softly. 'The Gospels have a *lot* to say on that. But most people don't listen.'

They were quiet again. Ferguson worried that the time had come for him to leave.

'So, are you an Episcopal minister?' asked Peri.

'Yes,' said Ferguson. 'I was ordained a couple of years ago.'

'We're Baptists,' said Peri. Ferguson nodded.

'Did you always know you wanted to be a preacher?' Peri asked.

'Probably,' Ferguson said. 'My father, my grandfather, an uncle, and a cousin are all priests. It's like the family business. Like barbecue is for your family. It was hard for me to imagine doing anything else with my life, and God always seemed so real to my father and to my uncle and cousin. I felt pulled in that direction.'

'Sometimes there's no escaping our fathers,' Peri said. 'Mine left me with a good business, which has provided some security for me and Wren. And I'm grateful for all that. But sometimes I feel trapped here in this place. Like I've got no other options.'

Ferguson nodded. 'Well, there's probably some poor soul out there who inherited a sewer-cleaning business from his father and he's looking at you and me thinking that he'd sure rather his dad had been in the wet 'n' dry ribs business or the God business.'

Peri laughed. 'When do you give your talk at the seminary?'

'Tomorrow morning at eleven,' said Ferguson. 'Why don't you come?'

Peri shrugged and frowned. 'I have to be here. We're pretty busy at lunch.'

There seemed to be nothing else to say. Ferguson paid

and got up to go. Peri stood up, too. Wren was asleep in the booth. They walked toward the door.

'Why don't you come to prayer meeting at our church tomorrow night?' Peri asked, surprising herself and Ferguson, too.

'I'd love to.' Ferguson smiled.

'Just meet me here at six thirty, and we'll go over to church together. Make sure to dress like a priest. All the old mothers will be impressed.'

Ferguson had news when he arrived at General Bar-B-Q the next evening.

'Dr King is here in Memphis,' he told Peri.

'I heard that,' said Peri. 'He's here to help our trash collectors with their strike.'

'Do you want to go over to hear him talk after prayer meeting?' asked Ferguson. 'Someone at the seminary said he'll be speaking at Mason Temple. Is that close to your church?'

'Close enough,' said Peri. 'I'd go a long way to see Dr King.'

Prayer meeting at Mount Gilead Baptist Church was held in the fellowship hall in the church basement. Rows of folding chairs faced a small wooden podium and a cream-colored upright piano. Most of the church members who had come for prayer meeting were elderly women, though there were a few older men, some younger women, and a teenaged white boy with cerebral palsy in a wheelchair. Ferguson Glen was the only other white person.

After twenty minutes of hymns, Pastor Duane Ellison led the gathered in a devotional study of the Gospel of Luke, chapter 12, verses 11 and 12:

'And when they bring you unto the synagogues, and unto magistrates, and powers, take ye no thought how or what

thing ye shall answer, or what ye shall say. For the Holy Ghost shall teach you in the same hour what ye ought to say.'

And also the Gospel of John, chapter 20, verses 20 through 22:

'And when he had so said, he shewed unto them his hands and his side. Then were the disciples glad, when they saw the Lord. Then said Jesus to them again, "Peace be unto you: as my Father hath sent me, even so send I you." And when he had said this, he breathed on them, and saith unto them, "Receive ye the Holy Ghost."'

As Pastor Ellison illuminated the meaning of his chosen text, Wren sat on the floor at Peri's feet coloring in a Donald Duck coloring book. She had completed six pictures of Huey, Louie, and Dewey, Uncle Scrooge, Donald and Daisy, and had worn her blue crayon down to a nub by the time Pastor Ellison concluded his meditation with these words:

'The Holy Ghost gives us supernatural power when we need it most. The supernatural power of the Holy Ghost supersedes the powers of those in authority to hold us captive, to oppress us, and to deny us our dignity and freedom.

'The Holy Ghost gives us supernatural power that supersedes the power of poverty, ignorance, drink, immorality, selfishness, hostility, and hatred.

'When the Lord Jesus Christ left us here on earth, he did not leave us alone. He left us with the Holy Ghost. And the Holy Ghost will always give us what we need, when we need it. But to receive the Holy Ghost we have to get close to Jesus. Close enough for him to breathe on us. The gospel says, *"He breathed on them, and saith unto them, 'Receive ye the Holy Ghost'."*

'So I ask you tonight, brothers and sisters, are you close to Jesus? Are you close enough to Jesus to receive his gift of the Holy Ghost? Are you close enough to Jesus to feel his breath on you? Do you have an intimate relationship with our Lord? Can you feel the warmth of his breath on your face? Are you close enough? If not, get closer. Get closer to Jesus.'

After devotions, Pastor Ellison led the group in singing 'Breathe on Me Breath of God', after which he asked that heads be bowed in prayer. He asked God's blessings on those gathered and thanked God for his steadfast mercies, then he asked for prayer requests.

The first several requests sought God's healing for those in the congregation who were sick, including two members with cancer, one with pneumonia, one with bursitis, one who was losing her thinking, and one with stubborn corns.

Ferguson heard Wren giggle at this. He opened his eyes and saw Peri reach over and gently squeeze her daughter's knee.

Then there were prayers for jobs needed, for the daughter in trouble at school, for the husband in jail, for the son who needed to get on the right road, for the water department that threatened to turn off the water at the apartment building, for the mother with a hard heart who needed to forgive and accept forgiveness, and for the family whose house burned down. Ferguson prayed to himself that he would feel the breath of God.

Finally, prayers were offered up for the striking Memphis sanitation workers.

The meeting was closed with the hymn 'Spirit of the Living God'.

'That's probably not the way you Episcopalians do prayer meeting is it, reverend?' asked Peri, as they got up to leave.

'No,' said Ferguson. 'But we don't do it any better.'

In Peri's car, on the way to the Mason Temple, Wren asked Ferguson about some words in 'Spirit of the Living God'.

Specifically she wanted to know the meaning of the phrase 'fall afresh on me'.

'It's like when something happens to you for the first time,' he said. 'Or maybe it's happened to you before, but you didn't notice, then it happens again and you do notice and it feels like it was the first time. It feels fresh. And sometimes if this happens suddenly and it surprises you, you just fall right down. Your legs go out from under you and *BOOM!* You fall. And that's how they came up with the expression "fall afresh on me".'

Ferguson looked at Periwinkle Brown to see if this explanation was going to fly or if he was going to have to try again. She smiled and shrugged. He looked in the back seat to see if he had satisfied Wren but she had turned her attention to changing the clothes on her Barbie doll.

Ferguson noticed, as if for the first time, that all the Barbie dolls he'd ever seen were white.

At the temple, they heard Martin Luther King Jr. tell his followers that he had been to the mountaintop, that God had allowed him to see the Promised Land, and that they would all get there someday. And though they might not all get there together, they would get there. He told them all that his eyes had seen the glory of the coming of the Lord.

Ferguson and Peri stood close as they listened. He felt the warmth of her body. His arm touched hers. Once, when the crowd moved and pushed against Wren, Wren took hold of Ferguson's hand and held it. Peri smiled at Ferguson and took hold of his other hand. The word 'afresh' came into his mind.

After the speech, Peri drove Ferguson back to the seminary. They sat in the car in front of the student union. In the back seat, Wren sang 'Soul Man' under her breath as she played with her doll.

Ferguson spoke first. 'I'd like to think those weren't the last ribs I'll ever have.'

'They don't have to be,' said Peri softly, looking out the window.

'Then maybe I'll come back,' said Ferguson. 'I'd like to come back.'

'That would be good,' said Peri.

They said goodbye.

The next morning Ferguson Glen boarded an airplane and returned to New York.

Back in his apartment he felt empty and tired. He lay down on his couch and slept until he was awakened by his telephone ringing. It was Walker Briggs, his editor.

'Ferguson, there's news from Memphis,' he said. His voice was taut. 'Turn on your television. King's been shot.'

Ferguson drank whiskey and watched the news reports in dumb silent horror. The hotel balcony. The hospital. The police and the reporters. The weeping and confusion. Then cities exploding in anger and grief. Detroit. Cincinnati. Kansas City. Memphis. He watched until the station concluded its broadcast day with the playing of the national anthem.

He was numb-faced and wobbly on his feet, but he stumbled to the phone and called Memphis information. There was no Periwinkle Brown listed in the Memphis phone book, but there was a G.J. Brown. Ferguson guessed that maybe Peri had also inherited her father's house so he tried the number. A man answered.

'Is Peri there?' asked Ferguson.

'No, she's not,' said the man. 'Who *is* this?'

'I'm a friend,' said Ferguson. 'Is she all right?'

'No! She's not,' was the hostile reply. 'She's not all right. She's at the hospital with her daughter.'

'Wren?' asked Ferguson, anxiously. 'Did something happen to Wren?'

'*Yes!*' the man shouted angrily. 'The girl was blinded by some tear gas or mace or something. The child can't see! *Who is this? Why are you calling here?*'

'I'm just a friend,' said Ferguson. He hung up the phone, went to the kitchen sink and vomited.

In Plum Grove, Texas, LaVerne Williams sat with his grand-mother Rose at her kitchen table listening to the news on the radio.

'This changes everything,' he said.

12

Cashier

The primary source of pride in A.B. Clayton's life is that LaVerne Williams trusts him. More than once Angela has pointed out to her husband that he has, over the last twenty years, become a mentor to A.B. LaVerne's typical response to this is to look away and mumble something along the lines of 'I don't know about that. But, yeah, he's a good kid.'

A.B. has earned LaVerne's trust by understanding the things that matter most to his boss; the top three being honesty, cleanliness, and punctuality. These are not values A.B. learned from his mother or any of her husbands or boyfriends. He learned them from LaVerne himself. A.B. has become the main enforcer of these standards, a responsibility that has, on occasion, challenged A.B.'s personnel management skills.

LaVerne is not a people person. He's most comfortable when he's alone in the kitchen cooking or tending the smoker. He has neither the interest nor the patience to closely supervise a crew of teenagers and parolees. So early on he began delegating many of the restaurant's human resources tasks to A.B., whom LaVerne felt was better suited to checking timecards, and providing instruction on the finer points of clearing tables and filling napkin holders.

'That's not the job of the CEO,' LaVerne told A.B., when A.B. complained to him about a cashier's chronic tardiness. 'As the chief *executive* officer, I'm in charge of long-range planning and product development. Day-to-day administration is the job of the COO – the chief *operations* officer. That's you, boy. You're operations. My right-hand man. You deal with this the way you see fit and I'll back you up.'

This seminar on corporate roles and responsibilities took place out back, by the dumpster. Both men were wearing greasy jeans and T-shirts. A.B., who hadn't shaved in three days, smoked a cigarette and idly scratched his butt. The back of LaVerne's shirt was tucked into his underwear, which rode up above his belt. A long piece of toilet paper was stuck to the bottom of his shoe.

For a friendly guy, A.B. doesn't really have any friends to speak of. If pressed, he might claim Del James as a friend, or perhaps Bob Dunleavy, because they kid around with him when they come in for lunch. But Del and Bob would be surprised by this news. Both men are old enough to be A.B.'s father.

A.B. knows lots of people at New Jerusalem Baptist Church, where he has attended worship nearly every Sunday morning for nearly two decades. But most of the other men his age have families, and after the service they go visiting or out to eat with their wives and children. A.B. goes home and takes a nap or maybe watches TV.

The only real friend A.B. Clayton ever had was Raymond Williams.

The truth is that his life is structured such that it's difficult for new friendships to take root and grow. Tuesday through Friday, he arrives at the restaurant at 6 a.m. to start the side dishes. About fourteen hours later, he turns out the lights, locks the doors, and goes home. On Saturdays, the restaurant is only open for lunch, so A.B. usually gets to leave at about 3:00 or 4:00 in the afternoon. Smoke Meat is closed on Sundays.

Several years ago, Angela insisted that LaVerne give A.B. Mondays off, which he did, though A.B. typically comes in anyway. He just arrives a little later than usual and leaves a little earlier. When LaVerne sees A.B. in the kitchen on Mondays, he'll shake his head and grunt, 'Damn it, boy. If Angela sees you here, she'll *kick* my ass.'

The only time A.B. goes anywhere other than the restaurant or church is when Mother Mary Weaver has a local gig. A.B. will almost always go to hear her wherever she's singing. As a result, he's become a blues enthusiast and Pug Hale has helped him put together a fairly good collection of blues CDs.

One Saturday night, Mary was the featured act at the New Cherry Blossom, a nightclub in Westport. A.B. was drinking a beer at the bar, thinking he liked Pug's guitar solo on 'Sinner's Prayer' even better than Eric Clapton's, when he saw Shawn Irwin.

Shawn Irwin was Smoke Meat's chronically tardy cashier. Even though LaVerne had given him authority to deal with such matters, A.B. hadn't taken any decisive action regarding Shawn's punctuality problem because A.B. liked Shawn and was hoping that regular reminders of the importance of being on time might remedy the situation, though the strategy had yet to achieve its objective.

Everybody liked Shawn. He was a smart, funny, good-looking kid; a junior at Parker Academy – Kansas City's high school for the performing arts – where he studied acting. All Shawn's teachers and classmates said he had a real shot at a career in television or movies and almost all conversations with Shawn eventually provided him with an opportunity to mention this fact.

Shawn was sitting at a table with some friends. A.B. waved at him. When Shawn didn't wave back, A.B. went over to the table.

'Shawn. How you doin' Shawn?' Shawn looked up at A.B., unsmiling, his eyelids drooping.

A.B. continued. 'So? You diggin' Mary's blues, Shawn?'

Shawn looked at his friends and grinned. 'Sure,' he said. 'I'm *diggin'* Mary's blues.' Shawn and his friends laughed. A.B. wasn't sure what at.

'Yeah, Mary's great,' A.B. said. 'She's the real deal. And can you believe Pug? He's awesome!'

Shawn agreed. 'Yes, *sir*! He's *awesome*!' Shawn's friends laughed harder.

'Him and me work together,' A.B. informed Shawn's friends. They nodded.

There was an empty chair at Shawn's table and A.B thought maybe Shawn would ask him to sit, but the invitation was not extended. A.B. decided that the chair must belong to one of Shawn's friends who was probably in the men's room.

'So, anyways, I'll see you at work on Monday,' A.B. said. 'We'll talk blues.'

When Shawn came in late on Monday, A.B. handed him a stack of CDs. 'Here, take these home and tell me how you like 'em. There are some rare cuts on some of these. Pug helped me find them. They're *classics*, man.'

Shawn took the CDs. 'Thanks,' he said. He put them on top of the filing cabinet next to the clock. Which is where A.B. found them when he was locking up the next night.

When Shawn came in late on Wednesday, A.B. reminded him of the CDs. 'Don't forget to bring those home, man. You'll love 'em. I'm serious.'

Shawn brought the CDs home and left them there for the next week, every day of which A.B. asked him if he'd had a chance to listen to them. Finally, Shawn had had enough.

'Look,' he said. 'I haven't listened to your CDs. And I'm not going to. I can't stand the blues. It's history. It's old. It's all "Oh, my baby left me. Don't know what to do." It's flaccid. The only reason I was there at that club was because I was writing a paper for school about African-American music traditions. It was an assignment is all. You and I got nothin' to talk about. You got your thing going on, and I got mine. So leave me alone, man.'

He walked off.

A.B went out back for a smoke. His hands shook as he lit his cigarette.

When he came back inside, Shawn was in the kitchen laughing with the busboy. There were customers lined up at the counter but Shawn didn't seem to notice. A.B. didn't say anything to Shawn. He just went over and started taking orders.

McKenzie Nelson, the sales rep at *KC.21*, was first in line. She ordered a sausage sandwich, then paused before going to her table to wait for her order.

'Forgive me for eavesdropping. But you can't let that guy talk to you like that.'

'What do you mean?' asked A.B., his cheeks on fire.

'I mean, if you let an employee talk to you like that, everyone else on your crew will see that you're a push-over. You can't worry about your employees liking you. They're your workers not your friends. You don't need them to like you. You need them to respect you.'

McKenzie went over to the soda machine and got herself a diet Coke. A.B. tried to breathe.

Later, LaVerne, who'd been out running errands, came looking for A.B., who was still working the counter.

'What are you doing here?' LaVerne asked. 'Isn't that Shawn kid supposed to be working the counter today?'

'I fired him, boss,' said A.B. 'He was always late.'

13

September Night

A young black woman in America in 1965 expected certain limits and impediments would be imposed on her by a society not yet convinced of her full humanity. But Angela Newton had not yet encountered many of those barriers, inasmuch as she had not yet broken through the barriers placed around her life by her parents.

Angela was convinced that when physicists put forth the conundrum of the irresistible force and the immovable object they had her parents in mind. The former being her mother, the latter being her father. She was also certain that her mother and father were squeezing every ounce of independence and individuality right out of her.

Graduation from high school – in most homes a rite of passage from adolescence to adulthood – with its accompanying rights and responsibilities, did not in Angela's case result in an appreciable increase in either. Her friends all had summer jobs and spent their summer nights cruising Swope Park. But Angela's father, the Rev. Dr Clarence E. Newton, senior pastor of the New Jerusalem Baptist Church, had forbidden her from working on the grounds that it was unnecessary and unseemly. Her mother, Alberta H. Newton, outlawed the cruising on general principles.

Angela's enrollment in college that fall also failed to

74

loosen her parents' restrictions. They insisted she live at home and that she observe a strict curfew. Because they were paying for her education, Angela felt she had little choice in the matter. She felt, in fact, that she had little choice in *any* matter.

She attended the University of Missouri-Kansas City where she majored in English, with the objective of becoming a high school teacher or perhaps a school librarian. She was passionate about books and literature, especially English novels, and could not abide the thought of a child growing up without the joy of reading.

The Rev. and Mrs Clarence E. Newton had deeply entrenched beliefs regarding the proper role of a Christian young woman; specifically that she should present herself as a willing and obedient servant to God by marrying a minister of the Gospel, bearing and raising his children, and supporting him in his ministry. But, above all else, a godly young woman must keep herself in all ways pure.

Therefore, in the Newton household there were strict prohibitions to which Angela was expected to adhere without complaint. First, there was to be no sexual activity of any kind before marriage. Additionally there would be no drinking, no smoking, no swearing, no card playing, and no dancing; and no dating boys who engaged in any of the aforementioned. Which meant that there would be no dating, since there were no boys – not even those whose families attended New Jerusalem Baptist Church – who abstained from each and every one of these activities.

Rev. Newton was a respected leader in the General Baptist denomination, and every year, during the third week of September, Rev. and Mrs Newton attended the annual General Baptist convention. When the children were young, the Newtons left them in the care of one of the families of the church when they went to the convention. When they were teenagers, they accompanied their parents to the gathering where they participated in Baptist Youth Fellowship events. But Angela's brothers, Luke and James, were grown and gone and she had classes to attend, so this year the Newtons reluctantly left Angela at home when they left for their annual meeting, which that year was in Detroit.

'Come right home after class,' Alberta Newton admonished her daughter as she kissed her goodbye on Wednesday morning. In the driveway Rev. Newton sounded the horn of his Oldsmobile. 'I bought all the groceries you could possibly need. So just come right home and watch a little TV and study your books. You'll be just fine.'

'I'm not worried about being fine, Mama,' Angela said. 'I know I'll be fine. Don't worry. I'm grown up now.'

Angela did go right home on Wednesday and on Thursday, but on Friday after class she didn't feel like going right home. The possibility of deciding for herself what she would do with her time, without having to explain or apologize for it, felt good. She decided to go to a movie.

She had wanted to see *The Sound of Music* for a long time and when the movie was over she cried. Then she went to the ticket counter, bought another ticket and went back into the theater and watched it again.

The next morning, Angela took the bus to the library; not to study or research an assignment for class, but to browse the stacks, flip through the pages of old atlases, read summaries of novels on brittle, yellowed, dust jackets and breathe in the musty, slightly mildewy air.

She stayed so long that she forgot to eat lunch. When she left the library and stepped out into the cool late afternoon she realized she was hungry. She realized that she was, in fact, hungry for burnt ends. She boarded the Vine Street bus with Arthur Bryant's in mind.

Bryant's was a Newton family favorite. Rev. Newton always ordered the ribs. Luke and Mrs Newton preferred the brisket. And James and Angela liked the crispy smoky burnt ends, with a mountain of fries and a red pop. At the counter, Angela thought for a moment about ordering a beer, but decided against it.

She took her tray into the crowded dining room. Virtually every seat was occupied, except for a chair at the end of one of the longer tables. At the other end of the table sat a skinny boy about her age. He was just starting in on a combo platter – burnt ends and brisket – with a mountain of fries and a beer.

LaVerne Williams saw Angela as soon as she walked into the room. Slender, with a nice 'fro, wire-rimmed glasses, and a shy smile.

His season with Birmingham had ended earlier that week, and the Athletics had given him a bus ticket to Kansas City so he could meet some of the team and watch their last few games. He'd never been to Kansas City before and didn't know much about it, but Blue Moon Odom, a pitcher who had just been called up from Lewiston, had recommended that he try Bryant's, which LaVerne did primarily to compare it to the barbecue back home in Texas.

Please sit here, he thought. *Please sit here.*

Angela sat down and for the next fifteen minutes both she and LaVerne ate in silence studying the barbecue in front of them as if they were inspectors from the health department.

Please say something, she thought. *Please say something.*

Finally, LaVerne spoke up. 'You live here? Here in Kansas City?'

'Yes, I do,' she said. She glanced at him then looked back down at her food.

'I'm just visiting,' he said. 'I'm with the Athletics organization.'

He waited for a response but Angela had just taken a bite of burnt ends. He proceeded. 'You like baseball?'

Angela nodded, her mouth full. 'I do,' she said, trying to swallow her food in a hurry. 'My whole family does. My father saw to that. He's maybe the biggest baseball fan in the world.'

LaVerne wiped his hands on a napkin and extended his right hand across the table. 'I'm LaVerne Williams. I'm from Plum Grove, Texas. Just north of Houston.'

'I'm Angela. Angela Newton. I'm from right here in Kansas City.'

She noticed that the palm of his hand was calloused, but the top of his hand was smooth and fine boned. His fingers were long and strong and graceful.

He noticed that her handshake was tentative and that his fingers wrapped all the way around her hand and that her fingernails were the shape and color of almonds.

They silently stared down at their food again, smiling and not very hungry for barbecue anymore.

Finally LaVerne spoke up again. 'So, you going to the game tonight?'

'No,' said Angela. 'But I read that Satchel Paige is going to be there.'

'He's not just going to be there, he's going to *pitch* tonight. That's just unbelievable,' said LaVerne. 'Do you want to go? To the game, I mean. I mean, *can* you go? Would you *like* to go? To the *game*. With *me*. Would you like to go to the game with me?'

Angela said yes. She marveled at how easy it was to make up her own mind without giving a thought to what her parents would say.

It was the 25th of September. The Kansas City Athletics were hosting the Boston Red Sox. Angela and LaVerne sat behind the Athletics dugout with a few other prospects from the club's farm teams. Blue Moon Odom waved to LaVerne on his way out to the bullpen. When he saw Angela sitting next to LaVerne he gave LaVerne the thumbs-up sign and grinned. Angela blushed.

The Athletics trotted out to their defensive positions and began warming up, tossing the ball around the bases. After a couple of minutes of this, Satchel Paige walked purposefully out to the mound and picked up the rosin bag. He was sixty years old.

In a move that was one part charity, one part recognition of Satchel Paige's genius, and yet another part gimmick, Charlie O. Finley had signed the old vet to a contract. This, together with the seasons he spent with Cleveland and St Louis twelve years previous, would give Paige enough playing time in the majors to allow him to collect a pension. Finley also hoped a 'Salute to Satchel Paige' night would sell tickets.

It didn't sell many. There were only 9,289 diehard baseball fans in Municipal Stadium to watch Satchel Paige pitch. The Kansas City Athletics never drew much of a crowd. They were the worst team in baseball, perhaps the worst team ever. If God himself had been the Athletics' starting pitcher that night, there might not have been many more people in attendance.

Paige retired the first two batters and murmurs of amusement tittered around the ballpark. Then Boston's slugger, Carl Yastrzemski, smacked a double off the fence in left-center. A groan went up from the crowd. LaVerne told Angela that if he'd been out there he'd have caught that ball. The next batter fouled out.

Satchel Paige befuddled the next six batters with his double-pump hesitation pitch, in which his right hand hovered over his head for just a bit longer than a batter thought it should, as if he were deciding whether or not to actually throw the ball. The old man had the crowd deep in the pocket of his glove.

But Charlie Finley decided to end the stunt while the legend was intact. As the first Red Sox batter stepped up to the plate at the beginning of the fourth inning, the Athletics' manager Haywood Sullivan signaled the bullpen and walked slowly out to the mound to relieve his starter. Together the two men walked back to the dugout. At the top step Satchel Paige removed his cap and bowed to the cheering crowd.

In the clubhouse, Paige took off his uniform and sat in front of his locker in his longjohns, staring at his feet. He heard the clatter of cleats in the tunnel and looked around. The batboy poked his head in the door.

'Mr Paige!' he yelled. 'They want you out there. They're calling for you.'

The old man stood, pulled on his jersey and pants and returned to the field.

The lights had been turned off, but the stadium was not dark. Little flames from thousands of matches flickered in the night. When the crowd saw Paige walk out onto the field they began singing the old folks favorite, 'Rockin' Chair'.

'Old rockin' chair's got me, my cane by my side. Fetch me that gin, son, 'fore I tan your hide.'

Satchel Paige stood on the first baseline, stone still, and though no one could see it, he was smiling.

Another song, 'Darling, I Am Growing Old', then floated out over the park.

'My darling, you will be . . . always young and fair to me . . . silver threads among the gold.'

Angela looked over at LaVerne. His eyes were filling up and his bottom lip trembled slightly. She turned away.

Finally, the serenade concluded with 'The Old Gray Mare'.

'The old gray mare, she ain't what she used to be, many long years ago.'

Satchel Paige waved his cap to the crowd and walked back into the clubhouse in the dark.

When the game was over, neither Angela nor LaVerne wanted the night to end. They stayed in their seats as the stadium emptied until they were the only two people left, except for the clean-up crew that had started sweeping the beer bottles and popcorn cartons out from between the seats. Somebody had put the radio on the public address system. The Four Tops were singing 'I Can't Help Myself'.

They were quiet for a while, listening to the music. Then Angela spoke. 'Thank you, LaVerne.'

'No. Thank *you*,' he said. 'Let me go down to the clubhouse and call you a cab. You shouldn't take the bus at this hour.'

'Can we just sit here for a while longer?' Angela asked. 'Maybe just talk?'

They did talk. Angela told LaVerne about her two older brothers, Luke, who was in seminary in Chicago, and James, who had just taken a position as an associate pastor at a church in St Louis, and how they had teased and tormented her when she was little, and how, when they were around, she felt pretty and calm and safe.

LaVerne told Angela about his mother Loretta and that she had been in prison off and on for most of his life and how he didn't really know much about her and how he didn't know who his father was and that his mother didn't know either.

He told her about his grandmother Rose and how hard she worked at Raylon Rice and Milling to keep him fed and clothed and how she made sure he went to church each Sunday at Plum Grove Second Baptist Church and how on hot Texas nights the two of them would sit outside on her porch and drink lemonade and listen to the radio.

Angela told LaVerne that she missed her best friend Lucille who had left two weeks earlier to attend Howard University in Washington, DC, and that Lucille wanted to be a lawyer and that she had met Thurgood Marshall. She told him about the brainy boy her age at New Jerusalem Baptist Church with the nappy hair and the one eye that looked in one direction and the other eye that looked in the other direction and how he had a crush on her, and even though she knew it wasn't Christian of her she wished his family would find another church to attend.

LaVerne told Angela about Delbert and Hartholz and the butcher shop and making barbecue and the smell of the cherry-wood smoke and the briskets and sausage and drinking whiskey and Delbert's blues. He told her about his high school baseball coach and how he taught him the fundamentals of the game and how to drive a car, and how to chew tobacco.

Angela told LaVerne that the pharmacist at the drugstore down on Troost had offered her a job for the summer, but her parents told her no, even though the pharmacist was a deacon at New Jerusalem Baptist Church. She told him about each of her classes at the university and how she didn't really like chemistry much, but her psychology class was interesting and how she would spend all day in her English lit class if they would let her. And she told him that there was a white girl named Elaine in her lit class that she had talked to a couple of times and that she seemed nice.

LaVerne told Angela about Birmingham and how he had seen a deputy sheriff set his police dog loose on a crowd of Freedom Marchers and how the next week that same man came to a ballgame and after the game asked him to autograph a baseball for his little boy.

Angela told LaVerne that she wondered sometimes if she might not suffocate under the weight of her parents' expectations and how she didn't really understand some of the rules her parents made her and the boys follow when they were growing up. Not dancing, for example. She and her brothers weren't allowed to dance. They weren't even allowed to go to the prom. But there was dancing in the Bible and so what, exactly, was wrong with dancing, anyway?

One of the stadium janitors, an older black man, came down the row and approached Angela and LaVerne. 'You kids about done? We'll be leaving in a half-hour or so.'

LaVerne nodded. 'Can you give us just a little more time? I'm with the team. We won't be long.'

The janitor smiled and left them alone. The radio was playing the Temptations' 'Dream Come True'.

LaVerne took Angela's hand and led her down onto the field. He put his arm around her waist and began to move her body slowly with his hand on the small of her back.

Smokey Robinson started singing 'Ooo Baby Baby' and LaVerne pulled Angela closer and Angela understood why her parents objected to dancing.

14

Outside Shot

When the guy in the yellow double-wide lost his job at the landfill he started picking fights with his friends at the bars and wanting A.B.'s mother to pay for his beer, and the relationship lost its spark. A.B.'s mom stopped going up to the trailer park in Sugar Creek. By then A.B. was smoking Camels every day. His mom knew about it but she had problems of her own.

Sammy Merzeti was the name of the big kid at the trailer park who got A.B. Clayton started smoking. Sammy was five or six inches taller than other kids his age, so people always thought he was older than he actually was. Kids his age were nervous around him because of his height and also the missing finger, and older kids picked on him and wouldn't let him hang around because he was younger. This all resulted in Sammy being pissed off much of the time. Except when he was playing basketball.

Because he was tall even the kids who avoided him or bossed him around wanted him on their team when they played pick-up games at the playground. Plus Sammy had a wicked jump shot, a reliable Kareem Abdul-Jabbar-style sky-hook, and could dribble behind his back and between his legs. When he was playing basketball Sammy felt light and forgetful.

A couple times he asked his mom to come to watch him play, but she said she couldn't think of a reason why she would go watch a bunch of kids play shitty basketball on a shitty playground basketball court where the hoops didn't even have nets.

'It's not like you're on a real team or anything,' she said.

Sammy had no reason to be any more optimistic than usual about how things would turn out when his mother first brought Rudy Turpin home with her. The other strays she brought home were only ever interested in one thing. And it wasn't Sammy.

For the first few weeks Rudy pretty much did have only that one thing on his mind. But during that time he was nice enough to Sammy that he felt could relax a little. Rudy even talked to him; asking him about school and girls and cars and sports. Sammy wasn't familiar enough with the first three topics to discuss them in any depth, but he was happy to talk to Rudy about sports. Especially basketball.

Rudy had dark bushy eyebrows, heavy horn-rimmed glasses with thick lenses, and an oversized nose. Sometimes when they were talking about the Lakers or the 76ers, Sammy would look at Rudy and imagine that he was wearing those fake glasses with the big plastic nose attached. Rudy never mentioned anything about his big nose or his thick glasses, so Sammy didn't either.

Rudy was also short, which was why he was particularly fond of the Houston Rockets' tiny superstar Calvin Murphy. Sammy was partial to the Kansas City Kings' Otis Birdsong.

'Well, then,' said Rudy. 'Maybe me and you ought to go to a Kings' game some time. What would you think about that?'

Sammy thought that it would never happen, that's what he thought. But he told Rudy that he'd like to go.

On November 27, five days after Thanksgiving, Sammy Merzeti and Rudy Turpin watched the Kansas City Kings beat the Houston Rockets, 117–115, at Municipal Stadium, in downtown Kansas City.

Rudy bought them hot dogs and sno-cones, and a lemonade for Sammy, and a beer for himself. On the way home, after the game, Rudy played the radio. He sang along on the chorus to 'Devil Went Down to Georgia' while Sammy played air fiddle during Charlie Daniels' solo. When Bob Seger's 'We've Got Tonight' came on, Rudy cranked it up loud and lit a cigarette. He offered one to Sammy, which he accepted.

Rudy talked about his job on the line over at the Fairfax plant making Chevy Blazers. He asked Sammy about his finger, and Sammy explained that it got smashed in a car door when he was eight years old. He didn't tell the part about his mother slamming the door shut because she was mad at him for stealing money from her purse. Sammy asked Rudy if he had any kids and Rudy said no, he didn't. He'd always wanted kids of his own, but things didn't work out that way.

On Sterling Road, about a half-mile from the entrance to Harmony Haven, was a 7-Eleven where Rudy liked to stop for gas and cigarettes. He pulled in and filled up. When he was done he poked his head in the car window. 'Come on in, kid. I'll get you a Snickers or something.'

They went in and Sammy picked out a Zero bar. At the counter, Rudy asked the clerk for a pack of Kools. As the clerk turned and reached for the Kools, another customer walked up and asked for a pack of Marlboros. The clerk turned back around, gave Rudy his Kools and the other man his Marlboros. The Marlboro guy handed the clerk a five-dollar bill. The clerk proceeded to ring up the sale for the Marlboros, which is when Rudy intervened.

'We was here first,' he said.

The other fellow glanced at Rudy impassively, then turned back to the clerk with his hand extended, expecting change from his five. The clerk looked anxiously at Rudy, but since he'd already made change he gave it to the Marlboro guy.

With a swift upward sweep of his left arm Rudy knocked the money from the guy's hand. The coins jangled on the floor by the ice-cream freezer. The competing customer gazed at his empty hand for a moment then made a move for Rudy, which Rudy intercepted with the point of a knife he produced from his back pocket. He held the blade of the knife alongside the man's nose.

'I don't think you were looking for trouble,' Rudy said. 'So I'm willing to give you the benefit of the doubt. But you need to work on your manners, mister. Seriously. You need to set a good example for youth who might be taking note.'

Rudy then delivered a hard open-hand shove to the man's chest, which sent him stumbling back into a display of key chains, car deodorizers, and disposable lighters. Rudy gave the clerk a ten-dollar bill, apologized for the inconvenience, took Sammy by the arm, and left.

It took Sammy a long time to fall asleep that night.

That weekend on his way into Harmony Haven to see Sammy's mom, Rudy drove past the playground and saw Sammy shooting baskets. He parked, got out of his car, went over and sat down on the bench, lit up a cigarette, and watched for a while.

Sammy was self-conscious at first and missed several shots in a row. Some didn't even hit the backboard, or the rim, or the net. But eventually he found a groove and started sinking nearly everything, at one point swishing four straight.

'Hop in the car, boy. I'll drive you home,' Rudy said, finally. 'Your mother's expecting me.'

In the car, Rudy smiled at Sammy. 'You got a deadly shot, kid.'

A week or so later, on an unseasonably warm December Saturday afternoon, Sammy went down to the playground to practice free throws. Five black kids about his age were there playing shoot-out, laughing and teasing. Sammy recognized two of them. One lived in a trailer over by the ditch. The other went to his school. They stopped playing when Sammy stepped onto the court, waiting in wary silence to see what he would do, which Sammy himself hadn't yet figured out.

At first Sammy thought he might ask if they were playing half-court. And, if so, could he use the other half. But he surprised himself.

'You guys need a sixth?' he asked. 'For three-on-three?'

They deliberated by looking at each other, watching for non-verbal cues, positive or negative. The kid who lived over by the ditch broke the ice. His name was Wesley. He nodded.

'You play with me and Reggie,' he said, indicating one of the other guys, a tall skinny kid wearing a dark blue wool-knit cap and a Detroit Lions jersey.

Sammy quickly realized that the others were a lot better than he was. Except for a cheerful chubby kid named Dwayne. Dwayne had lots of hustle, but was seriously uncoordinated and had no outside shot. Sammy decided that if he was going to stay in the game he'd have to go one-on-one against Dwayne.

The tactic worked well. Sammy stole the ball from Dwayne

at will, and Dwayne's attempts to defend against Sammy's jump shot and skyhook were ineffectual. Sammy was emboldened by his success and began to taunt Dwayne.

'Come on, Dwayne! That all you got?' he hissed in Dwayne's ear as Dwayne tried to block an inside drive.

'Hey, big boy! Watch this!' Sammy hooted, as he went in for a lay-up.

Sammy's cockiness made Wesley anxious. He grabbed Sammy's shirt.

'Cool it, man,' he said. 'This is for fun. And Dwayne is my boy.'

Sammy nodded and smiled. He breathed in and out hard and slow through his nostrils. There was a ringing in his ears and he wondered where it was coming from. His feet and hands felt tingly and electric and he thought that if he looked down at them they might be invisible. He felt a bead of sweat form on his forehead, swell up, then slide down between his eyebrows alongside his nose past the left corner of his mouth under his chin then down his neck, sternum, belly, and into the waistband of his underwear.

He backed off Dwayne, and Dwayne made a couple of lay-ups. His teammates shouted encouragement and glared at Sammy.

It was getting dark, the wind had picked up and it was feeling like winter. Sammy knew the game would probably not last much longer. By his count, the score was tied.

Reggie missed a long outside jumper and Dwayne managed to snag the rebound. He turned and started dribbling slowly down court. Encountering Sammy about halfway to the goal, Dwayne stopped and looked for someone to pass to. He threw the ball toward a teammate on his left, but with a quick flick of his right hand Sammy intercepted the pass. Dwayne twisted his body around, reaching for the ball, hoping to steal it back. Sammy elbowed him in the ribs knocking him to the asphalt. He heard Dwayne grunt. He went in for an easy lay-up and came down dancing.

'Oh, yeah! Oh, yeah!' He laughed.

He turned around grinning as Wesley struck him full force in the face with the base of his hand, breaking his nose. He staggered backward, hit the back of his head on the goal-post and slid to the ground. Blood spurted from his nose in thick short bursts.

Wesley bent over him. 'I told you this was just for fun, asshole,' he said.

He stomped Sammy in the balls. Then he stomped him in the balls again.

Sammy lay in the dark on the grass by the side of the basketball court for a long time. When he finally struggled to his feet he saw that the front of his T-shirt was soaked in blood. He started home, breathing through his mouth, cradling his testicles with both hands. His mother had earlier said that Rudy was coming for dinner. He hoped Rudy was still there.

His mother was standing at the sink with her back to the door when Sammy came in.

'Is Rudy here, Ma?' he asked stuffily, through broken cartilage.

'No,' said his mother, without turning around. 'He ain't comin'.'

'Why? I thought he was going to eat here tonight.'

'Well, he ain't. Not tonight. Not ever.'

'*Why?*' Sammy demanded. '*Why* ain't he coming ever?' His mother still had not turned to look at Sammy.

'Because he says he didn't like the way I was talkin' with a guy at the bar last night. Even though I said it wasn't nothing and I was just havin' a little fun, he didn't see it that way. So we got into it and he said we was done and I was a whore anyways.'

90

Sammy began to shiver. 'You *are* a whore.'

Sammy's mother whipped around to face her son. She gasped when she saw his broken face and bloodied clothes. And she gasped again when Sammy picked up the heavy glass ashtray from the kitchen table and swung it up against the side of her head with all that he had in him.

She wasn't dead. He could see that. She wasn't even bleeding that bad. He picked up the ashtray, went to the sink and washed it. Then he returned to the table, sat down, lit a cigarette, and looked at his mother.

His own wounds no longer hurt. He felt like there were possibilities. Like he could do things now he couldn't do before. Before his mother was on the floor.

He felt like taking a nap. He thought about what to do next. Maybe call Rudy. He wondered where his mother kept Rudy's number. His mother moaned. A glob of partially congealed blood fell from his nose onto the table.

He finished his cigarette, got up, went to the phone, and called 911. 'Yeah, my name is Sammy Merzeti. Somebody broke into our trailer and beat up my mom and me. Some black guys. My mom is hurt bad. She's knocked out, and my nose is broke, I'm pretty sure. It was black guys. Three of them.'

15

Thief in the Night

In 1983, the year after it opened, Smoke Meat was robbed three times. This almost convinced LaVerne and Angela that the restaurant business was too risky. At least in downtown Kansas City, and with Raymond spending so much time working there. But in 1984 there was only one robbery attempt, which failed when the robber slipped on some spilled barbecue sauce. LaVerne's and Angela's anxieties were allayed somewhat.

These days, when attempted robberies of the restaurant fail, the failure is usually due to a sudden collapse in confidence on the part of the would-be thief, resulting in rapid retreat or capture.

A few weeks after Raymond died, LaVerne was working the counter when a guy came into the restaurant at lunchtime, stood in line with everyone else and when it was his turn to order, pulled a gun out of his pocket, pointed it at LaVerne's forehead and demanded money.

LaVerne said no.

'I'm not giving you *anything*,' he said. 'Because I *got* nothing. I got *nothing* to lose. Nothing left.'

The guy with the gun appeared confused. This was the first time that pointing a gun at someone's forehead had not achieved the intended result.

LaVerne continued. 'Dying would be just fine with me. So if you want to shoot me, go ahead. I couldn't care less. But that's the only way you're going to get a dime from me, ass-hole.'

The guy with the gun began to sweat as he contemplated his next move. That's when LaVerne swept his right hand up and across, grabbing the gun. He jammed it up under the guy's chin, forcing him back on his heels.

'Don't kill me!' the suddenly gunless guy screamed.

'Then get the hell out of here!' LaVerne said, his jaws tight and clenching. He came out from behind the counter and the guy turned and ran out the door.

The next time somebody tried robbing the place LaVerne employed roughly the same tactics and they were once again successful. Thereafter this became LaVerne's primary theft-deterrent methodology. He kept the guns he collected this way in the safe in the office and turned them over to Pug Hale whenever he came in next.

LaVerne's approach did not work every time. Once, in response to LaVerne's refusal to hand over cash a robber clubbed him on the side of the head with his pistol, knock-ing him unconscious. Since then, LaVerne has used more discretion in how he handles robbery threats. If the thief appears at all unsure of himself, or if no gun is visible, La-Verne will stand his ground. If, however, the thief is cold and calm, with hard dead eyes, LaVerne will open the cash register and let the thief take the money. To minimize losses in such circumstances, LaVerne never keeps more than $100 in the cash drawer. The rest goes in the office safe.

Because more often than not LaVerne is not the one behind the counter, he instructs his employees to never resist a robbery. 'I don't expect any of you to lose your life or get hurt for minimum wage,' he says.

*

One Saturday, Bob Dunleavy surprised LaVerne by present-
ing him with a genuine autographed Rocky Colavito model
K55 35-inch Hillerich & Bradsby Louisville Slugger from
1964 – the one year Colavito played with the Athletics.

'I picked this up at an estate sale up on Ward Parkway, if
you can believe it,' said Bob, as he handed the bat to La-
Verne. 'It's the real deal. There's a note that came with it that
says this was really Colavito's bat. It's cracked on the handle
which is probably why he gave it away. It's even got cleat
marks. Can't you just see the Rock pulling this thing back
behind his shoulders before he steps up to the plate?'

LaVerne held the bat in his hands and grinned. 'Damn,
Bob, I can't accept this. You need to give it to your grandson
or something.'

Bob shook his head. 'LaVerne, my grandson doesn't
know who Rocky Colavito is and he doesn't even like baseball. I want *you* to have it. As soon as I saw it, I wanted you
to have it.'

LaVerne just grinned some more.

Later that afternoon he put the bat under the counter
by the cash register with the intent of showing it to Pug
next time he came in with Mother Mary. If LaVerne had
known that a genuine autographed Rocky Colavito model
K55 35-inch Hillerich & Bradsby Louisville Slugger from
1964 would sell for about $1,000 on eBay, he would proba-
bly have chosen a more secure place to store Bob Dunleavy's
gift. As it turned out this lapse in judgment thwarted the
theft of the $100 in the cash drawer.

A week or so later, A.B. was at the counter, when a burly
black man in an oversized hooded sweatshirt, with the hood
pulled up, baggy carpenters' jeans, and expensive sneakers
swaggered up to the counter and shoved a gun at A.B.

'I want all your money and cigarettes,' he said. 'Don't

mess with me, cuz I'll kill you. Just give me your money and your cigarettes.'

The request for cigarettes concerned A.B., because Smoke Meat doesn't sell cigarettes. And since he had left his own pack of cigarettes in the office he wasn't sure how he would comply with this demand.

He tried to explain. 'Well, I can give you the money but not the cigarettes because we don't sell cigarettes here. I used to try to get the boss to sell 'em because there are plenty of people who ask for them, including me, but the boss's wife won't do it. And she's probably right about that. It's not really healthy. We don't allow people to smoke in here anyways. I've tried to quit myself but I always start up again.'

About then LaVerne came out from the kitchen and saw the man and his gun. Without hesitating or breaking stride LaVerne snatched the Rocky Colavito model K55 from under the counter and with a quick single-handed swing swatted the gun from the man's grip, almost detaching the man's hand from his wrist in the process.

The man fell on the floor writhing in pain. '*Damn*, dawg! You broke my hand!' he cried. 'You didn't have to do that!'

LaVerne stood over him ready to use the K55 again if necessary. 'You didn't have to come in here and try to steal from us,' he said. 'Call 911, A.B.'

Twenty minutes later the whole thing was over. The police had come and hauled the perpetrator away and had taken statements from A.B., LaVerne, and a few of the customers. The place was empty except for Ferguson Glen and Del James.

LaVerne was pissed off. 'We should have just given him the hundred dollars because he chased away at least three hundreds' worth of business.'

He went into the kitchen, got himself a beer and went out back by the dumpster to drink it. A.B. sat down in a chair across from Del and took a deep breath. He wanted to go out back and smoke but decided it was best to leave LaVerne alone.

'You all right?' Del asked.

'Yeah,' said A.B. 'Whenever this happens it reminds of when I saw the angel.'

Del pointed to his ear. 'You'll have to speak up. I thought you said you saw an angel.'

'I did, Del. I did see an angel. That's how I got saved. That's when I accepted Jesus.'

'I have absolutely no idea what you're talking about, boy,' said Del. 'But I'm not really religious. That may be why.'

'It was September 6th, 1987. I'll never forget it,' said A.B. 'I was cooking briskets and butts for the next day, so it was late, like ten or eleven o'clock, and I went out back to get some wood for the smoker. I propped the back door open with a piece of wood like I always do so it doesn't close all the way, and I loaded up with logs.

'Anyways, I had my arms full and was trying to get the door open with my foot, when I hear something back behind the wood stack. So I'm trying to get inside quick because I think maybe it's a rat in the woodpile. Rats give me the willies.

'I get inside and put the wood down and turn around and there's this guy with a knife. A big knife. And I *know* the guy! He's the guy we got our wood from. He and his uncle had this big wood lot down in the Ozarks, and every two weeks he would drive his truck up here and sell wood to us and some of the other joints.

'So I say, "Billy, what's goin' on?" And he says, "Sorry, man, I wouldn't do this if I had a choice. But I don't. And just because we know each other doesn't mean I won't cut you up if you don't do what I say."

'So, Billy makes me go in the office and tells me to open the safe. I tell him I don't know the combination and he gets real mad. He puts the knife right up under my eye and tells me I'd better think of it real fast. I thought I was going to die. That he was going to kill me right there. Especially since I really didn't know the combination. That or he was going to cut my eye out.

'Anyways. Next thing I know, I see this flash of light. It blinds me. And everything is dark all around me, but I see this light in front of me and I hear a voice. A strong, but kind of quiet voice. And it says, "You're all right. You're safe. Keep your eyes on me."

'And I do feel safe. I don't feel afraid of Billy and his knife. The voice is telling me, "Stay with me, A.B. Stay with me. You're mine. And I need you."

'And then I see a man in white clothes. He's standing there in the light smiling at me with his hand out to me. He says, "Don't be afraid." And he calls me by my real name. Al Buddy. Nobody even *knows* my real name. Everybody just knows me by A.B. That's when I knew it was an angel.

'Then, I'm waking up in the hospital emergency room. And I'm okay, except I got a big ol' shiner.

'That's when I started going to church. Mrs Williams had been asking me to anyway. I figured if Jesus wanted me, then he was going to have me. If he sent an angel to save my life, then I was sure going to accept him as my personal Lord and Savior. That's when I got baptized. That's when I got saved.'

Del thought about all this for a moment. 'So, what happened to the kid with the knife?'

'Don't know,' said A.B. 'But he didn't get any money. A couple of weeks later his uncle came around to deliver wood and the boss told him to go screw himself, that we didn't want his wood anymore.'

Del shook his head. 'I'm not sure you saw an angel, A.B.

That sounds to me more like a medical experience than a religious experience. Sounds like you had a brush with death, not an angel.'

Del patted A.B. on the back and got up to leave. 'I'm glad you're still among the living.'

After Del left, A.B. sighed and looked over at Ferguson. 'Nobody ever believes me.'

Ferguson, who doesn't smile much, smiled at A.B. 'I envy you, young man.'

'Why would you envy *me*?'

'Because I *do* believe you.'

The two men sat in silence. A.B. felt like he might cry. Ferguson spoke. 'So? Is your name *really* Al Buddy?'

16

Direct and Indirect

LaVerne gets annoyed when people ask him for his 'secret recipe' for barbecue.

'There is no *recipe* for barbecue,' he snarls. 'There's a *technique* for barbecue. And it's no secret. Anybody who knows anything about barbecue knows the technique.'

Usually LaVerne's response stifles further discussion; however, if he's feeling charitable, he may offer that barbecue is a technique where certain cuts of meat are cooked slowly by the heat of coals made from a hardwood fire.

'Wood, meat, and time. That's what you need to make barbecue. It's no secret. There are lots of ways cooks add their own personal flavor to the barbecue, such as seasonings and sauces, but seasonings and sauces don't make it barbecue. They make it *your* barbecue.'

LaVerne Williams' barbecue is pretty straightforward. He prefers oak and cherry wood for his fire, though he'll use pecan and apple. And for seasonings, he uses salt, pepper, cayenne, and garlic powder. That's it.

'I'm not heavy on the seasonings,' he says. 'I let the wood and the smoke do most of the work.'

Maintaining a steady, reliable, supply of wood is one of the problematic aspects of the barbecue business. A few years ago, Smoke Meat struck a deal with a young farmer with a big wood lot down near Sedalia, who got into the wood business as a way of supplementing his cash flow during the winter months. He was punctual and honest and LaVerne liked him, but in the spring when the farmer realized he was actually going to need to use his grain truck to haul grain instead of wood, he called LaVerne and told him he was getting out of the wood business. For a couple of weeks, LaVerne bought wood from local suppliers. But most of the local woodyards sell primarily to competitive barbecue cooks and backyard enthusiasts and they charge more than LaVerne is used to paying.

The regulars at Smoke Meat knew that LaVerne was unhappy about his wood situation. So when Del James saw a sign advertising firewood up in northwest Missouri, he wrote down the phone number.

'It's about two hours from here, up near Worth, Missouri, on 169 Highway,' said Del. 'I saw the sign on my way back from my mother's place, up in Mount Ayr, Iowa. It may be too far. But you said were pretty desperate.'

LaVerne had A.B. call the number and ask what kind of wood they had and how much they charged for it.

'Looks good, boss,' said A.B., reporting back with the information. 'They got oak, apple, hickory, and maple. And the price is right. Only problem is, his truck is broke down so he can't deliver until it's fixed. If we want wood this week, we'll have to go pick it up. But he says if we do, he'll knock some off the price.'

LaVerne swore and slammed shut the walk-in door, but told A.B. to call back and make arrangements for them to pick up a load that Saturday.

Late Saturday morning, LaVerne and A.B. left on their errand, leaving Angela in charge of the lunch shift.

'I got a map from the Internet,' said A.B. proudly, climbing into the passenger seat of LaVerne's old, white, crew-cab Ford F-150. 'We're going to some place called Redemption Abbey, outside the town of Worth. We take Interstate 71 north to St Joe and then cut over on 169 Highway.'

'Why don't we just take 169 all the way?' asked LaVerne, skeptical of a computer's ability to provide accurate driving directions.

'Because it says here that the fastest way is 71,' said A.B.

'Well, I'm saying that's bullshit,' snapped LaVerne. 'We're taking 169.'

A.B. sulked for the first few miles. At about Gladstone, the silence finally got to him, and he reached for the radio, only to be jolted abruptly forward against his seatbelt as LaVerne pulled the truck over onto the shoulder and braked to a sudden stop, skidding a bit in the gravel.

'Jeez! Boss!' yelped A.B., unsure of what had just happened. 'Are you all right?'

'I'm fine,' said LaVerne. He opened his door and hopped out of the truck.

A.B. watched LaVerne look both ways for traffic and then walk out onto the road where he bent to pick something up. He crossed in front of the truck and A.B. got out to see what it was LaVerne had.

It was a turtle.

LaVerne held the turtle in his right hand, his arm extended all the way. Turtle pee dribbled out the back of its shell. Its legs moved like it was swimming in the air. LaVerne put the turtle down in the grass, which sloped into a ditch. It pulled its head and feet into its shell.

'Dang, boss,' said A.B. 'How'd you even know that was a turtle there in the road?'

'When I was a kid in Texas, we'd see 'em all the time,' said LaVerne. 'Sometimes you'd see 'em crushed on the road and I just hated that. They're so damn slow they're helpless.

I can't stand to see them crawling across a road, because you just know they're going to get smashed. So, when I see one, I always stop to pick it up and put it on the side of the road.'

LaVerne and A.B. watched the turtle tentatively poke its head out to assess the situation.

'I haven't seen one in a long time,' said LaVerne. 'But I don't get out of the city that much.'

The turtle decided the coast was clear and started down the slope toward the ditch.

Approaching Smithville, LaVerne and A.B. conferred with one another and decided they were hungry and drove into town for something to eat. The first place they came to was Humphrey's 'Fill 'er Up' BBQ, which was housed in an old gas station.

'Let's see what the competition is up to,' said LaVerne pulling the truck into the parking lot.

Inside, LaVerne inspected the menu and immediately began heaping scorn. 'Same old, same old. Fries, potato salad, slaw, and beans. None of these joints has any imagination.'

He ordered a brisket sandwich and beans. A.B. ordered the half-chicken, with fries and beans.

'Where do you think that turtle was going, boss?' asked A.B. while they waited for their food.

'I asked my uncle Delbert that same thing once when I was a kid, after he and I rescued a turtle from the road. He said, "Well, boy, he was goin' to the other side of the road." So I guess that's the answer. I mean, who knows what's in a turtle's mind? Their brains can't be any bigger than a pea. Then he said, "LaVerne, you never know what the result will be from something you do. You see a turtle in the road, and you worry it'll get killed, so you pick it up and you move it off to the side of the road and you think you done something good. And you probably did. But maybe that turtle was on its way home, and when you put it down on the other side of the road it got mixed up in its direction and got lost and never did find its way back home. Or maybe the turtle actually makes it across the road, but then a fox sees it and eats it. So, if you get the turtle out of the road, you're not saving it from the car running over it, but from the fox. But then maybe the fox goes hungry. Or maybe if you don't rescue that turtle, somebody driving down the road sees it up ahead and slams on their brakes and slides off the road and gets killed. You just never know when you do something what will come from it. So you just always have to do the best you can. You have to do what you think is right.'"

The food arrived, and LaVerne and A.B. ate in silence, until A.B. said, with his mouth full, 'This is pretty good chicken.'

LaVerne frowned.

'How's your brisket?' A.B. asked.

'It's okay.'

'How about the beans?'

'These aren't beans,' groused LaVerne. 'They're *candy*. Sticky, sweet candy. You can have mine if you want. I can't eat 'em.'

A.B. took the beans.

Back in the truck, LaVerne shook his head in disgust. 'I can't believe you liked those beans. Sometimes I wonder about you, A.B.'

'Well, I may as well tell you that I liked the fries, too,' said A.B., still smarting from the dispute over which highway to take. 'They were real good, in fact. They put some kind of seasoning on them. We should start serving fries like that. Our customers would like 'em.'

LaVerne glared at A.B. 'Unbelievable.'

They proceeded in tense silence and A.B. wished that the

farmer from Sedalia hadn't reneged on his wood contract. Finally, LaVerne spoke. 'What's the place we're going, again?'

'The guy called it Redemption Abbey,' said A.B. 'I have no idea what that is. Maybe it's a town. It sounds religious.'

'I don't know,' said LaVerne. 'I never heard of it.'

He looked up at the sky through the windshield. 'It's getting dark over to the west. Just our luck it'll start raining when we're loading up the wood.'

Just as Del had said, near the town of Worth, on the side of the highway was a sign painted on a half-sheet of plywood indicating that firewood was for sale six miles west, down a gravel side road. The first two miles of road cut through soybean fields. Then the cropland gave way to brush and scrub and LaVerne and A.B. could see in the distance a large red-brick church high atop a broad hill. Beside the church was another red-brick building, rectangular and not as tall.

The top of the hill looked as if it had pushed itself up by force of will out of a stand of trees that surrounded it on all sides for at least a half-mile in every direction.

'Dang,' whispered A.B.

'This doesn't look like a place that sells wood,' said La-Verne.

At the base of the hill was a driveway that split in two. One way went up to the front of the church. The other went up and around to the back of the other building. A small sign said that was the way to the wood. LaVerne drove up and around slowly, unsure exactly where he was going and what he was getting himself into. He stopped in a clearing near where another truck was parked under a massive elm tree. Two men and a boy were loading the truck up with wood. The boy looked like he was about twelve years old.

LaVerne and A.B. got out of the truck and looked around. There were neat stacks of split logs all around the clearing. Each stack was labeled with a hand-lettered sign designating the pile as oak, apple, hickory, or maple.

The younger of the two men walked over to LaVerne and extended his hand.

'Good afternoon,' he said. 'I'm Brother Ignatius. Call me Iggy.'

LaVerne and A.B. shook hands with Iggy.

'You guys from the restaurant in Kansas City?' he asked.

'We are,' said LaVerne. 'My man A.B., here, said you got oak at a good price. We'll take as much as we can put in the truck if you've got it.'

'I think we do,' said Iggy. 'Follow me.'

'So, what kind of place is this anyway?' asked LaVerne as he and A.B. walked behind Iggy to the stack of logs labeled 'OAK'.

'This is Redemption Abbey,' said Iggy. 'It's a Benedictine monastery.'

'Monastery. As in *monks* monastery?' asked LaVerne.

'Exactly. There are forty-eight of us monks here. This, here, is our dormitory. And that is our cathedral.'

He looked at LaVerne and A.B. 'You seem a little surprised.'

'A bit,' said LaVerne. 'I thought you guys just prayed all day and closed yourselves off from the rest of the world. I guess I didn't expect to buy wood from a monk. Plus, I thought monks wore those robes.'

'Well, we do pray a lot,' Iggy said. 'But we have to eat, too, so we support ourselves in a number of ways. Including selling wood. That's my job here. I cut it, split it, stack it, sell it, and load it. Once we get our truck running, I'll deliver it. And when I'm not on wood duty, I do wear a robe.'

He looked over at the western horizon. A long line of flat gray clouds was gathering. 'Hope we don't get wet.'

LaVerne backed his truck up to the oak pile and he and

A.B. started loading. The sound of logs landing in the truck bed reverberated in the still, cool, quiet air. After about twenty minutes of loading, A.B. needed a smoke. He walked away from the truck and stretched his back as he lit up. He noticed that the sky had turned a yellow shade of green that made him uneasy. He walked back over to LaVerne.

'This place gives me the creeps, boss,' he said. 'It kind of glows. It looks like the sky is coming right down on us.'

LaVerne looked up. Brother Ignatius and the other two were also looking at the sky.

Later, each one of them, when recounting the events of the afternoon, remembered that at that moment he felt a gentle breeze blow, heard leaves rustle, and thought about something he had said earlier in the day.

The wind surged upon them like a river rushing through a burst dam. A wide column of cloud, dense and black, closed in on the hillside. The branches on the trees around the abbey whipped about frantically. Dust and gravel rose up in swirling chaos. Brother Ignatius yelled instructions.

'*This way!*' He waved toward a cellar door that slanted out from the base of the building. '*This way!*' He held the door open.

LaVerne grabbed A.B.'s arm and ran toward the cellar. The other man and the boy followed. When they were all safely inside, Brother Ignatius bolted the door. Then he crossed himself. They stood there and listened to all hell breaking loose outside.

'Here,' said Iggy. 'Sit.' He motioned toward two benches facing each other along the narrow cellar walls. LaVerne and A.B. sat on one bench and the others sat on the other side.

'I'm Steve Hinman,' said the man who had been loading wood when LaVerne and A.B. arrived. 'This is my son Danny. I can't *believe* this. I *can not* believe it.'

LaVerne and A.B. introduced themselves.

Something big thudded hard against the cellar door. They all flinched and were quiet. Then there was a piercing crack and booming crash. They all flinched again and were quiet for several more minutes. Danny looked at LaVerne and whispered something to his father, who nodded and smiled.

'Are you the LaVerne Williams who played for the Kansas City Athletics in 1967?' asked Danny.

'That's me,' said LaVerne. 'You're the first person to ask me that question in about ten years.'

'This is *sweet*!' said Danny. 'I've got your rookie card. It's mint. This is awesome.'

'Well, son, you may have the only one left,' said LaVerne. 'My guess is that card is worth less than the bubblegum that came with it.'

'No,' said Danny. 'I saw on eBay that a mint condition LaVerne Williams' rookie card goes for thirty-five bucks.'

LaVerne smiled. 'I'll bet a mint condition Rick Monday goes for a lot more.'

'Not really,' said Danny. 'There's a lot more of those. They're easy to find. They sell for about two dollars.'

A.B. jabbed LaVerne with his elbow. 'You hear that, boss? You're worth thirty-two dollars more than Rick Monday.'

'Thirty-three,' said LaVerne.

Iggy interrupted. 'Listen,' he said. 'It's over.'

They listened. It was over.

Outside, they stood and breathed. The air was clean and calm.

The elm tree had split in two and one half had fallen on Steve's truck, only one tire of which could be seen. Steve said nothing. Brother Ignatius crossed himself again.

A.B. took out his pack of cigarettes and lit one up. Iggy looked at A.B.

'Can I have one of those?' he asked.

A.B. gave him one and lit it for him. Iggy's hands were shaking.

Iggy, Steve, and Danny went over to examine the smashed truck. LaVerne went over to his truck to check on its condition.

A.B. walked around to the back of the dorm. All the windows had been blown out but the building was intact. Bibles and prayer books were scattered around the clearing. A.B. saw a toothbrush, a pair of underwear and a framed photograph of a dog. Some of the other monks, some in their robes, others in jeans and T-shirts, had emerged from the building, dazed and concerned, embracing one another, picking up the strewn stuff of their lives. A.B. heard a low moan and turned, expecting to see an injured monk. It was a cow.

'Hey, Iggy!' A.B. called. 'Your cow got loose in the storm.'

The cow was eating grass on the edge of the clearing.

Brother Ignatius came over to see. 'We don't have a cow,' he said.

A.B. wondered if maybe it was the cow that had thumped into the cellar door.

'We didn't have any chickens either,' said Brother Ignatius. He pointed to the side of the dorm. At the base of the dorm wall were eight dead hens. It appeared as if they had been shot out of a cannon against the bricks.

LaVerne came over to report on the truck. 'Our truck seems fine. I hate to leave you and your monks like this, needing so much help like this, but I'm kinda anxious to get home and see if things are all right. What do we owe you for the wood, brother?'

Iggy shook his head. 'That's okay, Mr Williams, we'll be fine. We have lots of strong backs here. We'll settle up later. I'll call you to arrange a delivery and you can pay me when I come down.'

LaVerne and A.B. walked over to Steve and Danny. Steve was trying without success to make a call on his cell phone.

'I don't know what we're going to do,' he said. 'I can't get a hold of my wife. I don't know if she's okay. She doesn't know if I'm okay. And we're stuck here.'

'Where do you live?' asked LaVerne.

'Parkville,' Steve replied.

'We'll take you home,' said LaVerne.

There was no small talk in the truck, at first. They were all thinking about what had happened. They were all wondering what it would have been like to have died. Finally, LaVerne asked Steve what he did for a living. Steve said that he was a lawyer.

'My law firm has a barbecue team,' Steve continued. 'That's why I was up here. Getting wood for a contest we were going to cook in next weekend. I'm the team captain. I do most of the cooking.'

LaVerne has ambivalent feelings about competitive barbecue cooks. He's been to some of the contests and has had some of the barbecue and admits, if only to himself, that it's all been real good smoked meat. But he doesn't like the jealousy he feels at the quality of the equipment some of the cooks use and the lavish amount of time and money they spend at the contests.

'For them it's a hobby,' he told Angela once, after they returned from the American Royal barbecue contest. 'But for me it's my livelihood. Yet they got better stuff than I do. They don't depend on their equipment to make their living. But I do. Some of their cookers cost more than I make in a year.'

But LaVerne felt as if his life had just been spared and he wasn't inclined to be touchy about barbecue hobbyists, so he let Steve talk about his barbecue contests and soon they were engaged in a scholarly discussion of the relative merits of

Carolina-style direct smoking versus the Kansas City-style indirect method.

When they arrived at the Hinman house, Steve's wife rushed out to hug her husband and son. As she gushed thanks on LaVerne and A.B., wiping away tears of joy and gratitude, Danny went inside. He returned a minute later with his mint condition 1967 LaVerne Williams rookie baseball card.

'Will you autograph this for me, Mr Williams?' he asked, beaming.

Back in the truck, A.B. came down with a bad case of hiccups, which impeded conversation. LaVerne turned on the radio. The tornado had cut a swath a half-mile wide and five miles long through a corner of northwest Missouri farm country. Officials did not yet know if there were any fatalities. A.B. lit a cigarette.

'I'm glad you saved that turtle, boss,' he said.

17

Corroborated

Raymond Williams and A.B. Clayton were pretty much insepar-
able from the day they met until the day Raymond left for
college. Raymond always had lots of friends, but he liked
A.B. best. A.B. was the only one who didn't want anything
from him but his company.

A.B. didn't have any other friends.

Raymond wasn't just popular, he was idolized. By nearly
everyone. He was the kind of kid other kids wanted to be, and
the kind of kid other kids' parents wanted them to be. Raymond was in almost every way exceptional. Exceptionally
good-looking. Exceptionally intelligent. Exceptionally talented. And exceptionally tall.

At school, everyone wanted to walk the halls with Raymond, eat lunch with Raymond, and be seen with Raymond.
Even teachers made a point of saying hello to Raymond
when they saw him between classes. And though A.B. was
almost always by Raymond's side, Raymond's popularity did
not spill over onto him. If Raymond missed a day of school it
was as if A.B. had ceased to exist. Nobody spoke to him or
even looked at him until Raymond returned. Everyone knew,
however, not to tease or criticize Raymond's little friend lest
they be forever excluded from Raymond's company.

Mostly, everyone politely ignored A.B., which was fine

with him. He feared that interactions with Raymond's other friends would reveal the extent of his inadequacy. The comfort and security he felt in Raymond's presence remained intact only so long as he didn't have to actually say anything to anyone else.

Raymond was not perfect, however. Perhaps because so much came so easily for him, he tended toward laziness. And not infrequently he clouded over. When the black moods came on him, he pulled deep within himself behind a false front of cheer and charm. Only Angela and A.B. knew these aspects of Raymond's character. Everyone else, including LaVerne, saw in Raymond what they wanted to see. A.B. just saw Raymond.

When they were sixteen years old, Raymond and A.B. would usually go straight to the restaurant every afternoon after school to work until closing, except during basketball season, when Raymond had practice. On Wednesday nights, LaVerne had the boys lock up so he could leave early to go with Angela to prayer meeting. After the boys checked to see that the front door was locked, the walk-in fridge closed tight, the timers set on the smoker, and the lights turned off, they locked the back door and Raymond gave A.B. a ride home. A.B. was always quite careful about this procedure. Raymond, less so.

One Wednesday night, Raymond was impatient to get going. He'd been griping all evening about having to stay open until 7:00 even though there hadn't been any customers since 6:15, and about the smell of smoke and meat in his clothes and hair, and about how his dad didn't even like prayer meeting so why couldn't he stay on Wednesday nights.

'I just figured it out, Ray,' said A.B. 'You've got a date tonight. That's why you've been pissy all night.'

Raymond grinned. 'Maybe I do. Maybe I don't. I won't know until I get out of here and go see the lady in question.'

As A.B. closed up, Raymond waited out in the alley by his car. A.B. leaned against the back door, holding it open, and reached around inside to turn off the light switch.

'You set?' he called to Raymond.

'I've *been* set,' Raymond called back. 'Let's go!'

A.B. let the door close and they got in the car. Raymond patted his pockets for his keys – first casually – then with more urgency, and then in a panic. '*Oh, man!*' he cried. 'Did you pick up my keys? I don't have my keys! Where are my *keys?*'

A.B. hated it when Raymond got upset. He immediately started to problem solve.

'I didn't pick 'em up. So, let's think about where you had them last,' he said quietly and evenly, hoping to calm Raymond down.

Raymond slammed his head back against the seat headrest. '*Shit!* They're on top of the filing cabinet in the office!'

The reason this realization warranted a 'Shit!' was that when the back door to Smoke Meat closed, it automatically locked. To deter theft, the door had no exterior knob, handle, or key lock, just one solid flat surface with nothing to pick, pry, or jimmy. When LaVerne opened up in the morning, he unlocked the front door and came in that way. He and Angela had the only keys to the front door. When A.B. went out back for a cigarette or to get wood for the smoker he propped the door open with a log from the woodpile so as not to get locked out, which sometimes happened anyway if he accidentally kicked the log. Then he had to walk around to the front to get back in. LaVerne always snorted and smirked when that happened.

Raymond and A.B. got out of the car and went over to the window that looks out onto the alley from the little hallway between the office and the kitchen. The year before, LaVerne had installed steel bars in the window to prevent break-ins. Raymond pressed his face against the glass.

'I can't *believe* this!' he yelled, kicking at the gravel in the alley. A.B. went over and pressed his face against the glass as if his way of doing it might produce a better result.

Then they heard the sound of tires on gravel and the single whoop of a siren. The bright white of a floodlight covered them and voices shouted out from the light ordering them to put their hands up. Up where they could be seen. Raymond and A.B. immediately complied with these orders. Out from the light came two Kansas City police officers, guns drawn and aimed at the boys.

'Turn around and place your hands up on the wall and spread your legs,' commanded one of the officers. Compliance was again immediate. The officers frisked Raymond and A.B.

'You have any ID?' asked the one officer who seemed to be in charge. 'Don't reach for it. Just tell me where it is. I'll get it.'

A.B. and Raymond both said that their wallets were in their back pockets. A.B.'s was. But Raymond's was on the filing cabinet with his car keys.

'This is my father's restaurant,' explained Raymond, facing the wall. 'LaVerne Williams. I'm his son, Raymond Williams. This is A.B. Clayton. We work here and I left my keys and wallet inside when we locked up just now. We were trying to see if we could get back in to get my keys. That's my car.'

No proof of the car's ownership was found in the car but the officers called in the number on the plates and confirmed that it did belong to a LaVerne Williams.

'You could have stolen the car as far as I know,' said the officer in charge. 'Looks to me like you two were trying to break in here. Get yourselves a little drug money and maybe some ribs while you're at it. We're going down to the station and sort this out.'

Raymond and A.B. were put in handcuffs, put in the back of the squad car and driven to police headquarters where they were told to call their parents. Raymond knew there would be nobody at his house so he called New Jerusalem Baptist Church hoping somebody there would pick up the phone and get a message to his parents. After twelve rings he gave up.

A.B. went ahead and called his mother, though he knew nothing good would come of it. His mother answered the phone, but her voice sounded funny and she didn't seem to understand that it was her son on the other end of the line. She kept asking A.B. to repeat himself.

'It's me, Mom,' said A.B., louder each time. 'Ray and I could use your help. Ray, Mom. You know, from work. The restaurant, Mom, the restaurant. We need you to get us out of a jam, and talk to the police.'

After he mentioned the police, a man's voice came on the phone. A voice he didn't recognize.

'Who the hell is this?' the man yelled. 'We haven't done anything wrong! You want to accuse us of something, come here and say it to my face! If you call the cops on us, I'll kill your ass. I know who you are!'

A.B. went pale and hung up. 'My mom isn't going to be able to help us.'

He began to hiccup.

The officer asked A.B. and Raymond for their home addresses and phone numbers.

'We're going to check some things out. But you're not going anywhere for now.'

He led the boys down a narrow hallway to large room divided into two parts. The front of the room was open and in the middle was a large gray metal desk, where another uniformed officer sat talking on a telephone. Behind him were two large jail cells. Two women occupied one of the cells. A young black woman sat on one of the cell benches crying quietly into a wad of tissue. Across from her on the other bench, a middle-aged white woman sat scowling, her back against the wall, arms crossed.

A.B. and Raymond were put in the other cell. There were two other boys there already. A black kid, a year or two younger than A.B. and Raymond, sat on the floor with his back to the door. He clutched his knees to his chest and rocked back and forth, whispering something to himself. He wore a dirty baseball shirt and his large white sneakers had no laces. The other was a white kid, maybe eighteen years old, lying on one of the benches sleeping. He was skinny and shirtless and his head was shaved. He smelled like puke.

A.B. and Raymond sat on the other bench.

'What are we going to do?' Raymond asked A.B. in a low, urgent tone.

'I don't know,' A.B. admitted. 'Maybe they'll let us call again later when your dad might be home.'

They sat there quiet. The stinky white kid belched in his sleep. Then he raised up on his elbows and vomited. The spew slid down his bare chest. He wiped it off with his hand and lay back down. Raymond got up and spoke to the officer at the desk.

'Sir, this guy just threw up,' he said. 'He might be sick.'

The attendant didn't like having to interrupt his phone conversation. He came over to the door and looked in. 'Step back,' he told Raymond. He unlocked the door, went in and roused the sick kid. He helped him out of the cell, locked the door behind them and walked the boy down the hall.

Then the officer who had apprehended the boys in the alley behind the restaurant came in from down the hall carrying a clipboard. LaVerne came in behind him. The boys stood right up.

'Dad!' Raymond cried. 'Did they tell you what happened?'

LaVerne was signing paperwork the desk attendant gave him. He didn't look at Raymond. The officer from the alley walked over to the cell.

'We finally got a hold of your father and he collaborated your story,' he told Raymond. 'Be more careful next time. We see a black kid trying to break into a business establishment at night, well, bad things can happen.'

He looked at A.B. 'And you, you should know better. You need to be careful who you associate with.'

A.B. glared at the man. 'What's *that* supposed to mean?'

'You know what it means,' the cop replied.

LaVerne approached the cell.

The cop smirked. 'So which one of these is yours?'

LaVerne looked at A.B. and Raymond.

'They're both mine,' he said.

18

Side by Side

Once or twice a year a food or travel writer from an East or West Coast newspaper will come to town, visit half a dozen barbecue joints, scarf down half a dozen sandwiches, then dispatch a tale of discovery informing readers back home of the marvels of Kansas City barbecue. Smoke Meat has never been among the establishments included in these write-ups. One reason for this oversight is that journalists get their ideas mostly from reading what other journalists have already written. And since most newspaper and magazine articles about Kansas City barbecue tend to focus on the more well-known venues – Bryant's, Gates, Jack's Stack, KC Masterpiece, and more recently, Oklahoma Joe's – those are the places that continue to get most of the attention. When a writer wants to demonstrate an intimate knowledge of out-of-the-way off-the-beaten-path joints that only locals know about, they may also include Danny Edwards' place or L.C.'s. This is not nearly the original idea the writer thinks it is. Even though they're smaller, grittier, and a bit more difficult to find, these joints have also been frequently and thoroughly covered by out-of-town food and travel writers.

Another reason LaVerne's place is overlooked is that LaVerne has never made an effort to widen the restaurant's reputation beyond its own neighborhood. Nobody much knows about Smoke Meat except the regulars. LaVerne doesn't do any advertising beyond taping a typed copy of the menu in the front window.

Finally, LaVerne is generally suspicious of journalists. He never much liked the stories that the *Star* or the *Times* wrote about him when he was with the Athletics, especially when he got hurt. And he thought that Raymond's death deserved a lot more attention from the press. On the off chance an out-of-town writer happens in to Smoke Meat, LaVerne is likely to be cool and minimally responsive, bordering on rude.

Once when A.B. had to bring his mother to her podiatrist for one of her bunion check-ups, he picked up a copy of *Midwest Vacation* magazine while he waited in the lobby. The cover story was a review of Kansas City barbecue joints, including all the usuals, plus Danny Edwards' place. Smoke Meat was not mentioned. A.B. was steamed. He tucked the magazine into his jacket and brought it back to the restaurant to show LaVerne.

'Why should these guys get all the glory, boss?' A.B. demanded to know, jabbing his finger into the magazine's offending pages.

'Who knows and who cares?' LaVerne shrugged, immediately shifting the conversation to a more pressing matter. 'Did Rocco deliver the onions and cabbage?'

The fact that onions and cabbage were of greater concern to LaVerne than the magazine situation exasperated A.B.

'Boss, we got to get ourselves some of this kind of publicity. It says here these joints are "authentic Kansas City". We're just as *authentic* as any of these guys. Why did they get in here and not us?'

LaVerne was unruffled by A.B.'s indignation.

'Son, what's publicity going to get us that we don't already have?' he asked.

A.B. threw up his arms and let them flop back down at his sides. 'People will know who we are!'

'The people who eat here already know who we are,' said LaVerne, wondering how he was going to get the discussion turned back around to onions and cabbage. 'We don't need too many more people eating here than we already have. There's only forty-five seats in the place.'

A.B. could see he wasn't getting anywhere. He shook his head and went out in a huff to clear tables. LaVerne went back to the office to call Rocco's Produce.

A few months later, a travel writer from Boston happened to call the restaurant. A.B. answered the phone the way he usually does. 'Smoke Meat,' he said in the clipped, hurried way he felt implied the full authority of his position as second-in-command. The caller on the other end of the line paused and A.B. thought for a moment there was nobody there.

'Is this LaVerne Williams' Genuine BBQ and City Grocery?' the caller asked.

'Yes, sir,' said A.B. 'Can I help you?'

'My name is Ainsley Ponairi,' said the caller. 'I'm a freelance writer in Boston. I'm doing a piece on barbecue restaurants around the country and I'll be coming through Kansas City next week and was wondering if the owner or manager could spend some time with me talking about Kansas City barbecue. Would that be Mr Williams?'

'Yes!' A.B. yipped. 'That *would* be Mr Williams. *LaVerne* Williams. He's the owner and the manager. Well, I'm kind of the manager. But more like the assistant and I couldn't really talk to anybody about Kansas City barbecue. I mean, I grew up in Kansas City and I work at a barbecue restaurant, but I couldn't talk about it to a free writer. Or lancer. Whatever you said.'

'Freelance writer,' said the caller. 'May I speak with Mr Williams?'

'Yes! You can!' said A.B. 'I'll get him.'

A.B. sensed hiccups coming on and struggled to suppress them. He clamped the telephone receiver to his chest and motioned frantically to Vicki Fuentes, the recently hired college student working the cash register.

'Go get the boss!' he whispered fiercely, shooshing her toward the office with frenetic arm flapping. Vicki scurried off and returned a moment later with a visibly peeved LaVerne. A.B. thrust the phone at him and mouthed ITSAWRITER with great exaggeration. LaVerne scowled and shrugged. A.B. tried again. AWRITERFROMBOSTON. LaVerne sighed, shook his head and snatched the phone from A.B.'s grip.

'This is LaVerne Williams,' he said, already impatient.

Ainsley Ponairi explained to LaVerne that he was going to be in Kansas City in a week and would like to meet to talk about barbecue and maybe take a tour of the restaurant.

'Well, there's not much to see,' he said. 'We're a pretty small operation.'

A.B. hovered expectantly.

'I suppose,' said LaVerne without enthusiasm to a question posed by the writer.

A.B. nodded energetically.

'Wednesday would work,' said LaVerne. 'But you'd have to come after two o'clock and before four.'

A.B. held his hand up for LaVerne to high-five. LaVerne ignored it.

'That's fine,' said LaVerne and hung up. He started toward the office with A.B. close on his heels.

'So?' A.B. asked eagerly. 'Is he coming here? Is he going to interview you or something?'

'Looks like it,' said LaVerne.

When it dawned on A.B. that he wasn't likely to obtain

any more information from LaVerne on the topic he went out back for a smoke.

Ainsley Ponairi arrived at Smoke Meat promptly at 2:00. He was petite and perfectly groomed; perfectly pressed tan gabardines, perfectly pressed blue oxford shirt with open collar, perfectly fitting navy blazer with burgundy pocket square, and perfectly shined cordovan penny loafers with silky white socks. He approached the counter and announced that he had an appointment with Mr Williams.

Leon Noel was working the counter that day and he went to retrieve LaVerne. Leon was a parolee who started work at Smoke Meat a few months after serving a short jail sentence for writing a bad check.

'I think that boy got a bad rap,' LaVerne told A.B. shortly after he hired Leon. 'He can hardly read or write. He gets his letters all mixed up. That's probably why he wrote a bum check. He didn't know how to write it right. Angela says it's probably that dyslexia.'

Leon returned from the kitchen with LaVerne who was wiping his hands on his apron. He and Ainsley Ponairi introduced themselves. They sat, and LaVerne asked Ainsley if he wanted to order anything.

'What's your specialty?' Ainsley asked.

'Barbecue,' said LaVerne with only the slightest smile.

Ainsley looked as if he might actually try to explain that he meant to ask what specific item on the menu did LaVerne consider to be his specialty, but LaVerne waved his hand to prevent it.

'I was kidding. I know what you mean. My personal favorite is our pulled chuck. We're the only place in town that serves it as far as I know. But our brisket is real good also. We slice it thick. Lots of places here in Kansas City use a deli-style slicer and cut it paper thin. But we slice it thick, which is Texas style because that's where I'm from.'

Ainsley said he'd have the pulled chuck and LaVerne motioned for A.B. to come over to the table. A.B. had been pretending to be busy behind the counter while he watched over the interview hoping to discern its content and tone. He hustled over to the table.

'What do you need, Mr Williams?' he asked solicitously.

LaVerne rolled his eyes. 'Our guest will have a Big Charlie. And how about a short end, and some greens and potatoes, just to give him a sampling.'

'And an iced tea,' said Ainsley. 'If you have it.'

A.B. scooted off to the kitchen for the food.

'So, do you also sell groceries here?' asked Ainsley, looking around.

'We used to stock a few items when we first opened,' LaVerne explained. 'But for a long time nobody lived downtown, so we quit. Nobody was buying anything but the barbecue. Recently folks have been moving back so maybe we'll add some groceries again. But I don't know where. We've added tables and there's not much room.'

'How long have you been open?' asked Ainsley. LaVerne was about to respond when Del James came in.

'Anyone seen a chisel?' he bellowed. 'It's a five-tooth coarse Milani.'

Customers dutifully looked under and around their tables and chairs, but no chisel was found.

'Thanks anyways!' Del shouted as he exited.

'That's Del,' said LaVerne. 'He's an artist. He lives down the block and doesn't hear very well.'

Ainsley nodded and smiled and waited for LaVerne to answer his question but LaVerne had already forgotten what it was. Ainsley moved on.

'You said you came from Texas. What brought you here to Kansas City?'

'Well, I was playing baseball for the Kansas City Athletics,' LaVerne started to explain. 'That was in 1967 . . .'

Suzanne Edwards came in and said hi to LaVerne on her way to the counter. A.B. brought Ainsley's food. LaVerne looked at the writer.

'You came here from Texas . . .' Ainsley tried to keep the interview on track.

'Yes,' said LaVerne. 'That's where I learned barbecue. From my uncle. I always like to say that the best Kansas City barbecue actually comes from Texas. By that I mean Arthur Bryant's and mine. My wife doesn't like it when I say that. She grew up here in Kansas City.'

'Where did your wife go for barbecue when she was growing up?' asked Ainsley.

LaVerne didn't much care for the question. 'Bryant's. And Gates, too, I think. There was a place called Oven Bar-B-Q. Her family went there, too.'

Suzanne walked by on her way back out. She was carrying a big cardboard box full of food.

'That's Suzanne,' LaVerne said. 'She works at the furniture store across the street. Whenever they have an open house or a big meeting with clients they get their food from us. She's a good customer.'

'You were telling me about your uncle,' Ainsley said. 'What were his barbecue secrets?'

'Delbert didn't have any secrets, really,' said LaVerne. 'It was all real straightforward. Briskets and sausage mostly. He didn't put anything on 'em. Just salt and pepper. Sometimes garlic or cayenne. That's it. The rest was all smoke. He used oak. Cherry if he could get it. Plus, he sliced the brisket thick.

'Uncle Delbert and his business partner, Hartholz, had a

little butcher shop in the town where we lived and they made the barbecue out back behind the shop in a brick pit they built. On Saturdays people would drive up all the way from Houston to buy smoked brisket and homemade sausage. My cooker is more expensive and lots fancier than theirs but my barbecue isn't any better. Nobody's is any better.'

LaVerne was interrupted by crashing and breaking glass. Behind the counter A.B. sheepishly held the end of a roll of red butcher paper in his hands.

'It's okay!' he called to LaVerne. 'I pulled on the paper too hard and the roll came loose and knocked over a rack of glasses. I'm takin' care of it.'

He wiped sweat from his upper lip and forehead.

LaVerne went over to inspect and Ainsley ate some of his Big Charlie pulled chuck sandwich.

When LaVerne returned to the table Ainsley waited for him to continue talking about Delbert, but LaVerne was finished with the subject. He waited for Ainsley to ask another question.

'So, now that you've lived here in Kansas City awhile and have owned your own barbecue restaurant, how do you think Kansas City barbecue compares to Texas barbecue?' Ainsley asked.

'Well, there's a lot more to Kansas City barbecue,' said LaVerne. 'More kinds of meat and sauces. Kansas City style is its own thing now, but it originates from Texas and the Carolinas. Kansas City gets its beef style from Texas and our pork style comes from the Carolinas. That's not just my thinking. A lot of other people say the same thing.'

Suzanne Edwards came marching back in with her box of food, past LaVerne up to the counter. She was red-faced and unhappy. She plopped the box down next to the cash register.

'Where's A.B.?' she demanded of Leon. 'This order is all wrong! I need to talk to A.B.!'

LaVerne suspended his explanation of Kansas City-style barbecue to observe the goings on in the back of the restaurant. Ainsley sighed and took a forkful of the greens, then some red potatoes. Up at the counter, Vicki Fuentes stood wide-eyed biting her bottom lip. Leon, who had filled the order, looked like he needed to sit down. They stared at Suzanne in silent dread.

A.B. came in from the kitchen. 'Hey, Suzanne. What's going on?'

'A.B., I ordered three pounds of burnt ends, two pounds of turkey, two pounds of pulled pork, and one gallon of beans,' she said. 'Look what I got! You guys have never messed up before. Not *ever*! But on the day that we're pitching our biggest account yet, you give me six gallons of beans and two plastic forks! Is this some kind of *joke* or something?'

A.B. looked in the box. There were six gallon containers of beans in the box, and tucked in one corner, two plastic forks.

LaVerne got up and went over to the counter. Ainsley Ponairi started in on his short end.

'I know what you ordered, Suzanne, because I took your order over the phone,' said A.B., trying to figure out what went wrong. He reached around through the pass-through window for a clipboard of order slips and found Suzanne's. He turned to Leon and Vicki.

'Who filled this order?' he asked, his face flushed and damp.

Leon admitted that he had. At that point LaVerne intervened.

'A.B., get Suzanne the food she ordered,' he said. 'It's on the house, Suzanne. I'm sorry about this. We'll have it fixed in a few minutes. If you need to get back to your meeting, we'll bring the order over to the store for you right away.'

Suzanne nodded and left. A.B. handed the order slip to LaVerne and retreated into the kitchen. LaVerne read the slip. A.B.'s handwriting was sloppy but legible:

3 lbs burnt ends
2 lbs breast
1 gal beans
2 lbs pork

LaVerne held the slip out for Leon to see. 'Tell me what this says, boy.'

Leon leaned in to study the slip. 'Well, I wasn't exactly sure.'

He looked up to see if Vicki was listening. Vicki noticed Leon's discomfort and went to help A.B. with the order.

Leon sighed. 'I think it says three tubs of beans, two tubs of beans, one gallon of beans, and two forks. I wasn't sure what a tub was, but I figured it was a gallon. Anyways, I'm not real good at reading. It seemed like a lot of beans. I guess I should have asked.'

LaVerne frowned and put his hand on Leon's shoulder.

'It's not your fault, boy. It's an easy mistake to fix. Don't worry about it. Go back to work. And if you need any more help with reading, just ask me.'

Ainsley Ponairi had eaten everything in front of him by the time LaVerne returned to the table. He smiled at La-Verne.

'I don't think I've ever heard of vinegar pie,' he said. 'Do you recommend it?'

'Wouldn't be on the menu board otherwise,' said LaVerne. He called for Vicki to bring two slices of vinegar pie and some coffee.

Ainsley ate his pie in silence. He was either out of

questions or had concluded that he was unlikely to extract more than another sentence or two from LaVerne before another calamity befell. When he had finished, he pushed his chair back from the table and extended his hand to LaVerne.

'Mr Williams, I've got some other stops to make so I must be going now. It's been a pleasure. My story will probably be published next month in *The Blue*, the in-flight magazine of Northern Airlines. I'll send you some copies.'

LaVerne shook his hand and Ainsley turned to leave.

'Oh, one more thing,' he said. 'I'd like to arrange to have a local photographer come by and take a few pictures for the article. Would that be alright?'

LaVerne agreed, and that was that.

A week later a photographer called A.B. and set up a photo shoot for the following afternoon.

When the photographer arrived, LaVerne was cranky. He had wanted Angela to be in the picture, but she had left a message at the restaurant that morning to say that their pastor had called asking her to attend a meeting of the Ladies' Missionary Board at the church and she said she would.

The photographer, a friendly soft-spoken guy named Talbott, took some pictures of the interior of the restaurant, including one of LaVerne in the kitchen standing by the smoker. Talbott repeatedly encouraged LaVerne to smile, but his efforts were largely in vain.

A.B. had carefully assembled some trays of food so Talbott photographed those, then he asked if LaVerne and A.B. would pose for a shot outside in front of the restaurant.

LaVerne and A.B. stood side by side, squinting into the sun. Talbott counted down – 'One. Two . . .' Then, as he paused before 'Three', A.B. slung his arm around LaVerne's shoulder – an awkward move inasmuch as LaVerne is a foot taller than A.B.

As Talbott packed up his equipment he asked LaVerne if

he had any early pictures of the restaurant, maybe from when the place was just opened. 'The editors like to include old photos in the layout when they can. Gives the story added visual interest.'

LaVerne went inside and came back a minute later with a framed 8x10 which he gave Talbott. 'This is the only one I got,' said LaVerne. 'Be careful with it.'

Six weeks later, a package arrived from Ainsley Ponairi. In it were three copies of the airline magazine, *The Blue*, and a note from the writer which read:

> Dear Mr Williams,
>
> First the good news. Of all the barbecue establishments I visited in Kansas City, I enjoyed yours most, and I say so in my story.
>
> Now the bad news. As you may know, Northern Airlines has for many years struggled to remain solvent and was recently purchased by National Sky airline. Northern has shut down all operations and discontinued all flights. This means the magazine will not be distributed.
>
> I am deeply sorry for this turn of events. However, I am certain that word of your excellent food and warm hospitality will spread far and wide without my feeble efforts on your behalf.
>
> Yours truly,
> Ainsley Ponairi

LaVerne, A.B., Leon and Vicki each took a copy of the magazine. On the cover was a photograph of a plate of heavily sauced ribs with some corn-on-the-cob and fries on the side.

'Those ain't *our* ribs,' LaVerne snapped. He, A.B., Leon and Vicki flipped pages to the story inside.

The headline read, '*City Up In Smoke: Kansas City is*

barbecue capital of the world.' Beneath it was the photo of LaVerne and A.B. in front of the restaurant.

'Jeez!' said LaVerne. 'What were you thinking, boy, getting all snuggly on me like that?'

A.B. blushed. 'Well, I didn't think we should just stand there all stiff like we were soldiers. Anyways.'

Inset, inside the main photo, was the picture LaVerne had loaned Talbott. It was a snapshot Angela had taken the day Smoke Meat opened for business. It was grainy and faded, and in it LaVerne and Raymond stood side by side out in front of the restaurant. LaVerne had his arm over Raymond's shoulders. Barely visible through the window behind them was A.B. standing alone in the dining room, his hands pushed deep into his pockets, a cigarette in his mouth.

True to his word, Ainsley had indeed identified Smoke Meat as his favorite Kansas City barbecue joint, making specific mention of the pulled chuck, the greens and potatoes, and the vinegar pie, also making use of such clichés as 'off the beaten path' and 'best kept secret'.

He concluded his review with this observation:

Some of Kansas City's best known barbecue establishments go to great lengths to prove their authenticity. They demonstrate their respect for Kansas City's barbecue heritage by festooning their walls with historical photographs of barbecue joints of yore. They decorate in Old West or Urban Rustic motifs in homage to barbecue's traditional geographic roots. Though sincere, this is all quite self-conscious and ultimately distracting and superficial. Fortunately, none of this negatively impacts the actual barbecue, which is universally delicious, and more often than not the only authentic thing in the joint.

LaVerne Williams' place, on the other hand, is authentically authentic. It is the jointiest of joints. An honest-to-

goodness neighborhood hangout in an honest-to-goodness neighborhood. A regular kind of place with regular
customers. Williams' restaurant is not a barbecue shrine
or a barbecue museum. He's not in business to *honor*
barbecue. He's in business to *sell* barbecue. And the barbecue he sells is uniquely his own. It's also the best in
Kansas City.

LaVerne, A.B., and Vicki were quiet while they contemplated the words. Leon looked on, understanding that the
words must have said something important.

A.B. was pissed off. 'Well, that's just great. Just *great*. He
says we're the best and nobody will ever even read it.'

He stomped out the front door, lit up a cigarette and
paced up and down the sidewalk.

Vicki and Leon stood there a minute, then went back to
work. LaVerne went into the office and read Ainsley Ponairi's article a couple more times.

19

First Round

God and whiskey brought LaVerne Williams and Ferguson Glen together, and for a long time were their primary common denominators. Ferguson loves and hates both God and whiskey more deeply, but LaVerne has a better understanding of how each works.

The first time Ferguson Glen set foot in Kansas City was the day he arrived there to live, which is not to say that he came to make Kansas City his home. Ferguson Glen long ago gave up on finding home.

In July 2002, Ferguson was appointed to the John Stott Chair for Christian Literature at St Columba Seminary of the Midwest, in Kansas City. Since all discussions and interviews between him and the seminary's president regarding the job took place on the phone and via email, Ferguson never actually visited Kansas City until he accepted the position. He arrived in August 2002 for good.

The seminary's fall semester did not start until after Labor Day, so Ferguson spent his first weeks in town meeting seminary faculty and staff, settling into his office, and acquainting himself with the city. One of his first objectives was to befriend the staff of the seminary's library. He knew his position would require him to frequently enlist their efforts and expertise. Angela Williams had been the head librarian at St Columba for ten years. For the five years before that she was the assistant librarian.

When Ferguson first ambled into the library with a big bouquet of flowers, Angela recognized him immediately from the photo on his books' dustcovers. Angela had observed that Ferguson's writing was an acquired taste that not many seminarians had acquired. His books tended to circulate mostly among only a few members of the faculty, primarily those of a more contemplative nature.

'Good morning, Father Glen,' she greeted him as he approached her desk.

'Oh, my!' said Ferguson. 'Nobody's called me Father in years. Perhaps decades.'

'Well, then, shall I call you *Reverend* Glen?'

'Ferguson is fine. But I'm not crazy about Fergie.'

Angela laughed. 'What can I do for you today?'

'I just came in to introduce myself,' he said. 'My guess is I'll spend as much time here as anywhere else in Kansas City. So I wanted to make a good first impression. These are for you.'

'No flowers necessary. I've read your books. So you've already made a good first impression on me.'

Angela gave Ferguson a tour of the library during which he asked her about some of the faculty he'd met, about campus culture, then finally about Kansas City.

'Are you a native Kansas Citian?'

'Born and raised,' said Angela. 'Desperately wanted to leave when I was young, but never really got around to it. Though I did live in Texas for a couple of years. My father was pastor of a Baptist church here. And my husband and I have a restaurant here, so I guess I'm here to stay. Which is fine. Kansas City is a nice place. It's a good home.'

'Ah. A fellow preacher's kid.' Ferguson laughed. 'You appear to have survived it better than I.'

'You seem to have done alright.'

'Looks can be deceiving.'

Angela could tell he wasn't joking and she wondered what he meant by the comment.

'So? Have you found a place to live?' she asked.

'Not yet,' said Ferguson. 'They've put me up at the Raphael for the time being.'

'Are you looking for a house or an apartment?'

'I haven't lived in a house since I graduated high school,' he said, pondering the possibility. 'I guess I was thinking more of an apartment or a condo. Maybe a loft.'

'There're some nice lofts just down the block from our restaurant. You should come by for dinner or lunch sometime and take a look. And if you like barbecue, we've got the best barbecue in town.'

Ferguson thought about Periwinkle Brown and Wren and his first taste of barbecue.

'I do like barbecue. I like it a lot.'

A few days later, Ferguson Glen showed up at Smoke Meat. It was almost closing time and the place was empty except for A.B. and LaVerne.

LaVerne was tired and immediately annoyed that he'd have to clean up after another customer before locking up for the night, but A.B. cheerfully asked Ferguson what he'd like to eat. He ordered a combo plate – pulled pork and a short end. He took his tray to a table by the front window and ate while he watched workers hanging paintings in a small art gallery across the street. He wondered if there was a liquor store nearby.

After about a half-hour of unhurried dining, LaVerne approached Ferguson's table. 'We're going to be closing up soon. Can I get you a to-go box for that?'

Ferguson looked up from his meal. 'Oh. Sorry. Didn't mean to take so long. A box would be great. Thank you.'

When LaVerne returned with the box, Ferguson asked him if he was Angela's husband.

'I am,' he said, extending his hand. 'LaVerne Williams. How do you know my wife?'

They shook hands and Ferguson explained about his new job at the seminary and meeting Angela in the library.

'So you're the one!' LaVerne scowled in mock anger. 'Why, I oughta kick your ass for giving my wife flowers.'

'You wouldn't be the first,' laughed Ferguson. 'In fact, the real reason I'm here in Kansas City is that I'm on the run. There's a posse of pissed-off husbands chasing after me.'

LaVerne laughed. 'Hope the folks up at the seminary don't find that out.'

'So,' said Ferguson, 'I haven't found a place to live yet, and Angela said there are some nice lofts in this area. She also said you serve the best barbecue in town. I haven't had barbecue anywhere else in Kansas City, yet. But this sure was good.'

'Thank you,' said La Verne. 'You'll find out soon enough there are lots of other good places, too.'

'Is there a place here in the neighborhood where one can sit and enjoy a good glass of bourbon? If so, would you care to join me?'

LaVerne thought for a moment, then went back into his office, returning with an unopened bottle of Wild Turkey. He took a couple of glasses from a rack behind the counter, crossed the dining room, locked the front door, flipped the OPEN sign over to CLOSED and shut the blinds. He sat across from Ferguson and poured them each a glass.

A.B. poked his head in from the kitchen and called out, 'Goodnight, boss.'

Ferguson called back, 'You're welcome to join us, young man.'

A.B. shook his head. 'Nah. I'm going to catch Mother Mary's first set at the Levee. Thanks anyways.'

LaVerne saw that Ferguson was confused.

'Mary Weaver is a blues singer. She's a regular here. My man, A.B. there, is a big fan. Her nickname is "Mother".'

The men took long draws on their whiskey.

'You like the blues?' LaVerne asked.

'I do,' said Ferguson. 'Though I'm probably more of a soul and traditional R&B kind of guy. I'm kind of stuck in the sixties.'

LaVerne nodded. They each took another drink.

'Are you from Kansas City originally, LaVerne?'

'No. I grew up in Texas. North of Houston. I came here when I was twenty years old to play ball with the Kansas City Athletics.'

'What was that, around 1965 or '66?'

''67. The last year before they moved. You like baseball?'

'I liked the '68 Tigers. And I liked them again in '84. They haven't given me much to like since. I grew up in Michigan.'

LaVerne topped off their drinks.

'You and Angela have kids?' Ferguson asked.

LaVerne let his gaze drift to the wall behind Ferguson.

'Yes. A son. Raymond. He died in 1986. He was nineteen.'

Ferguson looked over at the menu board on the wall behind the cash register. He wondered what vinegar pie might be.

He wondered what it would feel like to lose a child. He wondered what it would feel like to have a child.

'I'm sorry,' he said quietly.

'That's okay,' said LaVerne. 'It took awhile, but God helped me through it.'

He held the bottom of his glass between his forefinger

and thumb and slid it back and forth sideways on the table. Ferguson held his glass with his fingers around the rim, slowly swirling the whiskey inside.

'You married?' asked LaVerne.

'Was,' said Ferguson.

They looked at each other and smiled small self-conscious smiles and shook their heads.

'That's okay,' said Ferguson. 'I'd like to say God helped me through it, but he's never seemed very interested in helping me. So I've stopped expecting it. In any case losing a seven-month marriage isn't much of a tragedy. I'd rather God spend his time helping people who've lost their children.'

'It'd be nice if he spent his time keeping children alive,' said LaVerne.

'I haven't yet figured out exactly what it is that God does,' said Ferguson. 'Maybe somebody over there at St Columba can help me.'

They drained their glasses and LaVerne poured a bit more into each.

'What do you think about the seminary?' LaVerne asked.

'So far, so good,' Ferguson said. 'Though I wouldn't have guessed in a hundred years I'd end up in Kansas City.'

'Me neither,' said LaVerne. 'And it's been almost forty years.'

Ferguson leaned back in his chair and stared at his bourbon.

'I taught for a few years at a small liberal arts college just east of Grand Rapids. It was an older school that was originally located downtown. But eventually they needed more space and some better facilities so, with some money donated by one of their alumni – who was also one of the Amway billionaires – they bought some land out in the country and built themselves a brand new school. It was beautiful.

State of the art. All glass and gleaming steel. And right in the middle of campus was this lake. Well, they called it a lake. But it was really just a big man-made pond, with pretty landscaped islands. And every once in a while as I'd be walking to class, I'd see a turtle on one of the rocks out on one of those islands. And I'd think, *How'd that turtle get there?* I mean, there were no other lakes or swamps or rivers anywhere near that school. So, if that turtle walked to that campus pond on its own, it walked a long way, which couldn't have been its plan. There's no way it could have known the pond was there. It probably left home one morning on some turtle errand and got distracted, or lost, or something, and ended up at the campus pond. The question is: Did ending up at that pond save his life or ruin his life? After all, if he hadn't found the pond he'd probably have died wandering around lost. On the other hand, he never found his way home either, did he?'

Ferguson took a deep breath.

'I guess the other possibility is that the landscapers who built the pond went out and bought a turtle wherever it is you buy turtles and put it in the pond to make it more like a real lake. Either way, the turtle didn't plan on being there.'

LaVerne was thinking about Delbert.

'I guess we're like turtles,' said LaVerne. 'Sometimes we get diverted and end up in a place we never expected to be.'

Ferguson finished his whiskey. 'Truth is, turtles probably don't even have homes.'

20

Broken

The next to the last day of his honeymoon was the last good day of Ferguson Glen's marriage. It was May 19, 1975, forty-three days after his editor Walker Briggs called to tell him his manuscript would likely be rejected, a month to the day after he and Bijou Serrée were wed, and one hundred and ninety-two days before their union was mercifully dissolved.

Ferguson's father, the Right Reverend Angus Mackintosh Glen, performed the wedding ceremony at New York's Cathedral Church of St John the Divine. Among the more than five hundred wedding guests were a dozen or so ambassadors, a handful of Kennedys, several members of Congress, the governor of Michigan, the chief executives of two of the Big Three American automobile manufacturers, a sitting Supreme Court justice, the Vice-President of the United States, Carly Simon, and about fifty of the most beautiful women in the world, who, at the reception that followed, received much attention from the Kennedys.

Bijou's father, Elliot Peabody, was a career diplomat and Cold Warrior of the Acheson School. Two months earlier, Gerald Ford had appointed him ambassador to Poland. Bijou's mother Estelle Serrée was a fashion designer and magnate, the formidable and flamboyant head of the House of Serrée, founded by Bijou's grandfather Louis Serrée in France, before the war.

Bijou began using her mother's maiden name when she was a freshman at Yale. She and her father had never enjoyed a particularly harmonious relationship and when she entered college their differences sharpened. They disagreed bitterly and loudly on almost every subject – music, vegetarianism, the war in Vietnam, and her spoiled younger brother Phillip. Bijou also had serious misgivings about the decadent, sexist materialism of her mother's fashion empire. But she concluded that distancing herself from her father better served her own long-term political ambitions so she dropped the name Peabody. Plus, she liked the sound of Bijou Serrée better than Bijou Peabody.

After graduating Yale, Bijou earned her law degree at Harvard and subsequently clerked for Justice Thurgood Marshall. At the time of the wedding, she was an aggressively activist civil rights attorney with a national profile and an ulcer. Elegantly severe in appearance and persona, Bijou was tall, bony, and pale, with fierce red hair. Her range of facial expressions was limited to righteous outrage, intense concentration, contempt, and patronizing bemusement.

The turnover rate among staff in Bijou's law office was nearly 100 percent. The same was true among her friends. Of both she expected unwavering loyalty, twenty-four-hour availability, and transcendent competence. Few measured up.

But Ferguson Glen disarmed her. He bought her a bicycle. He counted the freckles on her back. He sang Wilson Pickett and Al Green songs to her in the car. He gave her a subscription to *MAD* magazine. He memorized the names of her childhood pets. And he insisted that she do her own grocery shopping, a task kitchen staff or housekeepers had always done for her and her family. Once, he made her laugh so hard she peed her pants. Against her better judgment, he also compelled her to see the humanity and vulnerability of the defendants against whom she pressed her civil rights suits. He demanded she look past their calculated self-interest, their indifference, and even their hatred, to see their fearfulness, ignorance, and brokenness.

For her part, Bijou made Ferguson feel needed, which he had never before felt. Not as a child, though he had felt well fed, clothed, and cared for. Not in seminary, though he had felt respected by his fellow students and by his professors. Not when giving readings or signing copies of his novel, though then he felt idolized. And not marching in Selma, though he had felt welcomed and appreciated and part of something historic and monumental.

Even when celebrating the Eucharist he did not feel needed, though that came closest. When he raised the host and the chalice and spoke the ancient words he felt, if not exactly needed, that he was well and rightly used.

When celebrating the Eucharist Ferguson felt closest to God, but it was also then that he felt his silence most keenly. Ferguson had, all of his life, yearned for, and prayed for an encounter with God. He had all his life been told that one could have a 'personal relationship' with God, that one could 'walk with' God, that one should 'listen for' God, and 'watch for' God. But for all his watching and listening and walking there was nothing remotely personal about his relationship with God. He believed God was real, but not because any experience he had ever had caused him to believe it.

He had studied the Desert Fathers and the mystics looking for clues, searching for a secret path to an encounter with God. He had, for a time, attended a Baptist church because Baptists seemed so matter-of-fact about their relationships with God – *He walks with me, and he talks with me, and he tells me I am his own.* He saw the emotion in their worship and their certainty that what they were feeling was the presence of God himself. He wanted to feel that.

Yet, he, who had been raised by God's own servants, and who had chosen to devote his own life to seeking and proclaiming God, felt nothing. He could speak with conviction and clarity about God, but what he longed for was to speak with God. He longed for God to speak to him. This, perhaps more than anything else, was why, following seminary, Ferguson neither sought nor accepted a position as rector of a congregation. He was sure that he could not effectively guide parishioners in seeking what he himself had not found.

Still, he believed in that which he had not found. He had, at least, found Bijou. And he felt her love for him. And her loving him was maybe the next best thing to an encounter with God. These were the things he told himself.

Bijou and Ferguson first met at a mid-town Manhattan art gallery where they had attended an exhibit of works by the artists' co-op, Creativity Resistance and Peace. They were introduced by their mutual friend Carly Simon, whom Ferguson knew through publishing connections, and whom Bijou knew because their families' summer homes on Martha's Vineyard were just three houses apart.

Standing elbow to elbow contemplating a painting which depicted Queen Victoria in a red, white, and blue bikini, surrounded by Vietnamese children incinerated by napalm, Ferguson wondered aloud if the artists who staged the exhibit were aware that the acronym for their organization's name was CRAP. Bijou wondered aloud if they were aware that their art was crap. They finished their canapés and Chardonnay and went down the street for coffee.

She demanded the best from him. She insisted that he read to her from whatever he was writing and she told him the truth about it. If it was good, she told him it was good. And if it was shit, she told him it was shit. At public readings, he tended to read too softly with his head down. She coached him on projecting his voice, making eye contact with his audience, and delivering his words with authority. He admitted he should have learned all that in his seminary course on preaching, but confessed he hadn't really liked the professor much, and learning to preach wasn't why he went to seminary in any case.

When he drifted away from what he was writing, toward indifference and boredom, or his stacks of unread books, or the whiskey in the cabinet, she took hold of the tiller and turned him back on course. Bijou knew where he was weak and where he was strong.

She also knew where all the best restaurants were. She knew Brown v. Board of Education word for word. She knew Rudolf Nureyev's Paris street address, and she knew how to speak French. She looked good in a beret and she looked great naked.

Bijou Serrée and Ferguson Glen were engaged only as long as needed to plan and execute a wedding on the magnitude expected for two scions of American aristocracy. Their pending nuptials were the subject of spirited speculation in tearooms and saunas and on tennis courts and putting greens around town: *Could the soulful writer-priest breathe some life into the stone-cold courtroom diva of the New Left? And could the warrior princess save the melancholy minister from pissing away his talent?*

The popularity of and critical acclaim for *Traverse*, Ferguson's Pulitzer Prize-nominated first novel, and his high-profile involvement in the Civil Rights Movement had elevated Ferguson to the status of literary celebrity. But there were murmurs in the corner offices of New York's publishing establishment that Ferguson's second manuscript was in trouble. Word was that Walker Briggs' bosses had told him he would have to push his young writer harder. There had been a sizable advance and sizable expectations along with it.

Walker had tried to make clear to Ferguson that there was a fine line between a heralded Pulitzer nominee with a bright future and a forgotten Pulitzer also-ran with a bright past. The main difference being good writing and met deadlines, neither of which Ferguson seemed capable of.

There were signs Walker wished he'd seen earlier. Missed appointments. Promises to work harder, promptly broken. Defensiveness, distractedness, and depression. Late one afternoon he arrived at Ferguson's apartment to take him to dinner and found the door unlocked. Cautiously he entered, fearing he'd interrupted a burglary or worse.

Ferguson was passed out on the couch in the living room. On a coffee table by the couch was an opened, half-empty bottle of Jim Beam and a drinking glass half full. Walker would rather have interrupted a burglary. He had wondered and worried about this and now his suspicions were confirmed. In disgust, he kicked the couch hard. When Ferguson came to, Walker delivered an ultimatum: If your drinking means more to you than your writing, fine. Our lawyers will contact you about reimbursement of your advance. When he got back to his office Walker called Bijou, told her what had happened, and asked for her help.

Bijou could not claim to be surprised by Walker's story. She had her own suspicions. That night she confronted Ferguson and demanded that he quit drinking. If you don't, she said, the engagement is off. It's as simple as that.

So he quit. Until the next to the last day of their honeymoon.

Ferguson and Bijou honeymooned in Europe. They spent the first two and a half weeks in France, at Bijou's grandfather's summer home in Fontvieille, after which they traveled to Scotland for another two weeks.

In France, they slept late into the morning on the balcony overlooking the courtyard; made love in the choir loft of the church in the village while the priest was hearing confessions; rode bikes past fields of lavender and sunflowers; read books and newspapers on the terrace until the sun went down; and made love in a rowboat adrift in a tidal pool.

In Scotland, they stayed at a cottage in Haddington, where Ferguson's grandfather had pastored a congregation and where Ferguson's father was born. They rented a car, drove north to the coast and stood on a rocky bluff overlooking the sea until Bijou got cold and went back to the car. They hiked the hills and pastures around Haddington and one morning startled a flock of sheep, causing the farmer to curse colorfully as he rounded them up. They packed a picnic of cheese and apples, and after eating, fell asleep on their blanket under a gnarled gean tree.

As the end of their time in Scotland approached, Ferguson became increasingly apprehensive about returning to New York, knowing he must try to rescue his book. Hoping for inspiration and perhaps divine intervention, Ferguson arranged to visit the island of Iona, off the coast of Scotland. For devout Anglicans this religious community was revered as a 'thin place' – a place where the membrane between God and his creation is felt to be more permeable. Ferguson planned to spend time in prayer there while Bijou met with members of the community to discuss their work for peace and justice. But after two hours alone in the chapel, Ferguson emerged anxious and angry. He found Bijou in the library where she was struggling mightily to stay awake as three elderly members of the community droned on about their plans to meet with the Dalai Lama for the purpose of establishing inter-faith dialogue. From the doorway

Ferguson gave Bijou a 'Let's get out of here' look and she politely excused herself.

On the ferry back to the mainland, Ferguson went up to the deck and stood looking out at the sea.

Bijou followed him. 'What happened in there?'

'Nothing,' he said, wondering how cold the steel-gray water might be. 'Absolutely nothing.'

He rallied somewhat that evening. They ate dinner at a pub in the village and made crude jokes about haggis and bangers, laughing so loud they drew the smiling and knowing attention of other patrons.

Ferguson could smell the whiskey in their glasses.

The next morning after breakfast Bijou got a call from a lawyer with the Southern Christian Leadership Conference about a discrimination class-action suit in Florida. The lawyer was hoping to enlist Bijou's help with the case and, apologizing repeatedly, asked if he might fly to Edinburgh to meet with her later the next day. Bijou agreed and took the car into Edinburgh and stayed in a hotel there that night.

In Bijou's absence Ferguson's trepidation deepened. He called Bijou's hotel room, thinking that her voice might help him feel better but she wasn't there. He thought about calling Walker but remembered that it was the middle of the night in New York.

He went outside and stood. *This would be a good time to show yourself,* he thought. *Any little sign that things will be all right will do just fine.* He stood there in silence for a long time, then walked into the village to the pub.

He ordered a bottle of Laphroaig and over the next three hours drank half of the scotch at a table in the corner of the tavern. Occasionally the barkeep asked him if he wanted anything to eat but Ferguson waved him off. Finally he shoved the bottle into his jacket and walked back to the cottage where he finished the whiskey and passed out in a chair in the front room.

When Bijou returned late the next day, Ferguson was still in the chair, semi-conscious, his trousers stained and stinking of urine. Bijou gasped and stood paralyzed in the doorway. Ferguson heard her and tried to sit up. Bijou strode across the room and slapped his face with all the force she had in her. Ferguson made no effort to stop her or to defend himself. He didn't raise his hand to touch the place where she struck him. Bijou spoke quietly.

This won't work, she said. This is a betrayal. I can't believe you did this on our honeymoon. You promised me and you broke your promise. I love you, Ferguson. But you don't love *me* – you don't love *us* enough to keep your promise. I can't trust you.

This will not work in my life, Ferguson. Not in the life I want. I'm going back to Edinburgh to stay and then I'm flying to Florida. I'll meet you in New York next week and we'll see about getting an annulment.

This breaks my heart, she said. And she left.

21

Shim-sham Shimmy

If A.B. hadn't made such a big deal about Mother Mary Weaver's seventy-fifth birthday, most people wouldn't have had any idea how old she actually was. For about a week prior to her birthday, A.B. announced to nearly every customer who walked through the door, 'Hey, Mother's going to be seventy-five! Can you believe it? Seventy-five and goin' strong. A genuine Kansas City blues legend! Seventy-five years of blues greatness!'

Anybody else would have been flattered at first, then increasingly embarrassed by such lavish attention. But Mary can never get enough attention, her ego being even bigger than her body. If she happened to be at her corner table eating her burnt ends when A.B. started in with his proclamations, she'd grin a big toothy grin and nod in agreement. She left the being embarrassed part to Pug.

Kansas City police detective, Pug Hale – Mary's regular lunch companion, de facto manager, guardian, and lead guitarist – is a shy and unassuming man, in spite of the fact he's been cited by the department numerous times for bravery. So as Mary basked in the glow of A.B.'s adulation, Pug sat there as still as he could be, focusing on his ribs, hoping it would all be over soon.

In public, Mother Mary's prodigious head is always

helmeted in a goldish House of Hair wig. That, together with her soft, smooth, medium-brown complexion might lead one to assume she's younger than she is. But her arthritic knees and severely bloated ankles have so limited her mobility that, seeing her struggle to walk, even with Pug's help, many people might conclude that she's older than she is.

It was Pug who told A.B. that Mary was about to turn seventy-five, after a benefit performance for a community center out in Johnson County. Mary's set was short, but she was in good voice and A.B., who went along to help the band with its equipment, said so to Pug when they were packing up.

'Dang, Pug. I listen to her albums from back in the day, and she sounds as good now as she ever did.'

Pug nodded. 'Mother's talent doesn't seem to have noticed that Mother's body is getting old. She'll be seventy-five years old soon. I keep thinking maybe she'll quit. But she shows no interest in it.'

That was all it took for A.B. to spring into action. The next day after closing, as he and LaVerne were loading the Hobart with glasses and trays, A.B. laid out his proposal.

'Okay, boss. I got an idea. Pug tells me that Mother is going to be seventy-five . So, how about we throw her a big party? Maybe a surprise party.'

'How big is "big", A.B.?' asked LaVerne.

'Well, I been thinking about it, and I figure that if we invited the owners of the clubs where she sings, some of her friends from her church, some of the local blues musicians, and the regulars here at the restaurant, there might be about a hundred people.'

'You planning on renting a hall or something?' LaVerne asked. 'Even if we took all the tables out, we couldn't squeeze more than about sixty people in here. And then it'd be pretty tight.'

'I thought about that, too,' said A.B., pleased that so far he'd anticipated all his boss's questions. 'What if we asked Babaloo's if we could use their parking lot?'

Babaloo's is the strip bar across the alley behind Smoke Meat.

'And were you thinking that we'd charge admission or something, to pay for this party?' asked LaVerne.

A.B. scowled and said nothing.

'I thought so,' said LaVerne, with a slight smirk. 'So, what other big ideas do you have for this party?'

A.B. brightened up. 'Okay. Well, it wouldn't seem right to ask Mother to be the entertainment at her own party so I was thinking that maybe we could get Junior Provine to come play. Pug and the rest of the band would probably play for free. And maybe Junior would, too.'

Junior Provine is the best blues harmonica player in Kansas City history. He was born in 1928 in Woodville, Mississippi – in the Delta where the blues themselves were born – the seventh son of a guitar-playing sharecropper. Junior is Junior's real name, a name he shares with his father and three of his six brothers. In April 1950, after his discharge from the navy, Junior boarded a train in Chicago with a ticket to Jackson, where he planned to catch a bus home to Woodville. But in Kansas City, where he had to change trains, Junior's life took a turn.

Standing outside Union Station smoking a cigarette, Junior saw a handbill tacked to a telephone pole advertising the need for workers at a meatpacking plant in the Bottoms. The next day he stood in line with sixty-one other men to fill out an application and the day after that he was pulling cattle carcasses off the line. Within the month, he was sitting in with bands at after-hours clubs around town.

Out in the alley LaVerne thought about A.B.'s plan, while

A.B. turned out the light in the walk-in and went to double-check that the front door was locked.

When he came out and let the door close behind him, LaVerne said, 'Sounds like you got it all thought out, son. And Mother deserves it. If you can get Pug on board with it, we'll do it.'

Pug liked the idea, but didn't think the party should be a surprise. 'You get a hundred people jumping up and yelling, "Surprise!" all at once, and Mother's likely to drop dead of a heart attack. Besides, she'll get a big kick out of knowing that there's a lot of planning going for a big hoop-dee in her honor.'

Pug also agreed to ask Junior Provine if he'd perform. When he first joined the force, Pug sometimes moonlighted as a bouncer at nightclubs around town. That's when he met Junior, who had just begun making a name for himself. Pug even filled in occasionally for Junior's longtime lead guitarist who sometimes had to pull a double shift at the post office where he was a mail sorter. Junior and Mother didn't know each other well, but each respected the work of the other and they had mutual friends.

'I can probably get Junior to do it for free,' Pug told A.B. 'If not, he'll probably do it for a bottle of cognac and a hundred-dollar bill. He's got a fondness for Ben Franklin.'

Junior said he'd be happy to play at the party and didn't ask for money, but Pug gave him a bottle of Rémy Martin anyway.

The other members of Mother's regular back-up band were eager to participate. They're all young musicians, except for Pug, and playing on Mother's gigs has given them a chance to perform with an established professional. Seth Cropper plays keyboards. Seth is an officer with the Kansas City police department's K-9 unit. The other musicians call him 'Cropper the Copper'. Seth claims he's a distant cousin of Steve Cropper, the Stax studio guitarist, and he probably is. But because he's also quite full of himself, the rest of the band pretends not to believe him. Jake Green plays bass, usually an acoustic upright. Jake is a social worker at Catholic Charities, and is kind of quiet. He and Pug are pretty tight, but no one else knows him very well.

Jen Richards is the drummer. She works on the line at the Harley-Davidson plant and rides a Sportster Custom-XL 883C. Jen has a fine voice and sometimes sings duets with Mother.

Leon and Vicki agreed to work the night of the party after A.B. offered them time and a half. And Babaloo's said that if A.B. scheduled the event for a Sunday night he could use their parking lot since they were closed on Sundays.

Finally, A.B. called Brother Ignatius up at Redemption Abbey and invited him to the party. Brother Ignatius had become acquainted with Mother Mary on his monthly wood delivery visits. When LaVerne first introduced them, Iggy said he'd always prayed to the Blessed Virgin Mother Mary, but hadn't thought he'd actually meet her in this life. Mary laughed, 'I am blessed, Mr Iggy. That's a fact. But I sure ain't no virgin.'

When Iggy accepted the invitation, A.B. asked if he'd drive down in his wood truck, so that they could use the truck bed for a stage, which Iggy said he would do on the condition that he be allowed to bring his guitar and sit in on at least one number with the band.

Other than Raymond's funeral and his own baptism, A.B. figured that Mary's party was the most important event he had ever been a part of. Every person he cared about in the world was going to be there. Except his mother.

He asked his mother if she wanted to come, but, even

after he explained it three times, she wasn't clear on who the party was for or why A.B. had anything to do with it.

'You go ahead, Al Buddy,' she said. 'I don't know any of those people anyway. Besides, me and Rudy, we're goin' down to the boats and play the quarter slots.'

A.B. didn't know who Rudy was, and didn't ask.

After the lunch rush one afternoon, about a week before the party, A.B. walked over to Michael's Fine Clothing for Men to reserve a tuxedo for the night of the party. His thinking was that, even though LaVerne was paying for the party, he was, in a way, the host of the party since it was his idea and he had made most of the arrangements. A good host should look his best, he thought. Besides, he'd never worn a tux and this was as good a reason as any he might ever have.

'What's the nature of the event, sir?' asked the sales clerk at Michael's.

'It's a big birthday party.'

'Is it an evening event?'

'It is. There'll be live music and all.'

'Then I suggest a dinner jacket,' said the clerk. 'Just right for a summer evening affair.'

A.B. was disappointed. 'I was really thinking more about a tux.'

'Oh, it *is* a tuxedo,' the clerk assured him. 'It's formal wear with a white jacket is all.'

A.B. tried on a dinner jacket and liked the way it looked. He ordered one for the night of the party, along with a pleated-front shirt, bow-tie, cummerbund, trousers with a satin stripe down the leg, and black patent leather shoes.

Walking back to the restaurant he got the hiccups.

A.B. didn't get much sleep the week leading up to the party. He was too excited, plus he had to work late getting things ready.

Vicki and Leon helped with the cobbler and the pies, which they made a few days ahead. The chuck could be smoked the day and night before, but the greens would have to wait till the day of.

LaVerne helped by making the beans. After the meat itself, LaVerne cares more about the beans than any other item on Smoke Meat's menu and he wasn't comfortable letting Vicki or Leon make them. Especially for a big party at which there'd likely be some folks eating his food for the first time.

On the Sunday of the party, Leon and A.B. got to the restaurant early to start on the greens. While the greens simmered, Leon and A.B. carried tables from the dining room out to Babaloo's parking lot.

Brother Ignatius arrived at about two in the afternoon and helped set up tables and chairs. Then he set up a stage in the back of his truck. He and A.B. joked about flying cows and dead chickens. When the band arrived, Iggy helped with the sound system.

Jen Richards, the drummer, noticed the comfortable camaraderie between A.B. and Iggy. 'You a friend of A.B.'s?' she asked.

'Yeah,' said Iggy. 'We're friends. LaVerne and A.B. buy their wood from us, so I see them about once a month or so. A.B. has as pure a heart as anyone I've ever known.'

Jen smiled as she watched A.B. bring the chafing pans out to the serving tables. He stood back, looked things over, and checked something off a list on a clipboard.

When LaVerne and Angela arrived, Angela gave A.B. a big hug. 'A.B. you've done such a wonderful job of putting all this together. Mother will be thrilled.'

A.B. blushed. Angela and Raymond were the only two

people who had ever hugged him as far as he could remember. Angela hugged him almost every time she saw him.

About an hour before the party was to start, A.B. went inside, to the office, to change into his tux. He wanted to look like a proper host when guests arrived.

After putting on the trousers and shoes, he was surprised to discover that his rented shirt had no buttons.

'That's just great!' A.B. said aloud, letting his arms flop to his sides in disgust.

'What's just great?' asked a voice behind him.

A.B. turned to see Ferguson Glen poking his head in through the office doorway.

'It's this shirt that came with my tuxedo,' said A.B. 'All the buttons are missing.'

Ferguson nodded. 'May I come in?' He held up a bottle of bourbon. 'I'm replenishing LaVerne's office stock.'

After stashing the whiskey in the bottom drawer of the filing cabinet, Ferguson stood back and gave A.B. a once-over.

'Was there a small plastic bag or paper envelope that came with your tuxedo? Perhaps in the pocket of the trousers or maybe the jacket?'

A.B. fumbled around in his pants pockets and then in the jacket.

'You mean this?' He held up a small zip-top plastic bag. In it were ten shirt studs and a pair of cufflinks.

'That's it,' said Ferguson. 'Here, let me show you.'

Ferguson took one of the studs and, on the middle hole of A.B.'s heavily starched pleated shirt, demonstrated how it worked.

'I'll be damned,' said A.B. shaking his head.

Ferguson smiled. 'Did you also rent a bow-tie?' he asked. 'Those can be a bitch.'

A.B. searched the bag that contained the shoes and the cummerbund, and found the bow-tie.

'I could show you how to tie one of these,' said Ferguson. 'But we'd miss the whole party. It'll be simpler if I do it for you.'

He flipped up the collar of A.B.'s shirt, tied a perfect bow, and carefully turned the collar down and straightened the tie. Then he helped A.B. on with his dinner jacket, pulling on the shoulders to make sure it draped properly.

'Young man, you look splendid,' he said.

A.B. wished there was a mirror in the office, so he could see how he looked.

They went outside to see how things were shaping up. Vicki had covered the serving tables with white plastic table-cloths and Leon was taking bottles of barbecue sauce out of a carton and placing them on the tables next to stacks of paper plates. A.B. walked over to ask Leon and Vicki what more needed to done.

'Hey, guys!' he called. 'How's it goin'?'

Leon turned toward A.B. and, as he did so, placed a bottle of sauce down on its edge. It tipped over and rolled the entire length of the table, picking up speed as it went. It careened off the table in the direction of A.B. and exploded on the asphalt, splattering A.B. with LaVerne Williams' Genuine BBQ Sauce KANSAS CITY STYLE.

Leon, Vicki, and Ferguson stared in horror at A.B.'s pants.

'Shit!' yelled A.B. 'Shit! Shit! Shit!'

He turned and stomped back into the restaurant, slamming the door behind him.

In the office, he surveyed the damage. Only his slacks and shoes had been stained. Remarkably, his jacket and shirt remained clean. Even though LaVerne didn't usually allow smoking in his office, A.B. lit one up and considered his options. Michael's Fine Clothes for Men was closed. He didn't have time to go back to his apartment. And though LaVerne sometimes kept a spare shirt and pair of pants at the restaurant, LaVerne was at least twelve inches taller than he was. He decided to change back into the jeans and T-shirt he'd been wearing while setting up. But when he picked up the T-shirt he saw it was smeared with grease and sauce and reeked of sweat and smoke. He examined his jeans. They were fine.

A few minutes later, A.B. reemerged from the back of the restaurant wearing his white dinner jacket, pleated starched shirt with studs, cummer bund, blue jeans, and gleaming black patent leather shoes, freshly cleaned.

Suzanne Edwards and McKenzie Nelson were just arriving. McKenzie jumped back when she saw A.B. 'Look at *you*! You are *stylin'*, my man!'

A.B. stood there, trying to remember how to talk.

Leon and Vicki seemed to be handling the serving line without any problem. When Leon saw A.B. he hung his head in shame.

'Dude. I'm really sorry about your pants,' he said, looking down at the pavement. 'I can't believe that bottle did that.'

Vicki gave A.B. a long look. 'I kinda think it worked out better this way. Movie stars dress like that. Jeans with a suit coat. Or a tuxedo with a T-shirt. It looks like you planned it this way.'

'Thanks, Vicki,' said A.B., bewildered.

He walked over to Iggy's truck. Seth, Jake, and Jen were up on the flatbed testing their mikes and amps. Iggy was picking along on his '70s-era Martin as Seth played 'What'd I Say' to warm up.

Iggy grinned down at A.B. 'It's going to be a good turn-out, A.B. There's sixty or seventy people here already. Maybe more.'

In the corner of the parking lot closest to the restaurant there was a small commotion, then Angela came hustling on over to the truck. She reached up to Jake who helped pull her up onto the truck bed where she took a microphone in hand.

'Welcome, everybody!' she called out. 'Thank you all for coming tonight to wish happy birthday to a Kansas City music legend.'

The crowd cheered and whistled. Angela smiled. She looked down at A.B. and gave him a wink.

'Tonight we're gonna have us some *barbecue*!' Angela yelled. And there were more cheers.

'Tonight we're going to have us some *music*!' she shouted. And there were louder cheers.

'Tonight we're going to have us some rock 'n' roll, some soul, and some *blues*!' The cheers turned to screams and howls.

Angela waited for the crowd to settle down.

'But before we get this party started, let me direct your attention over there to the corner, for a few introductions. First of all, there's my husband, LaVerne Williams, who's feeding us all tonight.'

LaVerne waved. Almost everybody there knew LaVerne. They hooted, and clapped, and called out his name.

'With him is our musical guest for the night, the incomparable, the immortal, the one and only *Junior Provine*!'

Junior waved and bowed to rowdy acclaim. He wore denim bib overalls, a starched white dress shirt, and red snakeskin cowboy boots.

'And finally, everybody, give it up for our guest of honor, Mother Mary Weaver! Seventy-five years young!'

The cheering crescendoed. Mary stood next to Pug, clutching his arm. She beamed and waved to her well-wishers. Pug escorted Mary to a table in front of the truck. LaVerne took Junior by the elbow and they followed Pug and Mary. There,

Junior gave Mary a kiss on the cheek and LaVerne helped him up onto the truck-bed. Then he helped boost Pug up onto the makeshift stage. Pug sat on a chair next to Seth's keyboard, and took his Gibson cherry sunburst Les Paul out of a case by his feet. Junior approached the stand-up mike and removed a harmonica from the back pocket of his overalls. He looked down where Mary was sitting.

'Happy birthday, Mother. I hope you took your heart pills, because we gonna party tonight.'

Mother threw Junior a kiss. Junior turned and said something to the band, which immediately kicked up the intro to 'Kansas City'.

Though it's been cliché for more than five decades for Kansas City musicians and musicians performing in Kansas City to open their shows with this song, it still gets Kansas City audiences up out of their seats. Junior delivered the song in a low, guttural growl. When he got to the part about the 'crazy little women' he pointed at Mary with one hand and patted his heart with the other. Mother waved him off with an 'Oh, go on now!' gesture.

Next, Junior and the band launched into the Doors' 'Roadhouse Blues', urging the partiers to roll, roll, roll, thus thrilling his soul. All right.

A.B. went over to where Del, McKenzie, and Suzanne were sitting. As he chatted with them, Bob Dunleavy came over and clapped him on the back.

'Excellent, as always, A.B.! Great food. Great party.'

Three elderly ladies approached, on their way back to their seats from the barbecue table. One of the women took hold of A.B.'s hand.

'Young man, we're from Mary's church, Mount Zion Missionary Church. Mr Williams tells me that you're responsible for this get-together. I just want you to know that this means the world to Mother. The *world*. God bless you, child.'

A.B. sat down with his friends, his eyes welling up.

'What's wrong, boy?' Del shouted, making McKenzie and Suzanne wince.

'Nothing,' said A.B.

'What?' yelled Dell.

'Nothing!' A.B. yelled back.

After ripping through a few Big Joe Turner tunes, Junior Provine made an announcement.

'I'm a little tired from all this partying,' he shouted, grinning wide. 'I think I need a little help to carry on. Anybody out there that can *help* me? Anybody out there know how to sing the *blues*? Anybody out there a *blues singer*?'

The partygoers were quick to reply. They began chanting, 'Mother Mary! Mother Mary!' in rhythm. Mother may have been surprised by this, but she wasn't at all reluctant. She motioned to LaVerne, and he and Angela helped her to her feet and then up onto the stage. Pug offered Mother his chair and she sat.

'I heard you was lookin' for a blues singer,' she said into the microphone. 'Do I have that correct?'

The crowd answered as one. 'Yes!'

'Well then, Mr Junior Provine, let me see if I may be of assistance,' she purred.

The partiers let out with a whoop. She nodded at Pug who signaled the band which cut loose with the Bessie Smith classic 'Gimme a Pigfoot and a Bottle of Beer', one of Mother Mary's signature songs.

Mother's loyal fans knew to join in on the line, *'Check all your razors and your guns. Do the shim-sham shimmy till the risin' sun.'*

Mary followed that up with the blues standard 'Ain't Nobody's Business if I Do'. *'If I go to church on Sunday, and sing the shimmy down on Monday, it ain't nobody's business if I do.'*

Mary looked tired. The party had taken a lot out of her.

'I'm going back to my barbecue and vinegar pie in a minute here,' she said, catching her breath. 'But before I do I want to thank my good friend A.B. Clayton for this wonderful party.'

She pointed to A.B., who was standing with Ferguson, LaVerne, and Angela. She waved to him and threw him a two-handed kiss.

'Thank you, my dear boy.'

The crowd expressed its gratitude with applause and whistles. A.B. felt sweat form on his upper lip, forehead, and along his spine. He smiled and waved back at Mary. He thought about throwing her a kiss, but didn't do it. Angela put her hand on the small of his back and patted him. Then Mother started a steady rhythmic clapping, and the audience joined in. Then, softly, and at first without the band, she began to sing 'Come on Children, Let's Sing', Mahalia Jackson's gospel standard.

> *'Come on children, let's sing, about the goodness of*
> *the Lord.*
> *Come on children, let's shout, all about God's great*
> *reward.*
> *Guides our footsteps every day, keeps us in this narrow*
> *way.*
> *Come on children let's shout, how the Lord Almighty*
> *has brought us out.*
> *There's none like him, without a doubt.*
> *Come on children, let's sing, about the goodness of*
> *the Lord.'*

When she got to the bridge, Mother got up out of her chair and did a little side-to-side slide step, her hands raised in praise. The three older women from Mount Zion Missionary Church were also inspired to get up out of their seats and dance. At that point, nobody was left sitting.

> *'He has been my all and all. He will never let me fall.*
> *That is why I can sing. That is why I can shout.*
> *Because I know what it's all about.*
> *The goodness, goodness of the Lord, the Lord, the*
>   *Lord.'*

Mary led the party in five choruses, then with a wave of her hand signaled that she was going to wind it down. And, just as she had started it, she ended the song *a cappella*, but this time in a low, commanding voice.

> *'Because I know what it's all about.*
> *The goodness, goodness of the Lord, the Lord, the*
>   *Lord.'*

LaVerne and Ferguson helped Mother down off the truck and back to her table where, as promised, she helped herself to some more barbecue.

A.B. went to check on Leon and Vicki. The food was pretty much gone and people were leaving so the three of them started cleaning up. Junior was through for the night and sat down with Mother for a piece of vinegar pie. Except for Del James and Bob Dunleavy who stayed and helped with the tables and chairs, the remaining guests said their goodbyes and went home. When the parking lot was cleared and LaVerne had locked up the restaurant, A.B. thanked Leon and Vicki and sent them home.

Ferguson offered to let Brother Ignatius sleep on his couch for the night and Iggy took him up on it. Iggy locked up the truck and he and Ferguson walked across the street and down the block to Ferguson's apartment.

A.B. and Jen Richards were the only two left in Babaloo's parking lot.

'So, Jen, do you need a ride home?' A.B. asked. 'I've got my car.'

'No,' she said. 'I've got my bike. It's just nice and cool and quiet and I'm not quite ready to go.'

She hoisted herself up and sat on the back of the truck. A.B. did the same.

They were silent. Off in the direction of Union Station there was a single whoop of a police siren. A.B. took his cigarettes out of the inside pocket of his dinner jacket, removed one and lit it, inhaling deeply.

'Dang, Jen, This might be the happiest night of my life,' A.B. said. 'I do think God has blessed me.'

Jen nodded. 'It was a good one.'

He offered Jen a cigarette and she took one and he lit it for her.

'I'm not sure it can get any better than this.'

Jen turned to him and smiled. 'Maybe it can.'

They sat there on the edge of the truck bed and finished their smokes in silence.

22

Don't Look Back

LaVerne Williams has only one memory of his mother. She is walking up the path to his grandmother's porch. She is wearing a yellow dress. She is young and pretty. She smiles and waves at her son. He is playing with a grasshopper in a jar on his grandmother's porch steps. His mother bends down to embrace him and he reaches for her and the jar tips over and the grasshopper hops out onto to his mother's arm and she shrieks and jumps away from him. The hem of her yellow dress brushes against his cheek. That is all he remembers.

Except that sometimes he also remembers the dust that rises around his mother's feet as she walks toward him, and the sound of his grandmother's screen door as it squeaks open and clacks shut, and the heat of the sun on the back of his neck, and the tapping noise the grasshopper makes when it jumps up against the lid of the jar. And the stiff, stale-smelling stain on the hem of his mother's yellow dress.

Then sometimes he remembers only that once when he was a child he played with a grasshopper on his grandmother's porch.

There might have been more memories, if not for Delbert. For years, Delbert Douglass Merisier III watched in consternated silence as his niece, Loretta, desolated his sister Rose's life. The manipulating, lying, and stealing started early. While other little girls her age were mastering jacks and jump rope, Loretta perfected her ability to set one friend against another to her advantage. She honed her skills at extracting compliments and favor from her teachers and friends' parents. She practiced distracting her playmates while deftly tucking their toys into her pockets. When confronted with evidence of her misdeeds, Loretta was cunning and convincing in protesting her innocence.

'Rose, you know the child lies to you and everyone else,' Delbert would say. 'Why do you let her get away with it?'

'She's only that way because her daddy run off,' said Rose, referring to Big Bill Williams, who, as far as she knew, was still legally her husband though she'd not laid eyes on the man in five years.

'It's not that her daddy run off that's the problem, Rose,' said Delbert. 'It's that she's got too much of her daddy in her. He was no good. He was worse than no good. He was evil. Besides, lots of kids' daddies run off and they don't lie and cheat, all the while with a big smile.'

'I need to be a better mother then,' said Rose, reaching into her handbag for a handkerchief.

'I'm not sure you can love her out of this,' said Delbert. 'I'm not even sure you could beat it out of her. It's just *in* her.'

Rose couldn't bear to hear her brother talk that way. But he wouldn't quit. He couldn't bear to see Rose consumed by worry and shame.

Some time after she turned fifteen, Loretta started taking the bus into Houston on Fridays after school, returning on Sundays with money. Rose said nothing, but Delbert demanded to know where the money had come from.

'I worked for it,' snapped Loretta. 'Not that it's any of your business.'

'Worked for it, how?' Delbert snapped back.

'Maybe I got a part-time job down there,' said Loretta. 'There's nothing goin' on here in Plum Grove, and never will be. There's no money here. There's nothing for *me* here. So I go where *I* can get what *I* need.'

When she was sixteen, she quit school and began spending more time down in Houston. When she came home, it was only to eat and sleep. What little conversation there was between her and Rose ended in hostility and hurt. Loretta was hostile. Rose was hurt.

One Sunday afternoon Rose returned from church to find Loretta drinking coffee at the kitchen table.

'What a pleasant surprise,' said Rose. 'I wish you'd been home sooner. You could have come to church with me. Everybody would have been so happy to see you.'

Loretta grunted. Her eyes were red and puffy, and her hair was stiff and dry. There were three buttons missing from the back of her dress, and she smelled of sweat, mildew, and cigarettes.

Rose smiled hopefully. 'Would you like to help me out in the garden with the peas and lettuce?'

Loretta snorted in contempt. 'You gotta be *shittin'* me.' She got up to leave.

'Why do you hate me, Loretta?' Rose asked.

'Why do you care?' Loretta shrugged.

'Because you're my *daughter*,' Rose pleaded. 'Because I *love* you, child. I don't want to see your life go this way. It doesn't have to go this way. I don't want to lose you.'

'I'm already lost,' Loretta said. She went to her bedroom and fell asleep on her bed. When she woke up, she left the house without saying goodbye.

One morning Rose was awakened by the Liberty County deputy sheriff, Link Thompson, knocking on her front door.

'Miss Rose?' the deputy called at the door. 'You in there?'

Rose peered through her front window as she wrapped herself in her housecoat. When she saw who it was, she went to the door expecting news that Loretta was dead.

'Deputy Thompson,' she said. 'What do you have to tell me?'

'Miss Rose, we have your daughter Loretta over at the jail,' he said. 'They arrested her down in Houston for prostitution and brought her up here to us. They didn't have room to keep her. So they gave her to us and said we could do with her what we thought was necessary.'

Rose held her hands to her face.

'She was pretty sick when we got her, Miss Rose,' said Link. 'Drunk maybe, or high. She's got marks on her arms. We're not going to keep her. So you can come get her.'

Rose nodded.

'I'm real sorry about your girl, Miss Rose,' said the deputy, tipping his cap.

Loretta's pimp – who called himself 'Sweet' – prided himself in his ability to use charm and empathy to recruit and retain personnel. A smile, a kind word, a sincere personal question about family or school, and soon girls would be telling him their life stories – information he skillfully exploited.

'Darlin', sounds to me like your papa's holdin' you back. Makin' you sweep the floors and do all that cookin' for him. Where's that going to get you? You got dreams, don't you? You want to go somewhere, be someone special, don't you? Well, I'm tellin' you, you are special. You're young and beautiful and there are a lot of men out there, like me, who would appreciate spending time with a young woman such as yourself. These are good, decent, hard-working men, who are looking for companionship, and understanding, and affection. And they gladly pay to spend time with someone special and pretty. And the money they pay is money you can use to make your dreams come true.'

Sweet also knew how to bring his product to market. After long meetings at the hall, union members emerged weary and pent up, and on their way home, many were likely to encounter friendly young women out for a good time. After Saturday night cock fights behind the roadhouse, liquored-up contestants could expect that their victories would be celebrated and their losses consoled by nice girls looking to do a little something bad.

Sweet had a knack for scouting out special events that attracted men with spending cash – traveling carnivals, boxing matches, horse races, and such. In the fall of 1946, one of these unique business opportunities presented itself. After the Kansas City Monarchs lost the 1946 Negro Leagues World Series to the Newark Eagles, Satchel Paige, the Monarchs' star pitcher, joined up with Bob Feller, the Cleveland Indians' ace, for a barnstorming tour. Paige and Feller assembled teams of 'all-stars' from their respective leagues and together they hit the road, playing a series of games to sold-out crowds in big-city and small-town ballparks from coast to coast. Houston was one of the early stops on the tour, after which the teams were scheduled to play in Oklahoma City. However, a tornado in Oklahoma City kept the caravan in Texas a day longer than planned, so the promoters quickly arranged for a game at the ballpark in Humble, Texas, just north of Houston and south of Plum Grove.

Sweet got word of the game from a bookie in the Fourth Ward who was both a business associate and a regular customer. Sweet immediately mobilized his workforce, including Loretta who knew the area well.

The venture proved profitable. At least three dozen fans and players purchased services from Sweet's twelve girls over the course of the nine innings and after. Loretta was even invited into the Paige All-Stars locker room.

Two hundred and sixty-six days later LaVerne Williams was born. Seventeen days after that Loretta was arrested in Houston for stabbing Sweet in a disagreement over money. Sweet didn't die. But he did lose an earlobe.

Loretta's trial lasted about an hour, after which she was sentenced to two years and two months.

Rose was heartbroken. Delbert was relieved. Together they undertook to raise up LaVerne in the way he should go. For Rose it was a second chance. A chance to do things differently than she did with Loretta. A chance to get it right. For Delbert it was a chance to be part of a child's life. Loretta had never liked him. Maybe LaVerne would.

By the time Loretta was released, LaVerne was a healthy, happy, strong-willed child who more than anything else loved playing catch with his uncle.

In spite of Rose's efforts to find her a job at Raylon Rice and Milling, so that she might return to Plum Grove to live, Loretta went back to Houston instead.

'I'll be fine, Mama,' she promised. 'I'm not going back to that way of living. I'm all straightened up.'

Loretta said nothing about bringing LaVerne with her to Houston. In fact, she showed little interest in LaVerne.

'I'll come up and see you, Mama,' she told Rose. 'And the baby. He seems like a good little boy.'

She gave Rose no address or way to get in touch with her. It was six months before Loretta came back to Plum Grove. She stayed for three days. Most of the time she slept, and at no time did she hold or even touch LaVerne. One afternoon, as she sat on the back step smoking a cigarette, LaVerne came around from the front of the house with his ball.

'You want to play?' he asked Loretta.

She looked at him and smiled. 'You go ahead. I'll watch.'

LaVerne shrugged and walked next door to Delbert's house where his uncle was playing dominoes on the porch with his friend, Fred Hartholz.

That's the way it went. Loretta would arrive unannounced and leave without saying goodbye. Sometimes it was only weeks between appearances. Usually months.

When LaVerne was four years old, Loretta showed up on her mother's porch in a yellow dress, her face scrubbed, her hair pulled back. She was smiling and weepy.

'I been saved, Mama,' she told Rose when she came to the door. 'I been baptized and everything. It's going to be different now. I just wanted you to know.'

Parked out on the road was a shiny black Cadillac. There was a man in the car wearing a black suit, with a white shirt and black tie. Rose couldn't see his face from the porch.

'That's Hiram,' Loretta said. 'He's a preacher. He's the one who brought me to Jesus. We're going up to Tulsa for a tent meeting, Mama. And I wanted to tell you so you wouldn't worry about me anymore.'

She looked down at LaVerne who was sitting on the porch steps holding a Mason jar. She reached her hand out to touch the top of his head. Then the preacher sounded the horn and Loretta stopped. LaVerne looked up at her. She turned and walked down the path to the black car. Rose sat down on the steps next to LaVerne and they watched the car drive off.

It was three years before Rose heard from her daughter again. Delbert returned from town one afternoon with his and his sister's mail, and there was a letter from the Julia Tutwiler Prison in Alabama.

Dear Mama,

I am here because of prostitution and heroin and they say I hurt a man bad in a fight in the motel. I don't expect you to visit me. I only wanted you to know where I was.

Your daughter Loretta

LaVerne sometimes asked Rose about Loretta.

'Your mother is a lost soul,' she said. 'She can't seem to find her way. She always chooses the wrong road. I don't know why.'

Delbert was more direct.

'I don't believe your mother is lost,' Delbert told his nephew one summer evening as he and Hartholz and La-Verne were smoking briskets and sausage in the pit behind the butcher shop. 'She *did* choose the wrong road. But she *chose* it. She didn't wander down it accidentally. She chose the wrong road *because* it was the wrong road.'

Hartholz shook his head and spat on the ground.

When LaVerne was fifteen years old, one of the women at Plum Grove Second Baptist Church told Rose that she'd seen someone who looked a lot like Loretta in Houston at the bus station. Then one of the customers at the butcher shop told Delbert that he thought he'd seen Loretta at a juke joint in the Fourth Ward.

'It sure looked like your sister's kid,' he said. 'But I know she was in Tutwiler, so maybe it wasn't. Or maybe she's out now.'

It was late May. LaVerne's baseball team was winning most of its games and LaVerne was the team's star. Rose, Delbert, and Hartholz went to every home game. In fact, most of Plum Grove had come out for the home games, even white folks. Including Link Thompson, who had been elected sheriff.

Between the eighth and ninth innings of a game on a hot Saturday afternoon, Delbert left his seat and went out back behind the bleachers to buy shaved ice for Rose, Hartholz, and himself. Standing in line at the shaved ice stand, Delbert could see LaVerne sitting at the end of his team's bench. LaVerne was trying hard to watch the game, but a horsefly had fixed its attention on his neck, and no matter how vigorously LaVerne waved and swatted, the fly returned to bite the back of his neck. Finally, LaVerne hopped up and started flailing the air with his ball glove. This is when he noticed Delbert looking at him. They grinned at one another. Delbert mockingly flapped his hands, mimicking his nephew's frantic attempts to rid himself of the fly. LaVerne put his ball glove on top of his head, made a goofy face and sat down on the bench, leaning back, with his legs stretched out in front of him in a pose of exaggerated lounging.

On his way back to the bleachers with the ice, Delbert saw a man and a young woman talking under a tree out by where the cars were parked. Money was being exchanged.

Delbert observed for a moment, then walked over to Sheriff Thompson, who usually watched the games from behind the fence at home plate.

'Sheriff Thompson, there's something goin' on over by the cars,' said Delbert. 'It may be nothing. But it looks like whoring, or maybe they're selling reefer. But it shouldn't be happening where kids can see.'

'Well, Mr Delbert, let's go look,' said the sheriff. They started in the direction of the cars.

Link Thompson stopped several yards from where the man and the woman were transacting their business.

'Delbert, that's your sister Rose's girl,' he said. He turned and looked Delbert in the eye. Delbert didn't flinch.

'Like I said, sheriff. It looks like something unwholesome is goin' on. Something young people ought not to see. I certainly wouldn't want my nephew seeing such things. Don't you think you should investigate? It could be a crime is being committed.'

'I think you may be right, Delbert,' the sheriff said. 'I'll go take care of it.'

The shaved ice had mostly melted, so Delbert went back and got some more.

23

Remains

When Raymond died, A.B. felt as if his name was stripped away from where it was attached to his soul. So much of his identity was derived from being Raymond's friend he didn't know how to think of himself with Raymond gone. He was sad and anxious every day and every night he thrashed around in bed sweating and half-awake, hoping not to dream. So, when he saw the long black limousine with the black opaque windows parked in front of the restaurant one morning, about seven months after Raymond died, it reminded him of Raymond's funeral. He would have turned his car around and returned home, except that, as he was leaving his apartment earlier that morning, he saw something that so unnerved him the thought of going back to his apartment made him shudder and reach for his cigarettes.

It was not quite light when he locked his apartment door and went out to the street to his car that morning. It was gray and cold and A.B. could tell it was going to be one of those days when it would only get grayer and colder. His neighbor, Mr Avelluto, was out at the sidewalk picking up his newspaper. He waved at A.B.

It was then they both sensed something above them. They looked up and saw a crow lift off from the roof of the apartment house. It let out a short sharp caw and released something black it was carrying in its claws. The thing fluttered down in slow motion and fell with a soft smack on the sidewalk in front of A.B.

It was a bat, not yet dead; its pointy little leathery wings feebly flapping.

'Damn,' said Mr Avelluto. 'Is that a *bat*?'

A.B. hopped backward and stared down at the creature in horror. Its mouth gaped, showing tiny fangs.

'I think so!' he yelped.

'Damn,' said Mr Avelluto. He crossed himself and went inside with his newspaper.

On his way to work, A.B. turned up the volume on his car radio as loud as it would go in order to distract himself from what he'd just seen. And also from the new odor in his car.

A.B.'s car didn't smell good to begin with, what with the cigarettes, the frequently spilled coffee, and the three years of flatulence buried deep in the foam rubber of the driver's seat cushion resulting from daily consumption of LaVerne Williams' Texas-style beans. But for about a week, a very specific stink unrelated to cigarettes, coffee, or gaseous emissions had filled the interior of his car. And it was getting worse.

A.B. had searched under the seats, under the hood, and in the trunk, looking for the source of the odor, but had found nothing that would produce what was, by the seventh day, an eye-watering, stomach-turning stench. He did, however, find his lost cassette of Stevie Ray Vaughan's *Soul to Soul* album.

Driving with the windows open alleviated the smell only slightly, but it was the only thing A.B. could think to do. That, and smoke non-stop all the way to the restaurant.

A.B. parked out back, in the alley. He saw Angela's Honda Civic where LaVerne's truck was usually parked and

175

remembered that LaVerne was over at Bartle Hall for the day, signing autographs at a baseball collectibles meet. Several players from the old Kansas City Athletics were going to be there. Angela was in the dining room taking chairs off the tables. She heard A.B come in and went to say hello.

'Good morning, A.B. How are you this morning?'

'Fine,' he said. He went into the walk-in to get greens and ham hocks, came back out and started washing the greens.

'You all right, A.B.?' asked Angela. She took his chin in her hand and turned his face toward her.

His eyes filled.

'I'm okay,' he said trying to look away.

She kissed his forehead and let him go. A few hours later, just before the lunch rush, she saw him looking out the front window; his shoulders hunched forward, his hands thrust deep his pockets. When he realized Angela was watching him, he left the window and went out back by the dumpster for a smoke. Angela looked out the window. A black limousine was parked at the curb.

After lunch, as she and A.B. cleaned tables, Angela noticed that every few minutes he glanced out the window. Whatever it was he saw outside made him frown.

'Child, what on earth has you so worried today?' she asked. 'You're not acting yourself.'

'That car, that limo, has been there all day,' he said, scowling. 'What's goin' on, do you think? Why is it out there? I haven't seen anyone in it or by it. I can't figure out why it's out there.'

Angela smiled. 'I noticed that, too. We don't see many limousines parked on this block, do we? Maybe some rich businessman is buying artworks at the gallery across the street.'

'Maybe,' A.B. mumbled. He went into the kitchen and loaded the Hobart.

It's never busy at Smoke Meat from 2:00 to 5:30. Usually, A.B. spends that time cleaning up the dining room and counter area. Sometimes he goes out and sweeps the sidewalk. On the day he saw the crow and the bat, and his car stank, and the black limo was parked out front, A.B. spent most of the afternoon in the kitchen pulling pork and chuck, and slicing onions and cabbage. He also took a lot more cigarette breaks than usual, out back by the dumpster. Once he walked up to the front corner of the building and peeked around. The limousine was still there. He went back inside to cook the onions and cabbage for the next day.

Angela came in from the dining room, where she had been filling napkin holders.

'LaVerne told me there were problems again with Rocco last month with some of the produce. Did that get straightened out? Are we getting the cabbage and onions we need?'

A.B. nodded without looking up. 'Yeah,' he said. 'It was some problem with Rocco's supplier.'

Angela tried to keep the conversation going.

'It's surprising how often cabbage and onions cause problems for Rocco, isn't it?' She leaned in toward A.B. trying to get him to look at her. 'You wouldn't think they would be that difficult to find, would you?'

He glanced up at her, but couldn't muster a smile. 'Yeah. A few weeks ago I even had to go over to Scimeca's Market for some. Boss keeps sayin' he's going to get a new produce guy, but he never does.'

Smoke Meat's kitchen can get uncomfortably warm and humid, but Angela noticed that A.B. was sweating as if it were twenty degrees warmer than it actually was.

'A.B., let's go sit down and talk,' she said, taking hold of his arm. 'I'm worried about you.'

They went in and sat down at the corner table where

177

Mother Mary and Pug usually sit. A.B.'s eyes welled up immediately.

'What *is* it, child?' Angela asked, reaching across the table for A.B.'s hands. A.B. looked down at the table.

'It's like there's omens,' he said. 'Like something bad is going to happen. I think maybe God is telling me I'm going to die.'

'My goodness, A.B. What kind of omens?'

'This morning a crow flew off the roof of the apartment and dropped a bat right in front of me. A *bat*! Like a *vampire* bat! Mr Avelluto saw it, too. Scared the shit right out of me.'

A.B. blushed. 'I'm sorry, Mrs Williams. Pardon my French.'

Angela smiled and squeezed A.B.'s hands.

'Anyways, it was like a bad dream. The worst dream you could have. It was like something from hell. Then, lately, my car stinks terrible. Like something rotten. But I can't find anything in the car that would smell that bad. It's like death. Even though I've never actually smelled death.'

A.B. shivered and gulped in air, trying to suppress the hiccups he felt coming on.

'So, then I get here this morning and there's that black funeral car out there. All day. It doesn't move. There's no driver or passenger. It just sits there. It's like it's waiting for me.'

A.B started to tremble. Angela thought he was going to cry. Or maybe explode.

'I keep thinkin' that the devil is in that car. Or maybe the Angel of Death. These are like signs, Mrs Williams. I think these are signs that I'm going to die. Just like Raymond. But Raymond went to heaven. If *I* die I'm going to *hell*. Ray was good and he went to church and he did good things. But I don't go to church. My mom never took me to church. And I smoke and swear and stuff.'

Then A.B. did cry. He let out a long low sob and put his face in his hands. Angela scooted her chair over next to A.B.'s.

'That's not how it works, A.B.,' she said. 'That's not how it works. The devil doesn't drop bats off roofs to scare us or drive a big black limousine around lookin' to take us to hell. And God doesn't send us signs that we're about to die.

'A.B., you're hurting inside just like the rest of us since Raymond died. Lord knows, I cry almost every night still. We'll never get over it. None of us. He was too young and bright and beautiful. And when you lose something precious to you, it changes the way you see things. Sometimes it helps you see things more clearly. You see only the things that are most precious and important. Other times it clouds your vision and you can't see things clearly at all. You can't tell what's real and what's not. Everything seems worrisome and dark and frightening.

'You loved Raymond, A.B., and he loved you. I know your heart is broken like LaVerne's and mine. And I know you must be lonely. But you're not going to die. Not just yet. Everything is just fine. You're safe. Everything is fine.'

A.B. wanted to smoke. But he knew how Angela disapproved of it.

'But what about the crow and the bat?' he asked. 'And what about that hearse?'

Angela smiled. 'Crows and bats give me the creeps, too. But that crow was probably just trying to protect its nest or maybe hoping for a little breakfast. And that's not a hearse. It's just a car. Like your car, only long and black.'

'Except it probably doesn't smell like shit,' A.B. said, then quickly added, 'Sorry, Mrs Williams. I keep saying bad words.'

They sat quiet there at Mary's table. From the corner, they couldn't see if the limousine was still there.

'Why did Ray have to die?' asked A.B. after a bit. His voice was small and thin.

'Raymond didn't have to die,' said Angela. 'He just died.'

'Why did God let him die?'

'God did let Raymond die. But he's going to let all of us die. The only difference between you and me and Raymond is not *if* we die, but *when* we die.

'Dying isn't a bad thing, A.B. The way we die is sometimes sad or painful, and sometimes it's unjust or tragic. But the dying itself isn't bad. And God knows that. He sees this life of ours here on earth and our life in heaven as one life. Now we're living in one house and later we're going to live in another house. We just can't see that next house from here. But God sees it. Because it's where he lives. And just like if you left Kansas City and went someplace else to live, LaVerne and I would be sad; when people we love die, it makes us sad. We miss them. We want them back. But they're where they're supposed to be. They're home. And someday we're going home, too.'

Angela and A.B. sat there for a while longer. A customer came in and Angela got up and went over to the counter to take the order. A.B. went back into the kitchen.

After the last customer left, A.B. went to the window. The limousine was still there. Leaning against the right front fender was a short heavyset man wearing a black suit, white shirt, and black chauffeur's cap. His suit coat was unbuttoned and his red necktie was tied short, leaving an expanse of white between the bottom of his tie and the top of his pants, which were themselves too short, exposing white socks falling down around his ankles. A.B. noticed the man was eating a Smoke Meat sandwich, and that a long drizzle of sauce was sliding down his right pant leg.

As they were locking up, Angela turned to A.B. and hugged him.

'Thank you for talking to me this afternoon, A.B. I'm so grateful for you.'

'You're welcome,' A.B. said, unsure why he was being thanked.

Angela held A.B. by the shoulders. 'Come to church with LaVerne and me on Sunday.'

A.B. didn't hesitate. 'Okay, Mrs Williams. I will.'

On the way back to his apartment, A.B. listened to *Soul to Soul*, with his windows rolled down all the way for maximum ventilation. He sang along until the tenth track, 'Life Without You.'

'The day is necessary, every now and then, for souls to move on, givin' life back again.

Fly on, fly on, fly on my friend. Go on and live again . . .'

He turned off the tape and lit up a cigarette.

Three blocks from his apartment, A.B. felt the unmistakable thump-thumping of a flat tire coming from the left rear of his car. He let the 'Sh' part of 'Shit!' escape, but successfully suppressed the remainder of the word. He pulled his car over onto a side street, lit another smoke, and got out to change the tire.

He opened his trunk and lifted the liner to get at the spare, the jack, and the tire iron, and was immediately overcome by a rush of putrid fumes. He staggered back a step, his eyes burning. He bent over and dry heaved twice, and then a third time.

He feared the worst, without having any clear idea what the worst might be. Maybe, somehow, there was the body of a gangster in his trunk, or a horse's severed head, like in the movies. He clenched his nose with his fingers and cautiously peered in the trunk.

It was nothing dead. Only a clear plastic grocery bag from Scimeca's Market, with something in it. He reached in and picked up the bag. In it were the rotting liquefied remains of two heads of cabbage and five yellow onions.

24

The Father, the Son

Nothing of consequence happens at New Jerusalem Baptist Church without the knowledge and consent of the Ladies' Missionary Society. Founded in 1884 – the same year as the congregation itself – for the purpose of sponsoring missionaries overseas, the Ladies' Missionary Society has evolved over the decades into a de facto directorate whose moral support must be sought and earned for all initiatives by other church boards, committees, volunteers, and even the pastor. This seeking of support is conducted on a strictly informal basis, and the Society never actually meets to discuss or vote on such things they've been made aware of. However, while the Ladies would never presume to exercise a veto – since technically such authority belongs only to the deacons and trustees – if you happen to be a member of the New Jerusalem Baptist Church and you do not obtain their blessing for your new Sunday School class curriculum, your social outreach project, or your proposal for new wallpaper in the church library, your plan will shrivel and die like a worm on a hot sidewalk.

In 1984, the year of its centennial, there happened to be sixty-five ladies in the Society. Each of whom was accorded even more respect and deference than usual during the year-long series of special events New Jerusalem Baptist Church held to observe the anniversary.

These observances culminated with a day-long celebration on the second Sunday in November, beginning with an all-stops-pulled-out worship service. In addition to the New Jerusalem Baptist Church senior choir, choirs from the Troost Avenue AME Church and the Rosedale Church of God in Christ performed. Proclamations from the mayor and the governor, and letters of congratulation from pastors of churches throughout the metropolitan region were then read aloud. Following these felicitations, worshippers were roused by a soul-stirring sermon by senior pastor Rev. Orville Harris, who expounded for approximately fifty minutes on the last five verses of the twenty-eighth chapter of Matthew's Gospel. The congregation was then treated to an additional sermon, also full-length, by the guest speaker, the Rev. Dr Foster Yancey, an ordained medical missionary, home on furlough from his mission in Gambia. Dr Yancey chose as his text the entire twenty-first chapter of the Gospel of John.

After the worship service, a sit-down banquet was held in the fellowship hall, with the young people of the church serving as waiters.

After the banquet, the New Jerusalem Baptist Church children's choir performed a program of African hymns and Sunday School songs. This was followed by a slide show, narrated by Angela Williams, telling the story of the Ladies' Missionary Society and the overseas missions it had supported since its founding. In spite of Angela's attempts to convince the program committee to condense the script and reduce the number of slides, her efforts were ultimately futile. There were too many constituencies needing placation. Nearly every family in the congregation claimed a selfless and tireless female ancestor whose labors on behalf of the Society were decisive in the organization's success, thus meriting inclusion of a comprehensive biography. To the by-then-weary church membership, the resulting presentation felt much like a day-by-day accounting of the Society's hundred-year history. Angela tried various vocal inflections to maintain audience interest, but in the darkened and sound-deadened fellowship hall, most of the elderly and several of the children fell asleep. Gentle snoring could be heard whenever Angela paused for a breath.

The final event of the day was the raffle drawing. In addition to serving as waiters for the banquet, the youth of the congregation had been assigned responsibility for selling tickets for a chance to win a pair of season tickets to the Kansas City Chiefs' 1985 season. The proceeds of this sale were to be donated to the Rev. Dr Yancey's mission in Gambia.

Though, in the preceding season, the Chiefs finished last in their division with a record of 6–10, raffle-ticket sales were brisk. However, because ticket holders were required to be present to win, and because many congregants had snuck away during the slide show, and had gone home exhausted by the day's proceedings, six drawings were needed before a winner could be awarded the tickets. The winner was ninety-three-year old Mavis Thigpen, which greatly peeved LaVerne, who had purchased twenty-five tickets at five dollars apiece to increase his odds. He sulked all the way home.

'What a waste,' he grumbled to Angela. 'What's a ninety-three-year old woman who's mostly blind and deaf going to do with Chiefs season tickets? It's ridiculous. It's just a waste.'

'Maybe she has a grandson or nephew who'd like the tickets,' said Angela.

LaVerne snorted. 'I'll be her nephew if she needs one.'

*

One of the lesser celebrations of the hundredth anniversary of the Ladies' Missionary Society was the mother–daughter banquet, which was held on the third Wednesday in September of that year. LaVerne Williams' Genuine BBQ and City Grocery catered the event.

Smoke Meat had only catered one previous event – a party in Johnson County, hosted by a mutual fund manager, at which he and fifty of his closest friends watched the second and final game of the 1982–83 Big Eight basketball season between the University of Missouri and the University of Kansas. LaVerne's barbecue and side dishes had been well received, but the party turned ugly when several inebriated KU fans became overly agitated at the game's outcome and began throwing beer cans, not all of them empty.

The mother–daughter banquet promised to be more tranquil. The Ladies asked LaVerne to serve brisket, greens, red potatoes, onions and cabbage, peach cobbler, and sweet potato and vinegar pies. LaVerne, Raymond, and A.B. began preparation about forty-eight hours before the dinner. LaVerne smoked the briskets in two batches, and the boys made the desserts. Raymond and A.B. then started in on the greens, while LaVerne cooked the onions and cabbage. LaVerne wasn't yet comfortable letting his assistants prepare onions and cabbage. He had specific preferences regarding the ratio of cabbage to onions (five to three), the precise amount of lard to be used to cook the onions and cabbage (a lot), and the correct degree of caramelization to be achieved in the cooking process (a lot, but not too much).

Because Raymond and A.B. had school the Wednesday of the banquet, and LaVerne needed to work at the restaurant during the day, most of the final prep had to be done on Tuesday night. When Raymond and A.B. came in after school on Tuesday afternoon, LaVerne was loading chaffing dishes and utensils into the truck.

'I'm going over to the church to drop these off and set up the serving line,' he said. 'Then some guys from the men's fellowship are coming over to set up tables and chairs, so I'm going to get them started. You two take care of business while I'm gone, and when I get back we'll have to cook up some sauce. We don't have enough for tonight, tomorrow, and the banquet, too.'

It was a slow night. Eight nametag-wearing insurance underwriters, attending a convention, strayed in and stayed for two hours. There were only four other customers other than that, all of them carry-out. As Raymond and A.B. were cleaning up, LaVerne called from the church, mightily pissed off.

'Well, none of the forgetful, inconsiderate, irresponsible, lazy-asses who were going to come to set up tables and chairs showed up,' he barked into the phone. Raymond held the phone away from his ear.

'I'm going to have to stay and put the tables up myself,' LaVerne said. 'That means you and A.B. are going to have to make the sauce. You've never done the sauce before, but it's straightforward. Use the five-gallon recipe and put it in the walk-in when you're done.'

From across the kitchen, A.B. could hear LaVerne's instructions. He immediately went over to the bulletin board mounted on the wall between the stove and the Hobart and retrieved the five-gallon version of the recipe for LaVerne Williams' Genuine BBQ Sauce KANSAS CITY STYLE. All the basic recipes for the Smoke Meat menu were tacked on the board for the benefit of new employees, even though LaVerne didn't let any new employees use them.

A.B. pulled a big stockpot out from under the stainless-steel prep table and went into the office to gather up cans of tomato purée and pickled jalapeños, and bottles of vinegar and corn syrup for the sauce.

'This'll be fun,' said Raymond, grinning wide and rubbing his palms together. 'I've always wanted to do this.'

A.B. wasn't so sure. 'I don't know. Your dad has ways he likes to do things. We could screw it up.'

'We're not going to screw it up,' said Raymond. 'We might make a few improvements. But we're not going to screw it up.'

'Improvements?' A.B. squeaked. 'Jeez, Ray. Let's not fuss with anything. Let's just do it the way it's written down.'

Raymond put his arm across A.B.'s shoulders. 'Al Buddy Clayton, my man, you got to take risks in this world if you ever want to get ahead.'

A.B. shrugged. 'I don't really want to get ahead, Ray. I just don't want the boss to get mad 'cause we messed up his sauce.'

'We need some tunes for this kind of work,' said Raymond. He went over and turned on the boombox on top of the refrigerator. The artist known as Prince was exhorting and sermonizing his way through the intro to 'Let's Go Crazy'. When the guitars and drums kicked in, Raymond strode and slid in rhythm back over to the work table. A.B. grinned and shook his head, and tried to put LaVerne's inevitable reaction to their sauce experimentation out of his mind. He poured the cans of tomato purée into the stock pot.

Raymond rolled up his sleeves. 'The first thing we need to do is put a little more jump in this sauce. How much cayenne pepper does it say to put in?'

'Oh, boy,' A.B. said, anxiously. He looked at the recipe. 'One half-cup.'

'Okay. How about we put in one *whole* cup? That oughta liven' things up.'

'Ray. Seriously. That's too much,' A.B. said.

Raymond had already scooped up a cupful of cayenne and dumped it in the pot. 'How much garlic does it say?'

'Twelve cloves, crushed,' A.B. said. 'That's quite a lot. We probably don't need to add any more.'

'I think eighteen cloves will do quite nicely,' said Raymond. He proceeded to smash garlic cloves with the flat of his father's chef's knife, as he'd seen his father do. Eighteen in all.

'You know, A.B., in my African Heritage class we learned about African cooking,' Raymond said. 'Mrs Nelson said they use peanuts a lot. What if we paid a little tribute to our African roots by putting some peanuts in here?'

Raymond peered into the pot as if looking for just the right spot to add peanuts.

A.B. was near panic. 'Listen, Ray. We don't have any peanuts. Besides, your dad maybe won't notice a little more hot pepper and garlic. But peanuts? That's just strange. It won't even taste like barbecue sauce.'

Raymond opened the refrigerator and found the jar of peanut butter that Angela used to make sandwiches when she worked at the restaurant on Saturdays. Poised above the pot, he swiped a big glop of peanut butter out of the jar with a spatula. 'This should be about right,' he said, as he let the peanut butter slide into the bubbling sauce.

A.B. looked on in horror. Since his protestations were having no effect on Raymond, he went out back in the alley and it up a cigarette.

LaVerne made Raymond and A.B. wear black pants, white shirts, and neckties to the mother–daughter banquet.

'This isn't just church,' he told them. 'This is a job. We need to look like professional caterers.'

Raymond looked a lot better in his get-up than A.B. did in his. Raymond's clothes always fit well. His height and athletic build showed them off to their best advantage. A.B. hadn't worn his catering outfit since the basketball party in Johnson County and it looked as if the shirt and slacks had lain on his closet floor since that time. Not that it would have made much difference if they'd been freshly washed and pressed. A.B.'s small, bony frame made all his clothes look like a damp towel hanging on a bathroom doorknob.

The banquet program featured a before-dinner performance by the New Jerusalem Baptist Church choir and an after-dinner presentation by a motivational speaker. Her speech was titled 'The Power of One: Be your best self and change your world!'

The choir started with 'I Had a Talk With God', followed by 'God Can Do Anything But Fail'.

Only two songs into the performance and the assembled mothers and daughters were already standing by their seats at the banquet tables, clapping and dancing in place. The older women held their hands up in praise. This was sufficient encouragement for the choir director, Yvonne Maynard, to commence a series of James Brown-inspired hop-and-glide moves as she led her singers, her satin robe flowing and flapping.

Raymond and A.B. were standing in position behind the serving tables, on the far end of the fellowship hall, opposite the choir. Raymond, too, was in full gospel groove. He danced and clapped along with the rest, only when he did it, it looked better than when anyone else did it. A.B. also found himself moved by the music and initiated a modest head-bobbing, arm-swinging action. Raymond stopped, stood back, and watched his friend for a moment.

'Racial stereotyping is an evil thing,' he said, smiling. 'But it's true what they say – white boy can not dance. It's a good thing we're standing in the back here, where nobody can see.'

When the choir got to the chorus of its third number, 'He's Calling Me', a young man in the choir's back row began shouting 'Yes! Jesus!', and swaying out of time. He closed his eyes. His head rolled back and he began to convulse.

'What the *hell*?' A.B. whispered sharply to Raymond. 'That guy's having a fit or something.'

Raymond was unconcerned. 'Nah, that's just Lorenzo. He's being overcome by the Holy Ghost. It happens all the time. The Holy Ghost always seems to pick Lorenzo when it wants to overcome someone.'

The rest of the choir also seemed unconcerned. They continued singing without interruption. Then Lorenzo appeared to faint. Two other men in the back row helped him down from the risers and sat him on the floor. Three of the mothers went over and began to fan him with their banquet programs. When he was sufficiently revived, the two men helped him out of the fellowship hall. As all this happened, the choir kept singing. A.B. was relieved when, two songs later, Lorenzo and his helpers returned and took their places in the back row.

'Man, I'm glad he's okay,' he said to Raymond.

Raymond shook his head. 'It ain't over yet.'

Indeed, a few minutes later, when the choir had reached the bridge of 'Start All Over Again', its last song of the evening, the Holy Ghost took hold of Lorenzo once more. He began to pitch forward and was helped off the risers by the same two men. However, this time, instead of fainting, he fell to the floor, stiffened up and began vibrating and humming like a barber's electric clippers turned on and set on a table.

'Is church always like this?' A.B. asked Raymond.

'*Lorenzo's* always like this,' said Raymond. 'Don't worry. When the music stops he'll suddenly recover.'

Which is what happened. As the mothers and daughters applauded, and director Maynard bowed, Lorenzo got to his feet, straightened his robe and got back up on the risers under his own power.

Raymond got lots of compliments from the mothers and lots of self-conscious smiles and giggles from the daughters as they made their way through the serving line.

'My, my, young man. Don't you look handsome tonight.'

'Goodness, Raymond. You get taller every time I see you.'

'LaVerne, you and Angela sure did make yourself a pretty baby.'

'Hi, Raymond. See you in study hall.'

Even the president of the Ladies Missionary Society, Mrs Oleta Wesley, stopped to chat. 'Raymond Williams, where are your manners? Introduce me to your friend.'

'This is my best friend, A.B., ma'am,' said Raymond. 'We work together at the restaurant. In fact, he made the barbecue sauce for tonight.'

Raymond smiled and wouldn't make eye contact with A.B., who looked stricken.

'I can't believe you told that lady that,' A.B. hissed through gritted teeth when President Wesley had moved on down to the pie and cobbler.

'Who knows?' Raymond laughed. 'Could turn out good for you. The sauce might be a hit and then they'll name it after you. *"Al Buddy's Genuine BBQ Sauce AFRICAN STYLE".*'

LaVerne came by to inspect the serving line and detected levity, which he felt was unprofessional when serving barbecue in a church basement.

'Knock it off, you two,' he said, and went into the church kitchen to get more pie for the line.

About then, down at the other end of the hall, one of the

grandmothers present let out with a loud 'Wooooo!' Raymond and A.B. saw that she was gulping down ice water. A.B. started to sweat. Raymond laughed, but his laughter lacked confidence. They anxiously monitored the situation, and were relieved when the grandma took another bite of barbecue, which was also followed by a 'Wooooo!' and more ice water.

A few minutes later, another of the Ladies came up to the serving line, leaned across the table and took Raymond's arm. 'Tell your father that I really like what he did with his barbecue sauce,' she said. 'It's different, but I like it. You tell him I said so.' Raymond grinned and elbowed A.B. in the ribs.

Dinner was pretty much done and the event was winding down. LaVerne came out from the kitchen and told the boys to break down the serving line and start packing up the truck. As he was administering his instructions, Mrs Wesley came over.

'Mr Williams, on behalf of the Missionary Society I want to thank you for catering our banquet this evening,' she said. 'Everything was just delicious, as always. And your young men were so polite and hard working. Your family is a blessing to this church.'

Mrs Wesley handed LaVerne an envelope. As he took it, she stepped closer to him and whispered in his ear. 'LaVerne, dear, you may want to check your barbecue sauce. I think it's spoiled.'

LaVerne's eyes narrowed and his jaw muscles tightened. He said goodbye to Mrs Wesley and stalked over to where A.B. and Raymond were taking apart the chaffing dishes. A small pan of barbecue sauce was still on the table. He stuck his finger in the sauce and then in his mouth. A.B. and Raymond braced themselves.

LaVerne grimaced and struggled to swallow the offending condiment. 'What the *hell* did you two do to the barbecue sauce?'

Raymond and A.B. stood there mute, each trying to think of a suitable lie. As LaVerne burned, waiting for an explanation, yet another mother approached them.

'*Mercy*, LaVerne!' she said. 'Those greens and potatoes were just *wonderful*. The brisket was the best I've had in *years*. And that sauce . . .'

She paused to deliberate on precisely the right words to use.

'Well, the sauce was gourmet. It was unusual. But in a good way. I just wanted to tell you how much I enjoyed it all.'

She turned to leave. 'Keep up the good work, LaVerne.'

LaVerne clenched his fists and scowled. Raymond expected to be grounded, and A.B. expected to be fired.

'I don't know what you guys did to my barbecue sauce. But you'll never have the chance to do it again,' LaVerne said. 'From now on *I* make the sauce. And *only* I make the sauce.'

When Raymond and A.B. had finished unloading the truck at the restaurant, Raymond offered A.B. a ride home.

'Well, that could have been a lot worse,' said Raymond, as he drove up 17th Street to Grand.

'It was bad enough,' said A.B. He rolled down his window and lit a cigarette.

They were quiet. Raymond rolled down *his* window. 'It's a beautiful night, isn't it?'

A.B. didn't say anything. Raymond looked over at him. He was holding the tip of his cigarette out the window.

'So, Ray. Was that Lorenzo guy faking it? And what is the Holy Ghost, anyway? That's sounds spooky to me.'

'The Holy Ghost is another name for the Holy Spirit,'

Raymond answered. 'God sends the Holy Spirit to us to comfort us, or to inspire us, or to help us understand things we can't figure out on our own.

'And I don't know about Lorenzo. Maybe he's faking. But nobody's ever pushed him on it. It's probably just his way of expressing himself. He just lets the music take control. I know it looks foolish, but that's just Lorenzo. We all do foolish things. And where else is Lorenzo going to be Lorenzo if not in church?'

When A.B. got home, his mother was watching TV, drinking a quart of beer out of a paper bag.

'Where you been?' she asked.

'I had to work late,' said A.B. He sat down on the couch opposite his mother.

'Ma, how come we never go to church?' A.B. asked.

'What do you mean?' His mother sounded annoyed.

'Why don't we go to church?'

'Well, we went sometimes when you was little. You was baptized an' all.'

She didn't look up from the TV.

'I was baptized?'

'Yes. We're Catholics. All Catholic babies are baptized.'

'What do you mean we're Catholics? You never told me we're Catholics.'

'Well, we are.'

'Then how come we never talk about God or the Holy Ghost or Jesus? I've never heard you talk about God.'

A.B.'s mother took a long swig of beer.

'Well, goddamnit, I'm tryin' to watch my program.'

A.B. went to his room and opened his window and lay down on his bed. A September night breeze blew in. He felt like he should be angry with his mother, but he wasn't. The breeze was cool and comfortable.

25

Romantic Facts of Musketeers

Ferguson Glen's Pulitzer-nominated novella, *Traverse*, has slipped below the surface of public and critical memory. Out of print for years, it's now found only at church used-book sales or in the libraries of mainline denominational colleges and seminaries. It remains, however, the principal achievement of Ferguson's career, and he welcomes any opportunity to remind himself and others, that, at one time, he was capable of producing work that mattered.

One such opportunity was a conference hosted by DePaul University in Chicago titled 'Our Back Pages: Themes of Race in the American Literature of the Sixties: A Study in Black and White.' Ferguson was invited to deliver a reading from *Traverse*, and to discuss the public and critical response to the book at the time of its publication. He was also asked to sit on a panel of authors and academics which was to analyze the role of literature in the Civil Rights Movement.

Ferguson spends little time preparing for such events. After nearly forty years of readings, he has virtually every word of *Traverse* memorized, and knows on which page nearly every passage is printed. For Ferguson, readings are not readings as much as they are performances. He does, however, prior to these performances, devote considerable time deliberating on the matter of his clerical collar. The main consideration being its potential impact on women who may be in attendance.

Sometimes, on some women, the collar has something of an aphrodisiac effect. In these instances, the affected women are clearly intrigued by the notion that a man with Ferguson's intelligence, grace, and wit would devote those gifts to the service of God. Often these same women seem deeply curious about what it would take to seduce such a man. They wonder if the sight and scent of their bodies might capture and corrupt the soul of this man of God. Frequently, however, if Ferguson reciprocates the interest, it turns out that much of this spiritual and sexual curiosity is, in fact, academic. Nevertheless, in certain settings, the collar does seem to increase his chances of spending the evening in the company of a woman.

In other settings, on other women, the collar has a chilling effect. In these instances, the mere sight of a man in a clerical collar seems to arouse latent religious guilt, fear, and resentment, and, after a polite interval of stilted chit-chat, the affected women excuse themselves from Ferguson's presence, increasing his chances that he will spend the evening alone.

Though Ferguson has never been able to ascertain which conditions produce which results with which women, he decided to go collarless to the conference in Chicago.

The conference was attended by about one hundred academics. Most appeared to have read and fondly remembered *Traverse*, and the questions and observations during the discussion were informed and intelligent. Ferguson was pleased.

At the reception afterward, Ferguson was immediately ambushed by Colin Zimmerman, a fossilized, semi-retired liberal activist professor from the political-science department at Loyola University Chicago. Zimmerman cornered

Ferguson between the wet bar and a ficus tree, making escape impossible.

In the mid-sixties, Zimmerman was a minor advisor to the SDS and SNCC. However, as those organizations' tactics became increasingly violent, his pacifism put him at odds with their leaders and he fell out of favor with the militant Left. By then his association with those radical groups had made him an anathema to mainstream liberals. Shunned by Left, Right and Center, Zimmerman found himself politically homeless. He has spent the years since reliving his few glory days, desperately and futilely trying to rehabilitate his reputation.

Zimmerman's primary career-revival strategy was to write an authoritative history of the trial of the Chicago Seven. Critics were unanimous in their disdain for the book. The *New York Times Book Review* said, 'Zimmerman suffocates this vibrant period in contemporary American history under the weight of his bloodless, ponderous, and pedantic prose . . .'

The *New York Review of Books* used the word 'putresce' in describing Zimmerman's writing. No one who read that particular review, including Ferguson, remembered any other word in it except the word 'putresce'.

After twenty-five minutes of one-sided conversation, Ferguson concluded that the word 'putresce' also applied to Zimmerman's breath, wafts of which gusted up into Ferguson's face every time Zimmerman used a word beginning with W or H.

While Zimmerman held forth on his premise that John Froines and Lee Weiner were the true heart and soul of the Chicago Seven, and that Abbie Hoffman and Jerry Rubin were publicity whores, Ferguson speculated on the possible causes of Zimmerman's pungent breath. After deciding on gingivitis, Ferguson turned his attention to the outgrowths of stiff bristles erupting from Zimmerman's ears and nose.

Meanwhile Zimmerman shifted his monologue in the direction of Tom Hayden's marriage to Jane Fonda.

For Ferguson, the one benefit of the situation was his proximity to the bar. The bartender, a pimply graduate student, sympathized with Ferguson's predicament and kept him well supplied with bourbon. As Zimmerman started in on a critique of Judge Julius Hoffman's judicial career, an attractive woman approached the bar. She was in her mid-fifties, and had medium-length medium-brown and gray hair, bright green eyes and a green silk blouse with the top three buttons unbuttoned.

'I'll have some of that, if you don't mind,' she said, indicating the bottle of bourbon in the bartender's hand. 'No ice, please.'

She glanced over at Ferguson and surmised his plight. Drink in hand, she approached Zimmerman.

'Colin, go bore somebody else,' she said, shooing him away like a stray dog. 'You've tormented poor Father Glen long enough.'

Zimmerman looked at her blankly, and for a moment it appeared as if he might say something in his defense, but apparently thought better of it, and walked away.

'I'll have my accountant cut you a check in the morning,' said Ferguson to his rescuer. 'Thank you, thank you, *thank you*.'

He extended his hand and introduced himself. 'Ferguson Glen,' he said.

'Martha Garcia,' said the woman, shaking Ferguson's hand. 'Zimmerman and I are colleagues at Loyola. I teach twentieth-century American history.'

Ferguson smiled. 'Ah. A historian. Perhaps you could help me better understand the historical and cultural significance of Tom Hayden's marriage to Jane Fonda. I've always been curious about it.'

Martha Garcia pretended to choke on her bourbon.

'Oh, *my*,' she laughed. 'I am *so* sorry. If I'd known that Zimmerman was subjecting you to his Chicago Seven tirade, I would have intervened much sooner.'

'Actually, you were just in time,' said Ferguson. 'A minute or two later and I'd have passed out.'

Martha wrinkled her nose. 'Gingivitis,' she said, shuddering.

They both laughed. Then both were quiet. Then, self-consciously, both laughed again.

'I came over mostly to tell you that *Traverse* changed my life,' said Martha. 'I've always hoped that someday I'd meet you so I could tell you that.'

Ferguson smiled vaguely. 'Thank you,' he said. 'It changed my life, too. Though maybe not for the better.'

Unsure of what he meant, she continued. 'Seriously, *Traverse* made me see everything differently. It provided me with a metaphor for my life. I began to look at my whole life as a journey, like in the book, a cross-country train trip. And when I began to see the things in my life, my family, my religion, my country as I would if I were viewing it all from the window of a train, well, it changed me. It helped me understand that the journey and who you're traveling with is really what our stories are all about.'

Ferguson remembered that Bijou had once told him she was glad that they would be going on their journey together.

'That is very gratifying. I'll admit though that when I wrote it I didn't even really understand the story as fully as it can be understood.' He sighed. 'Turns out I only had the one story in me.'

Martha reached out and put her hand on Ferguson's arm. 'When it's a story as timeless and universal as yours, I'd say one's enough.'

Ferguson finished his bourbon.

'I was too young to appreciate the responsibility a writer has to his readers. Too young, really, to recognize the nature of my calling, as a writer. The story was a gift, and I didn't comprehend the nature of the gift. That came to me later. Too late.'

Martha finished her bourbon. '"Ah, but I was so much older then. I'm younger than that now."'

Ferguson laughed. She was smart, funny, and pretty, and seemed to have a sense of him.

'Ms Garcia, I'm wondering if you'd like to go get some dinner.'

Martha smiled somewhat tentatively. 'That would be wonderful. I'm here with Brad Schissler. Maybe you've met him already. He's on the faculty here at DePaul. I'm sure he'd be delighted if you'd join us for dinner.'

Ferguson felt his eyes wanting to close.

'You know, Martha, it would be hard enough for me to try to maintain intelligent, droll conversation with one professor over the course of a dinner. I'm quite sure two would leave me utterly exhausted. Perhaps another time.'

Martha's face showed regret and understanding. 'Of course. Brad will be disappointed.'

Ferguson forced a laugh. 'Maybe ol' Zimmerman needs some company,' he said. 'I wouldn't have to talk at all.'

They said goodbye. Ferguson went outside. It was cold. He thought, *If I smoked this would be a good time for a cigarette.*

A few of the conference attendees came outside. They greeted Ferguson and complimented him on his reading and commentary. Ferguson thanked them and they chatted about the facilities at DePaul University, the weather, and the White Sox. After a minute of this Ferguson realized he was bored and hungry.

'Where's good to eat around here?' he asked.

'Depends on what you're hungry for,' said a short heavy-set man with smudged glasses and a stained necktie. 'There's Nookies, which is Greek food. Then there's Butera, which is Italian. Butera is awesome. Then there's Café Bernard, which is classic French. And Tilli's which is kind of eclectic. They're all good. And they're all pretty close.'

'There's Robinson's,' said a woman who reminded Ferguson of Bea Arthur. 'If you like barbecue.'

Ferguson was quick to reply. 'I do like barbecue. I'm from Kansas City after all. How far is Robinson's?'

'About a half-mile,' said Bea Arthur. 'Just go south on Sheffield, here, about three blocks. Then east on Armitage, about six blocks. Best ribs in Chicago.'

Ferguson thanked the group for their recommendations and set out in the direction of Robinson's. At about the corner of Sheffield and Armitage, it occurred to him that he had never before said, 'I'm from Kansas City,' to anyone. Not even to himself.

The sign out front said, 'ROBINSON'S NO.1 RIBS RESTAURANT'. Ferguson had to admit they were good ribs – maybe number 3 on his list of favorite ribs, with LaVerne's being second. He ordered beans with the ribs, and liked those better than LaVerne's. Plus he had fries.

At his hotel, he stood at the elevator; not moving as the doors opened, closed, and opened again. Then, instead of going up to his room, he crossed the lobby to the lounge where he sat down at a small round table. When the waitress came he ordered a double bourbon, neat.

The featured entertainment was Bette Dion, a stout, chesty woman in a spangled peach-colored ball gown and frightening orange hair. Bette's favored genre was the Big Ballad. At one end of the bar, a pudgy middle-aged man with a goatee and an expensive suit straddled his stool, swizzling an olive around in his martini. At the other end of the bar, a heavily made-up middle-aged woman with a tight blue dress and a centerfold body coddled a Manhattan. In between them, two younger women wearing denim jumpers and convention ID badges on lanyards around their necks fixated on the band, mouthing the words along with Bette as she swept into a big key change to assert her belief that children are the future.

Ferguson watched as Expensive Suit established eye contact with Blue Dress. Expensive Suit then ambled over to Blue Dress's end of the bar and whispered something in her ear which resulted in the two of them leaving the lounge together. Ferguson looked for the waitress with the intent of ordering another whiskey, but when Bette arrived at the bridge of yet another anthem, he decided he'd had enough. He left money on the table and exited as Bette was taking it to the next level: '. . . *by the others who got rained on too, and made it through . . .*'

It was after eleven when Ferguson got to his room. He took off his suit jacket, tie, shoes and socks and stretched out on the bed, half expecting that he'd fall asleep. He let his mind drift. He pictured things Expensive Suit and Blue Dress might be doing. He wondered if Bette could sing the blues. He wondered who it was that proclaimed Robinson's ribs number 1 and what it was that made LaVerne's ribs better. He thought about how much he hated smudged glasses. He pictured Martha's green eyes and speculated about the contents of her green blouse. He disagreed with Zimmerman about Abbie Hoffman and Jerry Rubin. And he decided that the night wouldn't have turned out any different if he'd worn his collar. He wasn't anywhere near asleep.

He got up and looked inside the mini-bar refrigerator. There was the usual Scottish shortbread, Toblerone, honey-roasted peanuts, two bottles of Evian, two bottles of Heineken, two bottles of Bud light, and one miniature bottle each of Chivas, Skyy, Tanqueray, Glenlivet, and Jack Daniels. He opened the Jack Daniels and poured it down his throat. He turned on the television, lay back down on the bed, and flipped through the channels with the remote. There were sixteen channels, including HBO. And for $7.94 movies could also be viewed from the premium channels Starz or Xtaseez. The menu screen for Xtaseez made a point of informing customers that only the amount of their movies purchased – and not the names of movies viewed – would be recorded on their hotel bill.

He watched the last ten minutes of *American Chopper* on the Discovery Channel, and wished he'd tuned in earlier, inasmuch as the crew had been building a Zorro-themed chopper. When he was a boy, he was always Zorro on Halloween.

At midnight he flipped around the circuit again and landed on the History Channel which was featuring a program about the life and times of William 'Braveheart' Wallace. The show was an hour long, during which time he ate the Scottish shortbread, Toblerone, and honey-roasted peanuts, and drank the two bottles of Evian. After Wallace had been castrated, disemboweled, drawn, and quartered, Ferguson turned off the TV, took off his shirt and trousers, lay back down in his boxers and T-shirt and tried again to sleep. His flight back to Kansas City left at 8:20, which meant he'd need to be at O'Hare at about 7:30, which meant he'd have to be down front to get a cab no later than 6:15. If he fell asleep right now he'd still get a little more than fours hours in, leaving time for a quick shower and shave.

He lay there in the dark. He listened to the sounds of traffic down on the street. From a room one floor up, he heard a woman laughing, and then a man urgently asking, 'Now, baby? Now?' and then a minute or two later he heard the woman gasp, 'God!' and then in a low voice she said it again. He called room service and asked that a bottle of bourbon be sent to his room. A few minutes later, the whiskey was delivered. He poured some into one of the glasses from the bathroom.

On the Interactive Home Shopping channel, a young man in a golf shirt and pleated khakis was evangelizing about the qualities of a particular model of big-screen TV, specifically the advantages of the screen-within-a-screen feature. Watching TV about TV was not Ferguson's idea of entertainment, or even mindless distraction. He was about to flip on by when he noticed that the young man was wearing a toupee and a poorly fitting one at that. Ferguson found poorly fitting toupees both entertaining and mindlessly distracting, especially when accompanied by bourbon. He put down the remote and settled back to learn more about screen-within-a-screen technology.

Over the course of the next hour, he also learned about the health benefits of a diet rich in the nutrients present in vegetable and fruit juices produced by the JuiceMaxx 3000. He learned that once you start using Maka Helehelena face creame, made with Hawaiian-grown macadamia nuts, you can say 'Aloha!' to those creases and wrinkles around your eyes. And he learned that for all your weeding, hoeing, mulching, aerating, tilling, and cultivating needs, the GardenMaster X-treme six-in-one gardening implement is the tool for you. Finally, he learned that the best swords in the world are made by Peter Johnsson, and although the collection of swords being sold by the Interactive Home Shopping channel were not made by Peter Johnsson, they were nevertheless excellent swords, their maker having studied Peter Johnsson's techniques. The collection of swords featured a pair of samurai swords – one short, one long; Excalibur, the sword of Arthur; Anduril, the sword of Aragorn; a Roman gladiator's short sword; a Spanish conquistador's sword; a Civil War saber; and a claymore of the type used by William 'Braveheart' Wallace. Two folding knives and a Bowie knife were also included. All 'battle ready'. All for $394.

The whiskey having lowered his inhibitions, and because there were only twenty of these one-of-a-kind sword collections remaining, Ferguson called the Interactive Home Shopping toll-free number and bought one. Worried that he might next call and order a JuiceMaxx 3000, he changed the channel, and refilled his glass.

Three clicks of the remote later, Ferguson found the Rev. Joe L. Houston setting forth for his congregation God's principles of prosperity and fulfillment. To help his flock remember these principles, Pastor Houston had condensed them into six easy steps and had created an acronym as a mnemonic devise. To increase one's wealth and happiness one need only remember the word SPIRIT, which stands for:

Set your sights high
Prepare to succeed
Invest in yourself
Remember your goals
Invest in those who can help you succeed
Tell yourself 'you can do it'.

Ferguson watched for a while, assuming that Rev. Joe would pretty soon clarify how these six steps fit in with the things Jesus had to say in the sixth chapter of Matthew, verses 19–34. But this explanation was not forthcoming. Neither was Jesus ever actually mentioned in the sermon.

It was 2:30. He slumped back into the pillows. He flipped all the way through the channels nine times before deciding to give the Xtaseez channel a try. The on-screen menu presented him with several films from which to choose, including *The Girls from Ipanema*, *Girls Just Want to Have*

Fun, and *My Guard Stood Hard*. Ferguson chose *Cardinal Sins*, set in France in the time of King Louis XIII. The promotional description of the film promised a farcical and ribald romp telling the tale of a scullery maid who had attracted the attention of the powerful Cardinal Richelieu.

The story reached its climax about ten minutes into the movie, but it failed to stiffen Ferguson's resolve to come to grips with his restlessness.

He filled his glass then emptied it. By 3:30 he had passed out.

Ferguson was awakened at 10:30 by the sounds of a family with several loud young children hauling their luggage down the hotel hallway. His flight to Kansas City had left two hours and ten minutes prior.

He sighed heavily, showered, packed, and went down to get a cab to the airport.

At the American ticket counter, he arranged to fly stand-by on the 2:24, leaving out of Gate H. At the gate, he bought a newspaper, a tall Starbucks, and settled in to wait.

Across the concourse, a man dressed in a black wool suit and a black turtleneck sweater was composing music in a notebook, his head of bushy white hair bent intently over the pages. Seated three seats down, a mother breastfed her infant while her toddler son played on the floor with a Teenage Mutant Ninja Turtle action figure. Behind him a woman was talking to her mother on a cell phone.

'Yes, Mother. I'll take care of it when I get back this evening,' she said. 'The printer said they'll be ready in the morning.'

There was something distantly familiar in the tone and timbre of her voice. Ferguson turned to look.

She was a small black woman in her mid-forties. She

wore heavy, oversized sunglasses with dark lenses, a long tan-colored suede coat and black, knee-high, leather boots.

'No, it went well,' she said. 'I think they'll sign. We offered them a good package. The band's happy, the label's happy. I'm happy. Happy. Happy. Happy.'

She laughed. 'Okay, Mom. They're boarding now. I gotta go. I'll see you soon.'

There was a pause, during which the woman smiled knowingly. 'Yes, Mom. I am your little bird.'

She put her phone in her purse. Stood and straightened her coat, hoisted her carry-on over her shoulder and made her way tentatively to her gate. She held her left hand out from her side just a few inches, as if guarding against the possibility of bumping into something unseen. At the gate, she pulled her ticket from her purse, gave it to the attendant and boarded a flight to Memphis.

26

Homily

When the Rev. Julius E. Johnson left his position as senior pastor of the New Jerusalem Baptist Church to accept a call to serve as senior pastor of a church in Dearborn, Michigan, he left his former flock without a shepherd for nearly a year. While the search committee regularly reported its progress to meetings of the board of deacons, a parade of mostly mediocre pulpit fillers led the congregation in worship for forty-three straight Sundays, and LaVerne had had enough of it.

One Sunday, the guest speaker was the Rev. Deborah Middlebrook, who labored for forty minutes on the topic of 'Women Heroes of the Old Testament', focusing mainly on Rahab and Jael. Rev. Middlebrook's delivery was more scholarly than dynamic, and LaVerne left church complaining.

'I never even *heard* of Rahab and Jael,' he whined to Angela, as they got in the car.

'Well, now you have,' smiled Angela. 'It was educational.'

'If I wanted education, I'd go to college.' LaVerne said. 'Church isn't supposed to be school. It's supposed to inspire people.'

Angela laughed. 'I find the lives of Rahab and Jael very

inspiring. I think you just don't like seeing a woman in the pulpit. I think you have a problem with women in authority.'

'Well, *you* should know better than that,' LaVerne said. 'You're the authority in *our* house, and I don't have a problem with you. Unless you start spoutin' off about Rahab and Jael.'

LaVerne flicked on the car radio. 'Where do you want to eat?'

Angela had anticipated this question.

'I thought we might go to the Ethnic and Regional Folk Festival over at Shawnee Mission Park. They're going to have lots of different kinds of food, and dance, and arts and crafts. It'll be fun.'

'You want to go to the what, where?' LaVerne asked.

'The Ethnic and Regional Folk Festival at Shawnee Mission Park,' Angela said.

'Shawnee Mission Park?' asked LaVerne. 'That's over in Johnson County, isn't it?'

Angela nodded. 'Mm-hmm.'

LaVerne snorted. 'Last time I checked there was no *ethnic* in *that* regional.'

Angela's patience with her husband's grumpiness was wearing thin.

'Do you want to go or not?' she asked. 'If not, let's just go home. We can have tuna fish sandwiches or something.'

This was sufficient incentive for LaVerne. He decided that since he'd already spent the morning learning about Rahab and Jael, he may as well devote the entire day to furthering his education.

'Fine,' he said. 'But I'm not eatin' any weird shit like sushi or octopus. I'm tellin' you that right now.'

They listened to the radio. After awhile Angela spoke up.

'A.B. wasn't in church this morning. That's not like him.'

'Yeah, I noticed that,' LaVerne said. 'Maybe he was out

with Mother and Pug and the band last night. He probably just slept in.'

'I hope he's all right,' Angela said.

'I'm sure your boy's just fine, *Mom*,' LaVerne said.

Then, because they were both thinking about Raymond, they were quiet until they got to the park.

It was immediately apparent from the aroma in the park that many of the ethnicities and regions represented at the festival used large amounts of garlic and onion in their cooking, elevating LaVerne's optimism regarding his lunch prospects. This improved his mood, though the sounds of finger cymbals and sitar coming from the India tent made him uneasy, likewise the pennywhistle and fiddle from the Ireland booth.

He and Angela started up and down the rows of exhibits. Angela made them stop and look at all the craft items on display, which as far as LaVerne was concerned, was an unproductive use of time, since he had no intention of buying any such craft items nor of discussing them at length with their creators, which is what Angela apparently wished to do.

LaVerne was therefore relieved when he saw, down the way a bit, a sign announcing the availability of handcrafted Old World sausages. Though LaVerne serves sausage at the restaurant, his taste for it is never quite satisfied.

When he and Angela arrived at the booth, LaVerne immediately recognized cousins Joe and Jack Krizman, of the venerable Krizman sausage enterprise. The Krizman family arrived in America from Croatian Yugoslavia in the early thirties, and has been making sausage at the same location in the old Strawberry Hill neighborhood for almost seventy years. For the last twenty-three of those, it has been Smoke Meat's sole sausage supplier.

Joe and Jack greeted LaVerne with friendly handshakes, and LaVerne bought bratwursts for himself and Angela.

LaVerne piled his high with grilled onions and sauerkraut. Angela applied a dainty dab of mustard to hers. The three men exchanged enquiries about their respective businesses while Angela wandered off to inspect handwoven wool blankets at the Peru tent.

Halfway down the next row Angela and LaVerne saw a sign advertising, 'The West Kentucky Barbecue Experience! Taste it for yourself!'

'Let's go check it out,' chirped Angela. 'Your brothers in smoke.'

LaVerne shook his head and frowned. 'We went through West Kentucky when I was in the minors, and I had some of their so-called barbecue. It's mutton, mainly. Sheep. Maybe it's the Texas in me, but that's not what I call barbecue. Tastes like roadkill or something, as far as I'm concerned.'

He made a face.

'Have you actually eaten roadkill, LaVerne?' Angela asked as she examined a silver and turquoise necklace at the Navaho exhibit.

LaVerne admitted that, no, he hadn't.

The West Kentucky Barbecue Experience! booth was staffed by a heavyset man with longish white hair and a white Kenny Rogers-style beard. He wore jeans and a white T-shirt with a Jim Beam Black Label logo on it. As LaVerne and Angela approached he greeted them with a big smile.

'Y'all like barbecue?'

Angela gave LaVerne's arm a firm mind-your-manners squeeze.

'A little bit,' said LaVerne. 'We own a barbecue place downtown.'

'Do you now?' the man asked cheerfully. 'Well, then try some of this good Kentucky barbecue and tell me how it compares.'

LaVerne waved him off. 'I just had something to eat, thanks,' he said. 'I couldn't handle much more.'

The man persisted. 'Well, how about a little sample of our burgoo? It's like a stew. We serve it alongside our barbecue in Kentucky. It's an old tradition.'

LaVerne agreed, primarily as a means of abbreviating any further interactions with the friendly Kentuckian, but also because the aroma of onions and garlic was still beckoning. He was handed a small Styrofoam bowl filled with a thick meat-and-vegetable soup, and he took a big spoonful.

'This is really good,' he said, his mouth full. '*Really* good. What'd you call it?'

'It's called *burgoo*. It goes back two hundred years.' The jovial Kentuckian grinned and handed a bowl to Angela who thanked him and tried some of the stew.

'Oh, my,' she said. 'This *is* wonderful.'

'I knew you'd like it,' he said. He extended his hand, first to Angela and then to LaVerne. 'Merle's my name. Merle Jackson. You sure you won't try some barbecue?'

LaVerne shook his head.

'I don't care much for sheep,' he said. 'I'm from Texas and down there barbecue is beef. And that's all. When I got here to Kansas City, I compromised some and allowed that ribs and pork butt also make pretty good barbecue. But I can't really accommodate mutton. It's not barbecue to me. No offense. It's just my own taste.'

Merle Jackson thought about this a moment, then smiled wider.

'No offense taken, my friend,' he said. 'None at all. Truth is that as much as we like mutton where we live, it's not real popular anywhere else. But, the spirit of it's the same, isn't it? You make do with what you got. That's what barbecue's all about, right? Whether you're in Texas, or Kentucky, or Memphis, or Kansas City.'

LaVerne nodded slightly. These were things he himself had thought from time to time. Merle continued.

'Mutton ain't leg o' lamb or lamb chops, that's for sure. But brisket ain't no filet mignon, is it? And an ol' pork butt ain't no ham. The one thing all barbecue has in common, no matter where you're from, is that it all starts out with a tough ol' cut of meat that isn't much good for anything else and by cooking it a real long time over a nice little fire, you end up with the best food there is. You take what the fancy people don't want and turn it into something the fancy people will pay a lot of money for.'

LaVerne smiled. 'Mr Jackson, I may not like mutton, but I like the way you think. It's been nice meeting you. And I've got to say, you make good soup.'

He shoveled another spoonful into his mouth.

Merle chuckled.

'You know how we make burgoo, don't you?' he asked, slyly. 'In addition to all them good veggies and chicken and such? Squirrel brains. That's the secret ingredient.'

Angela's eyes widened in horror and LaVerne choked. Both quickly deposited the contents of their mouths into their little Styrofoam bowls.

'Just kiddin',' Merle cackled. 'They used to use squirrel brains back in the old days. Especially up in the hills. But after folks kept dyin' of mad squirrel disease, they quit it. Seriously, I was just funnin' ya.'

LaVerne and Angela said goodbye and, when they were safely out of sight of the West Kentucky Barbecue Experience!, disposed of their burgoo in a trash barrel.

On their way back to the car LaVerne bought a funnel cake and split it with Angela. A blues band was playing on a stage behind the craft booths, so they meandered over to check it out. It was Mother's back-up band – Seth Cropper, Jake Green, and Jen Richards – and a substitute lead guitarist filling in for Pug. He had tattoos on the backs of his hands and a long goatee that was braided like a pigtail. Angela and LaVerne listened while they finished their funnel cake, and after the set, they went up and said hello.

'Where's A.B.?' asked Angela. 'Doesn't he pretty much go wherever you guys go?'

Jen spoke up. 'I have no idea where he is. He was going to help us with equipment, but never showed. I called his apartment and nobody answered. I even called the restaurant. There was nobody there either. So your guess is as good as mine.'

Angela scowled. 'That doesn't seem like A.B., does it?'

LaVerne snorted. 'That mother of his probably called and wanted him to come over and turn the channels on her TV or get her a beer from the refrigerator. She's about the most helpless individual I ever heard of.'

When LaVerne arrived at the restaurant the next morning Leon was turning ribs in the smoker.

'A.B. in yet?' LaVerne asked.

Leon nodded. 'He's out front takin' chairs down.'

LaVerne went out to the dining room. A.B. was there. He glanced up when LaVerne came in, but didn't say anything.

LaVerne felt that A.B. didn't look right. 'Missed you in church yesterday morning, son.'

A.B. nodded. He took another chair down from atop a table, put it on the floor and sat in it. He stared past LaVerne into the kitchen.

'My mom died last night,' he said. 'She had a stroke. She called me in the morning and said she had a headache and would I come over and bring some aspirin because she had run out. And when I got there she was passed out on the kitchen floor. I called 911 and they brought her up to Truman Hospital and she died there a couple hours later.'

LaVerne took a chair down and sat next to A.B.

'I am so sorry, A.B.'

A.B. looked at LaVerne. His eyes were red. He hadn't shaved.

'My mom didn't go to church, boss. And I need to make plans for some kind of funeral, I guess. Or to bury her somewhere. But I don't know where. I don't know how you find out about that kind of thing. She – her body – is still at the hospital, but they told me I have to have somebody, a funeral home or somebody come get her. Plus, since Pastor Johnson left, there's not even a minister to say anything at a funeral. Plus my mom said we were Catholics, expect now I'm a Baptist, so I don't know if that matters or not. So, anyways, do you think Reverend Glen would do that? You know, say something?'

LaVerne put his hand on A.B.'s shoulder. 'We'll figure it out, boy.'

While A.B., Leon, and Vicki started the day's cooking and prep, LaVerne called Angela and told her what had happened. About an hour later, she and Ferguson showed up at the restaurant.

Angela hugged him. Usually A.B. responds with awkward hesitancy to Angela's hugs. But this time he returned the embrace. She patted his back. A.B. pulled away and rubbed his nose on his sleeve.

'Mrs Williams, I was telling the boss that I'm in a real bind. I don't know who should take care of my mom's body and how to do a funeral. This kind of thing has never happened to me before. Is there somebody I should call? And what about a grave? I don't know about any of that stuff.'

He looked at Ferguson.

'We know about that stuff, A.B.,' Ferguson said. 'Why don't you let us take care it?'

'Don't you worry about any of this, child,' Angela said.

'We'll take care of it all. Everything. We'll take care of the hospital, and the arrangements, and the funeral, and everything. So, go home and sleep. We'll call you if we have any questions. Just leave it to us.'

A.B. took off his apron, hung it on a hook in the office, and drove himself home.

Two days later, on a cool, cloudless afternoon, a small caravan of vehicles, led by a black hearse, arrived at a modest suburban cemetery set back from the road on a gentle slope. The hearse was followed by two black limousines, and a middle-aged white Cadillac with gold-spoked wheels. The hearse stopped at a prepared grave site. The earth excavated from the grave was covered with a large sheet of green felt. Fitted atop the grave itself was a casket-lowering device skirted with green velvet.

A professionally somber funeral director in a black suit stepped out of the hearse and opened its rearmost doors. His two identically attired colleagues emerged from each of the limousines and opened the passenger doors of their respective automobiles.

Bob Dunleavy, Del James, Pug Hale, Leon Noel, Brother Ignatius, and LaVerne Williams exited the first limo and walked up to the rear of the hearse. Bob, Del, and Pug stood on one side, Leon, Iggy, and LaVerne on the other. LaVerne, Pug, Del, and Bob all wore charcoal gray or navy blue suits, and all wore ties except Del. Leon had on black pants, a white shirt and a skinny black tie, but no jacket. Iggy wore a plain brown sweater and brown pants.

Angela Williams, Father Ferguson Glen, and Al Buddy Clayton got out of the second limousine. Angela wore a simple black dress with long sleeves. A.B. wore a black suit and tie. Ferguson wore white vestments with gold trim. They walked up to the gravesite, where Ferguson took a position at the head of the grave.

The Cadillac was Mother Mary Weaver's car, but Jen Richards was driving. Vicki Fuentes was riding in the front passenger seat and Mother was in the back. Jen and Vicki got out and Jen opened the trunk and removed a wheelchair, which she unfolded and wheeled to Mother's door. She and Vicki helped Mother into the chair and, together, labored to push her up to where the others were standing. Mother wore a black dress and a big wide-brimmed black straw hat. Vicki wore black slacks and a denim jacket over a pink blouse. Jen wore a plain navy blue dress. Her hair was pulled up in a tight bun.

The funeral director nodded at LaVerne and he and the other men leaned into the hearse and slowly pulled the casket bearing A.B.'s mother's body out of the hearse. They carried the casket to the grave and carefully placed it down on top of the lowering device. Then they stepped back from the grave and went to stand with A.B., Angela, and the others.

Then a rusted metallic blue Toyota Cressida without a rear bumper rumbled up the drive and stopped behind Mother's Cadillac. A short, bony man with thick glasses, and slicked-down gray hair, got out of the driver's side. He wore pressed, creased blue jeans and a baggy, red sweater pulled over a pronounced beer belly. From the passenger side came a chubby woman with stiff white-yellow hair. She wore sunglasses, a lime-green pants suit, and a black baseball-style jacket.

They walked up to the grave. The woman linked her arm through the man's arm. They looked at A.B. and smiled and nodded. A.B. didn't recognize either of them. He looked away, and noticed that the headstones of the nearby graves were engraved with the name Dunleavy. He looked over at Bob, who winked at him.

Ferguson raised his arms as if to embrace those gathered, and spoke sacred words.

> *'I am the resurrection and the life, saith the Lord,*
> *He that believeth in me, though he were dead, yet shall*
>   *he live,*
> *And whosoever liveth and believeth in me shall never*
>   *die.*
> *I know that my Redeemer liveth,*
> *And that he shall stand at the latter day upon the earth,*
> *And though this body be destroyed, yet shall I see God,*
> *Whom I shall see for myself and mine eyes shall*
>   *behold,*
> *And not as a stranger.*
> *For none of us liveth to himself,*
> *And no man dieth to himself.*
> *For if we live, we live unto the Lord*
> *And if we die, we die unto the Lord.*
> *Whether we live, therefore, or die, we are the Lord's.*
> *Blessed are the dead who die in the Lord,*
> *Even so saith the Spirit, for they rest from their labors.'*

Ferguson looked up from his prayer book. 'The Lord be with you.'

Only Angela and Brother Ignatius responded. 'And with thy spirit.'

'Let us pray,' said Ferguson.

'O God, *whose mercies cannot be numbered: Accept our prayers on behalf of thy servant, and grant her an entrance into the land of light and joy, in the fellowship of thy saints; through Jesus Christ thy Son our Lord, who liveth and reigneth with thee and the Holy Spirit, one God, now and for ever. Amen.'*

Ferguson and Iggy crossed themselves. Ferguson continued.

> 'Like as the hart desireth the water-brooks
> So longeth my soul after thee, O God.
> My soul is athirst for God,
> Yea, even for the living God.
> When shall I come to appear before the presence
>   of God?
> My tears have been my meat day and night,
> While they daily say unto me,
> Where is now thy God?
> Now when I think thereupon, I pour out my heart
>   by myself,
> For I went with the multitude, and brought them
>   forth into the house of God,
> Why art thou so full of heaviness, O my soul?
> And why art thou so disquieted within me?
> O put thy trust in God; for I will yet thank him,
> Which is the help of my countenance, and my God.'

Ferguson paused and closed his prayer book. He looked at A.B. and smiled. Then he looked at each of the others standing around the grave. He took a deep breath.

'We live our lives as strangers to one another, even to those we love most and know best.

'We are here on this hillside, on this clear blue afternoon, to lay to rest Mona Bennett. It is sad that she is dead. Sadder still, that my friend A.B. has lost his mother.

'It is also sad, that among those of us gathered here at Mona's grave, few knew her at all.

'I *say* that A.B. is my friend, because I have known him for three years, during which time I calculate I have eaten at least four hundred meals prepared by his hands at the restaurant where he works. I have spent countless hours in his company. And yet until he needed me this week to officiate at this service, I knew nothing at all about his mother. Not even her name. And that is beyond sad. That is *shameful*. What kind of friend does not know something so fundamental about another friend as his mother's name?

'Perhaps I did not want to know her name. When you learn somebody's name they are no longer simply an idea – an abstract concept. When you know someone's name they become a person, with a story. A person, like yourself.

'If I had known Mona's name I might have felt obliged to enquire as to her well-being in my casual conversations with A.B., and then our conversations might have become something more than casual. They might have become intimate. And we might have become even better friends. And better friends bear greater responsibility to one another than do casual friends. If I had known Mona's name, I may have felt obliged to do something if A.B. had said to me, "My mother isn't feeling well," or, "My mother needs someone to help her." True intimacy *requires* something of us. And I may have felt the need to help. Or, more likely, I would have felt guilty when I *did not* help. Perhaps I wish only to be friendly, without being friends.

'Because I never asked, I don't know Mona Bennett's story. But, in truth, none of us do. Not even you, A.B. You know some of it, of course. You are her son, after all. But you were only one part of her life. And just as your life consists of more than being your mother's son, your mother's life consisted of more than being your mother. She lived things you didn't live. She knew people you do not know. She feared things that you have not feared and dreamed dreams that were not your dreams. And though you were her only child, you knew only some things about her. But God knows them all. God knows *all* of Mona Bennett's story. He knows her, and he has called her by her name.

'Our stories and our names are our most intimate possessions. Our names are the words we use, whether we like it or not, to identify ourselves, both to others and ourselves. Your name is the title of your story.

'A friend of mine once wrote, "When someone knows your name they have a kind of hold on you. When they call you by your name, even from afar, you turn to see who it is that is calling you."

'God has that kind of hold on us.

'A.B. was talking to Angela about his mother this week, and he asked her if she thought that his mother was in heaven now. The answer to that question is found in what God tells about love and judgment.

'Love is hard. We *try* to love one another. But generally the quality and quantity of our love for one another is found wanting, because we find it difficult, if not impossible, to look beyond those things that are ugly and unlovable in those we try to love. Even though the things that are ugly and unlovable in ourselves are the very things that cause us to cry out for love.

'In talking with A.B. about his mother this week, it became clear to me that she was not a perfect mother. But then A.B. was not a perfect son. A.B. would be the first to admit it. None of us are perfect. Thank God, perfection is not a condition of Christ's love for us. Christ knows we are not perfect. Yet he loves us still. He loves us in our totality. He knows who we are. *He knows our names*. And he loves us. Better than we've ever been loved or ever will be. He remembers what we almost always forget, or never knew to begin with, that we are, all of us, more than the equation – the sum of our successes minus the sum of our failures.

'Because we cannot fathom the depths of such love, we live in fear of judgment. When once I was despairing that God's judgment of me would be fair and, therefore, in my case, harsh, a friend of mine reminded me that it is Christ who will judge us. He said, "The one who will judge us most finally is the one who most loves us most fully."

'So, A.B., is your mother in heaven? This is what I know: Christ loves your mother, A.B. He knows her and that is why he loves her. He loved her enough to die for her.

'I know that your mother was baptized, A.B., marked as one of God's own. And when the sheep are sorted he will recognize her as belonging to him.

'I know that Jesus tells us that he is the good shepherd. Jesus says, "I know my sheep. And my sheep know me. My sheep hear my voice. I know them, and they follow me."

'This week Jesus called Mona Bennett by her name. She knew his voice. And she followed him.

'My friends, let us be reminded that Jesus is our model of love and friendship. Let us not live our lives as strangers to one another. Let us love one another as Christ loves us.'

Ferguson glanced over at Mother and nodded slightly. Mother closed her eyes as if to pray and began to sing.

'*Sometimes I feel like a motherless child*
Sometimes I feel like a motherless child
Sometimes I feel like a motherless child
A long way from home, a long way from home.

Sometimes I feel like I'm almost gone
Sometimes I feel like I'm almost gone
Sometimes I feel like I'm almost gone
A long way from home, a long way from home.

Sometimes I feel like a mournin' dove
Sometimes I feel like a mournin' dove
Sometimes I feel like a mournin' dove
A long way from home, a long way from home.

Sometimes I feel like a motherless child
Sometimes I feel like a motherless child
Sometimes I feel like a motherless child
A long way from home, a long way from home.'

Angela, Jen, and Bob were crying, as were the woman and the man who arrived late. The others were all quiet. Except for Del, who leaned over to Bob and in a whisper loud enough to be heard by occupants of nearby graves, asked, 'Isn't that song in poor taste? I mean, the kid just lost his mother, for Christ's sake.'

Bob shot Del a look that shut him up.

The Rev. Ferguson Glen held in his right hand a length of brass chain from which was suspended a small, ornately cut brass globe – a censer. This he swung over Mona Bennett's casket as he walked around the perimeter of her grave. The fragrance and the thin blue smoke of incense was carried out over her casket and then over and around A.B. Clayton and the others.

Ferguson nodded at the funeral director who had been standing off to one side during the service. He stepped forward and with one of his colleagues began lowering the casket, by working a crank mechanism on the lowering device. A.B. made a small sound with his breath. When the casket had been lowered all the way into the grave, Ferguson raised his hands toward the sky and then spread them out over the grave.

'*O God, whose blessed Son was laid in a sepulcher in the garden: Bless, we pray, this grave, and grant that she whose body is buried here may dwell with Christ in paradise, and may come to thy heavenly kingdom; through thy Son Jesus Christ our Lord. Amen.'*

Ferguson then asked that the group join him in the Lord's Prayer, which they did, Del much louder than the others –

saying 'our debtors' when the others said 'those who trespass against us'.

Ferguson then bent and scooped a handful of earth from the pile mounded up by the grave. He let the dirt fall from his hand into the grave and onto the casket. He looked at A.B. who looked confused and a bit frightened. Angela took A.B.'s elbow and led him to Ferguson's side. A.B. then stooped and picked up a handful of dirt. He looked into the hole for a moment and then let the dirt drop onto the casket. A big sob welled up and out of him.

The others then followed. Each of them taking up earth with their hands and letting it fall into the grave. When they were done, Ferguson said, *'Rest eternal grant to her, O Lord.'*

Angela and Iggy responded, *'And let light perpetual shine upon her.'*

Ferguson continued, *'May her soul, and the souls of all the departed, through the mercy of God, rest in peace.'*

Angela and Iggy responded again with, *'Amen.'*

Ferguson then made the sign of the cross and delivered the final blessing.

'The God of peace, who brought again from the dead our Lord Jesus Christ, the great Shepherd of the sheep, through the blood of the eternal covenant: Make you perfect in every good work to do his will, working in you that which is well-pleasing in his sight; through Jesus Christ, to whom be glory for ever and ever. Amen.'

Ferguson glanced at Angela who bent and whispered something to Mother, who cleared her throat and sang:

'Why should I feel discouraged, why should the shadows come,
Why should my heart be lonely, and long for heaven and home,

When Jesus is my portion? My constant friend is he:
His eye is on the sparrow, and I know he watches me.

I sing because I'm happy,
I sing because I'm free,
For his eye is on the sparrow,
And I know he watches me.

"Let not your heart be troubled," his tender word
    I hear,
And resting on his goodness, I lose my doubts and
    fears;
Though by the path he leadeth, but one step I may see;
His eye is on the sparrow, and I know he watches me.

Whenever I am tempted, whenever clouds arise,
When songs give place to sighing, when hope within
    me dies,
I draw the closer to him, from care he sets me free;
His eye is on the sparrow, and I know he watches me.'

Angela hugged A.B. and so did Del, Bob, Vicki, and Jen. Mother reached up from her wheelchair and embraced him. Pug and Leon shook hands with him. LaVerne stood behind him with his hands on his shoulders.

The woman and the man who had come late approached tentatively. The woman extended her hand to A.B.

'You must be A.B.,' she said. 'I'm Lurleen Haysmith. Me and your mom was good friends. I am so sorry for your loss. I'm going to miss your mother. I'm really going to miss her. We was real close friends.'

The man stepped forward to shake hands with A.B.

'I'm Rudy Turpin,' he said. 'Maybe your mom told you about me. We been together for a while.'

His face seized up and his voice failed him. 'Anyways. Your mom and I were together. I loved your mom and I can't believe she's gone. I don't really know what I'm going to do now. I'm sorry for your loss.'

LaVerne had taken Leon, Vicki, and Jen aside and was talking to them. 'Why don't you all go back to the restaurant. Leon and Vicki, heat up some ribs, chuck, and pork, and greens and potatoes if there are any. We'll meet you there. Jen, thanks for driving.'

Leon, Vicki, and Jen pushed Mother back down to her Cadillac, put her in the car, and left for Smoke Meat.

LaVerne turned to the others, 'We'd like to invite everyone over to the restaurant for some food and fellowship. Lurleen and Rudy, will you join us?'

Lurleen and Rudy looked first at one another and then at LaVerne and said they'd be happy to come.

Leon and Vicki brought out three platters piled with pulled chuck, pulled pork, ribs chopped into two-bone pieces, and slices of white bread.

Leon informed LaVerne that there had been no greens or potatoes left in the walk-in, so LaVerne told him to make some coffee and bring out some vinegar pie, sweet potato pie, and peach cobbler.

They sat at a cluster of tables by the doorway to the kitchen; LaVerne, Angela, Bob, Del, Pug, Mother, Brother Ignatius, Jen, Rudy, Lurleen, and Ferguson, who had removed his vestments and was now in a black suit, with a black shirt and clerical collar. A.B. kept one eye on Leon's and Vicki's activities, but LaVerne and Angela told him not to worry about it, so he tried not to.

Angela spoke up first. 'Thank you all so much for coming. And thank you, Ferguson.'

A.B. looked at the floor and nodded. 'Thank you all for coming. And thank you, Rev. Glen.'

Del looked at Bob. 'What'd he say?' he brayed.

'He thanked us for coming,' Bob barked back.

'That was nice of him,' Del said, only slightly less loudly.

Rudy glanced around the dining room, then looked at A.B.

'This is a real nice place you got here, A.B. Your mom said you like makin' barbecue. I bet you're real proud.'

A.B. looked anxiously at LaVerne. LaVerne smiled. Angela spoke again.

'A.B., Lurleen, Rudy, if there are memories of Mona you'd like to share you're welcome to do that.'

Rudy's eyes widened and filled. He shook his head.

Lurleen stared at a handkerchief she twisted in her hands.

'Well, Mona, her and me worked next to another on the line-up at the Fairfax plant, for about ten years. And we was real good friends. We ate lunch together and we was always laughin'. We always teased her and called her Mona Lisa, even though her middle name wasn't Lisa. We teased her that way anyways. Even after she hurt her back and went on her disability we stayed friends. Lately me and my husband Vince, and her and Rudy here, we went up to the boats and played the quarter slots or blackjack, and we'd have us a real good time. She was a kick, Mona was. We always laughed a lot. We called her Mona Lisa. That's about all.'

She paused and took a breath. 'I'll miss her.'

A.B. had looked up from the floor and was watching Lurleen talk as if he were trying to understand someone speaking in a foreign language. He didn't say anything. Nobody else said anything.

LaVerne stood. 'I think we've had enough prayin' for one day, so let's just assume that God has blessed this food and go ahead and eat.'

They ate barbecue and pie and drank coffee. Soon they began chatting about the weather, and then about the Chiefs, and then about the differences between West Kentucky, Memphis, Texas, and Kansas City barbecue. After the pie, LaVerne went back into the office and returned with an unopened bottle of Wild Turkey. Vicki went to the kitchen and got glasses. LaVerne poured, and everybody had a drink, except Bob, who had another cup of coffee.

It was quiet while they sipped their whiskey, then Jen starting singing.

'Mona Lisa, Mona Lisa, men have named you
You're so like the lady with the mystic smile.'

Mother and Angela joined in, and then Lurleen.

'Is it only 'cause you're lonely they have blamed you?
For that Mona Lisa strangeness in your smile?'

The rest then joined the song, except Del, Leon, and A.B.

'Do you smile to tempt a lover, Mona Lisa?
Or is this your way to hide a broken heart?
Many dreams have been brought to your doorstep
They just lie there and they die there
Are you warm, are you real, Mona Lisa?
Or just a cold and lonely lovely work of art?'

A.B. put his face in his hands and cried. Rudy looked as if he might crumble. LaVerne put his hand on A.B.'s head.

After the singing, Del bolted up and blared, 'Well, I gotta go.'

Bob stood up, too. And then the others. They each thanked LaVerne and Angela for the food and shook hands with A.B. or hugged him. When Rudy came up to A.B. he paused and then spoke in a shaky voice.

'I know you and me have never met, but me and your mom, we was pretty serious. Like Lurleen there, we worked together. Down at GM. The Fairfax plant. I been there almost thirty years.

'Anyways, this is a real shock. We was even talkin' about getting' married. I ain't never been married an' I don't have kids. So I'd been kinda thinkin' it woulda been nice to have a stepson an' all. We could maybe have done things together. Not that I would be like a real father or anything. Anyways. Your mom always said you was a good kid. Maybe we could stay in touch. You and me. If you wanted to.'

A.B. shook Rudy's hand and tried to smile. 'It was nice to meet you, too, Rudy.'

Then Ferguson approached, his eyes wet.

A.B. wouldn't look at him. 'Thank you, Rev. Glen. For those things you said about my mom being in heaven and about her name.'

Ferguson embraced A.B. 'Maybe from now on you should call me Ferguson.'

LaVerne told Leon and Vicki they could go, and he and Angela started cleaning up. A.B. picked up some glasses to take them into the kitchen, but LaVerne told him to put them down. He stood lost in the middle of the restaurant.

Jen Richards, who had stayed behind to help when the others had left, took him by the elbow. 'How about I give you a ride home?'

'That was real nice,' he said, looking out the window of her car. 'Singing that song and all.'

'Thank you,' she said. 'I was glad I could be a part of this today.'

He fished around in the pocket of his suit jacket for a cigarette. He found one, put it between his lips and began looking for matches or a lighter. Finding neither, he sat back in the seat and breathed out a long breath and rubbed his eyes.

'You know, for a long time I only wished that my mother knew more about my life. Now I wish that I knew more about hers.'

They watched the road ahead, thinking about the day. Jen took a lighter out of the console and reached over and lit his cigarette.

27

Chumming

Behind the butcher shop, back where Delbert and Hartholz played checkers and sipped whiskey in the evening while the sausage and briskets smoked in the pit, there was an old wooden barrel that smelled like moonshine and pickles. It was a 30-gallon oak-stave barrel Hartholz used for making sauerkraut, until customer demand for the sauerkraut necessitated a move up to a 50-gallon barrel, at which point Delbert appropriated the smaller barrel for the purpose of fermenting grain for use in chumming for catfish.

Delbert learned chumming from his father, Delbert Douglass Merisier II, and when Delbert and Hartholz became friends, and started going fishing together, Delbert taught chumming to Hartholz, though Hartholz left the actual making of the chum to Delbert, which was fine with Delbert inasmuch as he had strong opinions regarding chum-making technique.

The recipe for the chum itself could not have been simpler. First Delbert dumped three pails of seed corn, two packages of dry yeast, and three bottles of beer into the barrel. This was then covered in water and stirred with a wooden paddle that Hartholz also once used in making sauerkraut. Delbert then tamped the lid down on top of the barrel and left it alone in the Texas heat for a few days, after which two more bottles of beer were added and the corn covered again with water. When the soured grain had been allowed to ferment for about another week, it was ready.

The other half of the chumming equation was the stink bait. Because Delbert's stink bait stunk so omnipresently, it could not be made nor kept on the butcher shop's premises, lest customers conclude that Hartholz was selling spoilt meat.

Spoilt meat was, in fact, the primary ingredient in Delbert's stink bait recipe, which he concocted in a 50-gallon drum that Rose brought home from Raylon Rice and Milling. Delbert buried the drum in his backyard, in a hole only as deep as the drum was tall, so that its top was roughly level with the ground. Into the drum Delbert deposited scraps of meat he brought home from the butcher shop, to which he added a quart or two of milk, a pint or so of vinegar, and a handful of apple peels. Delbert then put the lid on the drum, weighted it down with rocks, and let the meat mix rot until needed.

After LaVerne came to live with Rose, she insisted Delbert erect a chicken wire fence around his stink-bait pit, to prevent the boy from investigating and falling into the fetid hole.

Sometimes, early on Sunday mornings when it was still dark, Delbert would shovel some of the rancid meat out of the pit and into a big pail, then cover it all with a shovelful of clean dirt to mitigate the stench. This and several buckets of the fermented corn mash were then loaded in the back of Hartholz's 1937 Ford pickup, along with Delbert's old skiff, oars, cane poles, a tackle box, and a gunnysack in which Delbert put a block of cheese, some brisket sandwiches wrapped in waxed paper, a butcher knife wrapped in newspaper, a thermos of coffee, and a bottle of whiskey. The truck bed was then covered with an oiled-canvas tarp.

*

On the east bank of the San Jacinto, at a sharp bend just below the Cordy Branch, there was a still deep pool shaded by a venerable black willow, where Delbert and Hartholz liked to fish for channel cats. As was their practice, they arrived at their place in time to drink a cup of coffee while they watched the sun rise. Then, using an empty molasses can, Delbert scooped out some of the sour corn and flung it out onto the surface of the water. As the kernels sank slowly down, Delbert and Hartholz had another cup of coffee.

Delbert then threw another canful of corn out onto the water, and minutes later, small bubbles percolated up from the bottom. The scent of the chum had attracted the attention of catfish in the region. Down in the black, beyond sight, their sleek gray bodies slid slowly through the cool quiet depths, around sunken stumps and through mossy hollow logs, their wide flat mouths gaping open to take in the soured grain, their whiskers brushing up against the roots of the willow tree growing out of the riverbank into the water.

Hartholz took the cheese from the gunnysack and cut two chunks from the block and handed one to Delbert. Delbert pushed the dirt off the top of the stink bait, then he and Hartholz held their breath, reached into the pail, and took some of the rancid meat with their bare hands. Working quickly, they kneaded their handfuls of meat and cheese together into putrid, baseball-sized lumps. Carefully, they pushed their fishhooks into the bait and lowered them into the river, then rinsed their hands in the water.

Though he was eager to wash off the stench, Hartholz didn't like putting his hands in the river. 'Those catfishes might bite my hand off,' he said. 'They got lots of little teeths.'

It didn't take long for the catfish to begin nibbling on the bait.

'I must have gotten the stink exactly right on this batch.' Delbert laughed. 'These poor cats is actin' like they ain't eaten in a month. Maybe this time we'll catch us one of them blues.'

Delbert held out hope that someday he'd land one of the channel cats' bigger cousins – a blue catfish – some which were known to reach 100 pounds.

Within moments, Hartholz's cane pole was bent over, its tip pulled down hard, whipping back and forth. After several minutes of thrashing, the fish tired and Hartholz pulled it into the boat. After removing the hook, he carefully threaded a long rope stringer through the fish's bottom lip. Hartholz lifted the shiny gray fish up by the stringer.

'Feels like eleven pounds,' he said. 'Maybe eleven and a half.'

Delbert knew that if Hartholz said it weighed 11 pounds, it weighed no more than 11 pounds, 2 ounces, and no less than 10 pounds, 14 ounces. At the shop, he had seen his friend cut meat exactly to the weight specified by customers without using the scale until the cutting was completed and the meat wrapped.

'How *do* you *do* that, Mr Hartholz?' customers would ask, shaking their heads in wonder. To which Hartholz would shrug and smile. Though only Delbert would recognize it as a smile. Customers most likely thought he was suffering a bit of indigestion.

By ten o'clock, the men had caught nine fish – Delbert three, and Hartholz six. To deflect any potential gloating by Hartholz, Delbert reminded him every ten minutes or so that, while he may have only caught three fish, his biggest – at about 20 pounds – was almost twice as big as Hartholz's biggest. Delbert also accused Hartholz of underestimating the weight of his big fish so as to diminish the magnitude of his achievement.

Hungry and satisfied with their morning's work, they rowed to the near bank and tied the boat to the stump of a toppled old sycamore, their fish wallowing on the river bottom, strung together with ten feet of rope.

They stretched out on the grass and ate their sandwiches. Delbert took his harmonica from his shirt pocket and played Robert Johnson's 'Travelin' Riverside Blues', and then 'Ramblin' on My Mind'. Delbert always played these two songs while they ate lunch on their fishing outings. While Hartholz watched a great white egret hunting frogs on the far bank, Delbert fell asleep. Then Hartholz leaned back on the trunk of the black willow and he, too, fell asleep.

After their catnaps they got back in the skiff, pushed off, and let the boat drift back into the shade under the willow. There was never any urgency to their fishing, but often their excursions were lackadaisical to the point of somnolence. This was aided and abetted by the whiskey, the bottle of which Delbert retrieved from the gunnysack and took a slug from before passing it to Hartholz.

Most of the stink bait was gone at this point, and the catfish had either wised up or retreated to deeper, cooler pools. Delbert and Hartholz let their baited hooks sit on the river bottom, hoping maybe they'd get lucky. They shared the whiskey and talked idly about baseball, the price of beef, the new janitor down at the school, and Mrs Jenkins, the fair-skinned black woman who came in on Wednesdays to buy a roasting chicken and a pound of smoked brisket. Most folks guessed Mrs Jenkins was a widow. Nobody had ever heard anything about any Mr Jenkins, and Mrs Jenkins had never clarified the situation. She worked as a secretary at a lumber yard over in Cleveland, and gave piano lessons at her house. She was judged by both Delbert and Hartholz to be the prettiest woman in Plum Grove.

As sometimes happened, deer flies had begun to buzz

around them and bite, causing Hartholz to complain bitterly. 'It's your sweet disposition they're attracted to,' said Delbert. 'If you were just more of a sourpuss we wouldn't have this problem.' They pulled their lines in and began packing their gear in the gunnysack and the tackle box. That's when something jerked down on the right side of the boat causing the men to grasp the sides to keep their balance.

'That was some big deer fly that just landed,' laughed Delbert.

Hartholz didn't laugh. 'What do you think that was?' he asked, looking over into the water.

'Maybe my twenty-pounder is trying to get free,' shrugged Delbert, grinning.

The boat tipped suddenly hard to the right again, this time so far that water slipped in over the side. The boat began to move slowly out into the current as if it were being towed.

Hartholz went pale. He shouted, *'Delbert!'*

Delbert saw that the rope stringer was pulled taut and whatever it was that was dragging them had a hold of the rope.

'Something's on the stringer,' he said. 'You row us back to shore and I'll pull on the stringer.'

Hartholz thrust the oars into the water and pulled on them as hard as he could in the direction of the riverbank behind them. Delbert took the stringer rope in his hands and yanked it toward him.

'I think a big blue came by and tried to eat our little channel kitties,' grunted Delbert, straining to maintain his grip on the rope. 'He's a big 'un.'

Hartholz's face was flame red. He groaned against the oars, sweating heavily. The men struggled in silence for fifteen minutes to reach the shore, a distance that would normally have been achieved in seconds. When he finally guided the boat to within a few yards of the shore, Hartholz jumped into the water and tried to drag the boat up onto the bank. Delbert leapt out of the boat to help. Hartholz slumped to the grass when they successfully grounded the skiff, but Delbert wasn't done. He went to the front of the boat and continued to pull on the stringer.

'If this is a blue on the end of this rope, I'm not lettin' it go without a fight,' he insisted.

Hartholz cursed and got to his feet. He came up behind Delbert and seized him around the waist. Together they heaved themselves backward, and fell over on top of each other. Hartholz managed to get back on his feet quickly, but Delbert slipped as he tried to stand and he slid back down the bank toward the water. Something moved in the water and Hartholz yelled, 'Watch out!', grabbing Delbert's hand and yanking him to one side. Delbert turned around in time to see the massive, monstrous, green-gray face of a giant alligator snapping turtle lunging at him. The stringer rope extended out of its gaping mouth like a tongue. The glistening, pink, bony remains of a catfish draped over its bottom jaw. Three other fish flopped around on the grass, their bottom lips still threaded through with the stringer. The turtle made a low, huffing noise in the back of its throat, shot its head forward and snapped the head off the nearest fish. Delbert yelped, and jumped into the grounded boat. Hartholz followed.

The turtle was covered in dark green algae. Its shell was as big around as a truck tire, and along its back were three ridges of sharp peaks, each six to eight inches high. Its head was as thick as a telephone pole and around the thing's bullish neck were rows of stubby spikes. Its face was fierce and rhinoceroian.

'*Stegosaurus!*' Hartholz shouted. '*It is a dinosaur!*'

'That, my friend, is not far from the truth,' said Delbert,

keeping a wary eye on the beast, which was retching and hacking, trying to disgorge the rope. 'What we're lookin' at is the biggest damn Texas alligator snapping turtle I have ever seen.'

'What are we going to do?' asked Hartholz anxiously.

Delbert picked up one of the oars. '*This* is what we're going to do,' he said.

He stepped out of the boat and walked quietly and gingerly up behind the turtle which was not at all fooled by Delbert's attempt at stealth. It turned and pushed itself up as high as it could on its four squat legs. Its tail was at least eighteen inches long, maybe ten inches wide at its base, and pointed at the tip. Without hesitation, Delbert raised the oar above his head and swung it down hard on the turtle's head. And then he did it again. And then again, breaking the oar clean in two. The turtle's head lay still and bleeding on the grass.

Hartholz shuddered and looked like he might throw up.

'Let's get out of here,' he said.

Delbert nodded. 'Good idea. Let's get this thing in the back of the truck.'

Hartholz was horrified at Delbert's suggestion.

'*What?*' he exclaimed in near panic. 'It's not *dead!* What do we want with a dinosaur turtle, anyway?'

'We're going to eat it,' Delbert announced.

Delbert was the only person in the world that Hartholz trusted, but the idea of eating this grotesque brute tested his confidence in his friend's judgment. Delbert knew what Hartholz was thinking. He smiled.

'You'll see. Let's put it in the boat. Then we'll drag the boat to the truck and pull it up onto the truck bed.'

Hartholz shook his head. Delbert grasped the edge of the turtle's shell on one side, and Hartholz did the same on the other side. They strained and groaned and managed to get it over to the boat and shoved it in. It fell on top of the gunnysack and the remaining stink bait squirted out.

Hartholz breathed hard. 'That thing is two hundred pounds,' he said, wiping his face with his sleeve.

'I'm telling you, it's the biggest ever,' said Delbert, bent over, his hands on his knees.

They climbed up on the back of the pickup and, with monumental effort and much cursing, pulled the turtle-laden skiff up into the truck bed and covered it with the tarp.

Just north of Plum Grove, Hartholz noticed that a truck that had been following them for a half-mile or so was speeding up, as if to pass them.

'This one is hurrying,' he muttered, as he slowed his pickup to let the other truck by.

Delbert turned and looked out the back window at the passing truck.

'Oh, man,' he said. 'Let's hope he just keeps going.'

The truck drove on past. Hartholz looked at Delbert.

'Why?' Hartholz asked. 'Why did you want him to keep going?'

'Because the boy in that truck is Jimmy Neville Cray,' said Delbert. 'Because you're white, you've never had to deal with Jimmy Neville Cray. Let's just say he's the meanest son-of-a-bitch over in Montgomery County and he doesn't much care for us colored. In fact, he thinks the world would be better off without us. Some folks say he already sent one poor black soul to his home over Jordan.'

Hartholz pondered the possible meanings of 'over Jordan'.

Then, stopped there in front of them, blocking the road, was Jimmy Neville Cray's truck. Jimmy Neville Cray was standing in front of it, with a shotgun over his shoulder. Hartholz braked to a skidding stop.

Jimmy walked up to the driver's side window of Hartholz's truck and tapped on the glass with the barrel of his gun. Hartholz rolled the window down.

'Out for an evening drive, fellas?' asked Jimmy.

'We're just driving home to Plum Grove,' Hartholz said. 'Please let us go.'

Jimmy cocked his head sideways, like a dog trying to figure something out.

'You sound like one of them Nazi prisoners they got locked up at the fairgrounds,' he said. 'Is that right? You a Kraut? One of ol' Adolph's boys? Like was locked up in that camp?'

Hartholz shook his head vigorously. 'I am German,' his voice trembled. 'But I've been in America a long time. Before the war. I was not a Nazi or in a camp.'

Jimmy wasn't interested in Hartholz's explanation. He'd already turned his attention to Delbert.

'A Kraut *and* a nigger,' he sneered. 'Together in one place. Smells like trouble to me. You boys planning trouble?'

Hartholz was about to deny any troublemaking intent, but Delbert elbowed him and shook his head. Hartholz said nothing.

'That's right,' said Jimmy. 'It's probably best if you just shut the hell up.'

There was nothing remarkable about Jimmy's appearance. If you spent an hour alone with him in a room, an hour after leaving him you'd be hard pressed to describe him to anyone. He was of normal height and weight, had short brown hair, acne on his forehead, a bit of a mustache, and slightly larger than average ears. He wore a dirty white T-shirt, with a pack of cigarettes in the breast pocket, blue jeans, and worn brown cowboy boots. He leaned into Hartholz's window.

'So, where you all been?' he asked in a secretive hush.

'You been lookin' for women? You been lookin' for pretty white women?'

Hartholz shook his head. Delbert stared ahead. Without obvious movement, he felt with his right hand for the old pistol Hartholz sometimes kept down by the passenger seat. It was there and he held it by the grip and sat still.

'Wait a minute,' said Jimmy. 'Is that stink bait I smell? You boys been fishin' for cats, ain't ya? And you didn't invite me. Shame on y'all.'

He stepped back from the window. 'Get out the truck,' he said. His voice was flat and cold.

Delbert and Hartholz got out. Delbert left the revolver in the cab, planning how he might jump back in for it, if circumstances required.

'It just so happens that I been needin' me a new fishin' boat,' Jimmy said.

'But the boat is old,' Hartholz said. Jimmy shoved the barrel of his shotgun into Hartholz's belly, doubling him over in pain.

'I told you to shut the hell up,' Jimmy said.

He took a deep breath. 'So, I was sayin' I need me a fishin' boat. And praise be, here one is.'

He walked around to the back of Hartholz's truck. 'See? You was wrong. It may be a little old, but this lil' boat will do me just fine.'

Jimmy hopped up onto the truck bed, and looked the boat over, as if he were about to purchase a thoroughbred racehorse. He kicked at the tarp.

A loud guttural hiss came from under the tarp, and the pronged bloody head of the gigantic Texas alligator snapping turtle thrust out and locked its barbed jaws around Jimmy's right foot. Jimmy screamed and fell backward, letting go of his shotgun, which fell to the road and discharged, blasting buckshot into the truck's left rear fender.

The turtle retained its vise-bite on Jimmy's foot, preventing him from fleeing. He flailed and shrieked, half in the boat, half out, his head hanging upside down, over of the back of the truck.

Hartholz and Delbert jumped into the front of the truck. They looked back through the rear window in time to see Jimmy flop out onto the ground. The turtle, which had something in its mouth, remained in the boat, which remained in the truck bed. Hartholz jammed the accelerator down and the truck sped away, spraying gravel and dust behind it.

A few miles down the road, Delbert picked up the pistol and held it in his hands, thinking how their lives almost changed. He sighed.

'Good thing we didn't have to use this,' he said. 'There ain't any bullets in it.'

Hartholz and Delbert spent the afternoon cooking turtle meat over a slow apple-wood fire. They drank whiskey, and watched the smoke drift up, and fed turtle scraps to a gray tabby cat that had recently taken up residence in the smoke shack. Because the cat had six toes on each foot, Hartholz called it Six Toes.

'That's real clever, Fred,' Delbert told him.

All afternoon friends and neighbors stopped by to ask if the story they'd heard about Jimmy and the turtle was true. The attention made Hartholz anxious, but Delbert reveled in it. He embellished the story with each retelling. In an early version he had caught four catfish; by the end of the day, it was seven. He started out telling visitors that he reached for the pistol under the seat, but later implied that he might have fired a few shots at Jimmy as they were leaving the scene.

The facts regarding the turtle itself required no exaggeration. After sending the beast home over Jordan with a bullet from Hartholz's newly loaded pistol, Delbert and Hartholz had heaved the carcass onto the shop's meat scale. It weighed 198 pounds.

As Delbert and Hartholz cooked, Rose and six other church mothers gathered to begin preparing the turtle soup that would be served that evening at a church picnic.

The first step was the roux – butter and flour browned in heavy cast-iron skillets. Then, on three long wooden picnic tables behind the church building, the women chopped smoked turtle meat, onions, celery, peppers, garlic, tomatoes, and bacon. All this went into an 85-gallon cast-iron kettle suspended over a fire pit by half-inch steel chain looped over a timber frame constructed from old railroad ties. The kettle was filled most of the way with clean well water, to which the meat and vegetables were added, then bay leaves, thyme, nutmeg, cloves, several cups of Worcestershire sauce, one jar of Rose's homemade Louisiana hot sauce, and fresh lemon juice. When the soup was ready to serve, three dozen chopped hard-boiled eggs were stirred in.

After the members of the Plum Grove Second Baptist Church and their guest, Frederick Hartholz, had their fill of turtle soup, the adults sat in groups on the church lawn drinking iced tea and lemonade. The children gathered under a black willow and took turns swinging sticks at two objects – a pair of totems – hanging by lengths of twine from a low branch. One was the front half of a worn brown cowboy boot. The other was a big toe that had once been attached to Jimmy Neville Cray's right foot.

28

Halfway

Sammy Merzeti was released from the Jackson County Juvenile Detention Facility into the care and custody of New Hope Halfway House on March 23, 1984, having served thirteen months for robbery and assault. It was his seventeenth birthday.

The object of Sammy's robbery was Blax Wax, Ink., a record store and tattoo parlor popular with headbangers – a subpopulation of teenage boys of which Sammy considered himself a member. The subject of the assault was Richie Black, the store's owner.

It was not Sammy's intent to hurt Richie Black. He liked Richie. Richie let him and other kids who were into heavy metal hang out at the store. He let them buy cigarettes, even if they were under age. But in the middle of the night, when Richie came into the store, startling Sammy as he was loading up with cartons of cigarettes and a selection of albums by his three favorite bands – Slayer, Fear, and Venom – Sammy felt he had no choice.

He had used a rock to bust out the glass in the front door and let himself in, assuming that Richie would be home sleeping. What Sammy didn't know was that the back room of Blax Wax, Ink. *was* Richie's home. Richie stood in the doorway between the front and back rooms of the store in his BVDs and black AC/DC T-shirt, sleepily scratching his crotch.

'Man, are you *robbing* me?' he asked wearily. It wasn't the first time one of Richie's regular customers had taken advantage of his trusting nature.

Sammy's response was to smash Richie in the face with his fist and then run for it, hoping Richie hadn't gotten a good look at him. But the time Sammy was a block away Richie had called 911, providing police with a detailed description of his assailant, including Sammy's name. Sammy was apprehended about a mile from Blax Wax, Ink., scrounging around in the bushes behind a car wash looking for the Slayer album 'Show No Mercy', which he had dropped while trying to climb a fence.

The social worker at New Hope Halfway House assigned Sammy to a bunk in a four-bed room, which had one other occupant, a black kid named Ron. When Sammy and the social worker came in, Ron was lying on his bed reading. He was wearing black slacks and a white shirt and he smelled like meat grease and smoke. When the social worker saw that Sammy noticed the smell, he explained that Ron was working at Gates & Son Bar-B-Q as part of his probation program.

'I don't smell good when I get back from work,' grinned Ron, looking up from his book. 'But I eat good when I'm there.'

The social worker introduced the boys and gave Sammy a rundown of house rules and expectations. When he was finished, he put his hand on Sammy's shoulder.

'That's all for now. You've had a big day. Why don't you relax, get some rest, maybe go down to the common room and watch some TV. In the morning your probation officer will be here to talk with you about your work program.'

Sammy sat on the edge of his bunk and looked around the room. On a bulletin board by the door several typed pages of rules and schedules were posted. A handwritten sign tacked up at the top of the board said, 'DO NOT REMOVE'.

On the opposite wall was a poster of a mountain climber standing on a mountain peak, silhouetted against a sunset. Under the picture were the words, 'If you can dream it, you can do it.'

Over Ron's bed was another poster. It featured a photo of John Lennon at a grand piano, with the word 'IMAGINE' printed above it. On the wall above Sammy's bed was a poster of Malcolm X.

Ron put down his book. 'If I don't say anything, it's not because I'm not friendly. I'm just guessing that you're not really in the mood to talk much. I wasn't when I got here. But if you got any questions about how things are around here, I might know the answer. Then again, I might not. I only been here six weeks. Six weeks and three days.'

Sammy nodded, but didn't say anything.

Ron held up his book.

'I'm workin' on my GED.'

Sammy nodded again, but didn't say anything. He lay down on the bed and remembered it was his birthday.

Sammy's work program consisted of cleaning restrooms and emptying trash bins on the overnight shift at a twenty-four-hour McDonald's.

'The objective is to reintroduce you into mainstream society,' said the probation officer. 'Hopefully your fellow employees will become a support system for you.'

Sammy had no idea what a support system was and was unclear as to the meaning of 'mainstream'.

*

Since getting beat up at the trailer park basketball court three years earlier, Sammy was wary of black people. But Ron seemed like a nice guy and Sammy thought maybe they'd be friends, but they never saw much of each other because of their different work schedules. One afternoon, when Sammy was watching TV in the common room with some of the other boys, two young men came in and introduced themselves around. They wore jeans and T-shirts, like the kids who lived there did, but they looked newer and cleaner. One was about Sammy's age. He said his name was Zack. The other was older, maybe in his late twenties. His name was Evan. Evan said that he and Zack were from Family First Community Church, over on the Kansas side, in Johnson County, and were there to invite the residents to a 'youth jam' at their church on Saturday.

'It'll be fun,' said Evan. 'We're going to have live music, and munchies, and all. And don't worry about it being a preachy church thing. It's not going to be like that. We'll just be hanging out. It's just a chance for you to meet people. You don't have to decide now if you want to come. We'll bring a van by on Saturday. If you want to come then, we'll give you a ride there and back. We've cleared this with your supervisors here and they're fine with it.'

None of the other guys seemed much interested in it, so Sammy didn't say anything to Evan or Zack about going. But later he mentioned it to Ron.

'You should go, man,' Ron said. 'I been goin' to church since I got released and it helps me feel better about things. People are real nice and they don't ask me about the trouble I've been in or nothing. You should go.'

He smiled. 'Everybody needs Jesus, Sam.'

On Saturday, Sammy showered and put on a clean shirt, and waited for the church van outside on the steps. He wondered if any of the other guys would come, but when Evan drove up in the van, Sammy was the only one.

'Tell me your name again,' said Evan, apologetically, extending his hand to Sammy. 'I'm terrible at remembering names.'

'It's Sam,' he said, sliding into the front passenger seat.

'We appreciate your coming,' Evan said. He smiled at Sammy and Sammy tried to smile back.

On the way, Evan asked the questions Sammy expected he'd be asked. How long have you been at the halfway house? Are you from around here? Are you working any-where? Sammy wanted a cigarette, but there was a sign on the dashboard that said, 'NO SMOKING'.

When Evan ran out of questions, Sammy offered him one.

'Aren't you going to ask me what I done?' he said.

'Jesus doesn't care what you've done, Sam,' Evan said in a serious, even tone. 'If he doesn't care, neither do I.'

Sammy nodded. 'You ain't curious?'

Evan smiled. 'Of course I am. I'm just hoping it wasn't murder.'

'Not yet,' Sammy snorted. 'I hit a friend of mine while I was robbing his store.'

He really wanted a cigarette.

Evan was quiet for a time.

'Sam,' he said, 'I don't know what led you to do what you did. My guess is you've had a hard life. Certainly harder than mine. Mine's been pretty easy. And you've probably made choices you wish you hadn't. I know that's true of me, too. But everybody makes mistakes. Everybody needs second chances. I hope that things will turn around for you. The folks who run the halfway house seem like good people. So maybe they'll help. Anyway, I just want to say that Jesus will give you a second chance. And a third and a fourth. You can't run out of chances with him. Not ever. So maybe, if you give *him* a chance, things can turn around for you.'

Sammy wondered what that would look like if it was really true.

The youth center at Family First Community Church was located in the church basement. The cinderblock walls were painted with a high-gloss, pale green enamel and were decorated with lots of hand-lettered signs praising God and celebrating previous 'youth jams'. There was a poster from the musical *Godspell*, another depicting Jesus laughing, and one of Salvador Dali's surreal painting of the crucifixion.

Sammy looked away from the Dali poster with a shudder. It gave him the creeps.

There were about fifty young people there. They looked shiny and breakable. Sammy guessed that about half of them were younger than he was. It was noisy with laughter and the band was tuning up. Evan leaned toward Sammy.

'I have to check on some things with a few people,' he said. He put his hand on Sammy's back. 'Get yourself a soda and relax. I'll find you later and introduce you to some of the others.'

Sammy went over to a folding table that had been set up with coolers filled with canned soda and fished out a 7-Up. Everybody seemed to know everybody else. He wished he was back at the halfway house.

He saw an exit door across the room and went outside for a smoke. It was cool and damp. From where he stood, down in a stairwell on the side of the building, he could see the illuminated church sign in the front yard. The title of the next morning's sermon was spelled out in black plastic letters – 'THE HARVEST IS PLENTIFUL, BUT THE LABORERS ARE FEW'.

Under the sign, something moved. Sammy squinted to get a better look and saw a boy rolling over on top of a girl, their mouths pushed against each other; their hands grasping and groping for something hard to hang on to.

Sammy went back inside as the band was starting up.

Evan spotted him and came over. 'I was looking for you. You havin' a good time? You meet anybody?'

Sammy shrugged. 'Not so far.'

Evan looked a bit confused. It had not occurred to him that someone might not have fun at a 'youth jam'.

The band was playing a song titled 'Get Back to the Bible'.

Evan started bobbing his head in time. 'This rocks, does-n't it? It's by the band Petra. You heard of them?'

Sammy shook his head.

Evan was undeterred. 'They're a Christian rock band. People think Christians can't rock. But they're wrong.'

Sammy listened for a bit. The band consisted of two acoustic guitar players – one girl and one boy – another girl on a tambourine, and another boy on a pair of bongos. Sammy wouldn't have used the word 'rock' to describe what he was hearing, but thought that maybe the group was just getting warmed up.

The next song was 'Spirit in the Sky' which Sammy actu-ally knew and liked. Especially the fuzzy guitar hook. He was optimistic. But the two acoustics could not reproduce the hook, and Sammy quickly concluded that what people said about Christians and rock was probably right.

Evan, however, was enjoying himself. 'I *love* this song.'

Across the room, Zack – the kid who had come with Evan to the halfway house – was eating pizza with a pretty girl that Sammy assumed was his girlfriend. Evan saw them, too.

'Hey, let's go say hi to Zack,' he said. He started over toward the couple and Sammy followed.

'You remember Sam, don't you, Zack?' Evan asked. 'From over at New Hope?'

Zack glanced at Sammy then at Evan then back at Sammy.

'We didn't actually meet,' he said. 'How you doin'?'

Sammy nodded. 'I'm okay.'

Zack's girlfriend stared at Sammy, which Zack noticed and didn't like.

Evan put his hands on Zack's and Sammy's shoulders.

'I'm going to leave you two, so I can go mingle. Sammy, help yourself to some pizza. I'll check back later.'

Zack watched Evan leave, then turned back to Sammy.

'Glad you could make it,' he said managing an anxious smile. 'Hope you're having a good time.'

He took his girlfriend's elbow and led her away.

Sammy felt still and quiet and cold. He could hear his heartbeat in his left ear. He went outside and sat on the curb by the church van and smoked while he waited for Evan to come out and drive him back to the halfway house.

Evan was disturbed by Sammy's silence on the way back to New Hope.

'Seems like maybe you didn't have all that much fun, Sam. I'm sorry if that's the case. I hope nobody said anything to offend you. They're all good kids. They all love the Lord. Sam, I'd love for you to know Jesus, too. As your personal Lord and Savior. It would make all the difference in your life.'

Sammy looked out the window. 'Don't worry about it.'

Neither of them said anything for several miles. Finally, Evan spoke up.

'So, Sam. What happened to your finger? If you don't mind my asking.'

'My mom chopped it off with a car door.' Sam shrugged.

Evan didn't ask any more questions.

*

Sammy woke up the next morning as Ron was getting ready for church. He sat up in bed and reached for his cigarettes on the nightstand.

'How'd it go last night?' Ron asked.

'It sucked,' Sammy grunted.

'Sucked how?' Ron was concerned and curious.

'It sucked by sucking,' snapped Sammy. He pulled on his jeans and went outside for a smoke. Ron came out a few minutes later to wait for his grandmother to come take him to church. He stood next to Sammy.

'You want to come with me? I can get my grandma to wait a few minutes if you want to go get dressed.'

Sammy lit a new cigarette with the tip of the one still in his mouth.

'No, man. I *don't* want to go with you. This religion thing is bullshit. All hypocrites. They don't give a shit about anybody.'

Ron smiled. 'Am *I* a hypocrite, man?'

Sammy scuffed his foot in the dirt.

'I didn't say that. I just don't believe in all that *spirit in the sky* shit. Maybe *you* need Jesus. I don't.'

He turned and went back inside.

The manager of the night shift didn't like Sammy and Sammy knew it. The manager never said so in so many words, it was more of an attitude thing. It was the way he smiled and greeted everyone else as they arrived at work, but not Sammy. It was the way he stated his instructions in the form of a question to everyone else – 'Would you please restock napkins out front? How about some more catsup up here, please?' – but not Sammy. With Sammy, it was: 'There's a spill by the walk-in. Go mop it up. You left the lid open on the dumpster again. You need to keep it closed.'

Sammy just wanted to stay out of trouble and keep his probation officer happy, so he kept his mouth shut. But he hated the shift manager more every time he laid eyes on him and often entertained himself by imagining ways to hurt him.

On the Monday after the 'youth jam', Sammy was sweeping up under grill when he overheard two of the other employees talking about their plans for the week.

'I have to go to my stupid brother's band concert,' said Jason, a thick kid with greasy hair and frightening acne, who was frying burger patties. 'My parents are making me go.'

He rolled his eyes and wobbled his legs as if he could barely stand up under the pressure of family obligations. Jason was directing his humor at Heather, a beefy girl with red hair and freckles, who was standing at the deep-fat fryer cooking a batch of fries.

'I'm going to a skate party with my church youth group,' she chirped.

Sammy snorted contemptuously.

'Make sure you invite plenty of juvenile delinquents,' he said bitterly. 'They need *Jesus*, you know. Boy, oh boy, do they ever need *the Lord*.'

He punctuated his sarcasm with another snort and kept sweeping.

'What's your *problem*?' demanded Jason. He took a step toward Sammy. Sammy stopped sweeping.

'I don't have a problem,' he said, his eyes fixed steady on his co-worker.

'Then maybe you should stop making wise-ass remarks about somebody's religion,' said Jason. He took another step in Sammy's direction.

Sammy dropped his broom and stepped forward.

'The only reason you're defending her pathetic religion is you're hoping to get yourself a piece of somebody's fat ass.' He leaned in so his nose was just inches from Jason's.

Jason shoved Sammy backward – a move Sammy had anticipated. He grabbed a spatula from the grill and slapped it hard and fast against Jason's cheek, leaving a bright red welt. Heather screamed and Jason charged forward, hunched over like a linebacker bearing down on a quarterback. Sammy thrust his knee up into Jason's chest, knocking the wind out of him. He fell over gasping and moaning. The shift manager heard Heather's scream and came running in from the front where he'd been assembling Happy Meals. He saw Sammy standing over the writhing and wheezing Jason. He grabbed Sammy's shirt and pulled him close.

'You miserable son-of-a-bitch. I knew this would happen sooner or later. You guys can't be trusted. Get your sorry loser ass out of here.'

He wrenched Sammy toward the back door, but Sammy had decided he wasn't going without a fight. He took hold of the manager's wrist and twisted until the manager released his grip on his shirt. They struggled in a dance of wills, Sammy holding the manager's one arm high with both his hands as the manager slugged Sammy in the gut with his free hand. They crashed against the grill, spilling burger patties onto the floor. They then spun around, slipping on burgers, until the manager was backed up against the deep-fat fryer. Sammy gripped the manager's arm at the elbow. Seeing the manager's eyes widen, Sammy smiled, then shoved the manager's hand into the deep-fat fryer. Deep into the boiling grease. It popped and sizzled the same way it did when a basket of frozen fries was lowered down into it. The manager kicked frantically, screaming hysterically. Jason and Heather shouted for Sammy to stop, pulling at him from behind. Sammy noticed that a foam of spit had formed at the corners of the manager's mouth. This made Sammy happy. He let go.

He pulled himself free of Heather and Jason and walked outside, lit a cigarette and waited for the police.

29

Rocky

He remembers Delbert is driving. And next to his uncle, in the front seat, is his grandmother Rose. LaVerne rests against the door in the back seat, his head against the window. His head is hot and damp. The window is cool.

His grandmother turns and speaks to him. 'How you doin', child?' She smiles gently, and her chalky brown skin crinkles at the corners of her eyes. 'Now, the doctor may have to give you a little shot, but then you'll feel better. So you just be still. We'll be to Cleveland in a bit.' She turns back around and looks out the window. 'Look, LaVerne, the kids are out at recess.'

They are driving past the school. LaVerne sees William and John, the twins from down the road, playing on the monkey bars. Helen and Esther, who live in town, are jumping rope with the new girl, Maybelle. His best friend, Junebug, is tossing a baseball high up into the air then catching it. He stops to watch the car go by. He sees LaVerne and waves.

LaVerne leans back on the seat and closes his eyes. He hears Helen, Esther, and Maybelle singing, '*Hey, boy! Hey, boy! What did you take? A sweet potato pie and a birthday cake. Hey, boy! Hey, boy! Where you gonna go? You can't drive a car, an' you run too slow. Hey, boy! Hey, boy! What you mama gonna say, when the sheriff lock you up an' take you away?'*

LaVerne Williams has his reasons for feeling ambivalent about baseball. He has often felt that maybe if he hadn't blown out his shoulder, and then been let go by the Athletics, if things had been different that way, then maybe Raymond wouldn't have died.

That long throw from deep center changed everything. And skulking around on the dark edge of his understanding is a sense that everything went to hell on that warm Florida evening that smelled like cut grass and popcorn and pine tar and leather.

LaVerne shows little apparent interest in baseball in general, and even less in the Kansas City Royals. You never hear him ask his customers, 'How 'bout them Royals?' The radio on top of the filing cabinet in his office is never tuned to Royals' broadcasts during business hours. And he's only ever been to a handful of Royals games.

This appearance of apathy is due, in part, to the fact that the restaurant's other employees really couldn't care less about the Kansas City Royals, which tends to inhibit casual workplace conversation about the team. A.B. lacks interest in sports in general. Leon is more of a NASCAR kind of guy, and Vicki is more than a little intimidated by LaVerne, and therefore shy about discussing with him any personal interests she might have, sports or otherwise.

Another factor is that, for the last twenty-some years, since 1985 when the team won the World Series, the Royals have been, in LaVerne's words, crap.

But the real reason is the feeling he gets every April on opening day, when the players take the field, when he feels like their lives are all ignorant hope, beautiful and young, and his is all that it is.

The pangs of longing and melancholy slowly dissipate over the course of the summer and into the fall. By the end of October he's not so much gloomy as he is just his normal cranky self.

But, even though – as far as most people can tell – he doesn't appear to care about the Kansas City Royals, Pug Hale, Ferguson Glen, and Bob Dunleavy are aware that LaVerne knows the name, age, hometown, college and/or minor-league experience, position, batting average, slugging percentage, runs scored, and fielding percentage of every player on the Royals' roster at any given point in a season.

On a Saturday afternoon in October, LaVerne and Ferguson sat out in the restaurant's empty dining room and drank coffee listening to the radio broadcast of the last couple of innings of the next-to-the-last game of what was arguably the worst season in Royals history. A.B. and Leon were in the kitchen cleaning up.

They listened without much conversation or comment on the game until it was over – Royals 7, Toronto Blue Jays 6.

'What, exactly, was the point of *that*?' asked LaVerne, in disgust. 'Do they think that winning the next-to-the-last game of the year is going to prove anything? It's too late. They already proved to everybody what they're all about back in August when they lost nineteen in a row.'

Ferguson laughed. 'Yeah, they're nowhere near as good as the '67 Athletics were.'

LaVerne snorted. He went into the kitchen and returned with the coffee pot and refilled their cups.

'You ever hear from any of the guys you played with?' Ferguson asked.

LaVerne took a long slurp from his coffee.

'I used to hear from Catfish Hunter every few years or so, up until he died. Believe it or not, Reggie Jackson once in a while, before he went to the Yankees. Blue Moon Odom mostly. We were pretty good friends. We probably still would be if we lived anywhere near each other.'

Ferguson stirred several packets of sugar into his coffee.

'Present company excepted, I think my favorite Athletic of all time would have to be Rocky Colavito, though I liked him even better the four years before he went to the Athletics, when he was a Tiger. You ever meet him?'

'When I was coming up, I imagined myself having a career like Colavito's,' said LaVerne. 'Power hitter. Good fielder. Strong throwing arm. Those were what I had, too. I looked up to him. I wanted to be like him. Of course, he was a real likable guy. Popular with his team and with the fans. I was always too quiet and pissy to be popular. Anyways, he should be in the Hall of Fame. That's just a crime that he isn't.'

LaVerne and Ferguson listened to the clinking of Leon loading the Hobart and the groaning grinding of A.B. running the garbage disposer.

'I did almost meet him once,' LaVerne said. 'Back in '82 when we opened here, Colavito was the Royals' batting coach. One day Amos Otis calls me and says that he told Colavito about the restaurant and how I used to play for the Athletics and that Colavito wanted to come over after the game, with Dick Howser the manager, to check us out.

'So Raymond, A.B. and me, we get the place all lookin' nice and make sure we got cold beer in the fridge and fresh coffee and we wait and we wait and nobody comes. So finally we say, "Enough of this," and we go home.

'We find out the next day that he and Howser were arrested in a mix-up with the police out by the stadium. Some kid was driving drunk and crashed his car into the side of Rocky's car and things got pretty heated up. Rocky's son was there. Same age as Raymond. And supposedly the drunk guy was getting belligerent to the point that Rocky felt like he needed to protect his kid. The whole thing got physical and he and Howser were arrested and brung downtown. It was a pretty serious situation for those two. They weren't just slapped on the wrist and let go with a wink and a nod. They was actually sentenced to ninety days in jail, plus fined money.

'After the lawyers got involved, they got off with some kind of probation. And even though I don't think they were guilty of anything, if they'd have been black they wouldn't have got probation, I'm tellin' you that right now.

'So, anyway, I never did meet Rocky Colavito. But just like you, I always liked him. I always thought that I could have had a career like his.'

A.B. poked his head in from the kitchen.

'I'm outta here, boss,' he said. 'Leon already left.'

LaVerne and Ferguson said goodbye, then sat for a few minutes in silence.

'It's a good thing for them they didn't end up going to jail,' said LaVerne. 'They wouldn't have liked it much.'

LaVerne stared across the room. A crumpled napkin Leon's broom had missed lay on the floor in a corner. 'I know. I've been there.'

Ferguson looked into his coffee cup. It was empty. He stood and went into the kitchen and returned with the pot. He poured a cup for himself and one for LaVerne.

30

Exit 151A

When he returned home from his honeymoon without his wife or his marriage, the first thing Ferguson did was call his father. The Right Rev. Angus Glen's phone rang seven times before Ferguson hung up. At which point he went to the liquor cabinet, found a two-thirds-full bottle of bourbon, and poured himself a double. *What the hell,* he thought, *it's not like I have anything left to lose.*

About thirty minutes later, he discovered that the by-then-empty bottle of bourbon had been the only alcohol in the apartment, which prompted him to heave the bottle against the wall opposite the leather club chair where he'd been sitting.

He stared at the shards of shattered glass for several minutes before deciding that he'd better do something about it.

He stood, went over to the liquor cabinet, and picked up the crystal decanter his mother bought him when *Traverse* was nominated for the Pulitzer. He tossed it up into the air a few inches and caught it. Then did it again, assessing its heft. Then he flung it against the wall, aiming for the same spot where the whiskey bottle had hit. He followed this up with each of the eight matching glasses that had come as a set with the decanter. He felt a rush of bitter satisfaction when each glass disintegrated.

He crossed the room to the bookcase by the fireplace, and took from a shelf the Steuben vase that had been his great-grandmother's, and threw *it* against the wall. He noted that his aim was a little low and to the right.

Over the course of the next hour, Ferguson moved methodically and dispassionately through his apartment, destroying every glass thing he could find. Dishes, bowls, picture frames, a paper weight, three literary awards, the television, the bedroom window, the bathroom window, the oven window, the mirrors in the bathroom, and bedroom, and each pane in the French doors that opened to the balcony with the view of Central Park. Since some of these were fastened down and thus could not be thrown against the wall, he smashed them with a meat-tenderizing hammer he found in a kitchen drawer.

The hallway mirror was the last to go. Ferguson dispatched it with a backhand swing of the meat hammer, at which point a splinter of glass knifed into the muscle at the base of his left thumb, causing him to curse and bleed profusely. He went into the kitchen, wrapped his hand in a dishtowel, and sat at the table, trying hard not to think.

Then he cried for a long time.

When he was emptied out, he went into the bedroom, checked the bed for shards, lay down and slept.

When he woke, he realized that he had been sleeping on the pillow that had been Bijou's and that it smelled like the lotion she used just before bed.

He called his father again. This time Father Angus Glen's secretary, Julia Putnam, answered the phone.

'Julia, it's Ferguson. Is my father in?'

'I think so, Ferguson,' Julia said in a condescendingly sympathetic tone. 'Let me check.'

She came back on the line after a few minutes. 'Here he is, dear.'

Ferguson heard a click and then the sound of his father clearing his throat.

'Dad, it's me,' he said.

'Yes, Julia told me,' said his father.

Ferguson waited for him to say something else, but his father was silent. Finally, Ferguson spoke.

'Dad, I—'

Angus interrupted.

'You've made a mess of things, haven't you? Elliot Peabody called me and we think we can control most of the damage from this thing. It'll be best if you just stay out of it. We've got lawyers on it, and you'll get a call if they have any questions. I've got a vestry meeting, so I'm going to go now. Your mother is taking this whole thing hard, which is making life at home rather difficult for me these days. I'd wait awhile before calling her if I were you.'

Angus Glen hung up the phone. Ferguson went out to replenish his supply of whiskey.

When Angus Glen was ninety-four years old, Ferguson drove up to Charlevoix, in northern Michigan, to spend Thanksgiving with him.

Technically speaking, Angus Glen was retired. However, he remained active as an assisting priest at Christ Church, a small congregation that nearly doubles in size in the summer, when old-money Chicago bluebloods dock their sailboats and yachts at the marina, arriving at worship on Sunday mornings in sundresses, open-collared pink oxford shirts, and navy blazers.

Father Glen's status as a retired bishop lent considerable prestige to the parish, where he'd been given the official title of curate, which comes from the Latin *curatus*, meaning to be entrusted with the care of something. In Episcopal tradition, a curate is one entrusted with the care of souls.

Ferguson never used the word curate when referring to his father.

Christ Church's rector is Elizabeth Dardilly, called Mother Liz by her parishioners. Mother Liz is thirty-five years old and still aglow with cheery sincerity and passion for her calling. Christ Church is her first rectorate, having served as an assistant at St Luke's in Kalamazoo, and as a transitional deacon in student ministry at Western Michigan University.

Mother Liz was thrilled when Father Angus mentioned that his son was coming for a Thanksgiving visit. As far as she was concerned the best thing about Father Angus's service at Christ Church was his connection to Ferguson Glen, all of whose books she read when she was in seminary, and most of which she has reread since.

'Most of the books in the religion section at Barnes & Noble are filled with easy answers. It's all pop religion,' she said once, when recommending one of Ferguson's books to a parishioner. 'Like a Starbucks mocha frappuccino – a bit too sweet, mildly uplifting, and entirely predictable. But Ferguson Glen's writing is like a double shot of espresso – rich, complex, dark, and bitter. It's to be savored. It's an acquired taste, though, frankly, not many people have acquired it.'

Liz called St Columba in Kansas City and asked Ferguson to deliver the homily at Christ Church on the Sunday after Thanksgiving – the first Sunday of Advent. Ferguson accepted the invitation. When Liz told Father Angus that Ferguson would be their guest preacher, he looked at her as if he were going to ask a question, then shook his head and walked off.

Angus Glen lives in a house on the south shore of Round Lake, near Beaver Island Fry – the channel that connects Round Lake to Lake Michigan. He calls the place 'the cottage', in spite of the fact that it has 4,200 square feet, five bedrooms, four baths, three fireplaces, two kitchens, and a covered porch that wraps the entire house. Behind the house, at the bottom of a small slope, is a short wide dock, at the end of which is a two-story boathouse. The lower half houses a fully restored 1949 seventeen-foot Chris Craft Deluxe Runabout. Upstairs is a fully furnished two-bedroom guest apartment. Ferguson's parents bought the property with his mother's money, intending to retire there, but his mother died of stomach cancer seven months after they moved in. His father has lived alone there since.

Ferguson visits once a year. As his father approached his ninetieth birthday, Ferguson expected that perhaps he'd need to start visiting more often, but his father has never expressed a need for anything from his son.

It started to snow in Muskegon, and traffic on the interstate was slow. It was after ten when Ferguson arrived and he thought perhaps his father would be in bed. He unlocked the front door and let himself in, trying to be quiet. He put his suitcases down in the entryway and hung his coat in the closet.

'That you?' Angus called from the den.

'Yes, sir,' Ferguson replied. He went into the den where his father sat in a big leather club chair in his bathrobe, drinking a Scotch, watching CNN. 'I'm surprised you're still up.'

'I don't need much sleep anymore,' said Angus.

'It was snowing pretty heavy downstate,' Ferguson said.

'That's what they said on the weather,' Angus said. He sighed. 'I suppose you'd like a drink.'

Ferguson said nothing but went to the liquor cabinet and poured himself a bourbon. Neither man had yet looked at the other.

Ferguson looked out the window. The lake had begun to freeze over. Through the dark he could see light from a window in a house on the other side of the lake. He wondered who lived there and if it was warm in their house.

'Elizabeth asked you to do the homily on Sunday, did she?' Angus asked.

'She did. I was flattered. She said she invited us for Thanksgiving dinner.'

'Yes. She's quite an admirer of yours.'

Mother Liz Dardilly, her musician husband Chandler Tyner and their two-year-old son Peter, live in a second-story apartment above a fudge shop on Bridge Street, the main street of Charlevoix's picture-postcard, tourist-friendly business district. Chandler gives private guitar lessons and teaches a music-appreciation class at the middle school. Their apartment has a small living room in front and a narrow galley-style kitchen in back. In between the living-room and kitchen is a tiny dining room, big enough only for a little square table, four chairs, and Peter's highchair. When Ferguson and Angus Glen arrived for Thanksgiving dinner, Mystique, the family's sleek, black cat, was sitting in the living-room window, watching it snow.

Ferguson drove himself and his father to dinner in his father's SUV. He parked in front of the fudge shop and went around to help Angus out of the car.

'I got it,' said Angus, gripping the doorframe and pulling himself out and upright. He stepped up onto the curb. 'I'm old,' he muttered. 'Not crippled.'

As Ferguson watched his father walk slowly over to the staircase that led up to Liz and Chandler's apartment, he looked up and noticed the cat in the window.

Before the meal, Peter toddled around the apartment in wobbly pursuit of Mystique the cat. Each time Peter came within tail-grabbing range, the cat impassively got up from wherever it had been drowsing and trotted to another room to resume its rest.

Peter was not ready to quit this game when it came time to sit down to dinner, and he squirmed and yowled, 'Mmteek! Mmteek!' as Liz put him in his highchair and locked the tray in place. Mother Liz tried to appease and distract her son with turkey and mashed potatoes, but it quickly became clear that her strategy would not work, and she broke out in an anxious sweat. Chandler was in the kitchen carving the turkey and unable to assist. Ferguson and Angus watched in silence as Liz cooed and cajoled to no avail. Peter began to kick wildly, then to cry inconsolably. Angus looked away.

Chandler came in from the kitchen with a platter full of turkey. Liz looked at him helplessly. Chandler smiled and lifted Peter out of his highchair and bounced him in his arms. Peter twisted and tried to get down, but Chandler held him firm.

Liz poured wine, and she and Angus made small talk about the last vestry meeting. Ferguson watched Chandler pat Peter's back, and whisper in his son's ear. It made Ferguson feel like closing his eyes. After four or five minutes, Peter was calm and ready to eat. They each took their seats.

Mother Liz smiled. 'Peace be with you.'

Chandler, Angus, and Ferguson returned the peace. 'And also with you.'

After dinner, Liz dug deep into Ferguson's thinking about writing and liturgy and mega-churches and the quality and character of the current batch of seminary students. Chandler took Peter out for a walk in the snow, and Angus fell asleep in a recliner by the radiator in the front room.

Because it was the Sunday after Thanksgiving, many members of the Christ Church parish were away visiting family. The worship service was nonetheless festive. The nave was decorated in greens and garlands. The choir performed 'Come, Thou Long-Expected Jesus' and 'O Come, O Come Emmanuel'. The children's chorus sang 'O Little Town of Bethlehem'. And the acolytes lit the first Advent candle. The lection included passages from Isaiah 64:

> *But you were angry, and we sinned; because you hid yourself we transgressed.*
> *There is no one who calls on your name, or attempts to take hold of you; for you have hidden your face from us, and have delivered us into the hand of our iniquity.*
> *Yet, O LORD, you are our Father; we are the clay, and you are our potter; we are all the work of your hand.*
> *Do not be exceedingly angry, O LORD, and do not remember iniquity for ever.*

And from Psalm 80:

> *Let your hand be upon the man of your right hand, the son of man you have made so strong for yourself.*
> *And so will we never turn away from you; give us life, that we may call upon your Name.*

And from Mark 13:

> *. . . about that day or hour no one knows, neither the angels in heaven, nor the Son, but only the Father.*

It was from this last that Ferguson gave his homily.

'In the season of Advent we see the hand of God reaching through eternity, forward through the ages of history, back from all the possible futures, reaching out to gather his lost and rebellious children to himself.

'In the season of Advent, we see this strong and gentle

hand reaching out to us, and it begins to dawn on us at the other end of that hand is God himself, and we don't know whether to shout for joy or scream in terror. Will he rest his hand on our shoulders? Or tousle our hair? Or will he smite us with that mighty hand of his? God knows we have it coming.

'The prophet laments that God hides himself from us. Yet, when we see him coming, it is *we* who hide from *him*. We are lost, yet, when we see the one who has come to find us, we hide. We hide because we are ashamed. We are ashamed, for we know that we are lost only because, in our disobedience and foolishness, we have wandered off the path that God has made straight for us. We hide because we are ashamed of our rebellion. Our rebelliousness is not the proud and heroic revolt of the weak against the powerful. Ours is the sullen, indolent, empty rebelliousness of confused, pimply-faced, hormone-addled adolescents, nursing our self-inflicted wounds alone in our rooms, certain that nobody, least of all God, understands and loves us.

'But God *is* coming. His hand is on the doorknob.

'So we wait and we wonder, *When he sees me, will he recognize me? Will he know who I am? Will he remember my name? Will he like me?*

'We *hope* he will see us and recognize us and call us by our names. He is our Father, after all. Children crave the attention of their father. When he comes home after a long time gone, he is greeted at the door with eager hugs and kisses. Unless, of course, we are afraid. Afraid we will be punished for things we have done that we ought not to have done, for things we ought to have done that we have left undone. Then we await his arrival in dread and self-loathing.

'Even then, we hope.

'We hope our father will forget our transgressions, or decide they're not so bad after all. Though we deserve to be sent to bed without dinner, to be grounded for life, we hope all we'll get is a good talking-to.

'Then sometimes it's an aching, empty loneliness that makes us long for our father. We've been alone; alone in the house for a long time, while our father's been away. It's night. The house is cold and drafty. Outside the wind moans and the branches of the tree in the side yard knock against the bedroom window. We expected him a long time ago. But he's still not here. We wrap ourselves up in a blanket and hunker down to wait.

'Then the phone rings. It's him. "I'm on my way," he says. The house seems somehow warmer. We tidy the place up a bit. We turn on the lights. We straighten our clothes. Dad is coming home. He said so. He's on his way. We put on a pot of coffee.

'This anticipation is called Advent. The anticipation that soon our Father will be home. We will hear his voice. We will see his face. He will hold us in his arms. He will whisper, "Everything's all right."

'How do we know this? How do we know that God is coming to hold us, and not to extract the price of our sins and our sinfulness? We know because at Advent the hand that is reaching out to us is the hand of an infant, reaching up to us from the floor of a stable, reaching up to grasp our finger, in that way that babies do. We know that God has come to hold us because he comes as a infant needing, himself, to be held.'

He crossed himself and sat down.

Later, during the exchange of the Peace, he shook Angus's hand and noticed that his father's eyes looked puffy.

After the service, Liz hugged Ferguson and thanked him. 'You've made this such a special Thanksgiving. It was a perfect way to start Advent.'

Chandler was holding Peter in his arms. He shrugged sheepishly. 'It probably wasn't the most peaceful Thanksgiving dinner you've been to.'

Ferguson smiled. 'It was just right. Just the way it was.'

Ferguson drove Angus back to the house. Angus said nothing, except to comment that the lake was freezing over.

Ferguson had packed his suitcase that morning, before church. He carried his luggage out to his car. Because Angus is ninety-four years old, Ferguson understands that each time he says goodbye to his father it may be the last.

'I'm glad I came, Dad,' he said, taking Angus's hand in his.

Angus didn't look at him, but he held onto Ferguson's hand. 'Me too, son.'

Ferguson put his suitcases in the trunk. Angus opened the car door, and Ferguson got in.

Angus held the door open. 'It's not as simple as that.'

Ferguson nodded. 'Probably not.'

South of Chicago, Interstate 80 splits off from Interstate 94, heading west to Des Moines. Ferguson was tired when he approached the split, and considered staying on 94, going on up into Chicago; having dinner at Robinson's No. 1 Ribs and getting a hotel room. But he took 80, and a few miles later, at exit 151A, he saw a sign and turned his car south onto Interstate 57. The sign said, 'Memphis: 500 Miles'.

He was sure that it was Wren Brown he'd seen at O'Hare as he waited for his flight home after the DePaul conference in October. And he was just as certain that Wren had been speaking to her mother, Periwinkle Brown, on the phone there at the airport. He was going to Memphis to see; to see if it was them.

But probably only to see. Maybe from a far corner table

at General Bar-B-Q – if there still was a General Bar-B-Q. As certain as he was that it was Wren he had seen at O'Hare, he was equally certain that neither Wren nor Peri would recognize or remember him. Actually, Peri might remember him. But she would not recognize him. And he would not presume to give her that opportunity. He was a single page in a long book. God knows if she could find that page again even if she tried. He flicked on the radio and tried to find a station that might play some blues, or maybe some soul.

Ferguson got to Memphis at about ten o'clock on Monday morning, and found his way to General Bar-B-Q, which had not yet opened for the day. The neon 'BBQ & Whiskey' sign was gone. And the Coca-Cola sign, over the front door, now said, 'General Bar-B-Q Ribs Wet N Dry *Number 1*'. In most every other way the building looked the same.

He was exhausted and sore from the drive. He knew that if he waited in his car for the restaurant to open he'd fall asleep. He drove back out to the interstate and got a room at a Motel 6, where he slept for nine hours.

By the time he showered, shaved, and drove back to the restaurant, General Bar-B-Q was closed.

He got out of his car and peered in the front window. It looked like a light might be on in the kitchen, but he didn't see anyone. He turned to go back to the car, thinking maybe he should just go back to Kansas City, when he sensed something move off to his left. He turned and there was Periwinkle Brown.

She didn't recognize him. 'May I help you?' she asked.

She was small, and bright eyed, and deep cherry brown, just as he remembered, though her hair was now gray and she wore it in medium-length dreadlocks.

He stood silent, smiling.

Peri looked at him hard. 'I'm sorry, but we're closed here.

Our other place is open late, in East Memphis. It's a bit of a drive though. There're other barbecue places closer, if you were wanting someplace to eat.'

Ferguson shook his head. 'No. I'm fine.'

Peri continued to look at him. Ferguson thought maybe he saw a flutter of recognition in her eyes. But she said nothing.

'Thank you,' said Ferguson. He turned, got into his car, closed the door, closed his eyes and took a long, deep breath. He had hoped to see her, and he had. He turned on the ignition. Then Periwinkle Brown knocked on the car window. He rolled it down.

'Ferguson Glen,' she said. 'Ferguson Glen.'

He nodded.

'Get out of the car,' she said, firmly.

He complied immediately. They stood beside the car looking at one another. Periwinkle shook her head.

'Cast your bread upon the water,' she said, under her breath.

She unlocked the restaurant. They went inside and she started a pot of coffee.

'I didn't think you'd recognize me,' he said, leaning back on the kitchen work table, as they waited for the coffee. 'It's been thirty-eight years.'

Peri smiled. 'Well, Rev. Mr Famous Author, your picture *is* on the back of a few books which I happen to have on my shelves. And I've Googled you more than once.'

Ferguson was instantly ashamed that he had never thought to Google Periwinkle Brown.

'The thirty-eight years have been much kinder to you than they have to me,' he said.

'I'm looking at you and thinking you're right about that,' said Peri. 'But I'm happy to see you anyway. What brings you to Memphis? Conference at the seminary?'

Ferguson looked at Peri and thought about the question. 'No.'

Peri thought about his answer. 'I see.'

The coffee was ready. Peri poured two cups and they went out into the dining room and sat in a booth.

'You hungry? I could heat up some ribs or some sausage.' Peri stirred cream into her coffee.

'I'm fine,' said Ferguson. 'How's Wren?'

'She's wonderful.' Peri laughed. 'She's got her own record label, here in Memphis. Bluebird Records. Mostly old-school R&B and blues. She and her husband, Tyrell, have two girls; my grandbabies Ruby and Violet. Tyrell is a good man. He runs our East Memphis place. If I ever get up enough nerve to do something else with my life, the business would be in good hands with Tyrell.'

Ferguson sipped his coffee, and stared at a chipped place on the table. There was additional information he was waiting for.

Peri watched Ferguson's hands rotate his coffee cup in a small circle. 'What about you, Ferguson?'

'I'm afraid I don't have much of a story,' he said, not looking up. 'No family. Not much to show for the life I've lived. Mostly I've been looking for something. But I haven't found it. Probably because I'm not sure what I'm looking for.'

Peri scowled. 'What about your books? Your writing has touched people. God gave you a gift. Why would you look for anything else?'

Ferguson said nothing.

'Why are you here, Reverend?' Peri asked.

'To see you,' Ferguson said, finally allowing his eyes to meet hers.

'You think I'm what you been looking for?'

Ferguson shook his head, then shrugged. 'No. I don't know what I think.'

Peri persisted. 'You think maybe I can tell you where to find whatever it is you're looking for?'

Ferguson again shook his head.

Peri sighed and leaned in toward Ferguson. 'You came all the way here to see me because of two evenings in 1968? What makes you think that's all right? Did you consider that I might be married maybe?'

Ferguson nodded. 'I *did* come all the way here to see you because of two evenings in 1968. And I don't assume it's all right. I hope it is. But I think it may not be. And I did consider that you might be married.'

Peri leaned back in the booth. 'Well, I'm not.'

Ferguson wanted to breathe a big sigh of relief, but resisted. 'I don't expect anything. I was on my way back to Kansas City, where I live now. I was visiting my father in Michigan, and when I got to Chicago I just turned south and here I am. I just wanted to see you. I don't expect anything. This, having coffee with you, is more than I could have hoped for. I don't know. That's all there is to it, really. Nothing more than that.'

Peri smiled, just a little. 'Well, that seems like quite a bit, to me. I must have made quite an impression on you, Reverend Glen. I think I'm flattered.'

Ferguson nodded. 'You did.'

They were quiet again, until Peri spoke.

'You made quite an impression on me, too, Ferguson. It was just one day when you think about it. One day. But I've thought about you in these years. And you being here now, out of the blue, is maybe the biggest surprise of my life. I really don't know what to do or say. I really don't. But I'm willing to consider that maybe God has something in mind.

275

I should probably pay close attention to what's going on right about now. I should probably keep my eyes open.'

She took a napkin from the dispenser and wiped a spot on the table. 'Thirty-eight years is a long time between dates.'

Ferguson nodded. 'It is.'

Peri looked him in the eyes. 'I may not even like you once I get to know you better.'

Ferguson nodded. 'You probably won't.'

Peri nodded. 'Truth is, I've read all your books, and some of your writing online. And I've thought about you a lot. I feel like I know you pretty well already.'

Ferguson shrugged. 'Well, then maybe you can provide me with some clues.'

Peri tilted her head slightly and squinted. 'The black-and-white thing doesn't bother you?'

Ferguson gently shook his head. 'The black-and-white thing is what made me semi-famous. That's not an issue.'

Peri looked back down at the table and thought about things, then looked back up at Ferguson.

'Thirty-eight years,' she said in a whisper. 'Who ever heard of such a thing?'

'Not me,' said Ferguson.

Ferguson felt warm and remembered that he had remembered the yellow walls of General Bar-B-Q's dining room hundreds of times since April 1968.

He smiled. 'If you hadn't held my hand that night, none of this would be happening.'

31

Bob-Stones

About a half-block from Smoke Meat, up 17th Street, is a telephone pole that looks like it's melting into the sidewalk. Puddled around its base is a congealed pool of sealing tar that an over-industrious utility worker applied to the pole with too heavy a hand, resulting in its sliding off and hardening at the bottom like so much candle wax. A.B. passes this pole once or twice a week when he walks up to the convenience store at 17th and Grand to buy cigarettes. He always makes a mental note to say something about the pole to Leon or Vicki, but by the time he gets back to the restaurant he always forgets.

Late one night after closing, as he was getting into his car, A.B. checked his pockets for cigarettes and, finding none, drove up to the store to get a pack for the drive home. On the way up 17th Street, he glanced over at the telephone pole and saw a man working on the pole with tools. Thinking that it was late for someone from the telephone company to be out making repairs, A.B. slowed his car to check it out. The man looked up from his work and watched A.B. watching him.

He had a long thin face, long stringy dark hair, and large dark-rimmed glasses with lenses so thick they made his eyes look big and round. He glared at A.B.

A.B. swallowed hard and made a mental note to ask Pug, or maybe Bob Dunleavy, if they'd ever heard of the telephone company sending someone out to work on a telephone pole so late. But by the time he saw Pug and Bob next he'd forgotten.

About a week later, walking back to the restaurant from the store, with a Mountain Dew and a fresh pack of cigarettes, A.B. noticed that a steel plate about eighteen inches high, ten inches wide, and roughly a quarter-inch thick had been attached to the pole at about eye level. The plate was curved to conform to the shape of the pole and was fastened to the pole with two big bolts – one on the top and one on the bottom – that went all the way through the pole. Lock nuts were snugged down tight on the bolts on the other side. Welded onto the plate were raised steel letters arranged in four lines:

INLE

HRAIR

elil

OWSLAFA

A.B. decided the letters must be some kind of telephone company code. He lit a cigarette and stood there looking at the letters trying to think of what they might mean. His deliberation was interrupted by the horn of LaVerne's truck, which was stopped in the middle of 17th Street. LaVerne yelled at A.B from the truck.

'Boy, I don't know what the hell you're doing there. But you look stupid. In the future, when you're out in public gawkin' at telephone poles, kindly remove your official LaVerne Williams' Genuine BBQ and City Grocery T-shirt. I don't want you representing our establishment when you look stupid.'

LaVerne drove off. A.B. looked down at his T-shirt,

flicked his cigarette onto the sidewalk, stepped on it, and hurried back to the restaurant.

Several weeks later, A.B. was helping Jen unload her drums at Blaney's in Westport when he saw the man who'd been working on the 17th Street telephone pole. He was standing across the street, gripping a telephone pole as if he were strangling it. He was wearing a heavily insulated black parka, camouflage pants, and red Chuck Taylors. A.B. guessed the man was about his age. It was hard to tell. He appeared to be evaluating the sturdiness of the pole, a process interrupted when a beer truck pulled into the loading zone in front of the pole. When the beer delivery man got out of the cab and went around to open the truck's back door, the phone pole man looked both ways, pulled the hood of his coat up over his head and walked away, his shoulders hunched up around his ears. A.B. concluded that the man was not an employee of the telephone company.

The next day, after the lunch rush, A.B. walked up to the telephone pole on 17th Street to take another look at the steel plate with the mysterious inscription. He traced the letters with his finger. The welds were bumpy and rough. He tried pronouncing the words, but the odd combinations of vowels and consonants were awkward. He thought maybe Ferguson would know if the words were from some foreign language, but he knew he'd never remember them, so he copied them on the back of an order slip from the pad he kept in his back pocket.

INLE
HRAIR
elil
OWSLAFA

Ferguson didn't come in to Smoke Meat that day, so as they were cleaning up after closing, A.B. took the order slip from his pocket and asked Vicki Fuentes if she knew what the letters meant. He knew better than to ask Leon. Vicki went to college. She knew stuff. Plus she was Mexican. She looked at the four lines of letters and tried pronouncing them as words. She shook her head.

'I have no idea what they mean, A.B.,' she said. 'They're not Spanish.'

A few days later, Ferguson, Pug, and Bob Dunleavy all came in for lunch at about the same time. He went out, sat down next to Ferguson, and showed him the strange words on the order slip.

Ferguson put on his reading glasses and looked at the paper. He pronounced them out loud, slowly. Then again. Then once more, faster.

He snorted a small laugh. 'Sounds like I'm speaking in tongues. Except we Episcopalians don't speak in tongues, so I'm not really sure what that would sound like.'

A.B. looked at Ferguson. Pug fidgeted in his seat. Bob Dunleavy looked over at Pug and shook his head.

Ferguson frowned and cleared his throat. 'Where did you see these words, A.B.?'

'On a telephone pole up the street. I think I saw a guy put 'em there. They're on a metal thing. I thought maybe the guy worked for the phone company or something. But I saw him again down in Westport, and he didn't look like a phone company worker. It's kind of a mystery, don't you think? I wonder what it means.'

LaVerne arrived tableside. 'It means we could use a little help managing the restaurant. If it's not too much trouble.'

'Sorry, boss,' A.B. said. 'I just thought, since Rev. Glen is a professor and all, he might know what these words mean. Like what language they are.'

'It's the Lapine language.'

It was Bob Dunleavy who offered the explanation.

LaVerne, Ferguson, and A.B. all turned to look at Bob, who was wiping his mouth with his napkin, having just finished his pulled pork.

'It's the Lapine language,' he said. 'The language of rabbits.'

LaVerne shook his head and went back to the kitchen.

'Are you sure, Mr Dunleavy?' asked A.B. 'I'm pretty sure rabbits don't have a language.'

Ferguson nodded in slow recognition. 'I remember now. It's from *Watership Down*, right, Bob? The book.'

Bob nodded.

Ferguson turned to A.B. '*Watership Down* is a novel about a community of rabbits. I read it years ago.'

He looked at his watch. 'I've got to go. I've got a class to teach.'

He left without elaborating on rabbit communities.

Bob finished his diet Coke and also got up to leave.

'So, this book about rabbits must be a pretty good book,' said A.B. 'Did you read it, Bob? Is that how you knew the words on the phone pole were in rabbit language?'

Bob Dunleavy put on his jacket and turned to A.B.

'The young man you saw putting that sign on the telephone pole is my son, Warren. That's how I knew. He's mentally ill. He's not really dangerous or anything. But he's got serious psychological problems. And the whole rabbit thing is a part of it.' He sighed. 'It's a long story, A.B. I'll tell you about it some time.'

A.B. had felt a connection to the Dunleavy family since Bob gave him the gravesite in the Dunleavy family plot in which to bury his mother. So, A.B. was tormented by Bob's revelation about his son's mental illness.

'Bob Dunleavy has been coming into the restaurant for

years,' he told Jen. 'And I never knew this about him. I know lots of things about the people who come into the restaurant, but Bob never said a thing about this. Not once.'

'It's probably just too painful to talk about,' said Jen. 'I don't think anybody who hasn't had that kind of thing in their family can really know what it would feel like, how it would change everything.'

A.B. nodded and lit a cigarette. 'What kind of mental disease would make you put signs in rabbit talk on telephone poles?'

A.B. began looking for Warren Dunleavy every time he went up to the convenience store for smokes or a Mountain Dew, or whenever he was in Westport for one of Jen's gigs. On the way to and from work he made a point of glancing at every telephone pole along the way, hoping for a glimpse of Warren Dunleavy. A.B.'s surveillance resulted in several additional sightings of Lapine-inscribed steel plates, but no additional sightings of Warren himself.

Then one night, driving home after helping Jen and the band at one of Mother's charity performances, A.B. saw a man wearing camouflage pants and a black parka dart into an alley off Roanoke, just south of 45th. He was sure it was Warren. He turned into the alley, slowed his car to a crawl, and flicked on his brights. Without giving a thought to what he might do if he actually found him, A.B. continued down the alley looking for Warren Dunleavy. The alley was lined on both sides with dumpsters, loose newspaper pages, and multiple empty vodka and whiskey bottles. It looked a lot like the alley behind Smoke Meat.

A.B. rolled down his window, thinking maybe he'd hear Warren; maybe behind one of the dumpsters. He stopped his car and listened.

Then an arm in a black sweater sleeve thrust itself through the open window and the hand at the end of the arm grabbed A.B. by the collar and pulled him halfway out of the car and the face at the other end of the arm thrust itself into A.B.'s face and said turn off your car and A.B. flailed his right hand around feeling for the ignition and when he found it he turned it off and the face which was calm and was not Warren Dunleavy's face and had eyes that didn't blink asked what are you doing here. A.B. tried to speak but the hand was holding his collar so tight he could hardly breathe let alone speak so he just squeaked instead and the hand let him go and A.B. flopped back into the car bumping his head on the door frame and he realized he was about to pee his pants and he had to try hard not to.

'I asked you, what are you doing here?'

A.B. rubbed his throat. He looked out his window.

A white man in a heavy black sweater and black pants stood next to the car with his arms crossed. He had short-cropped almost-white gray hair. About a half-inch below each eye was a horizontal scar about an inch long.

'I thought I saw somebody I know come in here,' A.B. rasped, staring at the scars.

'I'm the only one here,' said the man. 'Do you know *me*?'

His voice was chill and even.

'No,' said A.B. 'I don't know you.'

'Then I guess this is goodbye,' said the man.

He pointed back toward the entrance of the alley and A.B. wondered if the man meant for him to back his car out of the alley, which would be somewhat tricky.

'Goodbye,' said the man.

A.B. put his car in reverse and carefully backed out. As he was about to drive off, he looked back into the alley. The man with the black clothes and gray hair stood under a streetlight waiting for A.B. to leave. Then, A.B. saw behind the man, down at the far end of the alley, Warren Dunleavy had stepped out of a shadow and he, too, watched for A.B. to go.

A bad case of the hiccups prevented A.B. from sleeping much that night.

Bob Dunleavy is not ashamed of his son's mental illness. Not anymore. But the spitefulness of it; the specific way it inhabits his son's life; the way it shoves his son's shoulders together and possesses his face and animates his voice beyond proportion; the way it shits on the floor of his son's once tidy mind; these he carries with him always, like stones in his pockets. They bruise and chafe when he walks. They are heavy and awkward, and because they are there, little else fits in his pockets. They knock together and he hears them and he is never not reminded of them.

They are made heavier by the fact that nobody knows they are there.

Actually, Pug Hale has known for a long time. But almost nobody else.

A few weeks after A.B. first spotted Warren and his mysterious signs, Bob Dunleavy was sitting down to lunch at Smoke Meat when A.B. rushed up to his table with the news that he'd seen Warren again and that he was quite sure that somebody was following him. Somebody dangerous. Like maybe somebody from the Mafia. Or maybe a spy, although he couldn't figure out why a spy would be following Warren around at night, because don't spies work for Russia or China? And why would the Russians or the Chinese be spying on Warren? Anyways, the guy was scary and was dressed in black and had really creepy scars under his eyes and shouldn't they maybe tell Pug about it?

This is when Bob decided that perhaps it was time to

share Warren's story with his friends, if for no other reason than to prevent A.B. from exploding.

After the lunch crowd was mostly gone and he'd finished his coffee and sweet potato pie, Bob motioned A.B. and LaVerne over to his table. Pug and Ferguson were there, so he waved them over, too.

'You guys know I'm kind of a private guy and that I don't talk much about personal stuff,' he said. 'That's just the way I am. Marge, my wife, thinks I should "open up" more. Whatever that means. I guess I've just always had the idea that you keep your problems to yourself. You got your problems. I got mine.'

LaVerne nodded. He was in agreement with this philosophy. Bob continued.

'Maybe some of you have heard me mention that I've got a daughter, Linda. She's married and lives over in Lawrence with her husband, Jim. They've got two kids, a girl and a boy. Well, as you now know, I've got a son, too. Though you've probably never heard me talk about him. Except Pug. And there's a reason for that.

'Anyway, the reason I don't talk about my son is not that I'm embarrassed or anything, but because it's complicated. And it's strange. And, well, it's a private thing. But I told A.B. about it a while ago, and there's no reason not to tell you guys.'

LaVerne squirmed a bit and wondered if it would be rude to excuse himself and go back to the kitchen and turn the briskets.

'My son Warren has a mental illness,' Bob said. 'It's a delusional disorder.'

He paused.

'He wasn't always sick. When he was in high school he was normal. I always thought he was a little too serious maybe, but he was smart and he liked movies and books and he had big ideas. Well, he kind of had a breakdown when he got to college. First semester. He stopped going to classes. He stopped showering. He got in arguments with his roommates. It was bad. If we had known what to look for, we probably would have seen it coming, but the truth is we probably couldn't have done anything about it. That's just the way these things are. You can't prevent these diseases. You can treat 'em, but you can't cure 'em.'

His voice got caught in his throat. He paused again. Ferguson put his hand on Bob's shoulder. Bob nodded.

'It's all right,' he said. 'It is. We've been dealing with this for almost twenty years. In my son's case, the way his illness is would be funny if it weren't so pathetic and sad. He's fixated on the book *Watership Down*. It's a novel about rabbits. Warren thinks the author, Richard Adams, is a prophet. Like in the Bible. He thinks that the book is like scripture and that the things in it are true, or will come true. Even though it's all about rabbits. He's always saying things like, "The prophet Adams saith this," or "The prophet Adams saith that." And he's always talking about, "When it comes to pass."

'The doctors say that maybe his name, Warren, has something to do with it. Because a warren is a rabbit community. Maybe that contributed to his fixation.

'So Warren thinks his mission is to spread the word of the prophet Adams. He thinks that secret police are out to destroy us all or something. So he sneaks around at night and puts signs on telephone poles in Lapine, which is the language the rabbits speak in the book, and these signs are supposed to warn us to beware of the secret police. The sign he usually puts up – "*inle hrair elil owslafa*" – supposedly means, "Fear the uncountable and unknowable enemy police." Another sign he has – "*inle efrafa owslafa*" – means

"Fear Woundwort's Gestapo". I'm not sure if those translations are exact.

'Marge and I have done all we can for him. He lives in an apartment by himself. It's not bad, and he actually keeps the place pretty clean. He gets Social Security. It's not that he can't function. He just doesn't have a firm grip on reality. Like I said, he's pretty smart. Lots of times you can actually have real conversations with him. He loves the Royals. We've got season tickets. He goes to almost every home game. Anyway, it's sad and it's difficult. But it's something Marge and I had to deal with. Lots of people have had worse things happen.

'I guess that's it.'

But it wasn't it for A.B. 'What about Pug?'

'I told Pug because I wanted him and the police to know that Warren is out there and what his problem is. He acts strange, but he won't hurt anybody. He's not dangerous. But if the police see him acting bizarre, I wanted them to know how to handle it.'

A.B. wasn't done. 'Bob, did you tell Pug about the guy I saw following your son the other night? He was scary. I don't know if he was going to rob your son, or what.' A.B. turned to Pug. 'I can tell you all about it, Pug. I can fill out a report if you want. It happened down by the Plaza. The guy scared the crap out of me.'

Pug looked at Bob. Bob nodded. 'A.B., that guy wasn't going to hurt Warren. He was there to protect him.'

He sighed. 'If I could, I'd follow Warren around myself to keep an eye on him and make sure nothing happens to him. But I can't. I've got a company to run. I've got a wife and a daughter and grandkids, too. They also need me. So, I hired somebody to be where I couldn't be. To keep an eye on my boy. Make sure nothing bad happens to him. That's who you saw. His name is Michael Zosimus Owen. We call him M.Z.

He was a Navy SEAL in Vietnam. An honest-to-goodness war hero. He lives in our guest house. His job is to watch over Warren.'

Bob had said all he cared to say on the subject of his son. He stood up. 'Thank you all for listening and understanding.'

LaVerne and A.B cleared the lunch tables in silence, until A.B. had to say something. 'Damn, boss. Poor Bob and his wife.'

LaVerne wiped barbecue sauce off the seat of a chair. 'He and his wife have done right by their son. Bob's a good man.'

A.B. stood at the front window. He could see the telephone pole up on 17th Street.

LaVerne pushed the chair up to the table. 'All I know is you'd *have* to be crazy to like the Royals.'

32

April 1968

Angela and her father, the Rev. Dr Clarence E. Newton, were waiting for LaVerne at the bus station. His return home from Plum Grove was delayed three hours when the bus he was to switch to in Joplin was late due to a flat tire. It was 1:30 in the morning and LaVerne could tell Angela had been crying. Her eyes were red and swollen. She clenched a white handkerchief in her left hand.

Rev. Newton stood behind his daughter with his hand on her back. He was wearing his black preaching suit, a starched white shirt, and a blue necktie. His eyes were cold and wary and his chin was thrust forward as it sometimes was in the pulpit when he was admonishing his congregation.

It was April 10. Kansas City's east side smoldered. Three nights of rioting and rage had burned away the city's thin skin of civility. Three National Guardsmen stood at the bus station exit watching LaVerne, Angela, and her father. One of them leaned over and said something to one of the others and they laughed. LaVerne pulled Angela close and held her.

'I saw that this was happening on a TV in the Joplin station.'

Angela nodded and dabbed her nose with her hanky.

'Five people have been shot and killed. And folks are

burning down their own neighborhoods. Raymond's at Momma and Daddy's. We're going to stay there until things are settled down.'

Rev. Newton tipped his head in the direction of the exit. 'Let's go.'

At the exit, Rev. Newton said, 'Excuse me, please,' to the Guardsmen but they didn't move. Angela, LaVerne, and Rev. Newton squeezed past them single file. LaVerne heard one of them say, 'That guy plays for the Athletics. I'm pretty sure of it. I wonder why he's not in Oakland.'

Outside, as they got into Rev. Newton's black Oldsmobile, LaVerne noticed the smell of burning tires. He heard sirens.

LaVerne, Angela, and Raymond stayed with Angela's parents for a week, until order had been mostly restored in the city, and LaVerne and Angela's neighborhood seemed safe enough for them to return.

LaVerne was bored and angry, and his shoulder hurt. He stalked around the apartment snarling and glowering like a caged leopard.

Down in Plum Grove, he had missed Raymond so bad it ached, but now everything about Raymond annoyed him – his insistent babbling, his runny nose, the way his applesauce dribbled down his chin, the way he smeared his peas on the tray of his highchair, his shitty diapers, and his constant need to be picked up and held. LaVerne's brooding festered, and after a day or two the contagion infected Angela. By then anything any of the three of them said or did resulted in an exchange of hostilities.

Curfews imposed to quell the unrest had kept everyone in their houses at night, and the fear of further violence inhibited almost everybody from venturing out during the day. But, finally, when their supplies of food and patience were depleted, Angela and LaVerne agreed that he should go get some groceries and a little time by himself out of the house.

The grocery store's windows were boarded up with sheets of plywood. Spray painted on one of the boards were the words, 'Opened for business'. On another was painted, 'MLK we will not forget'.

The aisles and shelves of the store were nearly empty, but LaVerne scrounged together a couple boxes of Kraft macaroni and cheese, three cans of chicken noodle soup, a can of SpaghettiOs, a package of hot dogs, a half-gallon of milk, and a loaf of Wonder bread.

On the way home, at the corner of 27th and Olive, LaVerne turned north on Olive, even though the way home was west on 27th. When he got to 22nd, he turned left and two blocks later parked his car outside Municipal Stadium.

It was abandoned. A temporary chain-link fence circled the stadium. He walked around to the players' entrance. From the fence he could see that doors were chained and padlocked. This is what he expected to see, but he wanted to see it anyway.

Back in the car, LaVerne drove north on Brooklyn. Eight blocks later he turned west onto Interstate 70. About three hours after that he pulled off at Salina, Kansas, and used a pay phone at a Sinclair station to call Angela to tell her he was on his way to Oakland, California. Also that she should probably go stay with her folks for a while.

'Angela? It's me. I just wanted you to know I'm okay.'

Angela was frantic.

'Where *are* you?' she shouted. 'I thought you'd been hurt. Or *worse*. With all the police and soldiers and crazy rioters. Thank *God* you're all right.'

LaVerne hesitated.

'You're not going to be thanking God when I tell you

this. I'm in Salina, Kansas. I'm going to Oakland, Angela. I got to talk to Finley. It's not right what they did. Just throwing me away. I can still play. They just need to give me some time. So, that's where I'm headed. I'm sorry about this, Angela. I didn't plan it. And I'll come back once I talk to them. I got seventy-two dollars. I checked. I'll be okay. Just take care of yourself and Raymond and don't be mad at me. I'll be back soon.'

Angela's voice was quiet and urgent.

'Nothing good can come from this, LaVerne. *Nothing*. This is selfish and irresponsible. You have a responsibility to your family. You can't just go runnin' off like this. You're a *black man* out there alone ten days after they killed Dr King, and dozens of others have died in riots.'

LaVerne felt hollow and dark. 'I just have to talk to them.'

Angela went cold.

'You *do not have* to talk to them. You're *choosing* this. You're choosing *this* instead of *us*. You need to be a *man*, LaVerne. You need to think hard about this. Real hard. You need to do what's right here and be with your wife and child at a time like this. You need to be a man and face facts. The fact is the Athletics don't *need* you anymore. The fact is *we do*. So you *choose*, LaVerne. *You* choose.'

She waited for him to say something.

'I love you,' he said as he hung up.

He stopped in Hays for gas and realized he was hungry, which reminded him of the groceries. The milk was warm by then, so he drank it, thinking that if he waited much longer it would spoil. Then he ate five slices of the Wonder bread.

By Limon he was hungry again. He wrapped three hot dogs in slices of Wonder bread and ate them like that, which made him thirsty so, when he stopped for gas in Bennett, he bought four bottles of Coca-Cola. When he went to the counter to pay, the attendant reached down under the cash register and retrieved a baseball bat which he put on top of the counter without comment, his left hand gripping the handle.

West of Denver he parked at a truck stop and slept the night in the car.

In the morning he was so cold he thought maybe he had frostbite on his fingers and toes. His shoulder hurt bad and he was stiff and sore all over. He hobbled inside to the truck stop restaurant for coffee. He wanted to stay inside for a while to warm up, but one of the truckers, who was paying for his breakfast at the cash register, put his hand on LaVerne's shoulder and said, 'Mister, I don't like having to give you this advice, but with all that's been going on the last couple weeks, I don't think it's safe for you to be here.'

LaVerne knew that driving through the Rocky Mountains for the first time should have been an experience he shared with Angela, so he tried not to look at them much. Their beauty was painful.

The radio in his '61 Ford Falcon Futura hadn't worked since they bought the car two years earlier, but he tried the on–off knob anyway. It still didn't work.

West of the mountains, somewhere along dusk between Rifle and Parachute, a large brown rabbit jumped out from the scrubby brush alongside the highway. In the moment before LaVerne hit and killed it, he thought to himself that it must be a jack rabbit like the kind he used to see in Texas because it was big and had tall ears and a black tail, not like the little rabbits with white tails that they have in Kansas City.

When he heard the thump, he quick-looked in his rearview mirror and saw the animal twitching on the road. He pulled over onto the shoulder, got out of the car and walked back to where the rabbit lay. It was still and blood was beginning to seep out from under its body. LaVerne cried off and on the rest of the way into Utah.

In Utah he looked for signs of life, but didn't see any. Only road and miles of red dirt and scrub brush.

East of Hinckley he pulled over to take a piss and almost stepped on a big black-and-white striped snake, which sent a shudder through him and hindered the completion of his task. He didn't consider a snake to be a sign of life.

At Salina, Utah, he turned onto US 50 and was reminded that it was in Salina, Kansas, that he had called Angela to tell her that he was going to California. This made him feel like crying again. But nothing came. So he screamed instead. Until his voice gave out. After which crying came easily.

Nevada was bleak, dry, and barren. Like Utah, only worse. LaVerne considered the possibility that at some point miles back he had missed an exit and was now on his way to hell.

Plus he was hungry. At the last truck stop in Colorado he had bought a can opener and had eaten the chicken noodle soup and SpaghettiOs out of the can with a plastic spoon. He still had the box of Kraft macaroni and cheese, but couldn't bring himself to eat the uncooked macaroni. He thought about mixing the envelope of powdered cheese with some water and drinking it. But he didn't have any water. The hot dogs and Wonder bread were long gone.

Around Carson City, it began to dawn on LaVerne that in a matter of hours he was going to be in Oakland, California, and that he had no firm plan of action.

It was late in the morning of Wednesday, April 24, 1968, when LaVerne Williams arrived at Oakland Alameda County

Coliseum to do whatever it was that he had come to do. A marquee at the main gate announced that the Athletics would play the Yankees that afternoon. It was the last of an eight-game home stand. LaVerne drove around until he found what looked like the players' entrance, parked his car and fell asleep.

A knock on the car window woke him up two hours later. An Alameda County sheriff's deputy was outside, motioning for LaVerne to roll the window down, which he did.

'You here for the game? Or you here to take a nap?' The deputy bent down and peered into the car.

LaVerne sat up straight. 'For the game, officer. Thank you.'

The deputy walked on into the stadium.

LaVerne saw Sal Bando and Bert Campaneris getting out of their cars. They followed the deputy through the gate. LaVerne got out of his car and went in behind them. He stopped inside the gate and breathed in the smell of grass, peanuts, cotton candy, and beer. Bando and Campaneris headed down a hallway tunnel off to the right. LaVerne watched them go. As he stood there, wondering if Charlie O. Finley was down at the end of that tunnel, somebody called him by name.

'Hey, LaVerne Williams! That *you*?' It was Blue Moon Odom, on his way in. He put down a large duffel he was carrying, went over and gave LaVerne a hug.

'*Damn*, man! You're a sight!' He grinned and slapped LaVerne on the back. LaVerne winced. At the entrance to the tunnel the deputy lit a cigarette and watched.

'Hey, Moon,' LaVerne said. 'It's good to see you, too.' He tried to smile.

'It's a shame about your shoulder, man,' Odom said. 'A real shame. I didn't think they'd cut you loose though. I thought they'd maybe send you down to play a little double-A ball or something, until you healed up. What'd the doctors say?'

LaVerne shrugged. 'They said my shoulder's messed up good. But I'm thinkin' with some time and rest and some good exercise, maybe next year, I might be able to come back and play. You know. If I took things slow.'

Blue Moon Odom nodded. It sounded like a good plan to him. He and LaVerne had been pretty good friends in Kansas City.

'So, here you are in California. Your pretty wife and baby with you?'

A commotion down in the tunnel interrupted them and they turned to look. Charlie O. Finley and some other men in suits were on their way up. In front was a short thick man in a blue windbreaker that said 'SECURITY' across the chest.

As Finley and his entourage approached, LaVerne stepped away from Blue Moon and toward the group.

He yelled. 'Mr Finley! It's me, LaVerne Williams! Your centerfielder back in Kansas City!'

Charlie Finley glanced over at LaVerne, but didn't seem to recognize him. He turned to continue an animated monologue he was delivering to a sweaty reporter who was frantically scribbling in a notebook. LaVerne moved closer.

'It's LaVerne Williams! I played for you just last season! Don't turn your back on me! Talk to me! Hear me out!'

The man in the blue windbreaker stepped toward LaVerne with his arms extended, palms out.

'Keep your distance,' he barked. 'Move back.'

The deputy took notice of these goings on and came up around behind LaVerne. Blue Moon took hold of LaVerne's arm to pull him back.

'LaVerne, don't,' he said. 'It won't do any good.'

LaVerne yanked his arm away, and stumbled toward the

man in the windbreaker, who grabbed him by the shoulders and turned him away from Finley and his men.

LaVerne yowled in pain. The security man wasn't finished. He shoved LaVerne in the back, propelling him toward the deputy. The deputy instinctively raised his arms up in front of his chest like an offensive tackle protecting a quarterback, clipping LaVerne in the chin.

LaVerne stood upright and held his chin. His shoulder throbbed and he realized he'd bitten his lip. Blood was dripping out of the corner of his mouth onto his hand. The deputy grabbed LaVerne's shirt and pulled him in close.

'Boy, let's you and I go back outside for a little chat.'

LaVerne heard Charlie Finley laughing. Maybe at *him*. Maybe not. But Charlie Finley was enjoying himself, and that felt to LaVerne like a mockery of his pain. He wrenched himself free from the deputy's grip, and the deputy fell backward. Backward and down. The deputy's head hit the concrete floor. His hat flipped up into the air and fell back down over his face. LaVerne saw the deputy lying there on the concrete floor, still and not moving. The deputy was not moving at all.

By the time the door of the holding cell at the Alameda County sheriff's department slammed shut, locking LaVerne deep inside himself, the Alameda County sheriff's deputy was home with an ice pack on his head and a cold beer in his hand.

LaVerne used his allotted phone call to contact Angela. He guessed that she would be at her parents' place, and she was. She cried a lot. Then she screamed at him and cried some more.

'I know I've ruined everything,' he said. 'I don't deserve you, Angela. If you don't come see me, if you just want to forget me, I don't blame you. I won't be mad. I just hope you know that I love you and I love Raymond. I'm so sorry I hurt you and let you down. They say that they're going to appoint a lawyer for me. A defender, they call it. So you don't need to worry.'

He waited. He could hear Angela sniffling and moaning softly.

'Will you please call Delbert for me?' he asked. 'I only have this one call. But he needs to know.'

Delbert was assigned a window seat, which he was glad for, inasmuch as this was the first time he had ever been on an airplane and he guessed it was likely to be the last. He hoped that they would fly over the Grand Canyon.

He thought about LaVerne. He wondered if he and Madeleine had had a son whether he might have been like LaVerne. He hoped so.

He had only one memory of LaVerne ever fighting anybody. LaVerne was twelve years old, and his best friend Junebug Whalen moved with his family to Detroit where Junebug's father was going to work making Fords at the River Rouge plant.

The Whalens left Plum Grove early on a Friday morning. They needed to be in Detroit by Sunday night so Mr Whalen could start his new job on Monday. LaVerne went to Junebug's house before school to say goodbye.

Later that morning, Esther Jones' big brother, Nate, saw LaVerne crying as they were all walking to school. Nate began to tease, calling LaVerne a sissy and advising him to wear a dress to school if he was going to cry like a girl. LaVerne endured this torment for several minutes before demanding Nate stop, which Nate declined to do.

Delbert was on his way to his job at Raylon Rice and Milling and happened to pass by the group of children just in time to see LaVerne land a roundhouse on Nate's left ear, at which point Nate delivered a swift punch to LaVerne's nose. LaVerne fell like a sack of rice falling off the back of a pickup.

Delbert stopped, scooped his nephew up, drove him back home, and left him with Rose.

On approach to the San Francisco airport Delbert looked out and saw Candlestick Park.

33

There Am I

The second thing Ferguson Glen did, when he got back from Memphis, was to Google Periwinkle Brown.

The first website in the search results belonged to Eye Max, the best-selling pure pigment eye shadow. Here, Ferguson learned that, because of its loose pigment form, Eye Max eye shadow is more dynamic and longer lasting than any of its leading competitors. Eye Max offers the same colors used by professionals and leading cosmetologists! Periwinkle Brown is one of Eye Max's line of metallic colors, along with Golden Sun, Peacock, Iced Brown, and Burgundy Boom.

The second site Google found was an eBay listing:

> Nine skeins of Brown Sheep Lamb's Pride 85% wool/
> 15% mohair worsted weight single-ply. The color is a
> gorgeous periwinkle. These yarns come from an estate.
> I have plenty of other yarns listed, so please check
> them out.

The third page was the official website for General Bar-B-Q Ribs Wet N Dry, which identified Peri as the proprietor. There was also a history of the restaurant, a reverent biography of founder General Brown, a menu, a Yahoo map link, and links to favorable reviews of the restaurant posted online by the *Commercial Appeal*, and the local television stations WHBQ and WPTY. Tyrell Davis was listed as the webmaster.

There were two more Google results. One was a Dutch-language site devoted to purebred field spaniels, one of which was named Periwinkle's Brown Babbler. Another was a review of a meal prepared by the twenty-nine-year-old executive chef, Fabio Trabocchi, of Maestro, the restaurant in the Ritz-Carlton in McLean, Virginia. Ferguson had to look hard for the words 'periwinkle' and 'brown'. He found them in a paragraph that made him laugh out loud.

> A recent dinner began with pan-fried Cape Cod scallops wrapped in crisp focaccia with Nova Scotia chanterelle mushrooms and salsa verde. It proceeded to liquid-center ravioli with organic egg yolk and monkfish liver with a periwinkle-brown-butter glaze and a Champagne sabayon. The fish course was wild Brittany Coast sea bass dusted with fennel pollen cooked en cocotte with sautéed fennel confit in a fennel-anise sauce. The meat course was Australian pasture-fed beef tenderloin Rossini. Maestro's cheese selection is one of the best in the region. The warm peppermint-chocolate soufflé is wonderful.

'Organic egg yolk', 'dusted with fennel pollen cooked en cocotte', and 'Australian pasture-fed beef' were the specific phrases that amused him. He smiled at the thought of the scornful and colorful things LaVerne would have to say about Australian pasture-fed beef.

The phrase 'periwinkle-brown-butter glaze' made him sigh.

The first thing Ferguson Glen did when he got back from Memphis was to call Periwinkle Brown. She answered the phone after one ring and Ferguson allowed himself to imagine that she was waiting for him to call.

'Okay,' he said. 'I was just calling to confirm that what I think happened actually did happen.'

'I can confirm no such thing,' Peri said. 'Because I don't know for sure myself what happened.'

'I think I asked you if you want to go steady with me,' Ferguson said.

'That's what I thought,' Peri said.

Ferguson thought maybe she would laugh at his 'go steady' line. She didn't.

'I don't think it will work, Reverend,' she said.

'Maybe not,' said Ferguson. 'Might be fun to try, though.'

'Oh, we're *going* to try,' said Peri. 'I just don't think it'll work. But we *are* going to try.'

Ferguson said, 'Whew!' and this time Peri did laugh.

'So here's my list of reasons why it won't work. One, we don't really *know* each other. We're *attracted* to one another. I'd say it was hormones workin', except I'm not sure I got any hormones left, and those I got don't seem to work all that well.

'Two, I don't have a real good track record with relationships. I suspect the same is true of you. So, we could just end up as failures on each other's long list of failures.

'Three, you better treat me nice or I'll kick your Episcopal ass. I know that's not technically a reason why it won't work. It's more a promise of what I'll do to you if you're being mean is the reason it doesn't.

'All my relationships ended poorly because men can't seem to treat me like a human being. There was one man who was nice to me. One. But it turns out he was being nice to three or four other women at the same time. Which is a shame because I really liked him. All the other men either wanted my money more than they wanted me or they didn't like having Wren around and didn't like that she was my main priority. There was one even raised his hand to hit me. But Jackson Reynolds, our cook at the time, stopped him. Jackson was about six foot ten inches tall and about three hundred and twenty pounds. He just picked up this man and put him out back by the dumpster and told him never come back. And he didn't.

'Four, we don't really even know each other. And what I do know about you and what I know about me, well, it wouldn't appear that we match up all that well. You're famous and rich and educated, and I'm not. Most of my own customers don't even know my name. I own the two restaurants, so I got enough money to retire if I don't live too long. And I went to community college for two years.

'Five, but I really truly am attracted to you, Reverend. I can tell you have a big heart. I can just tell. A big lonely heart. You're smart. And I like smart. You're funny and you seem to care about the right things. You still got most of your hair. You're not fat. And you're a man of God.

'Six, those are the reasons I don't think it will work.'

Ferguson held his breath before speaking.

There was never any shortage of people who had flattering things to say to him about his writing, or his lecturing, or his preaching. But it had been a long time since anyone had mentioned anything about his heart.

'Well, one, most of those things aren't really reasons why it won't work,' he said. 'Except maybe that we don't really know each other all that well yet. Which you mentioned twice, so that's not really six reasons anyway. Just five. And, two, now that you've told me all those things, I already know you better. So we're already making progress on that. Three, I'm really attracted to you, too, Peri. Seriously attracted. You're tough, but not hard. You're smart. And I like smart. And I'm actually only a semi-famous has-been. And my guess is that you've put your education to better use than I have mine.

'Plus, there's something in you, Peri, that's still and steady and easy. I'm at rest when I'm with you. And I can't imagine ever getting tired of looking at you.'

Ferguson could hear Periwinkle breathe in deep.

'You going to be nice to me?' she asked quietly.

'I will,' said Ferguson. 'I've never been mean to anybody or anything except myself. And I have lots of money, so I don't need yours.'

Peri said, 'Whew!'

'Then there's really only one remaining problem,' she said. 'That's the issue of barbecue. I'm led to believe that folks in Kansas City are of the opinion that Kansas City is the barbecue capital of America. I want you to know that's crazy talk, Reverend.'

Ferguson cleared his throat.

'Actually, ma'am, Kansas City is the barbecue capital *of the world.*'

'Well, then,' said Periwinkle Brown. 'Why don't you invite me out there so I can see for myself?'

After finishing his second *venti* cup of coffee, each with a shot of espresso added, and after reading the entire contents – minus the business sections – of the *New York Times*, *USA Today*, and the *Kansas City Star*, and after downing two cranberry orange scones from Starbucks, and after making six trips to the men's room, it occurred to Ferguson that perhaps he needn't have come to the airport an hour and a half early to wait for Peri's flight. He walked over to the monitor displaying flight arrival information. It said Peri's flight from Memphis was on schedule. Just as it had each of the previous dozen or so times he had checked.

One gate over, a flight had arrived and its passengers were emerging from the jetway. First came an elderly woman in a wheelchair, delicate and brittle, pushed by a younger man, perhaps her son, or maybe her nurse. Her eyes were bright and knowing. She wore a cream-colored pant suit and a mink stole around her shoulders. Her escort was attentive and solicitous. He wore a light blue seersucker suit, with a yellow polo shirt and flip-flops.

Next came a hurried parade of business-suited execs, wide striding and swift, tense and puffy eyed, insisting into the cell phones clamped to their ears that they would be home as soon as possible.

Then two soldiers. The first, a stout middle-aged woman in desert fatigues, instantly swarmed by her children: twin adolescent girls and a boy who looked like he was maybe five years old. Their father stood back a bit and watched for a moment, then stepped forward, threw his arms around his wife's neck and wept into her shoulder.

Next, a slender youth, perhaps nineteen years old, in an olive-green army dress uniform. He was greeted by an older couple, and a pimply-faced girl, about eight months' pregnant. The girl hugged the boy fiercely, as the older woman reached out and touched the top of his head and cried. As they moved away from the gate, the older man put his arm around the soldier's shoulders.

They were followed by a young woman in torn jeans and a *faux* vintage T-shirt carrying a guitar case. She stormed past, her lips pressed so tightly together they were white. A young man in torn jeans and a *faux* vintage T-shirt carrying a guitar case scurried after her insisting he'd been misunderstood, pleading for a second chance.

Ferguson's contemplation of the varieties of love was interrupted by an announcement over the public address system that American flight 4468 from Memphis had arrived.

She saw that he wanted to kiss her. But she knew him well enough already to know he was too much the gentleman to act on this impulse. She put her hand on the side of his face, leaned in close and whispered, 'Isn't it wonderful to be this scared?' He put his hand over hers and nodded.

By the time they got onto the interstate headed south to the city, they were chattering like squirrels. Periwinkle wondered about the enormous white plastic bull standing guard outside the headquarters of the American-International Charolais Association. Ferguson explained that Kansas City was once a cow town, and that she would be seeing more big plastic cows during her visit. As they crossed the river, Peri enquired as to the wonderful aroma of roasting coffee. Ferguson explained that downtown Kansas City is home to two – count 'em, two – coffee-roasting operations, Folgers for traditionalists and Roasterie for frou-frou types. As they headed down Broadway, Peri asked about the smell of oak smoke and cooking ribs. Ferguson pointed out that downtown Kansas City is, at last count, home to seven – count 'em, seven – barbecue joints. And furthermore that the greater Kansas City metropolitan region is home to more than 125 barbecue establishments, more per capita than in any other major metropolitan region in the U.S. of A.

'Of course, that was this morning. There may be more by now,' he said. 'However, the specific smoke you are now enjoying is emanating from LaVerne Williams' Genuine BBQ and City Grocery, known the world over as Smoke Meat.'

Peri harrumphed. 'Smoke Meat, what kind of name is that?'

'It's a name with a story,' Ferguson said.

It was too soon for dinner, and Ferguson felt that the conversation was just warming up, so he suggested that they go get coffee somewhere, to which Peri agreed.

'Traditional or frou-frou?' he asked.

'Frou-frou, if you please,' Peri said. 'I could use a white-chocolate mocha right about now.'

Ferguson obliged and headed for Coffee Girlz, over on the Boulevard in the Crossroads district. When they sat down with their drinks, the conversation that had been so lively and quick on the drive from the airport slipped into a lull. Periwinkle commented on the paintings hanging on the exposed brick walls.

'This neighborhood is a thriving artists' community,' Ferguson said. 'This shop always has local artists' works on display.'

Peri nodded. Ferguson stirred his coffee.

Peri used a stir stick to draw circles in the foam on the top of her drink. 'Did I read where your ex is running for Senate?'

Ferguson nodded. 'You did. She is.'

It wasn't that he expected that Bijou would never be the subject of discussion between them, but he hadn't expected it at that precise moment. He blamed himself for having let the conversation lag.

'So, do you ever see each other?' Peri asked.

'Every few years,' said Ferguson. 'We still have some friends in common, so once in a great while our paths cross.'

He looked at Peri, hoping to discern where she might be going with this line of questioning.

'What happened between you two?' she asked. 'Why'd your marriage fail?'

'It was me,' he said. 'I'm the reason.'

Peri thought about that. 'See, now that doesn't really tell me much, does it?'

'No, I suppose it doesn't,' said Ferguson.

'Why were *you* the reason?' she persisted.

'Because I was self-indulgent, scared, and lost,' he said. 'And I couldn't find my way.'

'That doesn't really tell me much either,' she said. 'Lots of people are self-indulgent, scared, and lost, but their marriages don't fall apart. And, by the way, my personal feeling is that since there's two people in a marriage, there's usually at least two reasons if it fails.'

Ferguson nodded and was quiet. He sighed and wondered if this would be the last cup of coffee he would have with Periwinkle Brown.

'It was my drinking that did it,' he said. 'Bijou told me to quit and I didn't. And that was the end of it. It was fair and reasonable of her and I made my choice. I ruined it.'

Periwinkle's face clouded over. 'Did you not quit because you couldn't, or because you didn't want to?'

'I don't know,' Ferguson said. 'I've never tried.'

'So you never did quit drinking even though it ruined your marriage?'

'No.'

Periwinkle got up and went to the counter to refill her cup. When she sat back down she leaned across the table.

'You remember what I said about not being mean to me? Well, in my experience, whenever some man decided he needed to yell at me, or push me around, or threaten me, he'd been drinking. So I don't have a real good feelin' about this.'

Ferguson watched the heavily pierced and tattooed barista make an espresso.

'I don't get mean when I drink. I get sad. And then I fall asleep. Mostly I drink when I'm alone. The problem is, I'm alone a lot. Alone is how I live.'

Peri was silent.

Ferguson went to get more coffee for himself. He sat down and Peri took his hand.

'I'm not up to rescuing you, Reverend,' she said. 'I'm looking to be with someone, not save someone. The only thing we lose if we quit right here is the idea that something good might have happened. Maybe we should quit.'

She sipped her coffee.

'But I'm not ready for that just yet. I've been believing that God is on the move here; the way things have happened. And I've been praying. And, well, here I am. This isn't an accident.'

Ferguson looked at Peri's hand holding his. His face felt heavy.

'All I know about God is what I've read and what others have said,' he said in a low near-whisper. 'I know a lot *about* God. Hell, I'm a professional expert on the subject. But I don't *know* God.

'I've wanted all my life to know God. To experience his presence. People talk about that. About feeling his presence. But I've never known what that feels like. I don't really have any idea what they're talking about. But this here, what you and I are doing right here, feels honest and dangerous to me. So maybe *this* is it. Do you think *this* is what they're talking about? Like you said, when God is on the move.'

She reached her other hand to his face and lifted his chin. She didn't smile or look away.

'Here I am.'

Outside the coffee shop, Periwinkle stopped and took a deep breath.

'Hickory and meat,' she said. 'Does it always smell this good around here? Or did you arrange this just for me?'

'This is just the way it is here,' Ferguson said. 'And it never gets old.'

They walked to the car. Inside, Peri turned to Ferguson. 'I was serious. This ain't no rescue mission. I can't save you. Only God can do that. But I do have a strategy. If being alone is your problem, then maybe I ought not let you be alone.'

He stood with her at the front desk of the President Hotel as she checked in, then walked with her to the elevators, where they agreed that they'd go out later for some live music.

Then he went back to his loft and, after twenty minutes of pacing, decided maybe he needed to rearrange the collection of swords he had displayed on his mantel.

They went to the Aldabra, a new club in the West Bottoms, where Mother Mary Weaver and her band play once or twice a month.

A.B. was there, sitting just offstage, watching Jen play drums. He saw Ferguson and Peri sit down and hustled over to their table.

'Hey! Rev. Glen! What are *you* doing here?' He stared at Peri.

Ferguson smiled. 'Well, I heard there was a halfway decent band playing here tonight, so I thought, why not check it out?'

A.B. was still looking at Peri. Ferguson saw that if the conversation was going to go anywhere, he would have to be the one to keep it going.

'A.B. Clayton, allow me to introduce Ms Periwinkle Brown of Memphis, Tennessee. Ms Brown, this is my good friend A.B. Clayton. I would tell you what the A. and the B. stand for, but I've been sworn to secrecy.'

Peri extended her hand to A.B.

'Pleased to meet you, A.B.,' she said. 'Are you in the band?'

A.B. blushed and shook his head. 'Oh, no. I just help out. The drummer is, well, she's my friend. And Mother is, too. Actually, they're *all* my friends. The whole band. But I'm not in the band. I just help out.'

He continued to stare at Peri. Ferguson cleared his throat.

'Young man, I detect that an explanation may be helpful here. Ms Brown and I are on what is known as a "date". A "date" is where one person asks another to accompany him and/or her to an event of some kind, such as a movie, or dinner, or, as in this case, some live blues. Generally speaking, the object of a "date" is to provide the two parties an opportunity to enjoy themselves in each other's company. It is perfectly understandable if you are confused and/or amused to see me in the company of a lovely woman on a "date", inasmuch as you usually only ever see me alone with my miserable self, a napkin tucked into my shirt and a dribble of barbecue sauce on my chin. Frankly, I'm as surprised as you are.'

A.B. looked at Ferguson as if Ferguson had just spoken in an ancient Chinese dialect.

Then he turned back to Peri.

'It's really nice to meet you, too, Miss Brown. Rev. Glen's a great guy. He comes into the restaurant almost every day. I don't understand half of what he says. But he preached at my mother's funeral and that was real generous. He's a great guy. Plus him and me talk about music all the time. So it's nice meeting you, too.'

He excused himself and returned to his place by the stage. Ferguson grinned at Peri.

'That was A.B. He thinks I'm a great guy. You should definitely listen to him. I've never known him to be wrong about these kinds of things.'

311

Periwinkle rolled her eyes. 'He also said he doesn't understand half of what you say, so maybe you just have him
fooled.'

Ferguson laughed. '*I* don't understand half of what I say.'

'So, what restaurant was A.B. talking about?' Peri asked,
'that you go to almost every day.'

'That would be "LaVerne Williams' Genuine BBQ and
City Grocery", known the world over as "Smoke Meat",'
said Ferguson. 'The very establishment whose name you
were so dismissive of earlier today.'

'I guess I shouldn't be talkin',' Peri said. 'It's not like
"General Bar-B-Q Ribs Wet N Dry" is exactly a normal
name.'

A server stopped at their table to take drink orders.

'I'll have a diet Coke,' said Ferguson, trying to sound
matter-of-fact.

Peri ordered a ginger ale.

After Mother finished a three-song set of Big Joe Turner
tunes, 'Well All Right', 'Tomorrow Night', and 'Chains of
Love', Peri nodded in approval.

'Woman can *sing*. *Yes*, she can.'

Ferguson nodded. 'I thought you might like Mother.'

On stage, Mother shifted her weight in her wheelchair
and pulled her microphone close.

'We're going to slow it down a lil' bit now with this one
from the late Otis Redding,' she murmured into the mike.
'We're gonna groove it low and slow. Like a ballad. Y'all
know what to do, now.'

The song was 'Love Have Mercy'. Peri took Ferguson by
the arm.

'Now *that's* what I'm talkin' about!' she said, pulling him
to his feet. 'This is *Memphis* music. And you and I are going
to dance.'

On the dance floor, she put her arms around his neck and he held her waist in his hands.

On the way back to the hotel, Ferguson directed Peri's attention to the large plastic Hereford bull on top of a tall tower-like pedestal on a bluff overlooking the Bottoms.

'See. I told ya,' he said.

Then, as they passed the Hereford House restaurant at 20th and Main, he pointed to the large plastic Hereford bull's head mounted on the side of the building.

'See. I told ya.'

At the hotel, Ferguson rode up the elevator with Peri and walked with her to her room. She leaned against the door and was quiet.

Then she sighed. 'What a day.'

Ferguson nodded. 'It was a "What a day" kind of day.'

Peri looked down at the floor and spoke softly.

'So, since you brought me here to see for myself if the so-called barbecue in this so-called Barbecue Capital of the World is any good, I guess tomorrow I best try some.'

Ferguson nodded. 'I think you'd best.'

She took hold of the lapels of his jacket and pulled him to her.

'How far is your condo from here?'

'Just a few blocks.'

'Well, if you start feeling too alone, just call me. We'll take it from there. You hear what I'm sayin'?'

Ferguson nodded. 'I hear.'

Next day, after breakfast at Coffee Girlz, a tour of St Columba Seminary, a leisurely walk on the Plaza, and a drive around Ward Parkway, and Eighteenth & Vine, Ferguson and Periwinkle arrived at Smoke Meat for lunch.

Pug Hale and Bob Dunleavy were seated together over at

Mother's usual table in the corner. They waved at Ferguson and he waved back. Suzanne Edwards and McKenzie Nelson were sitting by the window. They, too, waved and smiled broadly at Ferguson when they saw he was with Peri. A.B. was working the counter. When he saw Ferguson and Peri come in, he poked his head in the kitchen and motioned to LaVerne.

'Mr Clayton, you remember Ms Brown,' Ferguson said when he and Peri stepped up to order.

'Of course,' said A.B, flustered at the suggestion that he might have forgotten someone he'd met just the night before. 'Hello, Miss Brown. It's good to see you again.'

Peri smiled. 'It's nice to see you, too, A.B.'

She studied the menu board. 'So, tell me, what do you recommend?'

'It's all good, else we wouldn't put it on the menu,' said LaVerne, who'd come in from the kitchen, wiping his hands on his apron.

'LaVerne Williams, let me introduce Ms Periwinkle Brown, a successful barbecue entrepreneur like yourself,' said Ferguson. 'Ms Brown is proprietor of General Bar-B-Q in Memphis, Tennessee. She is on a fact-finding mission. She disputes our fair city's claim that we are, in truth, the Barbecue Capital of the World, and is here to offer you the opportunity to defend the claim. Although I've never been quite sure that you yourself believe in our barbecue supremacy, inasmuch as you hail from Texas, and, like all Texans, are of a mind that all things Texan are superior in all ways. Including barbecue.'

LaVerne looked at Ferguson.

Then he turned to Periwinkle and extended his hand.

'It's a pleasure,' he said. 'We don't often get other barbecue restauranteurs in our place. Be my guest and sample anything or everything from our menu, on the house. We don't have a real slick operation here. But we're proud of our food, and I'd be delighted to hear your opinion of it, professionally speaking.'

He looked at Ferguson again and shook his head. '"Inasmuch"? "Supremacy"?'

LaVerne asked Leon and Vicki to put together a sample platter. Just then Del James came in bellowing.

'I think I might have dropped a Dremel silicon carbide grinding bit when I was here earlier for lunch! Anybody seen it?'

Pug, Bob, Suzanne, McKenzie, and the other diners looked under their chairs and around on the floor, but no grinding bit was found.

'Okay! Thanks!' Del yelled as he exited the premises.

Peri glanced at Ferguson who provided the explanation.

'That was Del, the nearly deaf sculptor. His studio is across the street, in the same building I live in.'

They ate at a table near Pug and Bob, who, after they'd finished their lunch, stopped and introduced themselves to Peri. Pug flashed his badge and told Peri that if Ferguson got out of line all she needed to do was call and he'd take care of the matter.

As Bob and Pug left, LaVerne came over to the table – A.B. trailing behind.

'Well, ma'am, how do we compare?' LaVerne asked.

Peri sat back in her chair and looked at the decimated sample platter in front of her.

'First off, let me say that you've got a charming place here, Mr Williams. Really. And what a great neighborhood. All these wonderful stores and galleries.'

LaVerne frowned. 'Well, thank you. The area is getting a little too *la-tee-dah* for my tastes. Plus the company we lease from keeps jackin' up the rent. I think they'd be real happy if we just moved out. Then they could turn this place into some fancy-ass boutique that sells upscale "accessories for fine homes".'

Peri smiled sympathetically. 'Same kind of thing is happening in parts of Memphis. Hang in there. Even people who work and shop in fancy-ass boutiques need places to eat. And speaking of eating, this brisket of yours was a rare treat. Until recently, the only briskets in Memphis were corned beef like you find in the supermarket meat case. Never on the menu at a barbecue restaurant. So, this was a real joy. Tender, just the right amount of smoke. Nice smoke ring.'

LaVerne nodded. He liked where this was going. Ferguson sat back and grinned. Peri cleared her throat and continued.

'Same with the turkey. Not something we ever saw much of at joints in Memphis, up until recently. But this was lovely. Problem with turkey is that no matter what you do, it's always kind of dry. But a little of your sauce remedied that situation. Your sauce is a fine sauce, by the way. It's not as sweet as I expected a Kansas City sauce would be.'

Peri's comment about the turkey increased her credibility as far as LaVerne was concerned. He felt the same way about turkey. Plus he liked what she said about his sauce.

'That's a *Texas*-style Kansas City-style sauce,' LaVerne pointed out. 'It's got more vinegar.' Peri nodded in the manner of a scholar discussing research data with a colleague.

'Now we're getting into a tricky area,' Peri cautioned. 'Pulled pork is something we Southerners know about. But generally speaking it's favored more east of Memphis. So I can't claim to be an expert. But I can tell you that *this* was divine.'

A.B. nudged LaVerne, which LaVerne ignored.

Then Peri frowned. 'The ribs. The ribs. The ribs. I'd have to go back to Memphis and close down my restaurant if I said your ribs were better than mine. As a matter of business strategy, it's my responsibility to tell my customers that they're eating the best ribs in the whole wide world. So, Mr Williams, sadly, I must tell you that Memphis ribs rule.'

LaVerne smiled slightly and conceded the point.

Peri wasn't done. 'Then there's this pulled chuck roast. The reverend here tells me this is a house specialty. Well, all I can say is that it *is* special. Very special. If you promise never to tell anyone back home, I'll admit to you that this is the best barbecue I ever had.'

LaVerne grinned. 'Well, Ms Brown, that's a high compliment coming from another barbecue proprietor. You're welcome here as my guest any time. And I look forward to someday checking out the fine food at your establishment. Now, may I interest you in some cobbler or maybe some pie?'

Peri agreed to a slice of vinegar pie, which annoyed A.B., who feels strongly that vinegar and pie are incompatible concepts.

They sat with their coffee listening to A.B., LaVerne, Vicki, and Leon in the kitchen, cleaning up.

Peri patted Ferguson's hand. 'What you said yesterday? About being alone?'

He nodded. Peri gripped his hand and squeezed.

'You're not.'

34

April 1968

A men's room attendant at the airport told Delbert that there was a hotel about six or seven blocks east of the Alameda County sheriff's department where Negroes from out-of-town sometimes stayed when they came to visit or bail out their relatives at the County lock-up. So when he got on the bus that was headed downtown, that's where he told the driver he wanted to go. An hour later, the driver stopped in front of the Turner Hotel, a three-story brown brick building badly in need of tuck-pointing and new windows. The hotel's neon sign also needed fixing. The 'ner' in Turner and the 'Ho' in Hotel were broken and didn't light up.

The lobby of the Turner Hotel, such as it was – humid and dingy, with peeling wallpaper and worn wood floors – was occupied by three women of indeterminate age, two black, one white, each wearing skirts so short Delbert felt he should avert his eyes. One of the black women wore a lacy white blouse that, before he looked away, Delbert noticed he could see through. The women looked tired and hard. He thought about Loretta.

The furniture in the lobby consisted of a dented metal folding chair and a small lime-green upholstered couch with a crust of dried vomit where the seat cushions used to be. Nobody was sitting on either the chair or the couch.

Delbert smelled rotting fruit, disinfectant, and reefer. The latter a memory of his lost time down in Houston's Fourth Ward before the war. After they found Madeleine in the river. Before Rose led him to Jesus.

Opposite the front door was a sliding window that opened into a small office where the hotel manager sat. The window was made of thick Plexiglas, smudged and scratched to such an extent that it was nearly opaque. Delbert tapped on the window. The manager, a heavyset white man in an undershirt and stained chinos, was watching TV with his feet on the desk and his back to the window. He was, at first, unresponsive to Delbert's tapping, so Delbert tried again, at which point the manager pulled his feet off the desk, heaved himself out of his chair, and stepped to the window. His left eye was covered by a large square of gauze, adhered to his face with white medical tape. The bottom half of the gauze was yellowed and crusty. He slid the window open, and stood there.

'I'd like a room,' said Delbert. 'For three nights.'

The manager pushed a pen and a registration form across the counter to Delbert. When Delbert had completed the form, the manager took a key from a pegboard on the wall.

'That'll be twenty dollars a night. In advance.'

Delbert gave the man sixty dollars. The man gave Delbert a key to Room 203 and pointed in the direction of the stairs.

Delbert pushed the chest of drawers against the locked door, just to be on the safe side. It made him anxious that there was no lock on the window, but he told himself that there was probably nothing to worry about since his room was on the second floor.

He slept poorly that night, and only for brief periods. Outside there were sirens, barking dogs, yelling and cursing, screeching tires, and at least one gunshot.

In Plum Grove there were sometimes barking dogs, but never screeching tires or gunfire. Often there was laughing.

In the morning, as he was leaving to get a bus to the sheriff's department, Delbert noticed that the white girl he'd seen in the lobby the night before was sleeping on the lime-green couch. There were still no cushions on the couch and Delbert wondered if she was sleeping on the dried puke.

There was an *Oakland Tribune* newspaper box at the bus stop, and as he waited and wondered what he would say to LaVerne when he saw him, he glanced down at the newspaper displayed in the box window. The headline read, '*Panthers Demand Release of Assailant*'. The main photograph pictured several young black men on the steps of a large brick building. They were dressed in black pants, black leather jackets, and black berets, and they carried signs that said, 'Free our brother!', 'Justice NOW!' and 'A's = KKK'. One of the men was yelling into a bullhorn.

Delbert bent to get a closer look at the paper. There, next to the large photograph, was a smaller picture. It was a photo of LaVerne, from his Kansas City Athletics baseball card. The caption read '*Ex-Big Leaguer held in assault on officer.*' Delbert stood up straight. His heart beat fast and he felt sweat on his upper lip. He fished around in his pocket, found a quarter, put it in the box and took a copy of the newspaper, which he read on the bus.

The incident involving LaVerne and the deputy at Oakland Alameda County Coliseum had been witnessed by a stadium janitor who later recounted what he had seen to his older brother – a petty thief, heroin addict, and Black Panther Party hanger-on.

The Black Panthers were not in need of additional reasons for outrage. In addition to three hundred years of slavery, impoverishment, segregation, lynchings, and the assassination of Martin Luther King earlier in the month, there was the fatal shooting, just days before, of Bobby Hutton, one of the organization's founders.

On April 6, officers from the Oakland police department stopped two cars in which eight Panthers were traveling on their way across town. Both the officers and the Panthers were wary and suspicious after two nights of tension and violent outbursts following the King killing. Two of the Panthers, Bobby Hutton and Eldridge Cleaver, took off running and ended up cornered in a basement surrounded by police. A shootout ensued, resulting in the use of tear gas to flush the young men out of the building. Hutton was the first to escape the building, whereupon he was shot twelve times by the police and killed instantly. He was eighteen years old.

When the Panthers learned of LaVerne's arrest, they saw it as an opportunity to fuel the fire of rage they had kindled in Oakland, in hopes it would spread.

Delbert got off the bus at the corner, about a half-block from the sheriff's department. He could see that protestors had gathered again around the front steps of the building. He heard them chanting.

He knew about the Black Panthers from TV. He had seen them carrying guns and shouting about revolution on the news. One time Rose had asked him about it.

'Goodness, Delbert,' she said. 'What are those young men up to? Someone is going to get hurt. What have we come to?'

She speculated about their upbringing.

Delbert guessed out loud that the Black Panthers probably did not have parents who were much worried about them carrying guns and shouting about revolution.

'I can see why any colored person would be angry,' he said. 'That doesn't take any imagination. But the only progress I seen us make in this country is how Dr King was showing us. You disobey the laws that ain't just; that ain't right. But you know to begin with what the consequences are going to be and you take 'em when they come your way. It ain't that you don't believe in being law-abiding. You just can't obey laws that ain't right. You just want the law to be the same for everybody. You do what's right. And you pray for them that do wrong. Anyways, people start shooting and killing other people, things are going to get a whole lot worse. Not better.'

As he approached the steps, the group of young black men and women stopped their chanting and moved aside to allow Delbert up the stairs. This relieved Delbert's anxiety somewhat. He reached for the door to go inside and a uniformed deputy stepped out to block his entry. The deputy put one hand on Delbert's chest to keep him from moving forward. The other hand gripped the handle of his holstered revolver.

'Where do you think you're going?' he asked Delbert.

'Well, sir, I'm here to see one of your prisoners,' Delbert said.

Delbert looked down, his head bowed slightly. The Panthers moved in around Delbert and the officer.

'Who exactly are you here to see?' the deputy asked, eyeing the group warily.

'LaVerne Williams, sir,' Delbert said. He kept his head low and didn't make eye contact. One of the Panthers huffed indignantly.

'You don't need to be calling that pig "sir",' he growled. 'He ain't your *master*, is he?'

The deputy pulled Delbert into the building and locked the doors behind him. He led Delbert down a narrow hallway, then down a flight of stairs into a large room with a high ceiling and dull fluorescent lights. There were six holding cells; two on the facing wall, and two each on the left and right walls. On the rear wall were two doors that opened into rooms where prisoners and their visitors could talk at a table, separated by a tall Plexiglas barrier that divided the table lengthwise.

LaVerne was sitting on a bench in the far right corner cell, his back turned to the door. He didn't see Delbert come in. The officer led Delbert into the visiting room.

'Wait on that side of the table,' he told Delbert, pointing to the far chair, opposite the door. Delbert sat down. He said a prayer and waited.

There was a clock on the wall by the door. It was eight minutes past eleven. The room smelled like cigarette ashes and weak coffee. One leg of his chair was just a bit shorter than the others, causing it to rock slightly when he shifted his weight.

He waited and remembered the boy.

He remembered wiping the boy's nose as they waited on the Dibbs' front porch when they went to visit after Ronnie Dibbs was killed in Korea. He remembered buttoning the top button of the boy's Sunday shirt before the school talent show at which the boy performed magic tricks with his friend Junebug. He remembered the boy trying to catch smoke from the pit in a Mason jar. He remembered laughing with Hartholz and teasing the boy as he heaved and retched behind the smoke pit after swallowing a plug of chewing tobacco, having decided that real baseball players needed tobacco-chewing skills.

He remembered the seventh inning of the boy's last high-school game. When the boy was at bat and had already hit two home runs. And the pitcher, who had decided that he would not give up another home run, hit the boy hard on the hip with a fastball. And the boy trotted to first, then took a sharp left turn, raced across the infield and tackled the pitcher and managed to bloody the kid's nose and upper lip before the ump and the two coaches pulled him away.

He remembered listening to the boy sing in church. Too loud and off key. Sweet and sincere.

The deputy led LaVerne into the room. He was handcuffed and his face was crumpled up like a discarded paper sack. He sat down on the other side of the Plexiglas partition. His head and shoulders slumped and he cried.

'I can't believe you came, Uncle Delbert,' he sobbed. 'I can't believe you came.'

Delbert nodded. 'Well, boy, you're in a tough spot and you needed some family.'

LaVerne sank deep in the chair and put his forehead on the tabletop.

'I'm sorry, Uncle. I'm so sorry. I ruined everything. I ruined everything for everybody.'

Delbert interrupted. 'Enough of that. Nothing's ruined for nobody.'

'But it is, Delbert,' LaVerne moaned. 'It didn't happen the way they say it did, but it happened just the same. And if I hadn't come out here, if I hadn't left my wife and baby, it never would have happened. But you need to know, Delbert, I didn't attack that officer. I didn't attack him. I was just upset and I needed Finley to listen to me and he was acting like he'd never seen me before. But *he* was the one who signed me. When I signed my contract we even shook hands. Then when I tried to talk to him he just walked on like I was nobody. And that deputy had hold of me and wouldn't let go and Finley was laughing and I needed to talk to him so I pulled loose and the deputy just fell. He fell back and hit his head. I didn't *mean* to hurt him. But I *did* hurt him. And now it's all over. Everything good in my life is over and done with.

Gone. My family. Plum Grove. Baseball. All gone. They're going to put me in jail. They're not going to let a black man off the hook for something like this. Not when it involves a deputy. Not the way things are right now. Then there's those guys outside stirring things up. They're just making all these police even more mad. I don't know how they even heard about me and or why they're here. It's not that I asked them to do this. It just makes things worse.'

He wiped his eyes and sat up. 'Not that they can really get any worse.'

He was finished. He stared down at his shackled hands. Delbert was silent. He could hear LaVerne breathing.

'Nothing's over, son,' he said quietly. 'Nothing's gone. It's all still right here. This is just a little detour on the road.'

LaVerne didn't look up.

'LaVerne, I checked with Sheriff Link Thompson back home and he told me that they have to give you one of those public lawyers to defend you in the court. It's the law,' Delbert said. 'The lawyer will tell the truth. He'll explain that it was an accident.

'Here's the other thing, son. You got people who love you. Your grandma and me. And Angela and your little Raymond. Angela's folks . . .'

LaVerne shook his head at the mention of Angela's family.

'May as well take them off the list, Uncle. They were never too pleased that their daughter ended up with me. This will sink my boat with them.'

Delbert leaned close to the divider.

'Listen to me, LaVerne. This is what I want you to hear. It doesn't matter how this all turns out. You are *loved*. I love you. And I won't stop. Not *ever*. No matter what you *do* or what anyone else does *to* you. I know you feel lost, son. But you are *not* lost. Because *I* know where you are. I know right where you are.'

The officer came in to tell them the visit was over. He escorted LaVerne back to the cell.

'I'll be back, LaVerne,' said Delbert. 'It's all gonna be all right.'

The officer led Delbert back up the stairs.

'Next time you visit your nephew it'll be over at the county jail,' he said. 'He's being transferred over there after his hearing.'

As Delbert and the deputy stood at the exit, the officer turned to Delbert.

'Your nephew seems like a good kid. He hasn't made any trouble. And he seems real broke up about all this. I think he's got remorse. I hope things work out somehow.'

Delbert nodded. 'Thank you, sir. He *is* a fine young man. He made a mistake is all.'

The deputy held the door open for Delbert, and Delbert made his way down the stairs. The protesters had mostly dispersed. Among those who remained was the surly young man who had challenged Delbert for calling the deputy 'sir'. He was leaning against a tree near the sidewalk with one of the other demonstrators. As Delbert walked by, on his way back to the bus stop, the young man sneered.

'That's it, old man,' he snorted. 'Shuffle and step. Shuffle and step. Just like a good Nee-gro.'

Delbert stopped and turned. 'Who *are* you?'

The man lit a cigarette.

'I'm the Deputy Minister of Community Organization of the Black Panther Party. Who are *you*?'

'I'm Delbert Douglass Merisier III,' Delbert said. 'And I am LaVerne Williams' great-uncle.'

The man grinned. 'I knew I recognized you! You're Uncle Tom!'

Delbert stepped close to the Deputy Minister of Community Organization. He was at least five inches shorter than the younger man, but nearly fifty pounds heavier. He looked up directly into the man's eyes.

'Why are you here?' he asked in a cold even voice.

'The Black Panther Party demands justice for Brother Williams who has been wrongfully imprisoned by the white police state,' the minister recited.

Delbert's thick calloused right hand shot up and gripped the minister's Adam's apple. He heaved the minister against the tree and pushed his knee against the young man's testicles.

'As I pointed out, I'm Mr Williams' great-uncle,' Delbert hissed, his face inches away from the minister's. 'So I happen to know that you ain't his brother. I also know you're just using him. You don't give a damn about him or what happens to him. You're just marchin' around out here makin' noise tryin' to get folks to pay attention to your sorry ass.'

The minister's colleague reached inside his black leather coat. Delbert turned to him.

'I figured you might have a gun,' he said. 'Go ahead and use it, if you got the balls to do it. My guess is you don't. All mouth is what you are.'

He released his grip and spat on the ground. Then he turned and continued on to the bus stop. Sweat rolled down his back and he felt the urge to urinate.

Behind him the Black Panther coughed and shouted hoarsely. 'Go on back to the plantation, Uncle Tom. We won't be needing you, come the revolution.'

In his room at the Turner Hotel, he sat on the edge of the bed, and poured a glass of whiskey from a bottle he had bought at a corner grocery down the street from the hotel. Beside the bed was a nightstand with a drawer. Delbert pulled it open. In it was a Gideon Bible.

He settled back onto the bed and laid the Bible on his lap. He drank the whiskey and looked at the Bible. He wondered what Bible verse Rose would tell him was a good one to read at a time like this.

35

Tharn

Royals tickets have been progressively easier to come by every year since 1985 when the team won the World Series. When it became clear, last year, that the team would finish its third consecutive season with more than 100 losses, the few remaining season ticket holders became so disgusted they began giving tickets away – entire home stands at a time if necessary – just to be rid of them. Bob Dunleavy tried giving a pair of his tickets to LaVerne.

Bob and Pug Hale were finishing lunch when LaVerne emerged from the kitchen to fiddle with and swear at the thermostat. Bob waved LaVerne over to their table.

'You want tickets for Sunday's Royals game? They're playing the Indians. I was going to take a couple of guys from our Charlotte office, but it turns out they're not coming until next week. So, you can have two, if you and Angela want to go with Marge and me. Or you can have all four if you want.'

LaVerne contemplated the offer.

'Royals tickets, huh? Let me check my schedule. Nope, sorry, I'll have to pass,' he said without the slightest hesitation. 'Looks like I'll be busy watching a classic "Sanford and Son" episode. It's the one where Fred fakes a heart attack. Thanks anyway, Bob.'

He turned and went back to the kitchen.

Bob looked at Pug and shook his head. 'I get that a lot this season.'

A.B. was clearing tables. As Bob stood to leave he called out to him.

'A.B., you like baseball?'

A.B. turned around. 'Hey, Bob. Hey, Pug. As far as base-ball goes, boss talks about it a lot. So I've learned some things about it. But I never been to a game or anything.'

Bob grinned, and thrust two tickets at A.B. 'You want to go on Sunday?'

A.B. smiled and shrugged. 'Wow, that's nice of you, Bob. Maybe I can get Jen to go with me.'

Pug spoke up. 'Boy, you and that young lady are getting pretty tight, aren't you?'

A.B.'s face reddened. He closely examined the towel he was holding.

'I don't know if "tight" is what you'd call it, Pug. Maybe it is. I don't know.' He looked up at Bob. 'Anyways. Thanks for the tickets, Bob. This'll be fun.'

Bob put his hand on AB's shoulder. 'My pleasure, son. You'll probably be sitting next to me and my wife. Or maybe me and my son, Warren, who we talked about, if that's all right.'

A.B. thought about the telephone pole up on 17th Street, where he'd seen Warren post the sign in rabbit language. He went into the kitchen, cut up red potatoes and hiccupped for the next hour and a half.

A.B. was worried about getting a good parking spot, so he and Jen arrived at Kauffman Stadium about forty-five min-utes before game time. Jen had assured him that parking wouldn't be a problem, and she was right.

'We're going to be the only ones in the whole stadium,' she said.

It was Bat Day at the ballpark. At each gate, stadium employees in Royals jerseys and caps gave each ticket holder a '2006 Kansas City Royals Commemorative Edition' Louisville Slugger mini-bat, about 18 inches long.

'This is awesome,' said A.B., whipping the tiny bat back and forth. 'I wish the boss was here.'

Jen smirked. 'I would have thought you'd know LaVerne better than that by now. He hates this kind of thing. Especially when it's the Royals doing it.'

A.B. thought about this for a moment.

'You're right. In fact, I better not even bring my little bat to the restaurant. He'll make me throw it away.'

Jen was determined that A.B. experience the Whole Baseball Thing, so on their way to their seats they bought hot dogs and beer.

'Then we're going to have peanuts and Cracker Jack,' she said. 'I don't care if I never get back.'

On their way down the steps to their seats, A.B. saw that Bob was already there with his son Warren.

'Ah, Jeez,' he muttered.

'What's wrong?' asked Jen.

'I was hoping Bob would be here with his wife,' he said. 'I met her a few times and she's real nice. Instead he's here with his son, Warren. Remember, I told you about him? He's obsessed with rabbits and stuff. Bob told me about what's wrong with him. Something mental. Anyways, he gives me the creeps.'

'It'll be fine,' Jen said. She linked her arm in A.B.'s. 'He's here to watch baseball, just like you.'

Bob and Warren were laughing when Jen and A.B. arrived at their seats. A.B. was relieved. It seemed normal.

Warren wore khakis and a white polo shirt. His longish

hair was stylishly unruly, but clean. The thick glasses he was wearing when A.B. had seen him out on the city streets at night – the ones that had made his eyes look so big and frightening – were gone. He looked like the grown son of an affluent, suburban, country-club family. Which is what he was.

Bob stood and shook hands with A.B. and Jen.

'Hey, guys! Glad you could come.'

Then he smacked himself in the forehead with the palm of his hand in a mock show of self-recrimination.

'Darn! I meant to tell you to bring a game of Scrabble or Monopoly for us all to play starting in the third or fourth inning when the Royals are down by eleven runs. It helps pass the time.'

Warren grinned and nodded forcefully. 'You always say that, Dad. I love it when you say that.'

Bob smiled sheepishly at A.B. and Jen. 'I don't have any new jokes, so I keep recycling the old ones.'

Warren vigorously nodded some more. 'You always say *that*, too.'

A.B. and Jen took their seats and Jen leaned forward and spoke to Warren who was sitting on the other side of his father.

'Hi, Warren. I'm Jen Richards.'

Warren nodded and smiled. 'Nice to meet you, Jen.'

A.B. thought Warren's face seemed less fierce without his glasses and wondered if maybe he was wearing contacts.

A.B. reached across Bob to extend his hand to Warren.

'Hi. I'm A.B. Clayton. I'm a friend of your dad's. I work at a restaurant where he eats all the time.'

'I know who you are,' Warren said, without making eye contact. 'You're *yona*.'

A.B. looked anxiously at Bob.

332

'That's a good thing,' Bob said matter-of-factly. 'Means you're a hedgehog.'

The Royals were going through their pre-game warm-ups. Some were taking batting practice. Several were playing catch. Others were jogging around the outside edge of the field. Bob eyed A.B.'s hot dogs and beer.

'Dang. I'm getting hungry. And since you didn't bring any ribs with you, I guess I'll have to go get me a weenie or two and some suds to wash 'em down with.'

Bob went for his refreshments, leaving A.B. and Jen there with Warren. Which was what A.B. had specifically dreaded.

Jen sensed his discomfort.

'So, Warren,' she said. 'Is this year's Royals team the worst team in baseball history, or what?'

Warren pondered the question. 'The '67 Athletics were probably worse.'

A.B. was grateful LaVerne wasn't there to hear that remark. Though he probably wouldn't disagree with Warren's conclusion, he didn't like being reminded.

Warren cleared his throat. 'Actually, I think the new GM, Dayton Moore, is going to turn things around. Though it may not happen until next year. And, frankly, I think Sweeney has got to go. He's old and he's always getting hurt. The future belongs to guys like Grudzielanek, DeJesus, and that new kid Alex Gordon.'

He nodded, pleased with his analysis.

Bob returned with food and beverages. He handed Warren a bratwurst and a large soda, keeping a hot dog and a beer for himself.

'I don't drink beer,' volunteered Warren to no one in particular. 'It messes with my meds.'

To his surprise, A.B. had fun. The Royals racked up ten runs in the first inning. Even though it would mean nothing in the scheme of things, the crowd enjoyed the prospect of a Royals rout. A rarity at Kauffman Stadium. Laughter and cheering were heard, which was also rare.

Then, midway through the game, things took a turn for the normal. The Royals began racking up errors, instead of runs, and the Indians began to score. The bullpen, which had been the object of great hopefulness before the season started, and of great derision ever since, proved incapable of defending Kansas City's lead. The final score was a 15–13 Royals' loss in ten innings. The once jolly crowd turned surly. Curses and catcalls were heard.

A.B., Jen, Bob, and Warren got up to leave.

'Well, A.B., I wish your first major-league game had had a better outcome,' sighed Bob. 'But at least it was an authentic Royals experience. Dashed hopes and all.'

A.B. and Jen laughed at Bob's observation, but Warren was silent. Bob, who had expected him to respond, turned to his son, prepared to repeat the joke.

Warren's attention was fixed on the ball field. His eyes wide and wild. He began moaning in a low drone, breathing in hard through his nose. He swayed slightly forward and back, his body rigid. Bob stepped up close to his son and put his arm around his waist.

'What's the matter, Warren?' he spoke gently near his son's ear. 'What's upsetting you?'

He followed the direction of Warren's gaze. A small brown rabbit had somehow gotten onto the field and was frantically trying to find its way back out. The animal raced back and forth on the dirt track along the base of the stadium wall. A group of fans – boys in their late teens or early twenties – had spotted the rabbit and had gathered by the top corner of the dugout to watch its increasingly frenetic efforts to escape. The young men were shirtless and each had a big blue letter painted on his chest. They appeared to have consumed a great deal of beer over the course of the game, as evidenced by a tall stack of empty souvenir beer cups one of them was carrying, as well as by their loud behavior. The more panicked the rabbit became the more they enjoyed the spectacle. They leaned over and pounded the wall and flailed their arms to further frighten the rabbit. Then the one with the beer cups began throwing them.

The cups made poor projectiles. None landed anywhere close to the rabbit. This frustrated the rowdies who each took a turn at trying to hit the rabbit with a beer cup. Finally, when none were successful, one of them flung his '2006 Kansas City Royals Commemorative Edition' Louisville Slugger mini-bat at the rabbit, striking it in the head. Jen gasped and clutched A.B.'s arm. Warren shrieked and had to be restrained by his father from rushing to the rabbit's aid.

The rabbit lay twitching on the grass in front of a rolled-up tarp.

Exiting fans who had passively watched the taunting were suddenly outraged at its violent conclusion. They began to boo the young men who, sensing the negative sentiment of the remaining crowd, decided it was time to leave. Stadium security officers intercepted them on their way out.

A groundskeeper went out onto the field to examine the rabbit.

Warren Dunleavy began to tremble and sweat. His eyes fluttered and he began to chant.

'*Zorn inle hrair elil owslafa zorn emblay zorn owslafa inle inle inle inle inle.*'

'Help me get him out of here,' said Bob, taking his son's left arm.

A.B. took Warren's right arm, and Jen stepped in front of them and began to lead them up the stairs to the concourse.

At the top of the stairs, Warren wrenched his head around to look back at the field. The groundskeeper had scooped the rabbit's body up with a shovel and was dumping it into a trashcan.

Warren fainted.

For days after, A.B. was depressed and distracted by what he had seen.

'I don't know what to do, boss,' he told LaVerne. 'I feel like I should do *something*. I mean, I was *there*. I saw the whole thing. It was *horrible*.'

LaVerne shook his head. 'Well, I can't even imagine what that must have looked like. Bad, I'm sure. But I don't know what you can do about it.'

Angela knew exactly what to do. When A.B. told her what happened at the game, she called Bob to ask about Warren and to express support.

'We've got him over at Two Rivers,' Bob said. 'It's the best psych hospital around. He's been there before. They know him. It was a pretty serious setback, Angela. I won't lie to you. Who would ever have thought something like that would happen at a baseball game, of all places. Going to games was one of the few things we did that seemed normal. Normal father and son stuff. I doubt he'll ever want to go back. This is just heartbreaking. Marge is taking it real hard. And I'm sorry A.B. and Jen had to experience the whole thing. I really am sorry.'

Angela had Leon and Vicki bring some sliced brisket, pulled chuck, two slabs of ribs, some red potatoes, and a vinegar pie to the Dunleavys' house, along with some flowers and a note saying how everyone at the restaurant was praying for their family in their hour of need. Then she notified the leader of the prayer chain she belonged to at New

Jerusalem Baptist Church and asked that Warren Dunleavy and his family be added to the list of people to be prayed for.

The other thing she did was to tell A.B. that he should go visit Warren in the hospital.

'I don't know, Angela,' he protested. 'It's not like we're friends. I barely know the guy. And, I hate to admit, I get really uncomfortable around him.'

'Maybe what he needs most *is* a friend, A.B.,' Angela said. Her voice was gentle and firm. She looked A.B. in the eye.

A.B. looked away. 'But I don't know anything about rabbits.'

Angela held A.B.'s eyes with a motherly scowl, which made A.B. squirm.

'Except for Richard "Rabbit" Brown,' he said. 'I know about him. And Eddie Rabbitt. Him, too. I know about music stuff and those guys are both musicians. I don't think that counts as rabbits, though.'

Angela smiled. 'You might be surprised.'

Because it was a hospital, when A.B. arrived at Warren's room he expected to see Warren lying in a bed, in his pajamas. Maybe sleeping. Instead he was sitting cross-legged in an easy chair playing solitaire on a handheld electronic game. He was dressed in jeans and a clean, pressed, white T-shirt.

'*Yona*,' he said, without looking up. 'My father said you were going to come.'

A.B. stood in the doorway, unsure.

'You can come in,' said Warren. 'I'm crazy, but I'm not violent.'

'So, Warren. I came to visit you,' A.B. said as he moved tentatively into the room.

'I guess you did,' Warren's eyes were dull and his voice flat.

A.B. wished he hadn't come to visit Warren. He stood there not knowing what to do or say. He wondered why being a hedgehog was good.

'You can sit,' Warren motioned toward the other chair in the room. 'Go ahead and sit. I'm glad you came.'

Warren still hadn't actually looked at A.B. And A.B. only just barely at Warren.

A.B. sat down. 'So, are you feeling any better?'

Warren shrugged. 'I'm so heavily medicated I don't feel anything.'

A.B. shook his head. 'Jeez, Warren. I can't even imagine what that would be like. I'm sorry.'

Warren didn't say anything. A.B. shifted in his chair.

'So, I know you like rabbits and baseball, Warren. Is there anything else you like? I, myself, am kinda into music. Especially the blues. But I like other music, too. Country, and rock. Even some jazz. You like music?'

Warren shrugged again and nodded just slightly. 'I like music.'

He paused.

'As far as rabbits are concerned, it's not so much that I like them. At least not in the way that you're probably thinking of it. It's more that I understand them. I believe in them. Their role in God's plan is clear to me in ways that other people don't see. I know that my whole deal with rabbits is why people think I'm mentally ill. And if not being like normal people is the definition of mentally ill then I probably am. The doctors say that mental illness is a result of chemical imbalances in the brain. I know that my brain chemicals are messed up. That's clear to everybody. Including me. But have you ever thought that maybe if your brain has a little bit more of one chemical and a little less of another, it doesn't necessarily make you mentally ill, but maybe it makes you able to see things, perceive things, that normal people can't. Maybe some brain chemicals are like a blindfold that prevent us from seeing things in the world that are really there. And if those chemicals shift or are changed somehow, you see the world around you as it really is. I wonder about that. I think that's what makes prophets, like in the Bible, able to foretell the future. They see things. They see the hand of God at work in the world. I think that's maybe why I understand the importance of the rabbit world. Richard Adams understood it. He's a prophet. *Watership Down* is a book of prophecy. I understand that rabbits are like God's chosen people. Only they're not people. Obviously. But they *are* God's creatures. And he has chosen for them a special place in his kingdom. But I'd never own a pet rabbit. I don't like them in that way. Not like pet dogs or cats or gerbils or anything.'

A.B. took in a deep breath and let it out slow. He felt a bit nauseous. He felt hiccups coming on. He wished Jen were there with him. Even more, he wished he were with Jen, wherever she was.

'So? What kind of music do you like, Warren?'

Warren looked out the window. 'I like the Eagles. And Tom Petty. Johnny Cash quite a lot. Neil Young. And Bob Dylan. Only sometimes he makes me anxious so I have to quit listening to him.'

A.B. smiled. 'You have great taste in music, Warren. I didn't really know what you'd like, but I made you a CD. So maybe, you know, you could listen to it sometime.'

He handed Warren a plastic case with a CD in it. It was labeled, 'Rabbit Tunes'.

'I don't know about rabbits being God's chosen people or anything,' A.B. said. 'But I like going online and finding and downloading songs. My friend Jen, who you met at the

339

game, she and me do that a lot. So I made this. Some of the songs are kind of about rabbits or they have rabbits in the title or the musicians have rabbit in their name somehow. It's probably dorky to do a whole CD of rabbit music now that I think about it.'

Warren looked at A.B. and smiled.

'It's not dorky,' he said. He turned the case over and read the list of songs printed on the back.

Pet Rabbit – *Johnny Shines*
Rabbits – *Dave Bernstein*
The Rabbit Dance – *George Winston, 'The Velveteen Rabbit' soundtrack*
Rabbit Blues – *Robert 'Smoky Babe' Brown*
Rabbit – *Count Basie and the Kansas City Five*
The Rabbit – *John Hammond, Jr., Mason Daring*
Br' Rabbit – *Johnny Hodges*
Rabbit Song – *The Lost & Found*
White Rabbit – *Jefferson Airplane*
James Alley Blues – *Richard 'Rabbit' Brown*
Come with me to Rabbittland – *Eddie Rabbitt*

'I guess I never knew that there were so many songs about rabbits,' he said.

A.B. nodded. 'Actually there was a lot more. But most of them weren't very good. And some of them had, I don't know, bad words . . .'

Warren made a small laughing noise.

'The Jefferson Airplane song is a classic. Especially for us crazy people. We like the line, "*One pill makes you larger. One pill makes you small. And the ones that mother gives you don't do anything at all.*"'

Warren studied the song list.

'The only other song I know here is "The Rabbit Dance"

340

from *The Velveteen Rabbit*. That was one of my favorite books growing up. I watched the movie on TV lots of times.'

Warren stood and went over to the window and put the disk in a CD player sitting on the windowsill. Then he and A.B. listened to it all the way through.

36

Briefcase Full of Blues

After A.B.'s fourth rabbit-themed monologue in as many days, LaVerne laid down the law.

'Son, if you don't *shut up* about rabbits I'm going to lock you in the damn freezer,' he snapped. 'In fact, I have a better idea. Just plain ol' shut up. About rabbits, about *everything*. Just be quiet for a while. Long enough for me to remember what it feels like to think my own thoughts again.'

About a week after he started visiting Warren at the hospital on a regular basis, A.B. surprised everybody at the restaurant with a detailed oral biography of Baseball Hall of Famer Walter 'Rabbit' Maranville. Baseball not having been a subject he'd previously shown much interest in, in spite of LaVerne's background in the sport.

'I'm sure you probably heard of him, boss. Apparently he was this really aggressive little ball player,' A.B. said as he was washing greens.

'He played for twenty-three years, which is a really long time. All of it in the National League. He played mostly for the Boston Braves. He started out with them in the early 1900s and played with them until 1920. Then he went and played for the Pittsburgh Pirates for a while. Then he played for the Chicago Cubs and then the Brooklyn Robins. The Robins seems like a silly name for a sports team if you ask me. But when you think about it it's not really any sillier than the Blue Jays or the Cardinals. Which, by the way, is where Walter "Rabbit" Maranville played next. Then he went back to the Braves. Warren told me all this. It's really kind of amazing all the things he knows about. Anyways, I don't know a lot about baseball, as you know, boss. But Warren told me the Braves don't even play in Boston anymore. The team moved to Milwaukee and then to Atlanta. Or maybe it's the other way around. You probably knew that. So, this guy Rabbit was famous for his "basket" catches, which I don't really know what that is. Warren says the most interesting thing about him is that he was real little and that's why they called him Rabbit. Because rabbits are little. Plus he was quick like a rabbit.'

LaVerne scowled at A.B. 'Just because I played one year of pro ball doesn't mean I have personal knowledge of everybody who ever played the game. And it doesn't mean I have any interest in some rabbit guy who played almost a hundred years ago. Furthermore, your yammering on about it has caused a slow-down in your washing responsibilities.'

Later in the week, A.B. asked aloud, as he was turning briskets, if anyone else was as concerned as he was about the plight of the New England cottontail rabbits and the Columbia Basin pygmy rabbit.

Even though neither Leon nor Vicki said that they were concerned, A.B. decided it was an important enough issue that they should be apprised.

'Only three hundred New England cottontails are still alive in the state of Maine, which is where they live,' he explained. 'New England cottontails are the only true rabbits in Maine. There's some people trying to make a bigger area for these rabbits to live so they'll be protected. About four hundred and fifty acres by the Spurwink River. So that's good.

'But the Columbia Basin pygmy rabbit situation is real serious. The last purebreed male Columbia Basin pygmy rabbit died recently, leaving just two females in captivity, so the Oregon Zoo is going to try to breed the females with some Idaho and Idaho-Washington rabbits. But they won't be pure Columbia Basin pygmy rabbits.'

Leon said he was going out for a cigarette and Vicki said she was going out to clear tables.

On Friday, A.B. started in first thing in the morning with an explanation of how it was that the recently deceased World Heavyweight Champion Floyd Patterson got the nick-name of 'The Rabbit'.

'Basically, it was Muhammad Ali who first called him that. He called him that as an insult. Warren says that Floyd Patterson shouldn't have been insulted by it. He should have been honored by it.'

LaVerne shook his head. 'Boy, I didn't think insanity was contagious, but I think you been infected. You been hangin' out with Warren a little too much. I'm going to have to call Jen and pay her to take you out on a date so you'll have something else to do instead of going to listen to crazy Warren and his bunny stories.'

LaVerne went out back to get wood for the smoker. Leon and Vicki were in the dining room pretending to work, having realized that avoiding A.B. as much as possible was a good idea while he was on his rabbit jag. When A.B. eased a few words of rabbit language into casual workplace conver-sation, then later began to talk about the cruelty of giving rabbits as pets at Easter time, LaVerne put his foot down.

'Seriously, A.B.,' he said. 'I think it's good and Christian of you to be visiting Warren in the hospital and all. Angela is proud of you. So am I. And I'm sure Warren and Bob are grateful. But you got to be careful not to become too involved. You got a life you got to think about. Your work.

Your other friends. Jen. You and her got a good thing goin' on, boy. Don't get so carried away by doing a good thing that it turns out bad.'

On a Saturday morning, three or four weeks after Warren was discharged from Two Rivers psychiatric hospital, a limousine pulled up in front of LaVerne Williams' Genuine BBQ and City Grocery. It was a vintage 1967 Cadillac Fleetwood 75. Twenty feet long. Cream exterior, maroon leather interior, with seating for eight.

It was about 10:30, and though the restaurant was open, there weren't yet any customers in the place. A.B., Vicki, and Leon were in the kitchen, and LaVerne was out in the dining room taking chairs down from the tables.

Whoever it was who was driving the limo laid on the horn, which blared the first eight bars of 'Somewhere My Love' from the movie *Dr Zhivago*. Then whoever it was did it again.

This aroused LaVerne's attention.

'What the hell,' he groused, setting a chair down with more force than the situation called for. He went over to the window to see what all the commotion was about.

LaVerne's arrival at the window prompted a reprise of Lara's Theme.

'I *hate* that song,' LaVerne muttered. He went out to the curb to demand that the limo go somewhere else. As he was about to knock on the driver's window, the window slowly lowered. Bob Dunleavy was sitting in the driver's seat, wearing aviator-style sunglasses and a big grin.

'How do like my new wheels?'

Up to that point, LaVerne was so annoyed by the repeated choruses of 'Somewhere My Love' he hadn't actually noticed the car itself. He stepped back to take a look.

'Bob! This is a *sweet* ride, man!' he exclaimed. 'Where did you get this?'

He bent down to check out the inside and saw that Warren was sitting in the front passenger seat, which he had not expected. He paused, not sure if he should say something.

'Hi,' he said. 'I'm LaVerne Williams.'

Warren nodded. 'Is A.B. here?' he asked.

'He is,' LaVerne said. 'Would you like me to go get him?'

LaVerne looked at Bob. Bob smiled an 'It's okay' smile.

LaVerne went inside and a few moments later returned with A.B. behind him, wiping his hands on his apron.

Bob and Warren were standing curbside.

'Well, young man? What do you think?' Bob asked A.B., stepping to the side and sweeping his hands in the direction of the car, in the manner of a game-show hostess.

Warren spoke in a voice lacking animation. 'Cool, huh? What do you think, A.B.?'

His eyes were focused on some point down around A.B.'s knees. He seemed to be trying to smile.

A.B. grinned. 'No *way*, Bob! Warren! This is *yours*? This is the same year and make as the Caddy in the Blues Brothers movie! No lie!'

Warren nodded and succeeded in smiling. 'That was a good movie. Those guys were on a mission from God.'

'So, what's the story, Bob?' LaVerne asked. 'Where'd you get this big ol' barge?'

'Well, there was this "high society grande dame" that Marge knew who died about a month ago,' Bob said. 'She was never married and apparently had no heirs. This car is what her hired man used to drive her around in. But I guess he passed on several years ago and this baby's just been sitting in her garage since then. So, when they had the estate sale, I scooped it up for a song.'

Bob opened the back driver's side door. 'Come on, you two. Get in. Let's take this boat on a cruise.'

LaVerne stepped inside the restaurant and yelled to Leon and Vicki that he and A.B. would be back in a little bit. He got in the car. A.B. was about to, when he stopped and bolted for the restaurant door.

'I'll be right back,' he said. Seconds later he returned holding a CD. In the car, he handed it to Bob.

'If you've got a CD player in here, put this in,' said A.B.

Bob checked. 'You're in luck, A.B. Looks like it's been retrofitted.'

He slid the disk into the player. It was the Blues Brothers' first record, *Briefcase Full of Blues*. The first track was Otis Redding's 'I Can't Turn You Loose'. A half-hour later the Caddy pulled up in front of Smoke Meat and discharged its passengers and crew.

Three men in suits were outside the restaurant looking up and down at the building, as well as the other buildings on the block, the buildings across the street, and the street itself. Bob recognized one of the men.

'Hey, Ute Johansson,' he said. 'What are you doing in this neighborhood?'

Bob extended his hand to a tall burly man with blond hair and a broad ruddy face.

'Hey yourself, Bob Dunleavy!' the ruddy man replied, vigorously shaking Bob's hand. 'We're scouting out some properties. Hoping to get in on the action down here. Downtown is where it's all happening, with all these big projects you got going. You must be hauling the money to the bank in truckloads every night.'

He laughed loudly.

Bob didn't laugh. 'Ute Johansson, meet my friend LaVerne Williams. This is his restaurant. My favorite restaurant in all the world.'

347

Ute and LaVerne shook hands. LaVerne reluctantly so, having already sized up the situation and understanding it not to be in his favor.

'Nice to meet you, LaVerne,' said Ute, cheerily. 'I've always meant to come down here and check out your place. I hear it's great.'

LaVerne nodded. 'That's right.'

He looked at Bob, then back at Ute. 'Well, if you'll excuse me, I've got work to do.'

La Verne and A.B. went inside, leaving Bob and Warren out on the sidewalk with Ute and his colleagues.

LaVerne stormed through the kitchen, past Leon and Vicki, into his office where he swiped a bottle of barbecue sauce off the top of the filing cabinet and heaved it against the far wall, shattering the bottle, splattering his framed team photo of the 1967 Kansas City Athletics.

A.B. was right behind him. 'Are those guys out there going to buy this building? Is that what they're doing?'

'What does it look like?' LaVerne barked. 'They're not here to deliver flowers.'

'But they can't really buy the restaurant, can they? We've got a lease, right? So that would still be good with some other owner, right? That's what happened with my apartment building. They had to honor the lease.'

LaVerne paced in front of his desk. He glanced over at the wall where sauce and shards of broken bottle were sliding slowly down.

'I don't know. I don't know. All I know is it's out of our control and I don't like it. You scrape by, doing the best you can for twenty-five years then some fat-ass developer comes along and pulls the rug right out from under you. I should never have located in a building I couldn't afford to buy myself. This is just unbelievable.'

*

348

Outside, Bob pushed Ute Johansson regarding his intentions.

'We're looking to increase our holdings in this area,' Ute explained. 'With all the rehabbing and condo and office development, the galleries and such. We just want in on the action, like I said. We're actually in negotiations to buy this entire block. We're bullish on downtown, just like you. This block is ripe for some high-end retail. We envision a Pottery Barn, a Starbucks, a Chipotle, maybe a Border's.'

Bob interrupted Ute's reverie. 'What about the local homegrown businesses that are already here?'

'Oh, they'll be fine,' Ute said, with a dismissive wave of his hand. 'We'll pay to have 'em relocated to some other part of town. If they're really a healthy business, they'll survive. Their customers will follow them. It's a win-win.'

Ute and his cohorts excused themselves and walked down the block to continue their inspection.

Bob and Warren got back in the Caddy.

'I don't like that man,' said Warren.

'I don't either, son,' said Bob, shaking his head. '*Vair. Vair.*'

Warren nodded. '*Elil.*'

Almost immediately rumors began to migrate up and down the 1700 block of Walnut Street. One day at lunch Suzanne Edwards and McKenzie Nelson told LaVerne that they'd heard that Johansson's company was planning on locating a franchise of the Great USA Barbeque Company in the neighborhood somewhere.

'Well, that tells you all you need to know about their plans for LaVerne Williams' Genuine BBQ and City Grocery, doesn't it?' he sneered. He threw a dishtowel into the sink and stalked off.

The next day, LaVerne sat down next to Ferguson as he was finishing a pulled chuck sandwich.

'I been doing some research on this so-called Great USA Barbeque Company,' he said. He looked and talked as if he had a mouthful of turd.

'First of all they spell barbecue with a Q. Not B-B-Q, like we do. Not B-A-R-dash-B-dash-Q, like lots of other folks do. No, they spell it B-A-R-B-E-Q-U-E. That's a sissy-ass way to spell barbecue.

'Next of all, it was started up by some guy named Tony David, who used to be an accountant at ConAgra. You catch that? Accountant. ConAgra. They're that big food corporation. Good place to learn barbecue, huh? Plus this guy was born and raised in Wisconsin. *Wisconsin!* As if.

'Then, get this. Listen to their motto. "Best Barbeque in the World". Can you believe it? And if that ain't bad enough, they don't just have one motto, they have two. Their other one is "Legendary for Ribs". How do you like that? We don't even have *one* motto. Though maybe we *should* have one. How about this? "This is our barbecue. If you don't like it, I don't give a shit." Or maybe we could have two mottos like them. Here's our second one: "We've been here for twenty-four years, so take your so-called 'legendary ribs' and go to hell."'

Before Ferguson could say a word, LaVerne had huffed back to the kitchen.

As Ferguson left Smoke Meat he saw two men across the street. They had clipboards and tape measures, and they were looking at the restaurant from different angles, taking notes and talking on walkie-talkies.

37

Up in Michigan

About the same time Ferguson stopped asking LaVerne if he had any bourbon back in the office, LaVerne stopped offering to go in the back and get some. This didn't stop them from regularly staying behind after the restaurant closed, to sit at a table in the middle of the dining room and talk about things. It was just that drinking whiskey was no longer the pretext for it.

LaVerne sensed that Ferguson was done with drinking, without him actually having said anything to that effect. And Ferguson sensed that LaVerne understood better than anyone what it meant to give up something that had defined you and also ruined you.

'So. Memphis, huh?' LaVerne said, with a slight, sly smile, sitting down across from Ferguson. 'My, my, my.'

Ferguson shook his head. 'Strangest thing that's ever happened to me.'

LaVerne laughed. 'I think *you* may be the strangest thing that ever happened to *her*. I don't know of a black woman anywhere that's sittin' at home hoping or expecting that some rich white Episcopal priest-writer-professor is going to show up out of the blue someday and sweep her off her feet.'

'I don't know why not,' said Ferguson with a straight face. 'That seems perfectly plausible to me. Although I'll

351

admit that I don't know too many rich white Episcopal priest-writer-professors who are sitting at home hoping or expecting that some black woman barbecue entrepreneur is going to save him from himself, his past, and the hounds of hell nipping at his heels.'

LaVerne looked across the table at his friend. He never knew whether to be impressed or embarrassed by the way Ferguson talked.

'I'm guessing this is a serious thing. You two are too old to be wasting your time, flirting, and goin' on dates, and all the usual stuff.'

'It is. Serious.' Ferguson nodded. 'We probably shouldn't skip all the flirting and dating. But I think we both know that it's one of those things that we can't approach with caution. We can't be rational about it, because if we were we wouldn't even let ourselves consider it as a possibility. We have to jump right in with abandon. Head first. It'll either succeed spectacularly or spectacularly fail.'

LaVerne nodded as if he understood, even though he had only ever done one uncareful thing in his entire life and that had turned out badly. Everything before and after that one thing had been calculated and controlled. 'Abandon' and 'head first' were not concepts LaVerne embraced.

He got up, went to the kitchen and came back with a loaf of French bread and a box of Morton's kosher salt. He sat, broke the loaf in two and gave half to Ferguson. Then he poured some salt on a paper napkin, tore a piece from his half of the bread, pushed it into the salt, then ate it.

'Sometimes I get tired of the food on the menu. This right here tastes good to me. Simple.'

Ferguson pressed a piece of his bread in the salt and ate it.

'So what's the next step?' LaVerne asked. 'Goin' to meet the family?'

'Actually, yes. Next weekend, in fact.'

'I'll say this: she's one fine-looking woman.'

'She is indeed,' Ferguson said with conviction.

They drank coffee and ate their bread. LaVerne looked out the window.

'Don't you tell Angela I said that.'

Ferguson poured a packet of sugar into his coffee. 'Never ever.'

Ferguson's visit to Memphis to spend the weekend getting to know Peri's family got off to a bad start when his flight from Kansas City was delayed by the forced removal of a passenger whose grief over the death of his son – a college student whose body was being transported in the cargo bay of the aircraft – erupted in an alcohol- and guilt-induced rage, resulting in the injury of a flight attendant. Later newspaper accounts of the incident reported that the deceased had been drinking heavily and crossed the centerline driving back to campus from a bar where he and friends had been downing shots and shooting pool. One of the friends and a passenger in the other car involved in the accident were also killed. The young man had been a student at the University of San Diego and his father was escorting his body back to Portland, Maine, where the family lived and the boy would be buried.

Ferguson was standing in line at the gate with the other passengers waiting to board. He had come to the airport straight from the seminary, and was wearing what he always wore in his classroom – a black suit, black shirt, and clerical collar, with a silver chain and crucifix around his neck. As the bereaved and inebriated father was dragged from the plane by two airport policemen and an airline official, he grabbed Ferguson by the lapels of his coat.

'Forgive me, father!' pleaded the man, pulling Ferguson's startled face close to his. Ferguson smelled the sour floral smell of whiskey on the man's breath and remembered what that tasted like. 'I'm sorry. Tell him I'm sorry, father. Forgive me! I know I've sinned! I sinned against him. And the others, too. It was *me* who killed them! Not him! It's my fault!'

Instinctively, Ferguson reached out and placed his hand on the distraught man's forehead. He spoke with urgency and authority.

'Almighty God have mercy on you, and forgive you all your sins through our Lord Jesus Christ, strengthen you in all goodness, and by the power of the Holy Spirit keep you in eternal life. Amen.'

The police pulled the man's hands from Ferguson's suit coat. He looked back at Ferguson in anguish and gratitude as he was hauled away. Ferguson crossed himself, as did a nearby airline employee and another passenger. He flipped open his cell phone and called Peri to tell her what had happened and that his flight would be late.

The main event of Ferguson's visit was to be the traditional African-American Sunday doubleheader – church followed by family dinner at Grandma's house; Grandma being Periwinkle Brown.

'I don't know another grandmother who's as hot as you, Grandma Brown,' said Ferguson, as he and Peri drove to church.

'I *am* hot, Reverend,' she affirmed. 'And one of these days, you're going to get burned.'

'Is that a promise, Grandma Brown?' Ferguson laughed.

'You keep callin' me "Grandma" and you'll find out *exactly* what "burned" means.' Peri waggled her finger back and forth in mock warning.

Mount Gilead Baptist is no longer a small urban congregation, meeting in a crumbling downtown church building. It has grown exponentially in the nearly forty years since

Ferguson attended prayer meeting with Peri. The church has moved to a gleaming, golf-course-sized campus in the East Memphis suburbs, to better accommodate its more than 12,000 members.

The engine powering this growth is the Rev. Jerome Aaron Jenkins, who was appointed Mount Gilead's senior pastor in 1988, when he was thirty-two years old and the congregation's membership stood at 138. At six feet six inches tall and 340 pounds, Rev. Jenkins – who is called Rev. J.J. by most of his flock and 'J Dawg' by many of the church's young people – looks every bit the offensive lineman he once was at Tennessee State University.

Rev. Jenkins' preaching is as commanding as his physical presence. When he thunders forth from his pulpit that '*surely* the *Lord* is in *this* place', no one dares not believe it. And when he exhorts his congregation to 'go therefore and make disciples of *all* nations', they pretty much get up and go.

However, Rev. Jenkins' powerful personality and spiritual authority are only partly responsible for Mount Gilead's growth. Rev. J.J.'s entrepreneurial energy and vision have had at least as much to do with it. In interviews published in *Christianity Today*, *USA Today*, the *New York Times*, and the *Memphis Commercial Appeal*, Rev. Jenkins proudly pointed out that Mount Gilead was at the forefront of the trend toward large, ethnically diverse, suburban churches. 'We put the "mega" in the mega-church movement,' he said.

'It's impressive all right,' Peri told Ferguson, as they neared the campus. 'Miraculous really. And I was swept right along in J.J.'s rushing river with everyone else. But I've been worried for a while now that maybe it's all gotten too big. It's like a big business. It's not the Mount Gilead I grew up in. Not by a long shot.'

She sighed. 'But don't tell Tyrell I feel that way. This church is his life. Well, Wren and the girls come first. And the restaurants. But he's neck deep in the life of this church. He was chairman of the board of deacons for three terms. He's been president of the men's fellowship. He taught Sunday School. He coaches one of the basketball teams. Everything. He's in everything there. To be honest, I think he's the main reason I'm still there. Plus they have a great choir.'

She sighed again. 'Maybe I'll become an Episcopalian.'

Then Ferguson sighed. 'Well, that's just great. I was thinking of becoming a *Baptist*.'

Ferguson couldn't get the bereft father at the airport out of his head. He had prayed for the man during his flight from Kansas City to Memphis, and again during compline in his room that night. But the image of the man's contorted face and watery bloodshot eyes, and the strangled sound of his pleas, would not go away.

He had thought he would pray some more at Mount Gilead on Sunday, but, as he and Peri lowered themselves into plush theater-style seats, he understood that intimate time with God would not be one of the main features of the morning service. Intimacy was not the objective of worship at Mount Gilead. It was praise. Loud praise, and lots of it. Also exhortation. And, at Mount Gilead, praise and exhortation are done on one's feet, with one's hands either clapping or lifted towards the heavens. Only a very few minutes of the nearly three-hour-long service were actually spent sitting in the plush theater-style seats.

The praising commenced with the opening act, which was the gospel choir, accompanied by the rock band, leading the faithful in a hyperkinetic rendition of Psalm 68:

> 'May God arise, may his enemies be scattered; may his
> foes flee before him.

As smoke is blown away by the wind, may you blow
  them away;
But may the righteous be glad and rejoice before God;
May they be happy and joyful
Sing to God, sing praise to his name,
Extol him who rides on the clouds – his name is the
  Lord
A father to the fatherless,
God sets the lonely in families,
He leads forth the prisoners with singing.'

After the choir had concluded its frenetic choruses it was time for the exhortation.

Rev. Jerome Jenkins ascended to his pulpit from which he extolled his followers to 'live the *expectant* life'.

He took as his text the eleventh chapter of Luke, verses 9 through 13:

'*For everyone who* asks, receives, *and everyone who* searches, finds, *and for everyone who* knocks, *the door will be* opened.

'*Is there anyone among you who, if your child asks for a fish, will give a snake* instead *of a fish?*

'*Or if the child asks for an egg, will give a* scorpion?

'*If you then, who are* evil, *know how to give good gifts to* your *children, how much more will the heavenly* Father *give the Holy Spirit to those who* ask *him!*

'*So I say to you, ask, and it will be* given *you;* search, *and you will* find; knock, *and the door will be* opened *for* you.'

J Dawg paused to let the meaning of the Word soak in.

'When we *pray*, naturally we *want* God to answer our prayers. We *hope* God will answer our prayers. Most times we *need* God to answer our prayers. But we rarely *expect* God to answer our prayers.'

He whispered, 'Where is our *trust*?' And then thundered 'Where is our *faith*?'

Over the course of the next forty or so minutes, Rev. Jenkins admonished his congregation to 'ask for an egg, if an egg is what you want! But if you ask for an egg, you best *expect* an egg!

'Your faith in God is *revealed* in what you *expect* when you come to him with the needs of your life and the desires of your heart. If you *trust* God, you *won't* be expecting *scorpions*!'

Most of the congregation stood during most of the sermon, and cheered their pastor on as he preached, as they would the star of the hometown basketball team shooting three-pointers from the corner. The cheering was accompanied by much stomping and clapping. Rev. Jenkins was assisted by the organist who drove home key points with strategically placed chords and flourishes. As J.J. crescendoed to the finish, the organist's riffs got louder and more elaborate.

To help sustain the congregation's enthusiasm and the overall entertainment quotient, Rev. Jenkins improvised a few well-executed dance steps near the climax of his message.

'Expect God to make himself *known* to you!' he shouted, performing a syncopated shuffle, followed by a dainty two-step. 'Expect him to bless you with a new job, if *that's* what you need! God *knows* what you need! Expect him to bless your garage with a new *car*, if that's what you need. Expect him to bless you with a *garage*, if *that's* what you need.

'Expect him to make his *face* to shine upon you! Expect him to bless you in your coming *and* your going! Expect him to bless your children and your children's children to *all* generations!

'But, you need also to expect *God* to expect *something*

from *you*. God expects *you* to give *him* what's rightfully his. If he gives you *money*, you *best* give some back. If he gives you a new car, you best be giving folks a *ride to church on Sunday*. And if he gives you a job, you *best* be workin' in the *Master's* vineyard.

'Live your life in expectation that our Lord *is* coming back someday. Because someday he's coming back in *glory*. And *you* had best be ready.'

For emphasis and effect, Rev. Jenkins stretched out the words 'glory' and 'you' in his closing – 'glohhhhree!' and 'yewwww!'

Dinner was at Wren and Tyrell's big beige suburban house, and featured ham, macaroni and cheese, cornbread, fresh green beans with bacon, and homemade strawberry-rhubarb pie. Tyrell did the cooking. Ferguson was profuse in his praise.

After dinner, Peri listened contentedly as Ferguson and Wren chattered on about the current state of popular music. Wren asked if Ferguson had heard any of the new Dylan, which he had. Ferguson then asked Wren if she'd heard any of Solomon Burke's latest, and she had.

Tyrell had finished dinner clean-up, and was getting bored, so he tried steering the conversation in another direction.

'So, Brother Glen,' he said. 'How does our service at Mount Gilead compare to your Episcopal service?'

Ferguson laughed.

'That's easy. Compared to you, we look like we're dead. If we could capture all the energy at that service we could end America's dependence on foreign oil.'

Tyrell laughed, too, nodding in agreement.

'Seriously, though. I've never been to an Episcopal church. What's it like?'

'Well, there's more majesty and mystery in the Episcopal liturgy,' said Ferguson. 'But there's more joy in your worship. More joy and better preaching. Most Episcopal priests aren't nearly as gifted preachers as is your Rev. Jenkins.'

Tyrell liked hearing this. 'J.J. can bring it. Can't he? We're blessed to have him as our leader. We were praying for someone like him. We were about to shrivel up and die. But look at us now. It's like the passage from today says, "Ask and you shall receive."'

'That's true,' said Ferguson, smiling only slightly. 'Except for when it isn't.'

Tyrell wasn't sure he heard Ferguson right. 'Except for when it *isn't*?'

'Well,' Ferguson said. 'We don't get *every*thing we ask God for. Sometimes we ask for eggs and, while we may not get scorpions in return, we don't get any eggs either.'

Tyrell agreed with this, though somewhat tentatively and reluctantly.

'Right. But that's just God acting in our best interests. He knows better than we do what we need and what's best for us. We may not always ask for the things God knows we need.'

Ferguson nodded. 'Exactly. That's why I'm not sure we can call the things we enjoy or are grateful for "blessings". The logic of that is flawed. If we get what we pray for and call it a blessing, what do we call it when our neighbor who didn't pray gets the same thing? We thank God for the blessing of the sunshine, but Jesus says God causes the sun to shine on the righteous and sinners alike. So is the sunshine a blessing? Or is it just the sunshine?'

Periwinkle and Wren were quiet and attentive, as when anticipating thunder after lightning has hit.

Tyrell scowled. 'So, let me see if I understand what you're saying. Are you saying that there are no such things as blessings, in spite of the fact that blessings are mentioned throughout scripture?'

Ferguson realized that the conversation had gone down a path he wished it had not gone down. And he realized the only way out of it was back the way it came. He let out a long low breath.

'What I mean is that answered prayers and blessings aren't the same things. Think about the people who come to Mount Gilead's soup kitchen for a warm meal. Surely many, if not most of them have prayed for jobs, for homes, for health, for healing, wholeness, love, someone to notice them and take pity on them. And yet there they are. In line at a soup kitchen. So, are their prayers not good enough? Jesus never says that God's answers to our prayers are contingent on the quality of our prayers. He never says that our prayers have to meet some certain standard of excellence before God will answer them. In fact, the prayer he asks us to take notice of is the simple plea, "Have mercy on me, a sinner."

'It's easy to say that those folks are there in line at the soup kitchen because of bad decisions they've made, and it's probably true. But I've made just as many – maybe more – bad decisions in my life, and I'm not standing in line with them. So *why* are they there? Because God *chose* not to bless them? Why *wouldn't* he bless them? They're his children just as much as we are.

'I guess what I'm getting at is that I don't think we can necessarily make the connection between answered prayers and blessings. I think the only connection is that we are blessed when we pray – that the act of praying is itself a blessing. But I don't think it's safe to conclude that when we get what we pray for we can call it a blessing.'

He sighed and looked at his hosts apologetically. Then he added one final point.

'Besides, if you read the passage in Luke that Rev. Jenkins used as his text this morning, it is really more about the Holy Spirit than it is about getting God to give us what we want.

'*If you then, who are evil, know how to give good gifts to your children, how much more will the heavenly Father give the* Holy Spirit *to those who ask him!*

'When we come to God in prayer, he answers us by giving us the Holy Spirit. By being with us in the person of the Holy Spirit. So the answer to our prayers is God himself.'

Tyrell shook his head.

'I won't argue that. That's certainly true. But I won't concede that God doesn't sometimes answer our specific prayers with the specific things we pray for. And that when we prosper in this world, when we enjoy the good things that life has to offer, those are blessings from our good God who wants us to enjoy his abundance.'

Ferguson smiled. 'Well, I prayed that I'd be well fed, and I was. And it was abundant. And it was a blessing.'

Tyrell nodded. 'And I prayed for some intellectually stimulating theological give and take with my guest the priest and author, and I got what I prayed for. And it was a blessing.'

Tyrell and Ferguson shook hands. Peri and Wren raised their eyebrows at one another and breathed out.

Over coffee and pie there was more divisive discussion. This time regarding the relative merits of the Tennessee Titans and the Kansas City Chiefs. It was Wren who finally proposed the compromise around which formed a general consensus – that the Detroit Lions would never amount to anything.

They were basking in the glow of their agreement and watching the girls play with their Nintendos, when Ferguson's cell phone rang. He took it from his pocket and flipped it open. He recognized the area code, but not the number.

'This is Ferguson Glen,' he said.

'It's Liz Dardilly, Ferguson.'

Ferguson looked at Periwinkle and wished that they were sitting together drinking coffee alone in a booth in her restaurant's sunny yellow dining room. And that maybe she was reaching up to touch his face.

'Hello, Liz,' he said.

'Ferguson, it's Angus – your father. The hospital just called me. Just now. Apparently, he fell at the house. The housekeeper found him. I don't know the details yet. I'm on my way to the hospital now. I'm really sorry, Ferguson, but your father has died.'

Ferguson nodded. Peri searched his face.

'Thank you, Liz,' he said. 'I'll be there as soon as I can.'

He closed his phone and told Peri's family that his father had died. Up in Michigan.

Peri crossed the room and wrapped him in her arms. Tyrell took Wren's hand.

'Come, children,' he said. Then he and Wren, Ruby, and Violet stood in a circle around Periwinkle and Ferguson. They held hands, and Tyrell prayed aloud for Ferguson and for Angus Glen's soul.

On the way to Charlevoix, in the car they rented at the airport in Traverse City, Ferguson put his hand on Periwinkle Brown's knee and sighed.

'Thank you for coming with me. You didn't have to do this.'

'Of course I did,' Peri said.

They drove north along the shore of Lake Michigan. The lake and the sky were cold and gray, but Peri was warm and cherry brown. She put her hand on Ferguson's hand.

They went first to the hospital where Liz Dardilly had insisted Angus Glen's body be held until Ferguson arrived to see him and make arrangements. Liz and Ferguson embraced and Ferguson introduced Periwinkle.

'Peri, please meet Mother Elizabeth Dardilly,' he smiled. 'You could call her Mother Dardilly, or Mother Liz. Or Liz.'

The women hugged as if they were long-lost sisters. They went to the room where Angus was. Ferguson went in by himself.

He stood by the bed and thought how his father's body looked small.

He remembered a winter afternoon and his father pulling him on a toboggan up to the top of the hill the kids called Turtleback. He had wanted his father to ride down on the toboggan with him, but his father said no. I pulled you up here so *you* could ride, he said.

Ferguson put his hand on his father's forehead. He made the sign of the cross, bent low, and kissed his father's cheek.

Ferguson asked Mother Liz to officiate at Angus's funeral. At first she protested. Because Angus Glen had been a bishop after all, and an important, influential figure in the church, surely it would be more appropriate for the current bishop of the diocese, or even the presiding bishop, to conduct the service. But Ferguson insisted and Liz relented.

The current bishop of the diocese, and the presiding bishop, and many other church, business, and political dignitaries did attend the funeral. Ferguson thought maybe Bijou might show up, but she didn't, and Ferguson didn't know if he was sad about that or not.

It was late when they arrived at Angus Glen's house after the service and reception afterward. They sat in the car in the driveway.

'I don't feel much like going in there,' Ferguson said.

Peri put her hand up on the back of his neck and rubbed it.

Ferguson sighed. 'I think, if you don't mind, we'll stay in the boathouse tonight. There's two bedrooms.'

Peri leaned her head on his shoulder. 'Whatever you say.'

Ferguson lay awake in his bed. The window blinds were open and the lights from the marina reflected on the ceiling. The boats knocked against their docks.

I just wanted him to love me for who I was, he prayed. *Why didn't he see me and love me just for who I am?*

The silence of God and the lapping of the lake on the shore lulled him to sleep.

He had a dream. It was night. Black and cold, out on the lake. He had fallen out of a boat and he was in deep water, trying to swim back to the boat, but his arms and legs wouldn't move fast enough. There was a man in the boat whose face he couldn't see. He would finally struggle up alongside of the boat and the man would row it a distance away. He felt a hand on his back.

A warm strong hand on the skin of his back. The hand slid up under his arm and around his shoulder and held him tight and he understood that he was awake. He reached around behind him searching for more of the strength and warmth.

'I love you, Ferguson Glen,' breathed a voice in his ear, a strong warm voice. 'I love who you are.'

Then he wept. Not for what he had lost, but for what he had found.

It was Periwinkle's hands that woke him again in the morning, as she pressed herself against him, searching under his shirt and then his shorts for signs of life, which she found.

He turned over to face her. She smiled a half-smile, her eyelids half closed.

'Forgive me, father, for I have sinned.'

'We Anglicans don't do confession,' said Ferguson. 'But if you insist on doing penance for your transgressions, go thou and find a man whose soul has shriveled up inside of him and minister unto him. And then, after you've worked on his soul, minister unto anything else he has that may be shriveled up.'

Over coffee at a diner on Bridge Street, Ferguson said that he was going to have to reconsider his theological position on the question of blessings.

'Maybe I've been wrong. Maybe sometimes you ask for an egg, and you get an egg.'

Peri sipped her coffee and smiled. 'Sometimes, Reverend. Sometimes.'

They held hands as they walked back to Angus's house. Ferguson showed Peri around the house, telling her the stories attached to personal objects that accessorized shelves and occasional tables.

'That was the candy dish my mother put out every Christmas. She always filled it with those horrible hard candy ribbon things.'

'That was my grandfather's slide rule and drafting compass. My mother's father; he was an engineer and car designer for Fisher Body.'

'That was my mother's liquor cabinet – her favorite little corner of the world.'

When they arrived at the door of Angus's den, Ferguson sighed, went in and sat down at his father's desk.

Peri cocked her head slightly to one side. 'Would you like to be alone?'

Ferguson shook his head. 'I'd like *not* to be alone.'

He sat staring at the desk, wondering what Angus might have been working on or thinking about when he last sat there. Peri stood at the massive bookshelves browsing the volumes of histories, biographies, theological treatises, and spy thrillers.

'What's this?' she asked, holding up a small gold object.

'That, my dear, is a twenty-four-carat-gold divot tool,' said Ferguson. 'It's a golf thing. You use it to repair holes you make in the grass when you swing your club.'

'Was your father a big golfer?'

Ferguson nodded. 'My father was a Scotsman. All Scots are big golfers. They invented the game.'

Peri smiled. 'You're a Scotsman. Are you a big golfer?'

Ferguson frowned and shook his head. 'Nope.'

Peri squinted at him. 'Why not? Why don't you golf?'

Ferguson looked at the divot tool in Peri's hand. 'Because my father did.'

Peri looked at Ferguson as if she was trying to see through his forehead into his brain to figure out how it worked. She turned back to the shelves. On the middle shelf, just opposite the desk, were copies of each of Ferguson's books.

'Hey, you,' she said. 'Recognize these?'

When Ferguson didn't reply, she turned and saw that he had taken something from one of the bottom desk drawers and that the muscles in his face had gone slack and his eyes were closed. She went over to the desk.

Whatever it was, was wrapped in plaid woolen fabric – red and navy blue on a dark green background. The fabric was fastened with a round silver brooch, about five inches wide, simple and elegant, with a Celtic cross in the center. Pinned to the plaid was a note that said, 'For Ferguson.'

Peri put her hand on Ferguson's shoulder. His shoulder slumped under her touch.

367

'This is the Mackintosh tartan. The Glens are part of the Mackintosh clan. My father was immensely proud of that. This is his fly plaid, which he wore when he dressed in his full Scottish regalia, you know, the kilt and all that. The fly plaid goes over your shoulder. And this is the brooch that pins the fly plaid in place so it doesn't fly off. He always said that this brooch had been in the family for hundreds of years. Who knows if that's true or not. That's just what he always said.'

He unwound the fly plaid. Inside was a Bible, bound in thick black leather, with gilt-edged pages, dog-eared, and worn.

'This is my great-grandfather's Bible. He was the first priest in our long line of priests. He gave this Bible to my father at his ordination.'

He gently rubbed the leather binding, then placed the Bible on the desk, reached back into the drawer and removed a bottle of Scotch. Taped to the bottle was another note. It said, 'Raise a glass for me when I'm dead, son.'

Ferguson looked at the label on the bottle.

'This is ancient stuff,' he said. 'It's from the Isle of Jura. Angus used to say it was St Colomba himself who distilled it.'

There was a crystal tumbler in the drawer, and Ferguson poured an inch of the whisky into the glass. He put his nose to the glass and breathed in the peaty, briny aroma. Periwinkle watched him swirl the gold liquid around in the glass.

He looked up at her. Then passed the glass to her.

'You do it,' he said.

She took the glass from his hand, swirled the Scotch around in it as he had done, held it to her nose and drew in a deep breath.

Then she drank it. All of it.

38

Goin' to Kansas City

Sixteen months into LaVerne's prison sentence, his cellmate, Clyde, was transferred to another penal facility because of his repeated attempts to organize inmates to protest 'political conditions' by stripping naked. Clyde was serving ten months for stealing five cases of Fritos from a delivery truck parked behind a Safeway in West Oakland. LaVerne was serving two years for disorderly conduct and resisting arrest during the incident at the Oakland Coliseum – a charge reduced from the original charge of assaulting an officer. Stealing snack foods had landed Clyde in jail twice before. The first time it was Slim Jims. The second time, Little Debbie snack cakes.

To gain support for his proposed protest, Clyde began attending meetings held by some of the imprisoned Black Panthers and other militants. However, when they learned that his main grievance was the quality of the macaroni and cheese in the prison mess hall, they banished him from their meetings and wouldn't even let him stand near them in the prison yard.

'You see how easy the Man co-opts those so-called radicals,' Clyde bitterly complained to LaVerne. 'They don't understand that food *is* political. By keeping us unsatisfied in what we eat, they keep us from effectively organizing the

Revolution. Besides, all I'm asking is that they add a little hamburger and some canned tomatoes to their basic recipe. Or else use better cheese. And by stripping naked and showing our physical bodies to the authorities, we show we can't be controlled in our true selfs.'

LaVerne did his best to ignore Clyde, who persisted.

'So, do you think we should call it a "bare-in" like a sit-in, or should we call it a "bare-out" like a walk-out?'

LaVerne glared at Clyde. 'First of all, there is no "we". Because *I* ain't havin' no part in *your* dumb-ass, bare-ass protest. There's nothing political about macaroni and cheese. You got a food hang-up, man. Seriously. Getting yourself put in *prison* for stealing *potato chips*? Get real. At least those Panthers stand for something. They want to change the world. All you want to do is change the menu. You leave me out of it. I ain't getting involved with nothin' naked. Especially over macaroni and cheese.'

LaVerne's next cellmate was Josh Davidson, a twenty-year-old surfer from LaJolla who was serving a two-year sentence for refusing induction into the army.

At the hearing at which Josh's application for conscientious objector status was reviewed, the head of the San Diego County draft board had called him a 'spoiled snot-nose rich punk who doesn't want to get his pretty pink butt shot at'. All of which Josh admitted was true.

'I *am* a spoiled rich punk who doesn't want to get shot at,' he said. 'But you left out the important part. That I don't want to, and won't, shoot at anyone else. I'm trying to follow Jesus. And he wouldn't fight in the army. He says to love our enemies. I know that's hard, but that's what I'm trying to do.'

The chairman of the draft board denied the application.

Josh's feelings about war in general and Vietnam in particular also resulted in a great deal of tension and hostility between him and his parents. His mother was embarrassed and avoided any discussion of her son with her friends. His father, the city's pre-eminent plastic surgeon, was enraged, publicly and privately. In the months leading up to Josh's imprisonment, he and his father rarely spoke to one another.

When LaVerne asked him about this, Josh said, 'You don't really know what something's worth until you know what you're willing to pay for it. I have faith in what the Bible says, in what Jesus says. I guess the price for that faith is my relationship with my parents.'

LaVerne knew about ruined relationships. Though Angela had come to visit him eight times, and Delbert three, his grandma, Rose, and his in-laws, the Rev. Dr Clarence and Mrs Alberta Newton, had not come. Delbert assured LaVerne that Rose was only sad and tired, and that her love for him was as strong as ever. He brought letters from her, and puffed rice candy.

Angela gave no assurances of her parents' love. She was blunt, in fact, in explaining that her parents had urged her to divorce him and to have nothing more to do with him.

'They say they don't want their grandson raised by someone like you,' she said. 'I told them not to talk that way and that you're a good man and a good father, but Daddy won't hear it. He says he hopes he never lays eyes on you again.'

Angela's chin was set hard and her eyes were tired when she said this. She didn't like the spot she was in – being leaned on for support by LaVerne and pulled away from him by her father.

'I don't blame your father for saying such things. He's got a right to think that way after what I did. I wouldn't blame you if you felt that way either. I just hope you don't.'

Behind the heavy glass divider that separated visitors from prisoners, LaVerne hung his head and stared at his hands.

'Oh, shut up, LaVerne!' snapped Angela. 'I'm sick of hearing that shit! I been coming out here to see your sorry ass every two months since you been here. I've spent half of the last eighteen months on a damn train coming and going. So just shut up! I've proved how I feel. But you need to start getting your shit together. You're going to be out of here soon and you need a plan. You can't be all sad sack and down in the dumps. You need to be thinking about your life and how you're going to live it. And you best be figuring out how you're going to make things right with the Rev. Dr Clarence Newton, because I am not going to spend the rest of my life standing between the two of you! You need to be thinking about Raymond! That's what you need to be thinking about. So don't you tell me even one more time how sorry you are. I'm sick of it.'

LaVerne did as he was told and shut up about being sorry. But that left him without much to say. He had really only thought about one thing the entire time he'd been in jail, and that was how sorry he was.

The next time Delbert came to visit, LaVerne told him what Angela had said; that he needed a plan and that he needed to somehow get himself right with his father-in-law.

'Well, that Angela of yours is a smart woman,' said Delbert. 'I believe she's right in what she said. You should be thinking of what lies ahead. You're going to have a good long life, boy. Someday all this sadness and shame will fade. Unless you're determined that it won't. Unless, for some reason, you'd rather hang onto it. And as far as your father-in-law is concerned, Angela's right about that, too. And that starts with forgiveness. And that's never easy. Sometimes it's the hardest thing a person will ever do. But it's also the best thing a person will ever do. By the sounds of it, ol' Rev. Clarence has some forgivin' to do. And so do you. You have to start by forgiving yourself. Then you best be forgiving Mr Charlie Finley. Then Rev. Clarence.'

Delbert smiled. 'Have I left anyone out?'

LaVerne shrugged. 'Maybe Clyde. My old cellmate. He used to embarrass the hell out of me.'

Delbert nodded. 'You know, son, I never been up to Kansas City. But I always wanted to. They say they got good barbecue up there. Maybe I should go see if what they say is true. Maybe ol' Hartholz will want to come along. They say they got some good jazz there, too.'

LaVerne shook his head. 'Go if you want to, Uncle. But Rev. Newton is a proud man. Proud and hard. He's not likely to listen if you're going up there to change his mind about me.'

Delbert looked LaVerne in the eye. 'Is he a good man, son?'

'Yes,' said LaVerne. 'He's a very good man.'

'Then he already wants to forgive you. He just needs help.'

Visiting time was over and Delbert got up to leave. La-Verne stood, too.

'One more thing, Uncle Delbert. There's not much jazz in Kansas City these days. These days it's mostly blues.'

Delbert smiled. 'That's even better.'

Hartholz was delighted when Delbert asked if he'd like to take a train trip up to Kansas City.

'They have good jazz music, I have heard,' he said. 'Count Basie.'

'These days it's mostly blues,' said Delbert, with authority.

'And barbecue,' Hartholz continued.

'So they say,' Delbert nodded. 'I guess we'll find out.'

Delbert had called Angela to arrange the visit, which they

agreed would be positioned as merely a social visit attached to a business trip having to do with the butcher shop.

'Daddy knows you're coming, Uncle Delbert,' Angela said. 'But he's not thrilled. As far as he's concerned, everyone in LaVerne's family is guilty by association. He won't exactly be rude, but don't expect him to welcome you with open arms.'

'I understand, dear,' he said. 'We'll be staying at the YMCA. Downtown. We'll see you at church on Sunday.'

Hartholz declined the offer to attend church with Delbert at the New Jerusalem Baptist Church.

'I will go for a walk, I think. It has been a long time since I have been in a big city.'

Delbert was secretly relieved. He had worried that the presence of a cranky German butcher at a colored worship service would be a distraction to him and everyone else.

Delbert sat with Angela and Raymond in the front pew on the left side of the sanctuary. He noticed how attentive the child was to the sound of Rev. Newton's voice. On the other side of Angela, on the center aisle, was Mrs Alberta Newton. She wore a sky-blue dress with a matching wide-brimmed hat that featured white satin ribbon and white feathers, some of which were quite long.

The congregation of New Jerusalem Baptist Church was at least ten times larger than that of Plum Grove Second Baptist Church, and Delbert enjoyed the quality and volume of the music performed by the choir, the organist, and pianist. He had also enjoyed watching the white-gloved parking ushers direct traffic in the church parking lot. They wore identical suits and ties and conducted themselves with the seriousness and precision of a military honor guard. There was no parking lot at Plum Grove Second Baptist Church.

Rev. Newton had chosen for his text the Gospel of Mark

374

chapter 9, verses 17–29, which he read with the flourish of a classical Shakespearian actor.

'"*Master, I have brought unto thee my son, which hath a* dumb spirit; *And wheresoever he taketh him, he* teareth *him: and he* foameth, *and* gnasheth *with his teeth, and* pineth *away: and I spake to thy disciples that they should cast him out; and they could not.*" He answereth him, and saith, "*O* faithless *generation, how long shall I be with you? How long shall I* suffer *you? Bring him unto me.*" And they brought *him unto* him: *and when he saw him, straightway the spirit* tare *him; and he fell on the ground, and wallowed foaming. And he asked his father,* "*How long is it ago since this came unto him?*" *And he said,* "*Of a child. And ofttimes it hath cast him into the* fire, *and into the* waters, *to* destroy *him: but if thou canst do any thing, have* compassion *on us, and* help *us.*" *Jesus said unto him,* "*If thou canst believe*, all things are possible to him that believeth.*"'

Here, Rev. Newton paused for dramatic effect. He leaned forward across the pulpit, toward the congregation. He enunciated each word as if it alone carried the meaning of the entire sentence.

'*And straightway the father of the child cried out, and said with tears,* "*Lord, I believe; help thou mine* unbelief.*"'

Delbert knew how the father in the story felt. He had prayed prayers a lot like his. Rose was always certain that God was with her and would help her. Delbert was never quite so sure.

The main point of Rev. Newton's sermon was that the very thing we need most in life, belief and trust in Christ Jesus, we cannot ourselves produce. It was a point he made in a big, slightly nasal voice.

'The Bible says that "whosoever believeth in him shall not perish, but have everlasting life". But it is not the *quality*, nor is it the *quantity* of our belief that saves us from perishing. If that were true, then our salvation would depend on the strength of *our own* efforts. And that would mean that we can *earn* our own salvation, that our *works* might save us. But they *do* not and they *cannot*. It is Jesus Christ *alone* and his redemptive death and resurrection that saves us. It is Christ's works that save us. Not ours. Our works are *pathetic* and *puny*. His are *mighty* and *everlasting*.

'Like the terrified and grieving father in our Gospel passage this morning, we *say* we believe. Yet our belief is *inadequate*. It will *never be enough* to save us from our sins, from our *evil* ways, from our *empty* lives, from our *greed*, our *lust*, our *sloth*, our *covetousness*, our *blaspheming*, and our *idolatry*, our *disrespect* of our elders, our *neglect* of the poor, the *hungry*, the *naked*, and the *imprisoned*.

'So we must ask our Lord and Savior to *give us* the only thing he asks that we *give him*. Belief. Trust. Faith.

'Jesus asks us to *love* him. To *need* him. But our capacity to love him and to acknowledge our need of him is too *small*. We *can't* do it. We *need* him to help us *need* him. Only *his love* can help us *love him* in return.'

After church, at the front door, Angela introduced Delbert to her father. Rev. Newton tried to smile, but the result looked like he'd just gotten a whiff of cheese gone bad.

'Welcome, Mr Merisier,' he said. 'Welcome to our church and to our city. Have you ever been to Kansas City before?'

Delbert shook his head. 'No, reverend, I haven't. But I like what I've seen so far. Plus, I'm a barbecue man, and I hear you folks up here make pretty good barbecue. I'm looking forward to trying some.'

Rev. Newton nodded. 'Well, sir, you will not have to look long or far for good barbecue in this town.'

Angela looked at her father hard, which he noted but decided to ignore.

'Mr Merisier, we would love to invite you to dinner, but unfortunately Mrs Newton and I must visit the wife of the chairman of our board of deacons. She is in the hospital with a serious case of phlebitis. I am sure you understand.'

Rev. Newton returned Angela's glare. Delbert smiled.

'Of course, reverend. I understand. Maybe next time I'm in Kansas City. Maybe then we can have a cup of coffee, like family, and we can chat a little bit about that part of your sermon where you talked about neglecting people in prison.'

He turned and walked down the church steps. Angela followed.

Angela did not attend evening service at New Jerusalem Baptist Church that night, which alarmed her mother, but not Rev. Newton. He expected that his daughter would be angry with him.

Angela was waiting at her parents' house for them when they returned home from church. Raymond was asleep on Rev. and Mrs Newton's bed.

'Why, Angela,' her mother said, 'I'm so glad to see you. I was worried when you weren't at the service.'

Angela looked past her mother and spoke to her father.

'I'm ashamed to be your daughter,' she said in a low, even voice. 'I can understand your being angry at LaVerne. What he did was stupid and dangerous. But the way you treated his uncle Delbert this morning was shameful. It was rude, humiliating, and un-Christian. When LaVerne and I married – a marriage you performed, in case you forget – that kind old gentleman became a part of *our family*. And he *is* a gentleman. Unlike *you*. You're a pompous hypocrite. You're an *ass*hole.'

Alberta Newton gasped. 'Angela! Don't you *dare* talk to your father that way!'

Angela cast a look of contempt at her mother. 'You're just as bad.'

Rev. Newton raised his hand, his face twisted in hurt and rage. Angela moved toward him – her face inches from her father's nose.

'Go ahead, Daddy. Hit me,' she hissed. 'You can't hurt me worse than you already have. But I'm telling you this: if you ever want to see *me* or *Raymond* again, you find a way to make things right with LaVerne. And you can start with his uncle Delbert. If not, fine. I'll be moving to Plum Grove, Texas, to be with my *family*.'

Next morning, Delbert and Hartholz walked up to the City Market in downtown Kansas City's north end for breakfast and a newspaper. When they returned to the Y, there was a message at the front desk for Delbert. It was from Rev. Newton, asking Delbert to call him. Delbert used the phone at the front desk.

'Mr Merisier, I think it would be good for you and me to meet and talk,' said Rev. Newton. 'You said you are a barbecue man. Perhaps we could have lunch. Today. Before you leave town. One of our members has a little joint. I think you would like it. Some of the best barbecue anywhere. May I come by and pick you up at, say, eleven thirty?'

Delbert said that'd be fine, then went back up to his room, lay down on the bed and took a forty-minute nap. Hartholz finished reading the newspaper.

Nailed to the side of Betty Lester's white clapboard house, which was tucked in below a highway overpass in the Quindaro district of Kansas City, Kansas, was a hand-painted plywood sign that advertised, 'Mrs Betty's Bar-B-Q Kitchen "Pork barbicue the old South way".'

As they waited for their barbecue, coleslaw, potato chips,

and red pop, Delbert and Rev. Newton sat in silence for longer than either man felt comfortable with.

At one point Rev. Newton started to say something about the Royals, which had just finished their first season, but he decided against it. It would have led the discussion in the direction of LaVerne, and he wasn't quite ready for that.

'Do you follow football at all, Mr Merisier? Our Kansas City Chiefs are a force to be reckoned with.'

Delbert nodded and smiled. 'Oh, yes. I like the Chiefs. Of course, we still think of them as the Texans.'

Rev. Newton hadn't remembered that the Chiefs had moved to Kansas City from Dallas where they had played as the Texans, and he didn't like it that Delbert had. It felt to him that Delbert had somehow gained the upper hand in the conversation. He frowned deeply and changed the subject. 'Mrs Betty Lester has been making barbecue right here in her house for thirty years. Ever since her husband died. Apparently, he was a leader at the church. That was quite a bit before my time. There's a stained-glass window in his honor. Betty is at least eighty-five, eighty-six, years old. She's not really sure herself how old she is. But she is in good health and her mind is sharp. Her father was an escaped slave from North Carolina and her mother was a Wyndot Indian. She has a daughter and a son. Her daughter lives in Omaha. Her son is a mechanic for Braniff Airlines and was just transferred to Hawaii. His wife – Betty's daughter-in-law – is who kept the place running. I'm worried that Betty's going to have a hard time now that she's gone.'

Betty Lester herself brought their lunch order to the table. She was barely five feet tall and shy of ninety pounds. Her thinning hair was snow white and her skin was as crinkly as a wadded-up brown paper bag. She rested her hand on Rev. Newton's shoulder and smiled at Delbert.

'I see you brought a guest today, pastor.'

Clarence Newton grimaced. 'Sister Betty, let me intro-duce you to Mr Delbert Merisier of Plum Grove, Texas. Mr Merisier is here in Kansas City on business.'

Betty waited, as if expecting further information. Delbert obliged.

'I'm so pleased to meet you, Mrs Lester. The pastor's daughter, Angela, is married to my nephew, LaVerne.'

Delbert stared across the table at Rev. Newton who avoided eye contact.

'Yes, that's right, Sister Betty. LaVerne always said that his uncle here was like a father to him growing up.'

Betty smiled at Delbert. 'Well, LaVerne has himself a fine and handsome uncle. Yes, he does.'

She left them alone with their barbecue. The men wel-comed the excuse not to talk. They picked up their sand-wiches and began eating.

When he had finished his pulled pork – Carolina-style, topped with coleslaw – Delbert sat back in his chair and smiled.

'Rev. Newton, this is real good smoked meat. Texans rarely smoke a pig. In Louisiana, where my people originally come from, they're fond of pork, but I myself have never before tried barbecue pork "the old South way" until today. I'm glad I did.'

Rev. Newton wiped his mouth with his napkin. 'So, Mr Merisier, what business brought you to Kansas City? Were you able to get done all that you came to do?'

Delbert frowned. 'Not yet. But I'm hopeful.'

When they finished their lunch, Rev. Newton waved Betty over to the table.

'Sister Betty, do I remember correctly that you used to keep something in the pantry a little stronger than red pop?'

Betty nodded and smiled. 'Yes, pastor, you remember.'

She went into the kitchen and came back with a bottle of

Old Grand Dad and two glasses, which she put on the table. She winked at Delbert and returned to her work.

Rev. Newton poured whiskey into each glass.

'Let's talk about LaVerne,' he said.

Delbert sipped his whiskey. 'One of my favorite topics.'

Rev. Newton snorted and took a long draw on his drink.

Delbert smiled. 'I take it he's not one of yours.'

'Not lately,' said Rev. Newton.

Delbert shrugged. 'He made a big mistake. There's no doubt about that. Nobody would blame a father-in-law for being mighty angry if his daughter's husband did something as foolish as that.'

'I'm glad you understand,' said Rev. Newton.

Delbert nodded. 'Oh, I do.'

They were silent.

'Mr Merisier, are you familiar with the Apostle Paul's second letter to the Corinthians?' asked Rev. Newton. 'Specifically chapter six, verse fourteen? It advises Christians to "be ye not unequally yoked together with unbelievers. For what fellowship hath righteousness with unrighteousness? And what communion hath light with darkness?" That's the situation here, Mr Merisier. Angela and LaVerne are unequally yoked. They were from the start. This latest disaster just proves it.'

The muscles in Delbert's jaw tightened. His eyes narrowed.

'Sir, do I understand you to be using the words "unbeliever", "unrighteous", and "darkness" to describe my nephew? *Your* son-in-law?'

Rev. Newton flinched.

'That's not what I meant by using that passage. Not at all. What I meant is that Angela and LaVerne come from two different worlds. Angela has a strong family. She has an education. She's working on her master's degree. She's studying library science. She and LaVerne are not well matched. It was a mistake right from the start.'

Delbert leaned forward.

'And yet you blessed their marriage. As God's minister. With the power God gave you as a minister, you blessed it. And you blessed it as Angela's father. And you asked them to say the words "for better or worse".'

He drank from his whiskey.

'So I guess when young people marry each other they're supposed to promise "for better or worse" to each other, even though they're young and probably will do stupid things. Things they'll be sorry for. But *we* don't promise "for better or worse" to *them*. The grown-ups in their lives, the ones who are supposed to be looking out for them. For us it's *not* "for better or worse". It's just for better. If they mess up, we just cut them loose.'

He shook his head in disgust.

'You misunderstand me, sir,' protested Rev. Newton. 'I'm not condemning the boy. I'm just saying he and Angela need to be with people like themselves. They'll be happier in the long run if they're not burdened with a spouse that comes from a different background.'

Delbert laughed. 'Reverend, I get the feeling that you're trying to make things better. But you're only digging yourself deeper in a hole.'

Rev. Newton wiped his forehead with a napkin. He downed the remaining whiskey in his glass. He leaned toward Delbert, pounding the table with both fists.

'What that boy did was *wrong*. It ruined his future. And my daughter's and grandson's. Now he's a convicted *felon*. That'll never go away. That mark will be on him for ever.'

Rev. Newton crossed his arms across his chest and shoved his chair back from the table. Delbert watched Betty wiping the counter. They didn't speak, or look at one another. Betty, who'd been monitoring the situation, came to refill their glasses. Delbert cleared his throat.

'It might surprise you to know that LaVerne grew up in a loving Christian home, with a family that loves the Lord. There's nobody in this world who loves Jesus more than LaVerne's grandmother, my sister Rose. She studies her Bible every day. And she prays. She prays so hard that I worry sometimes her heart is going to break from it. But it only seems to make her stronger.

'LaVerne's natural mother was no good, I admit. That's one way that LaVerne and Angela are different. Mrs Newton is a good mother. I can see that. But Rose more than made up for her daughter's shortcomings. She gave LaVerne every kind of love a mother would have given him and more. And she worked double shifts at the rice mill to provide for him.

'I always did what I could to help. And I love the boy, too. Like a son. And Rose and me always taught the boy that if he trusts in the Lord things will work out.'

Rev. Newton's face relaxed a bit. He frowned, as if he wanted to say something, but couldn't get the words out. Delbert pushed on.

'Before me and Hartholz got on the bus to come up here for this visit, Rose and me talked about LaVerne and Angela and your family. Rose told me to remind you to read the seventeenth chapter of Luke where the Lord talks about forgiving people even if they sin against you seven times a day.

'Well, I've never had somebody sin against me seven times a day. Hell, I never had anybody sin against me seven times total. But that Loretta, LaVerne's mother, she sinned against Rose almost every day she was alive. And Rose forgave her every time. It seems foolish to some folks to forgive someone who keeps hurtin' you over and over like that. But as long as you keep being angry at someone, you can't ever get on with your life. Your mind can't be free.

'I'm going to say one more thing, reverend. And then I'm done. What I want to say is that I know about forgiveness. I was married once. Madeleine was my wife's name. And I loved her as much as any man ever loved his wife. Her people come from Louisiana, just like mine. And she was like a Tabasco pepper. Small and fiery.

'She worked at the Liberty County courthouse. In the cafeteria. And there was a sheriff's deputy who had an eye for her. And every time he came through the line he'd say something to her. First it was just harmless things, like, "Your hair looks nice today," or, "What a nice smile you have." But then it started gettin' more personal. The deputy would say things like, "Darlin', why don't you give me a little kiss with my hash browns?" And then it got worse. He started asking to see her after work. And he tried putting his hands on her. But she wouldn't have it. She told me all about him when she would get home from work. Most colored girls would be scared. But she was just angry. She wasn't scared of him, or nobody else for that matter. I told her to be careful, and she just said, "That deputy is the one who needs to be careful."

'Well, one day she doesn't come home from work. I wait for her till it's night and I drive over to the courthouse to see what's goin' on. Well, she wasn't there. Her boss says she left at the normal time. So I start askin' around and I see the deputy; Link Thompson was his name. And I ask Link if he seen her. He says he hasn't. Then he tells me that my wife has got a smart mouth on her and that someday it's going to get her in trouble. Trouble she may not be able to get out of.

'Few days later they find my Madeleine dead in the Trinity River. Her neck was broken.

'I thought about killin' that deputy. I thought about killin' myself. For years I could hardly think of anything else in the daytime and even in the nighttime my mind fixed on it. Nightmares so bad I woke up in a sweat. Screaming, sometimes. My whole self started coming apart. I couldn't laugh about anything. I couldn't enjoy music. I didn't get pleasure from food or whiskey. I was alive on the outside, but dead on the inside.

'Then I started noticing that the deputy was acting the same as me. He'd always been a fun-loving guy. Jokin' around. Smilin'. Liked to dance. But I saw that he'd become thin and sad and kind of empty lookin'. I couldn't look at that man without praying to God that he would die. But when I did finally look at him, really look at him, I saw a man who was alone in the world.

'That's when I changed my prayer. I asked God to help me forgive ol' Link. So we could *both* live again. I worried that God would ask me to tell Link face to face that I forgave him for killing Madeleine. Because I didn't know if I could do that. Because Link would probably say he didn't do it, and if I heard him say that, I *might* really kill him. With my bare hands. But God didn't make me do it face to face. He allowed me to do it in my heart. I forgave Deputy Thompson in my heart.

'And when I did, I saw a change in the deputy. Maybe he saw something different in the way I was, and that made him feel better. Not so guilty, maybe. Maybe God whispered in his ear that I had forgiven him. Whatever it was, after a while we were both able to smile and laugh again.

'Every day I was reminded of what I had lost and how I lost it. The deputy married a pretty girl from over in Cleveland, Texas. They had a couple of pretty daughters that both went to the school where I was a janitor. I saw them every day. If I had held onto all my hate and rage I'd never be able to look at those little girls and see them as innocent little girls, which is what they were. I would only ever see them as coming from the man who killed my Madeleine. I didn't want to live the rest of my life seeing the world through angry eyes.'

Delbert was tired. His face was puffy and his hands shook as he brought his glass to his lips.

'So I know about forgiveness, reverend. It ain't easy. But I recommend it.'

Rev. Newton took a deep breath. He spoke quietly. 'I'm a proud man. Too proud, some say. But you shame me with your story, Brother Delbert.'

Delbert shook his head.

'I didn't come here to shame you, pastor. I came here to help LaVerne. He feels hopeless. But you, more than anyone else in his life, can convince him that there is hope, if you tell him that you believe in him and that you'll help him get his life back together. He expects forgiveness and encourage-ment from Angela and from me. But if *you* take him back, he'll know he really can come back. And he'll work hard the rest of his life to prove that you didn't make a mistake by let-ting him back in.'

Rev. Newton looked down into his empty glass. He wanted more, but thought better of it. 'I guess we need a plan then,' he said.

Josh Davidson and LaVerne Williams lay on their bunks in their cell. Josh bounced a tennis ball against the wall, catch-ing it on the rebound first with his left hand then with his right. Typically this drove LaVerne nuts, but he was reading a letter – for the third time through – from his father-in-law, the Rev. Dr Clarence Newton. When he was finished, he put the letter down and stared at the ceiling.

Josh was intrigued. 'So, you going to tell me who that letter's from and what it says?'

LaVerne kept looking at the ceiling. 'You going to quit bouncing that damn ball?'

Josh caught the ball and held it.

'It's from my father-in-law, the Rev. Dr Clarence Newton,' LaVerne said.

Josh bounced the ball once and caught it. 'That's kind of a surprise, isn't it?'

LaVerne continued looking at the ceiling. 'That's puttin' it lightly.'

Josh bounced and caught the ball again. 'And?'

LaVerne smiled. And something caused him to remember that his uncle's truck smelled of German mustard, coffee, and 3-in-1 oil, when Delbert came to pick him up and take him home after Nate Jones had punched him and knocked him down, when Junebug moved to Detroit.

'He wonders if I might have any interest in the restaurant business when I get out. Seems there's a lady in his church who needs some help in her barbecue joint.'

Josh bounced the ball against the wall. LaVerne flicked his hand out and caught it.

39

From the Shadows

Four blocks south of Kansas City's ritzy Country Club Plaza shopping and dining district is Jacob L. Loose Memorial Park – a seventy-four-acre rectangle of grassy slopes, strewn with tall oaks and gnarled evergreens. Along the east side of the park is a pond, and on the day that A.B. Clayton and Jen Richardson finally got around to discussing the possibility that they were in love, there was a lone Canada goose gliding slowly and silently on the pond. A.B. watched the goose stretch its neck as he sat with Jen on a bench by the water's edge, feeling his heart fill with joy and fear.

'You snuck up on me, Jen,' he said. 'I thought we was just friends, then all of a sudden I realize we're not just friends. We're a lot more than that. I might've recognized it sooner, except that nothing like this has ever happened to me before.'

Jen took A.B.'s hand. She spoke softly and seriously.

'You're right, A.B. I did sneak up on you. I knew I couldn't come at you head on, or else I'd scare you away. I had to come at you from the side.'

She felt his hand get warm. 'Nothing like this has ever happened to me either, A.B.'

A.B. was quiet. He was worried he would cry if he tried to say anything. Or that he would get the hiccups. Jen noted the swipe of white that ran under the goose's chin and up the sides of its face, and how bright it was.

'I just thought I'd be alone in my life,' A.B. said, finally. 'You know, except for LaVerne and Angela. But here you are.'

Jen smiled and nodded. 'Yep. Here I am.'

They held hands and walked around the pond then up along Wornall Street, turning west on 52nd. As they approached the rose garden in the northwest corner of the park, Jen punched A.B. lightly in the shoulder.

'I bet I know more about Jacob L. Loose Memorial Park than you do,' she stated confidently.

A.B. snorted. 'Which is a safe bet, since I know exactly nothing. I didn't even know the Jacob L. or Memorial parts until just this second. I always thought it was just Loose Park. Like the opposite of Tight Park or something.'

Jen laughed. 'I wrote a research paper for my history class at Penn Valley. For example, I know that the landscape architects who designed the park were Sidney J. Hare and his son S. Herbert Hare. And the rose garden here was planted in 1931, and there are more than four thousand roses and a hundred and fifty different kinds. And the Battle of Westport was fought here. Right here on this land. It was the most important and bloodiest battle of the Civil War fought west of the Mississippi. And Buffalo Bill Cody and Wild Bill Hickok both fought for the Union in the battle, which the Union won.'

She smiled a self-satisfied smile. She looked at A.B. He was looking out onto the expanse of grass.

A.B. shook his head. 'Don't you think it's kinda weird, like in a really sad way, that a hundred years ago, or whatever it was, that soldiers died here in some terrible battle, that their blood was in this dirt, and here we are now, today, you and me, in this same place, being really happy?'

It was 10:30 on a Tuesday, just as Smoke Meat was opening for the day, when Ute Johansson showed up with Tony David, founder and CEO of the Great USA Barbeque Company.

A.B. was in back taking delivery from Rocco's Produce. LaVerne, who was at the smoker turning briskets, heard the door open and turned to look. He remembered Ute Johansson from their previous encounter and recognized Tony David from his company's website. The men stepped up to the counter, smiling expectantly. Tony David examined the menu board. Ute Johansson looked around the dining room. LaVerne ignored them.

Several minutes later, during which time LaVerne had still not acknowledged the presence of anyone in the restaurant other than himself and A.B., A.B. came in from the back and saw the two men at the counter. He frowned and addressed LaVerne in a hushed tone.

'Boss, you probably didn't realize there's customers out front.'

He pointed, in case LaVerne needed help remembering where out front was.

'Those are not customers,' LaVerne snapped. 'Those are the sons of bitches that want to shut us down.'

A.B. looked at the men at the counter, then back at LaVerne, his face scrunched in anxiety.

'Just the same, boss, they're standin' there.'

LaVerne kept his back turned and said nothing.

A.B. went out and greeted the men. 'May I help you?'

Ute Johansson spoke, louder than he needed to, looking past A.B. to where LaVerne had turned his attention to the ribs in the smoker.

'We just came by to introduce ourselves. You guys have got a good reputation here locally and we wanted to check see what you're all about. Seems like maybe you've heard things about some of our plans for this block and have made up your mind about them without even hearing what we have to say.'

A.B. stood mute. Tony David chimed in, trying to project his voice back into the kitchen where LaVerne was.

'Mr Williams, I'm Tony David. I own a chain of barbecue restaurants. The Great USA Barbeque Company. Maybe you've heard of us. We're seriously considering locating a unit here in Kansas City. I've researched this market, Mr Williams. I know you're one of the best operators in town. I have a lot of respect for you. I'd love the opportunity to meet you. You know, talk shop a little. Talk about the biz. No reason we can't be friendly competitors. A little friendly competition is good for everybody in the game. Right, Mr Williams? You're an old ball player. You know that. Keeps everybody sharp. No reason we can't all get along. It's a big enough pie that we can all get a piece.'

LaVerne had heard enough. He swung around, letting the smoker door slam shut behind him, then walked slowly and purposefully into the kitchen, like he was walking from the dugout into the batter's box. He walked past Tony David stopping in front of Ute Johansson, his chest nearly touching Ute's.

'Why don't you just admit why you're really here? It's to get a good look, isn't it? Like when you look at the bug on the sidewalk just before you stomp on it. I heard you talk to Bob Dunleavy like you and him are friends. Like you two are in the same business. But I know better. You and Bob Dunleavy aren't friends. He likes building things. You like owning things. And if you can't own it, you don't care about it. You'd just as soon destroy it.'

LaVerne turned to Tony David. 'And you. You talk about friendly competition, but coming here, into *my* place, with a man you know has plans to *shut me down*? What kind of "friendly" is that? And as far as competition goes, let me just say this, if you plan on opening a "unit" anywhere near here you *better* shut me down, because folks may stop in once or twice to try whatever it is you serve at your "unit", but once they come in here and taste some of my real barbecue, they'll never go back to the Great USA Barbeque Company. I'm telling you that. So you can shove your legendary ribs up your pearly white Wisconsin ass.'

Tony David swallowed hard and decided not to say anything at the moment.

Ute Johansson, however, had plenty to say. He glared at LaVerne.

'Downtown is coming back, my friend. And we're going to be a part of it. What you think of us is irrelevant. People who visit Kansas City and visit downtown are going to expect barbecue. That's what Kansas City is known for, and that's what we're going to give them. But this place of yours, this little *place* of yours just won't do it. It won't cut it. Get real. You only seat forty-four people. Hell, we'll seat more than that at one of our bars. And we'll have *three* bars and *two* dining rooms. We're going to give people a barbecue *experience*. That's what we're going to call it, in fact. The Barbeque Experience. Big, clean, entertaining.'

Tony David felt obliged to fill in the details at this point. 'Of course, we're going to be respectful of Kansas City's barbecue tradition. We've hired a top decorator to help us create the ambience of an authentic Kansas City barbecue joint. Plus, as I understand it, Ute's plan includes a nice compensation and relocation package for businesses in the development area. Considerably above fair market value. You could set up shop anywhere. Maybe build a new place. Maybe retire.'

LaVerne looked him in the eye.

'Eat shit,' he said, then he went into the kitchen, got a beer from the refrigerator and went out back by the dumpster to drink it. A.B. nodded emphatically as he watched LaVerne go. LaVerne's righteous anger had riled him up. He turned to the men at the counter.

'Furthermore, go to hell,' he said. 'And don't come back.'

Ute Johansson shrugged, turned and walked out. Tony David shook his head sadly and followed.

A.B. went out back, lit up a cigarette, and stood with LaVerne while he finished his beer.

That evening, A.B. and Warren had planned to go help Jen and the band set up for a gig with Mother Mary at the Blue Room down at 18th and Vine.

Warren seemed to enjoy unloading and loading the equipment. He nodded when Jen and the other members of the band joked around. And he smiled and murmured to himself, 'There she is,' when Pug rolled Mother into the room in her wheelchair. But mostly he liked sitting behind the stage with A.B. during the band's performances. Usually he just closed his eyes and listened, sometimes rocking slowly back and forth. Sometimes he'd say things like, 'That's a good song,' or, 'She sang that one last month, but not the time before.' And once in a while he would say a word that sounded like *'marli'* which A.B. didn't know the meaning of and preferred not to.

The first few times Warren went with A.B. to help with the band, they went together in A.B.'s car, with M.Z. Owen – the Vietnam vet Bob Dunleavy had hired to watch over Warren – following behind them in his black Land Rover Defender. But when Warren started helping on a regular basis, M.Z. offered to drive. This was a beneficial arrangement for all involved. There was a lot more room in the

Defender for Jen's drums, and M.Z. could keep closer watch over Warren. Plus, M.Z. liked Mother's music.

Jen called M.Z. 'Mike.' She said having to call one man in her life by his initials was fine, but two was too many.

After Smoke Meat closed for the night, Warren and Jen tried to hurry A.B. along by helping put the chairs up on the tables in the dining room, while Mike stood outside by the Defender.

'Why are you movin' so slow tonight, dude?' Jen teased A.B. 'If we don't get going soon, Pug's going to come down here and march us over to the club at gunpoint.'

A.B. tried to smile. 'Sorry. We had a disturbance here this morning, and it's on my mind.'

He told them about the confrontation with Ute Johansson and Tony David.

'I thought LaVerne was going to smack one of those guys,' he said. 'The whole thing is scary. What if they really *are* going to shut us down? What'll LaVerne do? What will *I* do? I never worked anywhere else. I don't know how to do anything but this.'

Warren had been smiling and nodding at Jen's teasing, but this turn of events upset him. He shook his head and grunted and looked at the floor. A.B. turned off the lights and locked the restaurant. Mike held open the front door of the Defender for Warren, and Jen opened the back door and got in. As A.B. started to slide in next to Jen, a smallish man stepped out of the shadows at the corner of the building and said, 'A.B. Clayton?' Then he took a step closer.

M.Z. Owen didn't like the feel of the situation. In one stride, he closed the distance between himself and the man from the shadows. He thrust his arm out and stopped the man's forward progress with his fingertips, which he placed gently and non-negotiably against the man's chest.

'Back up,' he said.

Typically, when Mike Owen suggested someone change course, they responded promptly, without protest or question, and with quite a lot of stammering and rapid blinking. This man was different. He just stood there, looking up at Mike through heavy-rimmed glasses perched on an oversized nose. He was skeleton thin, except for a protruding beer belly. His hair was oily and slicked back.

'Is that A.B. Clayton?' he asked. 'I've been waiting for him out here. I'm his stepfather.'

'He says he's your stepfather, A.B.,' said Mike, keeping his eyes fixed on the man's eyes.

'Well, I've had more than one of those,' said, A.B., coming around to see who it was. Jen had come and was standing behind A.B.

'It's Rudy,' she said. 'Rudy, from your mother's funeral.'

A.B. nodded. 'I thought you said you and my mom weren't married.'

Rudy shrugged. 'Well, technically we wasn't married. But we was together for a long time. Like what they call a "common law" marriage. Anyways, like we was saying – you and me – after Mona's funeral, I was thinking maybe we could get together once in a while. Get to know one another. Maybe go up to the boats. You know, have a good time. I think your ma would like that. You ever gone to the boats?'

A.B. frowned. 'No. I never have. Angela told me it's a sin to gamble away your hard-earned pay. Besides, why were you waiting for me here outside the restaurant?'

Rudy smiled and tried to take a step closer to A.B., which Mike prevented.

'Like I said, you and I had talked about maybe gettin' to know one another. And so I came over here, but the place was closed and I saw that you was cleaning up, so I just waited.'

It wasn't clear to A.B. what he should do or say. He turned to Jen.

'Rudy, my band is playing at the Blue Room tonight,' she said. 'We're on our way over there right now. You're welcome to meet us there.'

Rudy shook his head. 'That's all right. I don't mean to barge in. I'll catch up with you another time, A.B.'

He backed away from Mike, then turned and walked north on Walnut.

In the Defender, on the way to the club, A.B. held Jen's hand and stared out the window.

'This has been some kind of day, Jen,' he said. 'I didn't like it much.'

Warren fidgeted in the seat next to Mike. 'That guy? He wasn't afraid of M.Z. Most people are.'

40

Feeling Something Slide

Sammy Merzeti was given his new name three days after he slid a knife into the heart of the one they called the Rabbi.

The knife he used was an eight-inch piece of cyclone fencing, straightened, sharpened, and wrapped at one end with duct tape for a handle.

Sammy's naming rite took place in a corner of the prison yard claimed and protected by the Fellowship of the Sword and the Fire. The corner was called Zorn's Church by most of the inmate population, but Zorn himself called it the Altar of the Almighty.

Zorn was the name convicted murderer Harold Pickle gave himself when he anointed himself High Evangelist of the Fellowship of the Sword and the Fire, which he himself founded 'in order to purify the True Peoples of the Almighty's Last Nation'. Which were, in Zorn's words, 'the Caucasoids of North America'.

'Zorn is the Aryan word for rage,' said Harold Pickle at his self-conducted naming ceremony. 'The Almighty has given me this name because he is enraged at the corrupted seed of his True Peoples.'

Later, one of the guards who had witnessed the ceremony said to another guard, 'Yeah, Zorn is enraged all right. He's enraged that his real name is Harold Pickle.'

The name Zorn gave Sammy was Degen, which Zorn said was the Aryan word for sword.

'For you shall be the Sword of the Almighty's Wrath,' he proclaimed as the four other members of the Fellowship used the knife that Sammy killed the Rabbi with to carve the letters of his new name into the flesh of his right shoulder.

Sammy was surprised by how easily the knife had glided up under the Rabbi's ribcage. 'Just like pushing an ice pick into a watermelon,' he told Zorn afterward.

Zorn put his hand on Sammy's shoulder. 'The Almighty quickens the hand of the righteous,' he said solemnly.

Sammy was also surprised that killing the Rabbi had resulted in nothing more than his initiation into the Fellowship. When Sammy stabbed him, the Rabbi opened his mouth as if to speak and looked at Sammy like he was trying to remember something. When Sammy pulled the knife out, the Rabbi took a few steps forward. Then he fell, first to his knees, then slowly onto his face. By then Sammy had casually moved far enough away that when the guards and inmates began yelling that a man was down, he was able to join the crowd that had gathered to see what all the commotion was about without raising suspicions. He had expected that he would be charged with the Rabbi's murder, found guilty, and sentenced to spend the rest of his life in prison. But nothing happened at all.

Though he was in the seventh year of a ten-year sentence for aggravated assault, and, technically, eligible for parole in eight months, Sammy hadn't really thought much about what he would do once he was out of prison. After he fell in with Zorn and the Fellowship he began to wonder if prison was maybe where he was supposed to be. That maybe he was finally home. Which is why, when Zorn told him that killing the Rabbi would be the price of admission into the

Fellowship, Sammy didn't consider the price too high, even if it kept him in prison for the rest of his life. Life inside wasn't much different to life outside, as far as Sammy was concerned. Except maybe inside was safer.

Zorn was forty-eight years old and serving a life sentence, without chance of parole, for killing his wife and his wife's parents with a tire iron. He had a bushy gray goatee and a shaved head. He had lifted weights in the exercise yard nearly every day of the twenty-eight years of his incarceration, and his body was as bulked up as a professional wrestler's. On his chest was tattooed the image of a black wolf that appeared to be eating its way out of his body, his heart in the wolf's mouth; dangling arteries dripping blood. Sammy wanted a tattoo like Zorn's.

Other than purifying the True Peoples of the Almighty's Last Nation, Zorn's main interest was playing guitar, at which he was reasonably good. Though prisoners were prohibited from owning guitars – because the strings could be removed and used as garrottes – Zorn was allowed to play a guitar in the recreation center, under close supervision. He liked Merle Haggard, Waylon Jennings, and Willie Nelson, but his favorite was Kris Kristofferson. Zorn had a nice strong baritone, and he could make it purr or growl, as the song required. Once, Sammy cried while listening to Zorn sing 'For the Good Times'.

'I feel stupid cryin' like that,' he told Zorn. 'It's not like I ever had a woman, like in the song. It just made me feel things, that's all.'

Sammy worked in the prison laundry, mostly sorting and folding. Sometimes, if other inmates who worked there didn't show up because they had been paroled or punished or were sick, he would have to stay late to get all the work done himself. Usually he didn't mind. There was nowhere else to go and nothing else to do. But if he knew that Zorn was going to be playing guitar, he wanted to be there, and didn't like being late. Which is what happened when Jah-nel Greene missed his shift in the laundry due to a scheduled conjugal visit with his wife.

Sammy hurried across the yard and through the door to the rec center. He could see Zorn over by the ping-pong tables sitting by himself with his back to the door, guitar in his lap. Other inmates were playing cards and dominoes, or watching TV.

Sammy walked over to Zorn and sat down and felt his foot slide on something slick on the floor and looked and saw that it was blood and that there was blood all over the floor all the way under the ping-pong tables. 'Goddamn, Zorn,' he said, 'what the hell?' And he looked at Zorn and saw that the blood was coming from a long black slit that ran across Zorn's throat and that the razor-thin strip of plastic milk jug that had been used to make the slit was still there. In Zorn's throat.

When Sammy started screaming, some of the other prisoners turned to look. Most just kept playing cards and dominoes, or watching TV.

41

When Love Came to Town

LaVerne's customers tell him all the time how much they love his barbecue, and, as much as any other restaurant owner, he appreciates knowing that people like his food. But he gets uncomfortable when people go on and on, as they often do. That's because he didn't get into the barbecue business because he loves barbecue, though he does still, even after all this time. That was never the point of it. Or the purpose. He got into the barbecue business to save his life. It was what he had to do, and it was something he could do. Delbert and Hartholz and Mrs Betty Lester, they taught him how. So, though he's proud of his product, he doesn't provide much encouragement to his customers when they lay the flattery on thick. 'It's not about the barbecue,' he told Angela once. 'This place is about making something good out of something bad. It was about turning things around. But that's not really something you can explain to folks when they just want to tell you how much they like the brisket they just ate.'

It is something he has given considerable thought to.

A.B. left work early one night to go with Jen to the grand opening of a new Harley dealership north of the river. Vicki Fuentes had a class, and Leon had the day off, so LaVerne was stuck doing the closing chores by himself. Ferguson stopped in to say goodnight as he sometimes does when he teaches late classes at the seminary, and saw that LaVerne was alone, so he offered to help. LaVerne told him to go ahead and put the chairs up on the tables and he would start the mopping.

They worked in silence for a time, then LaVerne said, 'It's interesting how the things that make barbecue taste so good are the things that by themselves are so bitter.'

He let this observation hang there, as if the truth of it was self-evident and required no elaboration.

Ferguson found the statement interesting, but more interesting was that LaVerne offered it up out of the blue as he did. LaVerne was not one who regularly volunteered random philosophical contemplations.

'Please explain.'

LaVerne obliged.

'Take smoke, for example. It's a product of fire. Which only happens when something is being consumed. Destroyed. If you breathe in too much smoke it can choke or even kill you. And there's nothing that stings your eyes worse than smoke. You get smoke in your eyes, it blinds you.

'Same with salt. You get salt in your eyes, you'll be cryin' until your tears wash it away. A little salt tastes good, but too much of it will ruin your food. And you can't unsalt it. Once there's too much, it's just ruined.

'Then there's vinegar. Even just a little sip of vinegar makes your teeth tighten up and your eyes come out of your head. Vinegar is horrible by itself; straight up. They gave vinegar to Our Lord to drink, to torment him when he was dying on the cross.

'But you can't have barbecue without those three things – smoke, salt, and vinegar. Those are what make barbecue, barbecue. Without 'em it's just plain old cooked meat.

'How can that be? How can things so bitter make something so sweet?

'I'll tell you how. Patience and faith. That's how. And a willingness to learn.

'After you put a piece of meat in the cooker you can't rush it. It won't be done until it's done. It's going to take as long as it takes. You can make the fire hotter, but that'll just burn it and make it tough. You can take it out of the cooker sooner, but it won't be any good and all that time will be wasted. If you make the fire too hot or take it out too soon it's because you don't trust that the wait will be worth it. You're worried that cooking it for a long time over a low fire won't produce the desired results. It's a lack of faith.

'You have to learn to be patient. Patience and faith are related. They're almost the same thing. You have to learn how much salt to put on the meat before you put it in the cooker, and how much to put on after it comes out. You have to learn how to control the fire, to manage it so it produces the kind of smoke and the amount of smoke you need. Then you have to learn how much vinegar to use in your sauce. Some parts of the country use only vinegar. Other parts, like here in Kansas City, use it with other ingredients. Either way it's not barbecue sauce without it. Vinegar is what gives it its zest, its kick.

'But too much of any of these things, or not enough, and it's ruined.

'I've always thought that's interesting.'

Ferguson had never heard LaVerne talk so long or with as much reflection about anything. 'Thank you for sharing that . . .' he started to say.

LaVerne shot him a look.

'Damn it. I wasn't "sharing". I was just saying things that occurred to me. If you're going to make it into "sharing" then shut up.'

Ferguson obliged.

*

LaVerne and A.B. were out back stacking wood, when Mike Owen came out into the alley from the back door.

'Leon said I'd find you back here. I have something for each of you.'

He handed each an envelope embossed in gold foil with the logo of the R.L. Dunleavy Construction Co.

A.B. held his in his hands as if it was a consecrated offering to be laid at an altar. LaVerne ripped his open. It was an invitation, which LaVerne read aloud:

> *It is our sincerest wish that you will honor us*
> *By joining us for an evening of festivities,*
> *food and entertainment*
> *At 8:00 p.m., 4 December 2007*
> *In celebration of the opening of Sprint Center*
> *Downtown Kansas City, Missouri,*
> *Dress is semi-formal.*
> *R.L. Dunleavy*

Ferguson and Pug also received invitations, and so on the night of the event LaVerne and Angela, A.B. and Jen, Pug and Mother Mary Weaver, and Ferguson and Peri, who flew in from Memphis for the occasion, joined Bob Dunleavy and his wife Marge in one of the two Dunleavy skybox suites at the arena. Six other couples were there, mostly Bob's associates at the construction firm. In the other suite were another dozen or so Dunleavy employees and their guests.

'Warren gets anxious at things like this,' Bob explained to A.B. and Jen. 'He and M.Z. went to a movie tonight.'

A.B. had worried to the point of hiccups about not having any semi-formal clothes, but Ferguson told him that, for men, semi-formal meant a dark business suit.

'Is a dark church suit okay?' A.B. asked. Ferguson assured him it was.

LaVerne had been secretly worried about the same thing,

and was also relieved when he overheard Ferguson explaining things to A.B.

The men all looked sharp in their suits and the women lovely in their dresses. When Ferguson saw Peri in her little black number he suggested that maybe there were better ways to spend the evening than a social event in an arena with a bunch of people from a construction company.

Dinner in the Dunleavy suites was catered by Stroud's, Lidia's, and the American. A.B. went back through the buffet line so many times Jen finally felt it necessary to comment.

'You act like you haven't eaten in a month,' she whispered in his ear. 'Save some for the others.'

A.B.'s face reddened. 'I've never had food that tastes this good before. And I may never again. This is the fanciest thing I've ever been to.'

The night's entertainment featured several opening acts, all local, including Willie Arthur Smith's World Famous Marching Cobras youth drill team; a roping, riding, and barrel racing exhibition by the Flying D$\underline{X}$ Kansas Junior Rodeo; and performances by honkytonkers Rex Hobart and the Misery Boys; and hip-hop artist Tech N9ne.

Then the arena went dark, while the stage was set for the main act.

In the Dunleavy suite, the laughing and animated chitchat that had carried the evening forward slowed. Glasses were refilled and second helpings of dessert were had.

A.B. gave Jen an anxious look. She smiled and nodded. A.B. stood.

'Folks. We have an announcement to make, Jen and me. So. Well. You all have known for a while now that we, Jen and me, have been, well, you know, dating. But it's more than that, really. At least now it is. Now it's serious. Not like sad, serious. Good serious. Anyways.'

Jen put her hand on A.B.'s back. He cleared his throat.

'Well. You're our best friends,' he said. 'And we wanted you to be the first to know that we're getting married. Jen and me. We thought a special night like this would be a good time to tell you. Hope you don't mind, Bob.'

A.B.'s and Jen's friends crowded around them, dispensing hugs, handshakes, and backslaps.

'Young man, I'm delighted you picked this night to make your announcement,' said Bob Dunleavy. 'Warren will be thrilled.'

Ferguson embraced A.B. and whispered in his ear, 'Peace be with you, A.B. God's peace be with you both.'

Pug winked at Periwinkle, nodded in Ferguson's direction and asked, 'So? You two next?'

Angela smothered A.B. and Jen with kisses. LaVerne stood behind her waiting his turn to extend his good wishes. But, when Angela stepped aside, LaVerne didn't move. He looked at A.B.

A.B. tried to smile. 'Boss,' he said.

LaVerne nodded.

'Do you think Raymond would be happy?' A.B. said in a voice nobody heard but LaVerne.

LaVerne nodded again. '*I'm* happy, son,' he said, quietly. '*I'm* happy.'

Bob raised his glass and proposed a toast to the couple. There was a glow about the place and A.B. and Jen basked in it.

The main act was blues master B.B. King, a crowd-pleaser in Kansas City and, especially, the Dunleavy suite. Mother Mary, Periwinkle Brown, A.B., and Jen sang along with several songs, including the final encore, 'When Love Comes to Town', which Ferguson said was his favorite song of all time.

*

Outside the arena, when it was over, they were all quiet and content, their hearts and bellies full. Bob and Marge Dunleavy thanked their guests for coming and their guests thanked them for the invitations. They shook hands, hugged some more, and departed.

In the car, A.B. and Jen lit cigarettes.

'Everybody seemed really happy about our news,' A.B. said.

Jen smiled and nodded. 'Of course, A.B. Like you said, they're our best friends.'

They thought about their news and their friends and about the night and the music.

'We need to quit smoking, A.B.,' said Jen. 'Before the wedding.'

A.B. took a long draw on his cigarette.

'I been thinkin' the same thing.'

He flicked the ash from the end of his cigarette out the window.

'You know that Rudy guy? The one from my mom's funeral who came up to us outside the restaurant that one time? Well, he stopped by after work the other day and asked me again if I wanted to go with him up to one of the casinos. I didn't really want to, but I couldn't think of a reason why not, so I said I'd go. We're going tomorrow night. I hope that's okay. I didn't really want to go, but he and my mom were together an' all.'

Jen squeezed A.B.'s knee. 'You don't need to explain. I think it's nice you're going with him. Just don't lose all your money playin' craps.'

A.B. knew that his mother liked going to gamble on the floating casinos – the 'boats' – docked along the Missouri River, but he had never been to one and was anxious about it.

'I don't know what to wear or how much money to bring,' he told Jen. 'And I don't know how any of the machines or games work. When you think about it, I don't really know anything at all about the whole deal.'

Jen said he didn't need to worry about any of it. All he needed to do was to go and have fun with Rudy.

The plan was that they would meet at the Ameristar, eat dinner first at one of the casino's restaurants, gamble a little, then maybe check out one of the bands at one of the bars. Rudy was pacing in front of the main entrance when A.B. arrived. He smiled and took A.B. by the arm and pulled him inside.

'Great to see you, A.B. I think it's great we're gettin' together like this, don't you? I think your ma would be real pleased. I really do. Mona, she was great. I miss her all the time. I think she'd be happy we was spending time together.'

A.B. noticed that Rudy hadn't yet let go of his arm.

'How about we go over and get us a steak there at that Great Plains Cattle place. They got good steaks. I'm tellin' you what. It's on me. My treat.'

A.B. said steak sounded good and they made their way down an interior mall 'streetscape' of false nineteenth century-style storefronts and streetlamps toward the restaurant.

A.B. had a beer and Rudy drank a double gin while they waited for their steaks. A.B. was curious about some things and figured it was as good a time as any to ask his questions.

'So, how long were you and my mom together, anyways?'

Rudy looked across the room, out toward the gaming floor. 'Well, we actually was what you would call a couple for almost two years. Pretty long. It was serious. We was practically married.'

He finished his drink and ordered another.

'We knew each other a long time before we got together. We worked together at GM. And we used to run into each other sometimes at a bar up in Sugar Creek. We both had friends at a trailer park over there.'

A.B. nodded. He remembered going to a trailer park when he was little and wondered if it was the one Rudy was talking about.

'You never had kids?'

Rudy shook his head.

'No. I never did. Never worked out that way. Never got married.'

Rudy's interest in conversation didn't last beyond the arrival of their steaks. He ate with his head down, looking only at his plate. When the check came, A.B. offered to pay, but Rudy wouldn't have it.

'No, sir. I was the one suggested we do this. You was nice to come.'

He paid with a credit card.

They played the slots first. First nickels, then quarters. Rudy won a jackpot of $50 having spent only $10.

'I'm ahead forty bucks.' He grinned. 'And we haven't even been playin' for more than fifteen minutes.'

A few minutes later he won a jackpot of $200. He hopped around like a leprechaun.

'This is my night! I can just feel it! I think you're bringin' me good luck, son.'

A.B. didn't like it that Rudy called him 'son'. That's what LaVerne sometimes called him. A.B. lost $20 on the slots and considered calling it a night, but Rudy suggested they try roulette.

At first, Rudy's luck seemed to shift in a negative direction. He lost all the money he won at the slot machines in the first few spins of the wheel. He tried laughing it off.

'This sometimes happens. Ol' Lady Luck gives you a little bit, then she takes it away, hoping you'll give up. But you have to stick with it. You can't let her chase you off.'

Rudy's persistence paid off. Soon he was up $1,000. A small crowd gathered to watch him bet. A.B. lost another $50 and quit playing. He felt hiccups coming on.

Rudy ordered drinks for the other players at the wheel. Then, with a flourish and a 'Yee! Haw!' he bet all his winnings at once and lost.

He began sweating. The thick lenses of his big glasses fogged up. He looked at A.B.

'See what I told ya? She gives it to ya and then she takes it away. You just have to hang in there. I only lost what I won so far. So I'm still even. The night is still young.'

As far as A.B. was concerned this was a sign that it was a good time to go home and he suggested as much.

'I don't think so,' Rudy said. 'This is still my night. I know it. I think we just need to change tables.'

An hour later Rudy had lost $500 at craps. He turned to A.B.

'How much money did you bring? I hate to ask. But I only need a little. This is about to turn around. I'll pay you back. This sometimes happens. But it always turns around.'

He was biting his lower lip and he didn't look at A.B.

'I don't know, Rudy. It's not that I don't think you'll pay me back. It's just that you probably shouldn't play anymore. Even if you do pay me back, it's money you still lost.'

Rudy brought his eyes up to A.B.'s. 'What do you care if I win or lose? It's my goddamn money not yours. If you're going to loan me some, then give it to me. If not, then don't. But this night was goin' good and I want to get it back, so I need to know.'

A.B. took out his wallet and gave Rudy ten $20 bills.

Rudy looked at the money. 'I'll pay you back, son.'

A.B. felt like he needed to go to the bathroom.

Three rolls of the dice later and the $200 was gone. Rudy went pale.

'Really, A.B., you know I'm good for it. Can you loan me a little more? How much have you got on you?'

A.B. shrugged. 'I don't have any more, Rudy. I just gave you all I have.'

'Okay, then. Well, if you don't want to stick around then that's fine. You said you wanted to leave anyway. I'll come by your restaurant with your money.'

They walked out to the main entrance. Rudy said good-bye and went back inside. A.B. wondered what Rudy was planning to do in the casino if he didn't have any more money.

He lit a cigarette.

He told Jen what had happened even though he was afraid that it might result in their first argument.

'Sounds like he has a gambling problem,' she said. 'I'm just glad you didn't bring more money with you.'

'I didn't really want to go in the first place,' A.B. said. 'I don't feel all that comfortable around him. I was just trying to be nice. Since he and my mother were together an' all.'

He didn't tell Jen that Rudy kept calling him 'son'. He didn't like thinking about it, and he didn't want to say it out loud.

42

Outer Darkness

Conservative students at St Columba Seminary of the Midwest don't know what to make of the Rev. Ferguson Glen because, though there is not a single word or assertion of the Nicene Creed – the fundamental statement of the Christian faith – that Father Glen does not believe to be both true and factual, putting him squarely in the conservative camp on questions of basic orthodoxy, they deeply distrust his left-leaning political views and generally liberal interpretation of Pauline doctrine.

Liberal students are equally uneasy. They endorse his politics and his willingness to challenge traditional interpretations of Scripture, but they view his unbreakable embrace of the Creed as rigid, limiting, and unimaginative.

Ferguson makes no attempt to convert students from either group to his points of view. 'I'm here to teach them to think and to write, not to validate their politics or their theology,' he told Angela in the seminary library's break room, over diet Cokes and Ho Hos. 'They want me to take sides. They want to enlist me in their causes. But I'm done with side-taking. The older I get the less important political and theological ideologies are to me. They're just temporary. This right here, what we're doing right now. This is what lasts. Sharing a moment with a friend. Enjoying sodas and tubular crème-filled snack cakes coated in a waxy chocolate-like substance. That's eternal.'

After the Sprint Center opening, Periwinkle Brown stayed in Kansas City for another few days. There were things she wanted to see. She wanted to see the Edward Hopper paintings at the Nelson-Atkins Museum of Art. She wanted to see a Kansas City Chiefs game. She wanted to see the corner of 12th Street and Vine. And she wanted to see Ferguson Glen teach a class at the seminary.

'I'm afraid, my dear, only the paintings will meet your expectations,' Ferguson said. 'The rest will be disappointing.'

Ferguson had given the seven students in his advanced homiletic writing class the assignment of writing a poem or short piece of fiction based on Matthew 25, 14–30; the Parable of the Talents. Peri sat in the back of the classroom as Ferguson's seminarians discussed the assignment. Some questioned the message of the parable: Was Jesus saying that heaven is the reward for those who successfully carry out God's commands?

Peri studied Ferguson's face as he responded to the comments and concerns of his students – an arched eyebrow, a sad smile, a knowing nod, a delighted grin.

How did I get here? she wondered. *If I were home, I'd be sorting through invoices and writing checks. Alone at my desk in the back of the restaurant. How did I get* here *from* there?

'The conventional interpretation of this passage,' Ferguson was saying, 'is that how we invest the talents God gives us determines whether we get into heaven. After all, the first two invested well and were rewarded. But the third servant, the one who buried his talent, was thrown into outer darkness.

'Is it just me, or is this completely at odds with the gospel message: that we're saved by grace? Here's another thing: why is getting into heaven so often stated as the goal of our spiritual journey? Like that's the only thing we're in it for? The reward. The prize at the end of the race. The gold watch when you retire. Do you see how that puts the emphasis on how hard we try? On the quality of our effort?

'I don't think this story is about earning a good return on investment. I think it's about humility and understanding what we've been given, who gave it to us, and what it's to be used for. It's safe to say that the parable tells us we are not to use what we've been given for ourselves, since the story makes it clear it doesn't really belong to us in the first place.

'Ultimately, I think, this is a parable about fearfulness, and the consequences of fearfulness. Was the fearful servant punished for not earning interest on the money he'd been given? Or for his fearfulness? And wasn't his fearfulness its own punishment? Wasn't he already trapped in the outer darkness of his own fear?

'The real reward comes at the end, in the invitation, "Enter into the joy of your master." We are invited into an intimate relationship. No authentic loving relationship can be based on fear. Fear is the opposite of love.'

Peri was quiet in the car on the way to the airport. Ferguson supposed it was because she had been to an arena opening, a Chiefs game, had toured an art museum, and had to sit through one of his classes all in the space of four days. He reached over and rubbed her neck.

'Don't be depressed. I warned you that the corner of 12th and Vine would be disappointing.'

Peri laughed. 'You got that one right, Reverend. There was nothing there at all.' She sighed. 'I'm okay. I was just thinking about the parable. I think I'm wasting God's gift. Or I will be if I don't change things.'

She looked out the window. Ferguson felt as if he'd swallowed an ice cube.

Peri went on. 'Ferguson, one of the reasons I was so willing to be so foolish and let you into my life, when you showed up at my restaurant out of the blue that night, is that I had come to a place where nothing was happening. Every day was the same as the one before. Nothing was happening to me, and I wasn't happening to anything. Or anyone. Wren has been grown and on her own for over twenty years. She's fine. I think I over-mothered her because of what happened to her eyes. And being her mother was my purpose in life. It gave me focus and meaning. Then when the grandbabies came along, that was where I put all my love and energy. Into them. But they're getting older and Wren and Tyrell are their parents, not me. Tyrell is doing a great job with the business, and the fact is that I never chose the barbecue-restaurant business. I just inherited it when my daddy died. It's been good to me. It provided a good living for me and Wren. But I'm tired of it. And it's not really mine anymore anyways.'

She was quiet again. Ferguson waited. And prayed.

'You breathed life back into me, Reverend. I feel like you're a reminder from God that I still have a life to live. You're my invitation to a *new* life. And if I don't accept that invitation, well, then I'm wasting a gift God gave me. I'm burying it in the ground.'

Ferguson spoke softly. 'What do want to do, Periwinkle Brown?'

She smiled and looked at him. 'The first thing I want to do is travel around the world. With you. I want to see the world with you, Ferguson. I've never been anywhere but Memphis, Kansas City, and a few times to New York and

Los Angeles with Wren when she went there on business. And maybe when we're out there seeing God's big wide world, he'll give us an idea of what I should do – what we should do – next. How to use this gift he's given me.'

LaVerne was reading the newspaper at the desk in the office when A.B. got to work that morning, which was unusual for two reasons. Mainly because A.B. was always the first one to arrive at the restaurant each morning, but also because LaVerne almost never sat at the desk and almost never read the newspaper at work, and for him to being doing both at once made A.B. anxious.

'What's up, boss?' he said.

LaVerne didn't look up.

'I used to get a good feeling when I read or heard about some new business or condos goin' in near here,' he said. 'Made me feel like we were part of something growin' and maybe all that time we were down here almost all by our-selves was worth it after all. But now I just get more pissed off. Did I tell you I got a notice that they lowered our rent? The letter said that the Preservation and Restoration Com-pany owns the whole block now. Can you believe that asshole Johansson calls his company that: the Preservation and Restoration Company?'

He sighed and stared at a bottle of LaVerne Williams' Genuine BBQ Sauce KANSAS CITY STYLE as featured on the *Morty Pavlich Show* sitting atop a stack of bills and invoices.

'You know, I used to think that one day I'd leave this business to Raymond. But, well, when it was clear that he was going to go to college and play ball and be a minister, that changed that. Lately, I been thinkin' that maybe you, or you and Jen, might want it. But now I don't know if there'll be anything to leave to anybody. I've thought about what that asshole said; that maybe we should take the money and relocate somewhere, maybe in East Jack or Johnson County. Then I also wonder if I should just take the damn money and retire. I don't feel ready yet. But, I don't know.'

He went into the kitchen and checked on the ribs.

This got A.B.'s day off to a bad start. After the lunch rush, it got worse. Rudy Turpin showed up at the counter, but not to order barbecue.

'Oh, hi, Rudy,' A.B. said. He smiled even though he didn't feel like it.

'Hey, A.B.,' said Rudy. 'Can I talk to you a minute? Outside?'

A.B. felt like he needed to take a deep breath. 'Sure, Rudy.'

Out on the sidewalk in front of the restaurant, Rudy handed A.B. an envelope.

'It's the money I borrowed from you that night at the boats. I told you I would pay it back. It's all there. Count it.'

Rudy didn't look happy about paying his debt.

A.B. took the envelope, but didn't look inside. 'Gosh, Rudy. This is good. Thank you. This makes me feel better about things.'

Rudy shrugged. 'So, maybe we can do it again sometime. Go to the boats, that is, now that you know that I'm good for the money, like I said. Only maybe next time I'll have better luck. I'm due.'

A.B. didn't know what to say to be polite. He nodded and said thank you again. Rudy seemed to be expecting something more.

LaVerne came to the rescue by stepping outside to tell A.B. he was going to Bichelmeyer's for some briskets. This was the only good news A.B. had heard all day.

'I gotta go in now, Rudy.'

'I should go, too,' Rudy said. He extended his hand to A.B. and A.B. shook it. Rudy walked away, south on Walnut.

On the other side of the street, a tall muscular man with a shaved head watched Rudy and A.B. for a moment, lit a cigarette, then turned and walked up 17th Street. A.B. noticed that the man had an odd tattoo on his neck and head. He got a shiver and walked around back by the dumpster for a smoke.

The first thing Sammy Merzeti did his first full day out in the world was to go get the tattoo he'd been planning since Zorn was murdered. He had sketched the design so many times on sheets of prison-issued notebook paper it was already tattooed on his brain. It represented the name Zorn had given him – Degen – which Zorn said meant, *Sword of the Almighty's Wrath*.

Sammy's tattoo started on his lower back; the bottom of the sword's handle just above his belt line. The blade of the sword extended up along Sammy's spine, up the back of his neck, over the top of his shaved skull, then down onto his forehead, where the tip of the sword ended at a point between his eyebrows. The blade of the sword was blue. Orange and red flames spread out from the blade across Sammy's back. A scroll was wrapped around the handle of the sword; inscribed with the words 'Sword of the Almightys Rath'.

Sammy was not a good speller. Nor was the tattooist.

Sammy was surprised to be out of prison. He had expected that sooner or later he'd be connected to the Rabbi's murder and that he'd then spend the rest of his life behind bars. But that never happened, and now he was standing at the corner of 17th and Walnut, across from a restaurant with the words 'SMOKE MEAT' painted above the door. It was one of the places on the list his parole officer had given him of businesses known to employ parolees. He smoked a cigarette as he tried to think of the words the parole officer told him to use to ask for a job application.

On the sidewalk outside the restaurant, a short older man with slicked-back hair, a protruding beer belly, a big nose, and thick heavy-rimmed glasses, handed an envelope to a scrawny guy in a greasy white apron.

He had a thought about his mother and about playing basketball. He thought the man with the big nose and thick glasses looked familiar.

A tall black man, also wearing a greasy white apron, opened the front door and said something to the scrawny one. That must be the guy that runs the place, thought Sammy. No way I'm workin' for no nigger. He turned and started up 17th Street and the name Rudy Turpin came into his head.

He remembered that his mother said Rudy was never coming back. That was just before he hit her with the ash-tray.

43

Marked

In the dream he had after Raymond died and was buried and was still dead every morning when he woke up, LaVerne is sitting high up in the bleachers in an empty, soundless gymnasium. Soundless. Not quiet. Hartholz is sweeping the gym floor. His broom makes no sound. LaVerne is holding an empty jar in his hand. He thinks there is supposed to be something in the jar. He tries to ask Hartholz about it, but when he speaks, there is no sound. Even his thoughts have no sound. He wants to ask Hartholz if Delbert will be coming soon. But he can't form the question. Sitting up in the stands on the other side of the gym is his best friend Junebug. Junebug doesn't see him. He wonders, *Am I a child now? Is that why Junebug is here?* He wants to ask Hartholz if he is a child now, but he cannot ask it. Hartholz does not look at him. On the other side of the gym, Junebug is gone. There is supposed to be something in the jar. He hopes Delbert will be here soon. There used to be somebody sitting in the stands on the other side of the gym but he can't remember who it was. He looks down where Hartholz is sweeping. Hartholz points to the door at the far end of the gymnasium. There is somebody waiting on the other side of the door but he doesn't know who it is and the door is closed. He reaches for the door but his arm has no sound. He can't remember the name of the person who is sweeping the floor. There used to be something in the jar.

After receiving the letter saying that the restaurant's rent had been reduced, LaVerne began having the dream again. The first time it woke him up, sweating and confused, Angela had to call his name three times before he could get his bearings. That morning he and Angela had a long talk about their life.

'There were times in those first few years that I hated that restaurant,' LaVerne said. 'It represented all the things I hated about my life. That I wasn't playing baseball. That I needed your father's help. But after a while, after I got good at it, it got to be a part of me. And I was proud of it. It was always hard work, but it was honest and it was mine. Recently, I've been thinking that maybe when we retire we'd sell the place to A.B. and he and Jen could keep it goin'. A.B. practically runs it anyway. But now what? What's A.B. going to do if the place shuts down?'

Angela started to say that she had faith that God would take care of A.B., but LaVerne knew where she was going and he wasn't going there with her.

'That's just crap, Angela. God doesn't give a damn about the restaurant or if I own it or A.B. owns it or asshole Johansson owns it. I'm not sayin' God doesn't love me, or A.B., or even asshole Johansson. I'm just sayin it's our souls and our eternal salvation he cares about, not where we work for a living.'

Angela scowled. 'He does care, LaVerne. Jesus says God knows when a sparrow falls from the sky and if he cares about one little sparrow then certainly he cares for you and every part of your life.'

'I didn't say he doesn't care about me,' LaVerne snapped back. 'I'm saying he doesn't care about my job. He doesn't care if I own a restaurant or if I drive a bus. Jesus never said

God cares if the sparrow has a nest in a tree or in a bush. He only just cares about the sparrow. And you know the other thing Jesus doesn't say? He doesn't say God does anything at all to keep that sparrow from falling from the sky. He lets the sparrow fall and die. He knows about it. But he doesn't stop it. He knows about that asshole Johansson is about to close down the restaurant, but I don't expect him to do a damn thing about it. That's just not his deal.'

Discussions like this became more frequent over the course of several weeks until eventually they dried up, and there was nothing left but sighs. Angela worried that La-Verne might retreat to the place he had gone before, when the Athletics let him go, and when Raymond died. But instead of becoming remote and hostile, he exhausted his anger early, leaving him only tired and sad.

Whenever Bob Dunleavy came into the restaurant, he'd say things to LaVerne like, 'Cheer up, friend. Don't worry. It'll all work out. At least for now you're not paying as much rent.'

Mother Mary Weaver's response to Ute Johansson's plans was to call him a son of a bitch whenever the subject came up. Pug just shook his head.

Suzanne Edwards and McKenzie Nelson started a 'Save Smoke Meat' petition drive and brought the signed petitions in to show LaVerne. LaVerne looked at them and started to say thanks but the words wouldn't come out so he just nodded. Leon and Vicki were there and they signed the petitions.

Jen and A.B. set a date for their wedding and had begun making plans, but A.B. was distracted by the restaurant situation and by LaVerne's response to it. Jen understood the significance of it all, but found herself increasingly irritated that eventually all conversations ended up at the corner of 17th and Walnut.

'You know, A.B., for most of my adult life I thought I'd never get married. Then you come along and we fall in love, and now that I actually have a wedding to think about and plan for, you and everybody else can't think about anything but that restaurant. I know it's important and all, but the timing sucks.'

Angela also noticed the effect all the worry had on A.B. and Jen. On a Wednesday night after prayer meeting at which LaVerne hadn't prayed, Angela decided the time was right to address the problem.

'You need to start thinking about someone other than yourself, LaVerne. You need to quit moping around with your head down and your ass draggin' like a whipped dog. You said yourself that you wanted to leave the business to A.B. when you retired. So, do it. You're in the barbecue making and selling business. If you can't do it in the building you're in now, then find another building to do it in. Find a part of town that needs a barbecue joint and set one up. You owe it to A.B. The only job he's ever had is working for you. If you just quit and walk away, the only choice he'll have is to go work for some other barbecue place. How will you feel about that? You're the one who said you were worried about what he would do if the restaurant shut down. Well, you can do something about it. You have a responsibility to that young man. Especially now that he's getting married. You need a plan, LaVerne. You need a strategy.'

This lecture had a familiar ring to it, as did the disagreeable feeling LaVerne had that Angela was right.

His response was to pretend that he no longer felt that the rug was about to be pulled out from under him. He went to work in the morning determined not to say a thing about asshole Johansson or any related subject matter. Instead he asked A.B. how the wedding plans were going, which he regretted after the third hour of an A.B. monologue on the subject of rental halls.

Jen Richardson's parents are in their late seventies and live in Florida, so Jen's mother did not take on the usual mother-of-the-bride role in planning the wedding. Jen pretty much did most of the planning herself, with A.B.'s and Angela's help. Jen and her family didn't go to church when she was a child, so there was no home church for her to get married in. She'd been attending New Jerusalem Baptist Church with A.B. and the Williams since she and A.B. had become a couple and was even thinking about joining the choir, so she and A.B. decided the wedding would be held there, with the Rev. Norton B. Timms officiating. Warren and Leon would be A.B.'s groomsmen. Jen's bridesmaids would be her cousin, Sharon, who lived in Higginsville, and her friend, Clarissa, from the Harley plant.

'Do you think it's okay that we get married in a Baptist church?' A.B. asked Ferguson. 'I mean, my mom said we were Catholics. I was baptized when I was a baby and everything. Even though I was baptized again later at New Jerusalem when I was saved.'

Ferguson smiled. 'God doesn't care where you get married, A.B. God's not a Catholic, or a Baptist, or even an Episcopalian. God's not even a Christian.'

A.B. was reassured, right up to the point where Ferguson said that God wasn't a Christian, which concerned and confused him, and which he decided not to ask about.

'So, does he care about baptizing? And why are there different ways to do it? I don't get that.'

'Both ways of baptizing are deeply sacred symbols of our relationship with God,' Ferguson said. 'They're more than symbols, actually. Something real happens when we're baptized. It's a mystery. But it's real.

'Immersion, when a person is brought all the way under the water and back up, is the way Jesus himself was baptized. That's why Baptists do it that way. It symbolizes death and resurrection. And it symbolizes being washed of one's sins.

'But Jesus was also brought to the temple as an infant to be presented to God and marked as one of God's chosen. And that's why Catholics baptize babies. It's a mark that assures us that God will recognize that person as his very own.'

Ferguson gave A.B. a light slap on the back.

'So, A.B., when you die, you're going straight to heaven. No doubt about it. You've been baptized twice – washed of your sins *and* marked as God's own. You're twice blessed.'

A.B. thought about this. 'I've been blessed more ways than I can count,' he said.

A.B. and Ferguson had just concluded their theology seminar when Pug came in for a slab of ribs to take to Mother Mary. As A.B. wrapped the ribs in red butcher paper, Pug and Ferguson exchanged small talk.

'LaVerne tells me that you and Ms Brown are taking a trip together. That right, Rev.?'

'It's true, detective. We're going to Kenya, right after A.B.'s and Jen's wedding.'

Pug grinned. 'Things must be getting pretty serious between you two. Maybe we all ought to be keeping our wedding clothes handy.'

A.B. handed the ribs to Pug, who turned to go, then turned back.

'By the way, there was a fellow across the street a bit ago I didn't like the looks of. Tattoo up the back of his head down to his eyes. He was studying the restaurant here real hard. Maybe he was casing the joint, or waiting for somebody. In any case, I went over there and showed him the badge and asked him what he was up to. He just looked at me and didn't say a word. I told him he best be on his way and not to come back unless he had specific legitimate business. So, if you see a suspicious-looking character hanging around, give me a call, I'll take care of it. Like I said, evil-looking tattoo. Plus, he's missing his index finger on his left hand.'

44

It is Well

There is a shady place under a tall wild cherry tree on the west bank of the Trinity River where Delbert went to be apart from his cares. To be by himself. Sometimes when he went there he brought his harmonica or his fishing pole or a flask. Sometimes he'd fall asleep on the cool grass.

Rose knew Delbert had this place and asked him once if it was where he went to pray. But it was not a place for praying. Praying made him think of all the things that needed praying about, and the reason he went there was to not think of those things. Just sitting there watching the water was prayer enough.

It's where he decided to ask Madeleine to marry him. And near where they found her floating face down, broken and bloated. He didn't go back to the place under the cherry tree after that. He understood that it was lost to him. But sometimes, when life pushed down hard on him, he wished there was another place like it where he could go.

When LaVerne was fourteen years old, Pastor Elmer Jackson of the Plum Grove Second Baptist Church came to Rose and asked if perhaps LaVerne was ready to be baptized. Rose had been thinking about this as well. LaVerne went to church with her and Delbert every Sunday without complaint.

He sat attentively in the pew and sang the hymns with a strong, clear voice. He didn't curse and didn't appear to be in danger of straying off onto the path his mother had taken. But he never talked about God. He didn't ask questions about being a Christian. And Rose had never seen him read the Bible that children at Second Baptist are given when they reach the third grade.

Rose asked her brother his thoughts on the matter.

'I don't know why you're asking me, Rose. Seems like you should ask LaVerne. The boy's incapable of telling a lie. If he's ready, he'll say so. But if you're waiting for him to bring it up, well, don't. That's not the kind of thing the boy talks about. He doesn't talk about much to begin with.'

Rose did ask LaVerne, out on the porch on a humid summer night after he'd come home from the butcher shop where he'd worked all day with Delbert and Hartholz smoking briskets and making sausage. His clothes and hair smelled of smoke.

'Yes, Grandma, I probably am. I believe in Jesus. I know he died for my sins.'

Rose embraced her grandson and wept. The joy of loving and raising this child had filled her soul, pushing the sorrow of losing Loretta into a small dark corner. If allowed to choose, she would not change a thing about her life.

Pastor Jackson had also recruited for baptism William and John, the twins from down the road; their younger cousin, Esther; Mrs Irma Sykes, who had come to the Lord at the tent meeting that spring; and Mr Roosevelt Washington, Mrs Sykes' father, who decided that if Jesus was good enough for his daughter, he was good enough for him. The time and place for the baptizing were set by the deacons and the mothers of the church: 3:00 in the afternoon, the last Sunday of August, on the west bank of the Trinity River, with a picnic to follow in the churchyard.

If Delbert had thought about it beforehand, it wouldn't have surprised him, as it did, that the baptisms were going to be at the Trinity River.

'I don't know if I can go back to that river,' he told Hartholz. 'But I can't miss the boy's baptizing. It's an impossible situation.'

He knew what Rose would say if he expressed his misgivings to her: 'Brother, I know that river saddens you, but this will be the most important day in his young life and you need to be there to bless and support him.'

Hartholz was inclined to agree with Rose. 'Lutherans don't baptize in a river. So I don't know about it. But if your sister says it is important, it must be. She doesn't ask for much. You must be brave in your heart and do what she asks. She is your sister.'

There were only three people in the world whose opinions mattered to Delbert. Two of them said he must go, and it was for the sake of the third that they said so. He resolved he would go, but lay awake nights worrying about it.

After worship, the members of the congregation got in their cars and trucks and drove the fifteen miles to the Trinity. The Trinity was chosen for the baptism because it had been a hot dry summer; most of the creeks in Liberty County had dried up and there was more water flowing in the Trinity than in the San Jacinto.

They parked their vehicles back a ways, in order to leave enough distance for a proper procession to the river bank. Three deacons led the way, each holding a long wooden staff. The families of the candidates for baptism followed the deacons. Some of the women carried open umbrellas to shade themselves and their children from the Texas sun.

As they approached the river, a collective moan came up from the members of the congregation, and they began to clap in rhythmic unison. A woman began singing.

> 'Take me to the water
> Take me to the water
> Take me to the water
> To be baptized.'

Then she was joined by the others.

> 'None but the righteous
> None but the righteous
> None but the righteous
> Shall be saved.'

The mothers of the church followed the families. They were dressed in long white cotton robes and wore white cotton head coverings. Walking behind the mothers – also in long white cotton robes – were the candidates for baptism: William, John, Esther, Mrs Sykes, Mr Washington, and LaVerne.

> 'So take me to the water
> Take me to the water
> Take me to the water
> To be, to be baptized.'

Last in the procession was Pastor Elmer Jackson, wearing a black suit, white shirt and black necktie. He carried his Bible.

> 'I'm going back home,
> Going back home
> Gonna stay here no longer
> I'm going back home,
> Going back home
> To be baptized.'

The deacons walked into the river and poked the long poles into the river bottom, looking for holes, sunken logs, or catfish. When they found a safe and steady spot they stuck the poles into the river mud, forming a triangular space in which Pastor Jackson stood.

One by one the candidates waded into the water, where Pastor Jackson took them by the hand and pulled them to himself and put his arm around behind their shoulders. He called them by their names and asked them if they had come to be baptized and they said yes. He asked them if they loved the Lord with all their hearts, souls, and minds, and again they said yes. And then one by one he covered each of their faces with a clean, dry, white handkerchief and lowered them into the Trinity River, saying in a loud voice, 'I baptize thee in the name of the Father, and the Son, and the Holy Spirit. Amen.'

Delbert watched as one by one they were lifted out of the water. Emerging from the river, Irma Sykes let out with a whoop and a 'Halleluiah!' William got a bad case of the giggles.

When LaVerne came up from the river he wasn't smiling. He was shining – the sun reflecting off the water streaming down his calm and quiet face.

As the newly baptized made their way to the shore, the congregation began singing:

> 'When peace like a river, attendeth my way,
> When sorrows like sea billows roll;
> Whatever my lot, thou hast taught me to say,
> It is well; it is well, with my soul.
> It is well, with my soul,
> It is well, with my soul,
> It is well; it is well, with my soul.'

Delbert felt the words move in him. On the far bank he saw a small turtle, no bigger than the palm of his hand, sunning itself on a log. Something had changed. The Trinity had been redeemed. The boy had baptized the river.

45

Crixa

Sometimes when Rudy Turpin got in over his head he prayed. Other times he stole valuables from the women he was living with at the time. When he prayed, he promised he'd never gamble again if God would just help him this one time to find a way to pay his marker. When he stole, he broke into the house to make it look like a burglary, trashed the place up a bit, and, just to be sure no one would ever suspect him, he always stole some of his own belongings.

Generally, Rudy found stealing more expedient than prayer in getting what he needed.

Sometimes he felt guilty about stealing from his lady companions, especially since it usually involved taking their jewelry, which they all seemed to have sentimental attachments to. But jewelry was so much easier to conceal and fence than, say, a big TV, that, as a practical matter, he really had no choice. Usually, however, by the time his financial situation got to the point where he had to resort to robbing his girlfriends, his gambling had pretty much ruined the relationship, so he didn't feel as guilty as he otherwise might when he made off with their stuff.

Rudy made good money at the GM Fairfax plant, but still lived paycheck to paycheck. The bank had foreclosed on a house he'd owned, and had repossessed two cars because of missed payments due to gambling. He had a studio apartment, but had to hock most of his furniture and appliances. Living with a woman was the only way he could live comfortably. Some of them he became quite fond of; maybe even loved. But sooner or later they all ended up telling him to quit going to the casinos, which was something he never succeeded in doing.

Rudy's bad-luck streak started when Mona Bennett died. He had a good thing going with Mona. She and her friends liked going to the boats and having a good time. There was always lots of laughing and drinking. She had a nice house and some pretty good jewelry. He checked.

After Mona died, he had a hard time developing a lasting relationship with another woman. This made for a lonely life, devoid of TV, dependable transportation, and cash advances. He got panicky when he thought about it. He knew he was in a sorry and unattractive state. He needed to make himself presentable to the opposite sex. He needed new clothes and some dental work too, but was unlikely to get either unless he scored some cash.

Bob Dunleavy arranged ahead of time that, on the Saturday of A.B.'s wedding, Mike Owen would drive him and Warren around in the Cadillac Fleetwood to pick up A.B., LaVerne, Ferguson, and Leon, and deliver them to the church where the groom and his groomsmen would change into their tuxes and get ready for the ceremony.

'If you gotta go, you may as well go in style,' he teased, throwing his arm around A.B.'s shoulders.

A.B.'s apartment was the first stop on what Bob was calling the 'Wedding Express'. A.B. got in the car, hung his tux bag on the little hook above the door, and immediately started apologizing.

'Jeez, Bob, you won't believe this, well, you probably

will believe it, because I do this kind of thing all the time, but I left the shoes that go with my tux at the restaurant. I picked it up yesterday afternoon, and then when I went back to work, I brought it into the restaurant because I didn't want to leave it in the car in case someone stole it or something. Anyways, I noticed this morning that the shoes were missing. They're on top of the filing cabinet in the office. I know that for sure because I remember putting them there so I wouldn't forget. But obviously I did forget. So, I'm really sorry but we have to stop at the restaurant so I can get 'em. It was stupid that I forgot 'em.'

Bob laughed. 'Whoa! Relax there, fella. You've got wedding-day jitters. Everything's fine. We're going right by the restaurant anyway. We've got to pick up Ferguson, remember? It works out great.'

Warren nodded. 'Unless you want to get married in your bare feet.'

Medication was a tricky business for Warren on occasions such as this. Too much and he was lethargic and non-responsive. Not enough and he was anxious and obsessive. It was too early to tell how the day would go.

The next stop was LaVerne's house. Even though he was not officially a member of the wedding party, Jen had bought him a forest-green silk tie that matched the fabric of her bridesmaids' dresses. Angela came out to the car with him and gave the knot of his tie a final adjustment. She wore a light green dress with a forest-green silk scarf.

'See you all at the church in a little bit,' she chirped, bending to peer in the open car window at the other passengers on the Wedding Express.

'I forgot my shoes,' A.B. announced unprompted. He shook his head, trying to come to grips with his oversight. 'They're at work.'

Angela took A.B.'s hand and squeezed it. 'Aren't you going right by there anyway to pick up Ferguson?'

A.B. nodded. 'I guess.'

'He could go barefoot,' LaVerne suggested.

Warren grinned. 'That's what I said.'

Ferguson was waiting in front of his condo building when the Fleetwood pulled up. He was decked out in full Scottish regalia – Mackintosh tartan kilt, black short-waist formal jacket, starched white shirt with wing collar, black bow-tie, cream-colored knee-length woolen socks, and a tartan fly plaid over his shoulder, pinned in place on the left lapel of his jacket by his father's silver Celtic cross brooch.

'Damn it, Ferguson,' LaVerne said as his friend got in the car, 'you look like one of the bridesmaids.'

'You're just jealous because your legs aren't as pretty as mine.' Ferguson sniffed, nose in the air.

'I forgot my shoes,' A.B. informed Ferguson. 'We have to stop over at the restaurant, if you don't mind. They're on the filing cabinet.'

'That's, okay, A.B.,' Ferguson said. 'I'll pick up a slab of ribs to go while we're there.'

What Sammy Merzeti was most curious about was whether Rudy remembered him; if he remembered going to the Kings game or singing in the car. He wondered if Rudy remembered his name. That's why he kept going back to the corner of 17th and Walnut. Maybe he'd see Rudy there again. Maybe Rudy knew that guy who worked at that restaurant. That's why he went there again on Saturday. To wait for Rudy. To find out if he remembered. He would use the gun in his pocket to jog his memory if he needed to.

He stood across the street from the restaurant, smoked a

cigarette and wondered what things might have been like if his mother and Rudy hadn't split up.

Even though it was early in the afternoon, it was dark inside the restaurant. He hadn't noticed anyone going in or coming out. He crossed the street to take a look. There was a piece of paper taped to the door. It said, 'We will be closed Saturday do to a wedding. Sorry for the inconvenients.'

Sammy spat on the sidewalk and turned to leave and there was Rudy; approaching the restaurant. He glanced at Sammy as he passed. He went to the door and read the note. He tried the door handle, then leaned close to the window to look inside.

Sammy stepped up behind him. 'Looks like nobody's home, Rudy.'

Rudy spun around. 'Do I know you?'

Sammy put his hand in his pocket. 'Do *you* know me?'

Rudy didn't like the way this punk was getting in his face. 'I know you're a inked-up freak. Now get out of my way.'

Sammy had hoped that Rudy would recognize him and that maybe things would be different than they were about to be. He slid the gun out of his pocket and punched it into Rudy's ribs.

'Let's go around back and talk about old times.'

Sammy grabbed a fistful of Rudy's jacket and pushed him around the corner of the building toward the alley behind Smoke Meat. They stopped between the woodpile and the dumpster where Sammy slammed the handle of his gun into Rudy's head and shoved him up against the back door of the building. He held the muzzle of the gun against Rudy's temple.

'Are you sure you don't remember me?' he hissed.

Rudy's glasses were sliding off. 'Look, if this is about money I owe then just tell me who you work for and I'll make it right.'

'It's too late to make it right,' Sammy said. 'But, since you don't remember me, please allow me to introduce myself. My name used to be Sam, but you can call me Degen.'

The Wedding Express had arrived. A.B. hopped out of the Fleetwood, unlocked the front door of the restaurant and scurried back to the office to retrieve his tux shoes from the top of the filing cabinet.

As he turned to leave he heard a loud bang and a thump on the back door.

He put his hand on the doorknob and listened.

He heard moaning and someone say something.

He opened the door and Rudy Turpin's bleeding body fell onto him.

'Jesus!' A.B. screamed, jumping back. Rudy's body flopped onto the office floor. A.B. looked down in horror. 'Jesus, Rudy!'

Sammy put the end of his gun under A.B.'s chin and lifted his head up to face him. 'Did you know this guy?'

'I did. I do,' A.B. wheezed, trying to breathe. 'Rudy Turpin.'

Sammy pushed A.B. backward through the office into the restaurant, with the nose of the gun under A.B.'s chin.

Sammy shouted, 'How did you know him?'

A.B. shouted back, 'He used to live with my mother! That's all! I didn't know him very well! Why? Why are you doing this?'

Sammy kept pushing A.B. backward with the gun, into the dining room.

LaVerne, Ferguson, Bob, and Warren had heard the shot and were there just inside the door.

'You will not hurt that boy,' LaVerne growled.

'*Really?*' Sammy sneered. There was movement behind him and he swiveled, pulling A.B. around in front of him. A man was striding toward him, confident and calm. Sammy shuddered and shot the man.

As Mike Owen staggered back and fell behind the counter, Warren screamed. '*Zorn! Zorn!*'

Bob Dunleavy grabbed his son to prevent him from charging the tattooed man holding a gun on A.B.

Sammy's voice stretched to a desperate cry. 'What does he mean, "*Zorn*"? How does he know *Zorn*? Zorn came to purify the Last Peoples of the Almighty. How does *he* know him? *I'm* the one. *I* knew them. *Both* of them. They knew *me*.'

Bob stepped forward. 'He *doesn't* know Zorn. It's just a word from a book he likes. It's rabbit language.'

Sammy's shaved head was red and wet with sweat. The veins on his temples pumped.

'Shut up!' he roared. He pushed A.B. aside and leveled his gun at Warren. Bob lunged toward the gun and a bullet ripped through his throat.

A.B. stumbled forward. LaVerne threw his arms around him. Ferguson tackled them both.

Sammy whipped around and managed to shoot twice more before Mike Owen crushed his skull with one swing of the Rocky Colavito model K55 35-inch Hillerich & Bradsby Louisville Slugger.

LaVerne felt a familiar fire in his right shoulder and saw A.B. standing outside, in front of the restaurant, watching Raymond up on a ladder with a paintbrush and a pail of paint.

Ferguson understood there was a hole in his chest and found himself in a yellow room and wondered if it was heaven.

A.B. sensed something warm and wet on his face and raised his hand to wipe it off. He was holding his tux shoes.

He wanted to ask Jen if they should have invited Rudy to the wedding.

Warren sat on the floor holding his father in his arms, rocking back and forth whispering, '*El-ahrairah. El-ahrairah. El-ahrairah.*'

Michael Zosimus Owen stood guard, listening for the sirens.

46

SMOKE MEAT

Three weeks after Bob Dunleavy's funeral, his widow Marge called A.B. Clayton, Jen Richardson, and LaVerne and Angela Williams and asked them to meet her and her attorney at her home. A.B. had never personally met with an attorney and the idea of it made him sweat.

'I'm never gonna be able to quit smoking, if horrible things keep happening,' he told Jen, as he lit another cigarette.

A.B. had been inconsolably depressed and anxious since the incident at Smoke Meat. Nearly every conversation ended with him expressing his guilt over having forgotten his shoes. The restaurant had been closed since the killings there, and A.B. had nothing to do with his time except fret and frequently cry.

Marge Dunleavy hugged each of her guests as they arrived, except LaVerne whose shoulder was still in a sling and heavily bandaged. She escorted them into Bob's den, where her attorney, Andrew James, was waiting.

When they were seated, Marge Dunleavy looked at each of her guests and cleared her throat. She held a white handkerchief in her hands.

'First, I want to thank you all for your graciousness to our family during this time. Especially to Warren. His doctors say he's stabilized. The medication and therapy seem to be working, and perhaps he can start coming home on weekends. I know your visits and emails have meant the world to him. Especially from you, A.B. You're such a blessing to him.'

Jen squeezed A.B.'s hand.

'Andrew and I have been reviewing Bob's will this week. There are some provisions that affect you, LaVerne, and you too, A.B. Andrew will go over the details with you, but I wanted to tell you myself what Bob has done and why.'

She turned to LaVerne.

'Obviously, LaVerne, you and Angela have become dear friends. I remember after the first time Bob had lunch at your restaurant. He said it was the most wonderful "little hole in the wall".'

She smiled apologetically at LaVerne. 'I hope you're not offended by that description. That's why he loved it so. It was a comfortable place where he felt welcome. He felt no need to impress anybody. He could go there with his foremen and their crews and just be himself. And he loved the food. I was always jealous when he said he'd had lunch at Smoke Meat. And I was always thrilled whenever he brought some of your barbecue home for dinner.

'When Ute Johansson's company expressed interest in pursuing development projects in your area, Bob became concerned, as you were, about the future of the restaurant, as well as the other small locally owned businesses on the block. So, he bought the block himself. The Preservation and Restoration Company is Bob's company. He wanted to be sure that the neighborhood stayed a neighborhood. He's been your new landlord for a while now. That's why your rent went down.

'I knew that he had done this, and of course, I was thrilled. We've been blessed with the means to do many

442

wonderful things for our community. This had the added benefit of doing something wonderful for our friends. But what I didn't know, until this week, was what else he had done.

'Because of Warren, Bob and I have always taken great care to keep our legal affairs in order and up to date. We need to make sure that Warren is well cared for after we're gone, and even though we're in good health . . .'

She stopped and twisted the handkerchief.

'We wanted to be sure that if something should happen to either one of us, things would be in order.'

She took a deep breath.

'LaVerne, in his will, Bob left the restaurant to you. The building and the lot the building sits on are yours. You no longer have to worry about your rent or losing the place to an unscrupulous developer. It's yours.

'That's not all. A.B., Bob and I have been so grateful for your friendship with Warren. Warren has never been so happy and, well, so normal. We were worried that we would lose him; that he would get lost inside his own mind. But you cared enough to be a friend. Just a normal friend.

'A.B., in his will, Bob left the 1700 block of Walnut to you. From Walnut to Main, from 17th to 18th, that block of property is now yours.'

Both A.B. and LaVerne looked as if they wanted to speak. Marge lifted her hand.

'There is one more thing. Bob's desire was that the two of you should own and control the businesses and property in the neighborhood, but there are strings attached. LaVerne, if you should decide that you want out of the restaurant business and would like to sell your property, A.B. has first right of refusal. If he wants to buy the property, you must sell it to him at fair market value. If he doesn't want to buy it, right of refusal goes to the Watership Foundation, which is a charitable foundation we've established to fund mental-health programs. If the foundation waives its right of refusal, you're free to sell it to the buyer of your choice.

'Likewise, A.B., if you choose to sell any part or the whole of the property you now own, LaVerne gets first right of refusal. If he chooses to waive his right, then the property must be offered to the foundation. If the foundation does not wish to buy the property, you may sell to whomever you wish.'

Marge bowed her head and her voice lowered to a near whisper.

'It gave Bob great joy to do this. And it gives me great joy to share this news with you. Bob was the connection between us. I would never have known any of you if it weren't for him. I pray that now he's gone we will still see one another often. It'll help me stay connected to him.'

A.B. couldn't bear any more. He let out a loud sob. La-Verne buried his face in his hands and wept. Angela and Jen felt a weight of love as heavy as any sorrow. They stood and went to Marge and took her into their arms.

LaVerne and A.B. went to the restaurant that night for the first time since the murders. The cleaning service had done its job well; it looked the same as on any night after closing. There was no sign of what had happened.

LaVerne had called ahead to ask if Ferguson would meet them there and within a few minutes he knocked on the front door and let himself in. He had been discharged from the hospital only a few days earlier and, under his shirt, his chest was wrapped with layers of gauze. He moved carefully. In his hand he carried his father's silver brooch. He held it out for LaVerne and A.B. to see. There was a hole about the size of a dime in one of the bars of the Celtic cross.

'This is what saved me,' he said.

LaVerne and A.B. took turns holding the brooch, each sticking his pinkie in the hole, shaking their heads in disbelief.

Ferguson eyed LaVerne's sling. 'How's the shoulder?'

LaVerne snorted. 'Doctor says he cleaned up all the old scar tissue. Says I could play outfield for the Royals if I wanted to. I told him I'd pass.'

They sat at a table by the window and were quiet for a time.

A.B. spoke first. 'I don't want this property. I want Bob back. He wouldn't be dead if it wasn't for me.'

'You aren't responsible for Bob's death,' said Ferguson. 'Forgetting a pair of shoes never killed anybody. That poor tormented young man killed him. He made the choice to take Bob's life.'

'Why couldn't God prevent him from doing that?' A.B. asked.

'God could have, A.B. And he could have prevented you from forgetting your shoes. And he could manipulate time and space to put things back the way they were a month ago. But then all of creation would be meaningless. The only meaning there is in all the universe is love, A.B. And love can only exist of its own free will. If God manipulates all our choices and decisions; if we're nothing more than his playthings, then we have no real relationship with him. A child's toy cannot love the child. It's only when we're free to commit monstrous acts of murder, that we're also free to love God and each other.'

They were quiet again and then LaVerne spoke.

'Son, this is what I know in my heart; to God there is no difference between here and there; heaven and earth. This life and eternal life; it's all the same to him. Raymond and Bob were here, now they're there. We're here now. Pretty soon we'll be there. There's not much separating this place from that place. I have to believe that if I reach out my hand I can touch my boy. Believing that is pretty much the only thing that has kept my mind whole.'

A.B. shook his head and stared down at his feet.

LaVerne reached over with his good arm and took A.B.'s hand in his.

Ferguson crossed himself. 'A thin place,' he said. 'We're in a thin place.'

Epilogue

The Peace

In a near-empty sanctuary, the sweet thin blue smoke of incense rises up like whispered prayer. Gathered around a baptismal font at the back of the nave are LaVerne and Angela Williams, Marge Dunleavy and Warren, Pug Hale, Periwinkle Brown, and A.B. and Jen Clayton. The Reverend Ferguson Glen, in his liturgical vestments, holds his hands over the water in the font and prays.

'*We thank you, Almighty God, for the gift of water. Over it the Holy Spirit moved in the beginning of creation. Through it you led the children of Israel out of their bondage in Egypt into the land of promise. In it your Son Jesus received the baptism of John and was anointed by the Holy Spirit as the Messiah, the Christ, to lead us, through his death and resurrection, from the bondage of sin into everlasting life. We thank you, Father, for the water of baptism. In it we are buried with Christ in his death. By it we share in his resurrection. Through it we are reborn by the Holy Spirit. Therefore in joyful obedience to your Son, we bring into his fellowship those who come to him in faith, baptizing them in the Name of the Father, and of the Son, and of the Holy Spirit.*'

Ferguson pauses and listens. Someone is speaking the words in unison with him. It is a voice he knows. He looks

447

at the faces of those around him, these people he loves. Was one of them speaking the words together with him? He lowers his hands and touches them to the water.

'*Now sanctify this water, we pray you, by the power of your Holy Spirit, that those who here are cleansed from sin and born again may continue for ever in the risen life of Jesus Christ our Savior. To him, to you, and to the Holy Spirit, be all honor and glory, now and for ever. Amen.*'

He hears the voice again. It is one with his voice, and gives power to his voice. Those around him smile expectantly. They wait for him to continue. He extends his hands to receive the infant who has been brought here for baptism.

Ferguson cradles the child in the nook of his right arm and touches the baby's cheek. The baby reaches for his hand, grasping at his wedding band.

Ferguson dips his hand into the water and speaks as he pours the water onto the child's head.

'*Robert Raymond Clayton, I baptize you in the Name of the Father, and of the Son, and of the Holy Spirit. Amen.*'

Ferguson knows now who it is who is saying the words with him. He knows that those standing near him are not hearing his voice, but the voice of the one who speaks with him, and in him, and through him. He knows that this is the voice he has waited a lifetime to hear. He knows it is well with his soul. 'Let us pray,' he says.

'*Heavenly Father, we thank you that by water and the Holy Spirit you have bestowed upon this your servant the forgiveness of sin, and have raised him to the new life of grace. Sustain him, O Lord, in your Holy Spirit. Give him an enquiring and discerning heart, the courage to will and to persevere, a spirit to know and to love you, and the gift of joy and wonder in all your works. Amen.*'

With his thumb, Ferguson makes the sign of the cross on the child's forehead.

'*Robert Raymond Clayton, you are sealed by the Holy Spirit in baptism and marked as Christ's own for ever. Amen.*'

He turns to his friends. Their faces shine. He invokes the blessing.

'*The peace of the Lord be always with you.*'

And they return the blessing to him.

'*And also with you.*'